ARISTAENETUS, EROTIC LETTERS

Society of Biblical Literature

Writings from the Greco-Roman World

David Konstan and Johan C. Thom, General Editors

Editorial Board

Number 32

Volume Editor
Patricia A. Rosenmeyer

ARISTAENETUS, EROTIC LETTERS

Introduced, translated and annotated by

Peter Bing and Regina Höschele

Society of Biblical Literature
Atlanta

ARISTAENETUS, EROTIC LETTERS

Library of Congress Cataloging-in-Publication Data

Aristaenetus, author.
    Erotic letters / Aristaenetus ; introduced, translated, and annotated by Peter Bing and Regina Höschele.
        pages cm. — (Writings from the Greco-Roman world ; volume 32)
      ISBN 978-1-58983-741-6 (paper binding : alk. paper) — ISBN 978-1-58983-742-3 (electronic format) — ISBN 978-1-58983-882-6 (hardcover binding : alk. paper)
      1. Aristaenetus. Love epistles. I. Bing, Peter. II. Höschele, Regina. III. Aristaenetus. Love epistles. English. 2013. IV. Series: Writings from the Greco-Roman world ; v. 32.
    PA3874.A3E5 2013
    880.8'.03538—dc23   2013024429

Printed on acid-free, recycled paper conforming to
ANSI/NISO Z39.48-1992 (R1997) and ISO 9706:1994
standards for paper permanence.

Contents

Text and Translation

ABBREVIATIONS

GENERAL

f.	folio
fl.	*floruit*, flourished
fr(s).	fragment(s)
scil.	*scilicet*, namely
v(v).	verse(s)

PRIMARY RESOURCES

Ach.	Aristophanes, *Acharnians*
Am.	*Amores* (Ovid, Pseudo-Lucian)
Anth. pal.	*Anthologia Palatina*
Anth. plan.	*Anthologia Planudea*
Argon.	Apollonius of Rhodes, *Argonautica*
Ars	Ovid, *Ars Amatoria*
Carm.	*Carmina* (Catullus, Horace, Sidonius Apollinaris)
Charm.	Plato, *Charmides*
Chron.	John Malalas, *Chronographia*
Cod. justin.	*Codex justinianus*
Cycl.	Euripides, *Cyclops*
Demetr.	Plutarch, *Demetrius*
Dial. Court.	Lucian, *Dialogues of the Courtesans*
Ep.	*Epistle(s)* (Aelian, Aristaenetus, Synesius)
Epigr.	*Epigrammata* (Callimachus)
Eph.	Xenophon of Ephesus, *Ephesiaka*
Epitr.	Menander, *Epitrepontes*
Ethop.	*Ethopoieiai* (Libanius, Severus of Alexandria)
Fam.	Cicero, *Epistulae ad familiares*
Gyn.	Soranus, *Gynecology*

Hal.	Oppian, *Halieutica*
Her.	Ovid, *Heroides*
Hermot.	Lucian, *Hermotimus*
Hipp.	Euripides, *Hippolytus*
Hymn Apoll.	Callimachus, *Hymn to Apollo*
Id.	Theocritus, *Idyll*
Il.	Homer, *Iliad*
Imag.	Philostratus the Elder, *Imagines*
Lys.	Aristophanes, *Lysistrata*
Metam.	Ovid, *Metamorphoses*
Nat. Child	Hippocrates, *On the Nature of the Child*
Nat. Hist.	Pliny, *Natural History*
Od.	Homer, *Odyssey*
Parm.	Plato, *Parmenides*
Phaedr.	Plato, *Phaedrus*
Protr.	Clement of Alexandria, *Protrepticus*
Pyth.	Pindar, *Pythian Odes*
Rep.	Plato, *Republic*
Soph.	Plato, *Sophist*
Symp.	Plato, *Symposium*
Theaet.	Plato, *Theaetetus*
Theog.	Hesiod, *Theogony*
W. D.	Hesiod, *Works and Days*

Secondary Resources

Adler	Adler, A., ed. *Suidae Lexicon.* 5 vols. Leipzig, 1928–1938.
CMG	*Corpus medicorum graecorum.* Leipzig/Berlin, 1908–.
CPG	*Corpus paroemiographorum graecorum.* Edited by E. L. Leutsch and F. G. Schneidewin. 2 vols. Göttingen, 1839–1851.
CSHB	*Corpus scriptorum historiae byzantinae.* Joannis Malalae Chronographia. Edited by L. Dindorf. Bonn, 1831.
de Boor	de Boor, C. *Excerpta historica iussu imp. Constantini Porphyrogeniti confecta.* Vol. 3. Berlin, 1905.
de Falco	de Falco, V., ed. *Iamblichi theologumena arithmeticae.* 2nd ed. Stuttgart, 1975.

Felten	Felten, J., ed. *Nicolai Progymnasmata*. Rhetores Graeci 11. Leipzig, 1913.
FGrHist	*Die Fragmente der griechischen Historiker.* Edited by F. Jacoby. Berlin-Leiden, 1923–1958.
Garzya	Garzya, A., ed. *Synesii Cyrenensis epistulae*. Rome, 1979.
Gow-Page	Gow, A. S. F., and D. L. Page. *The Greek Anthology: Hellenistic Epigrams*. 2 vols. Cambridge, 1965.
Helmreich	Marquardt, J., I. von Müller, and G. Helmreich, eds. *Claudii Galeni Pergameni scripta minora*. 3 vols. Leipzig, 1884–1893.
Kassel-Austin	Kassel, R., and C. Austin, eds. *Poetae comici graeci*. 8 vols. Berlin, 1983–.
Kühn	Kühn, K. G., ed. *Galeni Opera Omnia*. 20 vols. Leipzig, 1821–1833.
Kühner-Blass	Kühner, R., and F. Blass. *Ausführliche Grammatik der griechischen Sprache*. Vol. 1. 3rd ed. Hannover, 1890–1892.
Littré	Littré, E., ed. *Oeuvres complètes d'Hippocrate*. 10 vols. Paris, 1839–1861.
Lobel-Page	Lobel, E., and D. L. Page. *Poetarum Lesbiorum Fragmenta*. Oxford, 1955.
Merkelbach-West	Merkelbach, R., and M. L. West, eds. *Fragmenta Hesiodea*. Oxford, 1967.
Patillon	Patillon, M., and G. Bolognesi, eds. *Aelius Theon, Progymnasmata: Texte établi et traduit*. 2nd ed. Paris, 2002.
Pfeiffer	Pfeiffer, R. *Callimachus*. 2 vols. Oxford, 1949, 1953.
PG	*Patrologia graeca.* Edited by J.-P. Migne. 162 vols. Paris, 1857–1886.
PMG	*Poetae melici graeci.* Edited by D. L. Page. Oxford, 1962.
Radt	Radt, S., ed. *Tragicorum graecorum fragmenta*. Vol. 3: Aeschylus. Göttingen, 1999.
Snell-Maehler	Snell, B., and H. Maehler. *Bacchylides*. Leipzig, 1970.
Voigt	Voigt, E.-M. *Sappho et Alcaeus*. Amsterdam, 1971.
West	West, M. L. *Iambi et Elegi Graeci*. 2 vols. 2nd ed. Oxford, 1989–1992.

INTRODUCTION

FROM THE OFFICE OF DEAD LETTERS: THE REDISCOVERY OF THE EPISTLES

The year 1492 saw two notable discoveries, one greater and one lesser: Columbus came upon the New World while sailing across the Atlantic, and Janus Lascaris reported that while he journeyed through Apulia he found a manuscript[1] containing fifty letters by a previously unknown author. Some years later, this manuscript was bought by the humanist, doctor, and court historian in Vienna, Johannes Sambucus (1531–1584), who published the text for the first time in 1566.[2] The manuscript, dating from the twelfth/thirteenth century and coming from the region of Otranto,[3] made its way, like many other manuscripts acquired by Sambucus, to the imperial library in Vienna. Known as the *Codex Vindobonensis philologicus graecus* 310, it constitutes our sole witness to the text.[4] Its original

---

1. The coincidence in date is also noted by Arnott (1974, 353). For the text of Lascaris's reference to the Aristaenetus codex, cf. Müller 1884, 402, and also Bianchi 2008, 138–39.

2. Ἀρισταινέτου Ἐπιστολαὶ ἐρωτικαί· Τινὰ τῶν παλαιῶν Ἡρώων Ἐπιτάφια; E Bibliotheca c.v. Ioan. Sambuci (Antwerp: Plantin, 1566). See Mazal 1968 on this and other early editions.

3. A good summary of the manuscript's character and date is provided by Drago (2007, 9–10). Its *terminus ante quem*, as well as a link to the vicinity of Otranto, is established by the presence at the end of book 1 (on the verso of f. 40) of two poems by Nicolas Nectarius of Otranto (1155/56–1235), abbot of the nearby monastery of St. Nicolas of Casole between 1219 and 1235. Written in cursive, in a hand roughly contemporary with, or only slightly later than, that of the manuscript, these were first noted and published by Bast (1796, 7–8 n. 2). In the same note, Bast also mentioned a rendering of Aristaenetus, *Ep.* 1.22, in iambics in the lower right-hand margin of the manuscript (recto of f. 32). Jacob (1988) identified the hand as that of Palaganus of Otranto, datable to the early thirteenth century.

4. On this manuscript and the transmission of the letters, see Lesky 1957.

cover page is lost, but a copyist seems to have replaced the title (or what he thought the title ought to be) at the top of the first page—obscured though it is by stains and corrections. It appears to read Ἐπιστολαὶ Ἀριστ^{αιγετ},[5] which Lascaris and almost all subsequent editors have taken as Ἐπιστολαὶ Ἀρισταινέτ[ου (more on the rationale for this title in a moment). It has hence been customary to call the author of these fifty charming erotic letters "Aristaenetus" ever since.

Sender Unknown

The name Aristaenetus, however, is probably just a placeholder for the more apposite "Anonymous." For although some have asserted his reality and even attempted to identify him with a particular historical personage,[6] "Aristaenetus" seems more likely to have been fictitious, entering the ranks of ancient epistolographers as the result of guesswork, probably because a copyist speculated about the authorship of the collection.[7] That precisely this sort of speculation prompted its attribution to Aristaenetus is plausible in light of the following considerations: (1) all but two of its texts start with a heading, listing the letter's author and recipient; these are overwhelmingly fictional *sprechende Namen* (signifying names) wit-

---

5. Cf. Mazal's (1971) note on the title of book 1 in his apparatus. His reading has been forcefully confirmed by Bianchi (2008, 137–38). By contrast, Vieillefond (1992) (who relied on a microfilm of the manuscript, not autopsy) claims in his apparatus to the title to be able to read no more than the letters "arist ..." (or "Arist ..."), followed by two characters obscured by a stain—possibly ων—over which appears the correction αι, scil. ἀρισται. In this he is followed by Drago (2007, 16 n. 38).

6. Thus Lucas Holstenius (1596–1661) proposed in a letter to Lambecius (*Ep.* 63) from the year 1646 that we identify the author with that Aristaenetus known as one of the orator Libanius's closest friends and most frequent correspondents before his untimely death in an earthquake in 358 (see Boissonade 1817, 331–35, esp. 334). The identification is most unlikely given internal chronological indicators in the letters of Aristaenetus, on which see below. It is worth considering, however, whether our Aristaenetus might have adopted the persona of the learned friend and avid letter writer with whom Libanius shared both thoughts and books (see Gallé Cejudo 1999, 19). Drago (2007, 17) notes that others have—without justification—suggested identifying Aristaenetus with the figure mentioned by Synesius, *Ep.* 133 (Garzya) as having held the office of consul in the east for the year 404.

7. For the sake of simplicity, we refer to the author as Aristaenetus throughout the rest of the introduction, as opposed to placing the name in quotation marks or calling him Pseudo-Aristaenetus.

tily characterizing the speaker and his addressee; (2) Aristaenetus, who appears as author of the first epistle of book 1, which occupies the most prominent location in the text, perfectly fits this category, as his name means "Praiser of the Best,"[8] an apt description of one writing here in praise of the charms of Lais, which are supreme; (3) from this position at the head of the first letter, it was an easy step to place Aristaenetus at the head of the corpus as a whole.[9]

Postmark Unclear

It may strike us as fitting that Aristaenetus turns out to be a fictitious author of a collection of fictitious erotic letters, yet (as we have seen) one would more accurately call him Anonymous. He is an Anonymous, however, whose letters contain clues helping us situate him in a particular time and cultural environment. Internal indicators point to a date around 500 c.e. In *Ep.* 1.26, we find two important historical references. First, the narrator describes himself as a "public courier" (τῆς πολιτείας ἱππεύς), "acquainted with the new Rome and the old" (καὶ πρός γε τῇ νέᾳ τὴν πρεσβυτέραν ἱστόρηκα Ῥώμην). Since Emperor Constantine officially established Constantinople as the "new Rome" in 324 c.e., the title provides a secure *terminus post quem* for the collection. This letter, however, also contains a reference to the famous pantomime Karamallos ("Wooly Head," a designation likely pointing to the type of wig worn by the mime).[10] A celebrated pantomime of this name appears in a poem by Sidonius Apollinaris datable to the years between 463 and 466 (*Carm.* 23.268–271). He may or may not be

---

8. Lesky (1951, 8) and Drago (2007, 17) suggest that the compound should rather be taken passively, that is, describing the author as worthy of the best praise; see also Arnott's translation "Bestpraiseworthy" (1982, 293). But verbal adjectives ending in -τος, and their derivative names, can be either passive or active in sense (cf. Kühner-Blass 1.2:288–89).

9. No one would dream of taking "Aristaenetus" as anything other than fictitious if this letter did not come at the start of the collection but was located elsewhere. Zanetto (1987, 197–99), however, argues that because the collection includes several letters playfully purporting to be by Aristaenetus's epistolographic models (see xxii below), we cannot rule out the possibility that the author would have wanted to take his place at the head of his work among these illustrious literary predecessors.

10. On the term ἔμμαλος with reference to mimes and various compound names ending in -μαλλος designating mimes, see the passage from Malalas cited below, as well as Maricq 1952, 362–68 and Gager 1992, 52 (with n. 27).

the same Karamallos depicted on a "contorniate medallion" from the reign of Emperor Valentinian III (425–455) bearing the Greek inscription "May you be victorious, Karamallos."[11] Complications arise, however, regarding the reference in Sidonius since John Malalas (*Chron.* 15 [*PG* 97:573; *CSHB* p. 386:17–20]) notes how in the years between 478 and 481/82[12] Longinus, brother of Emperor Zeno, presented to the Green circus faction of Constantinople a bewigged (ἔμμαλος) Alexandrian dancer, Autokyon, nicknamed Karamallos (along with another, Rhodos, nicknamed Chrysomallos ["Goldilocks"]: ἔδωκε δὲ τοῖς Πρασίνοις ἔμμαλον τὸν Αὐτοκύονα τὸν λεγόμενον Καράμαλλον ἀπὸ Ἀλεξανδρείας τῆς μεγάλης, καὶ τὸν Ῥόδον τὸν λεγόμενον Χρυσόμαλλον). This Karamallos is unlikely to have been the same who bestrode the stage in Sidonius, since Malalas, writing about events some twenty years later, appears to envision a performer considerably younger and less established than others of his time or than the one highlighted by Sidonius.[13] The complications multiply, moreover, as possibly still another Karamallos is referred to in the collection of historical excerpts made by Emperor Constantine VII Porphyrogenitus (*Excerpta de insidiis* [170 de Boor]) in connection with events of the year 520 as being a particularly celebrated pantomime at the circus of Constantinople at that time. Perhaps, as scholars have suggested, these two or more Karamalloi belonged to different generations within the same theatrical family, an artistic dynasty,[14] or perhaps they refer simply to a character type common among pantomimes of this period. Which Karamallos did Aristaenetus have in mind? There is no sure way to tell. These "wooly mime" stories, however, offer a range of possibilities between about 425 and 520 C.E.

A date in this general range harmonizes with the language of Aristaenetus. He emulates the Attic style of such classical authors as Plato and Menander, favorite models both, while also regularly drawing on second and third century C.E. Atticists such as Alciphron, Lucian, and Philostratus

---

11. On "contorniate medallions" (coins with a deep furrow on the edge, which were struck in the fourth and fifth century C.E.) depicting mimes in general and on the Karamallos medallion in particular, see Jory 1996, 6–8, and Drago 2007, 28.

12. On the date, see Burri 2004, 86 (with n. 18).

13. Earlier in the passage cited above, Malalas says that the wig-bearing pantomimes brought by Longinus were young (ὀρχηστὰς ἐμμάλους μικρούς) since he had set free Constantinople's older, more famous ones, after giving them many gifts (ἦσαν γὰρ οἱ ὀρχούμενοι ἐν Κωνσταντινουπόλει εὔφημοι παλαιοί, καὶ ἐποίησεν αὐτοὺς λῦσαι, πολλὰ χαρισάμενος αὐτοῖς). Cf. Burri 2004, 86.

14. Cf. Burri 2004, 86–87; Drago 2007, 28.

the Elder. Yet "as with so many writers of late antiquity his aim often fell far short of the target, and his Greek abounds with solecisms," as Arnott puts it (1982, 295). Prose rhythm is another factor placing Aristaenetus in the fifth century or later: he is one of the earliest authors to use accent-regulated clausulae, that is, a prose rhythm at the end of his sentences or before a sense pause that avoids "sequences of words there with one or no unaccented syllables between the last and penultimate accents, and favoring sequences with two or four such syllables" (Arnott 1974, 355).[15]

One final clue that may push our author's date to the later end of the spectrum comes in *Ep.* 1.19. Here, the musician Melissarion bears a child to her lover, Charikles. He, in turn, "considered it the greatest injustice for his beloved, the mother of such a child, to still be called hetaira. So he liberated her at once from that shameful profession and made his beloved his wife, so as to plant in her the seed of legitimate children." Mazal (1977, 3–4) has argued that this story presupposes the existence of the *Lex de nuptiis* enacted by Emperor Justin between 520 and 524, which specifically permitted actresses (*scaenicae*) to wed men of any rank provided they give up their dishonorable profession.[16] Vieillefond (1992, x–xi) has objected that tales of young men raising up poor, socially inferior women so as to make them their legitimate wives are "un thème éternel dans la littérature comme dans la vie." Yet the letter would undoubtedly acquire added point and topical significance in light of the recent promulgation of this law, since Melissarion's transformation from actress/hetaira to legitimate wife finds a striking parallel in the life of the notorious actress/hetaira

---

15. Fundamental on this topic are Meyer 1905 and Nissen 1940. The latter demonstrates how Aristaenetus regularly modified the phrasing of antecedent texts he was quoting, so that they would follow this rule of prose rhythm.

16. *Cod. justin.* 5.4.23: "Thus since it would be unjust that slaves should be able to receive their freedom by imperial indulgence and be restored to their natural rights so as to live, upon bestowal of imperial beneficence of that kind, as if they had never been slaves and had always been free born, but that women who have been on the stage [*mulieres autem, quae scaenicis quidem sese ludis ǀmmiscuerunt*], but who have changed their mind and have abandoned a dishonorable profession, should have no hope of imperial beneficence which might lead them back to the condition in which they might have lived if they had not sinned, we grant them by this beneficent imperial sanction the right that, if they abandon their dishonorable conduct, and embrace a better and honorable mode of life, they may supplicate our majesty, and they will unhesitatingly be granted an imperial rescript permitting them to enter into a legal marriage" (Blume 2009).

Theodora, who by means of this law was to become the bride of the future emperor Justinian. Mazal's argument for a date after 520 thus gains a certain plausibility, the more so as it would place Aristaenetus in the context of the revival of classical literature in the reign of Justinian.[17] But though suggestive and appealing, Mazal's proposal is by no means conclusive. We do best, therefore, to remain flexible: a date somewhat before or after 500 C.E. seems appropriate.

Intimate Correspondence

Recent years have seen the publication of several translations that label Aristaenetus's epistles *Lettres d'amour* (Vieillefond 1992), *Lettere d'amore* (Conca and Zanetto 2005; Drago 2007), or *Lletres d'amor* (Pagès 2009). "Letters *about* love" they are, indeed—love letters they are, for the most part, not. Only a few texts in the collection grant us glimpses of an intimate correspondence between lovers, while a significant number bear only the slightest resemblance to actual letters: containing neither epistolary formulae nor references to the medium, to the composition of the message, its delivery, or its reception, they offer third-person narratives with no visible connection to either sender or recipient.[18] In numerous instances nothing besides the heading (*X to Y*) and the context of the collection indicates that we are to envision the text in front of us as part of a written correspondence. As we shall see, the epistolary framework is indeed meaningful to Aristaenetus. Yet one can often lose sight of it, as the author's emphasis appears to lie more in presenting his readers with erotic tales or anecdotes, which would function equally well without their epistolary trappings.

The majority of Aristaenetus's letters are concerned with the description of extramarital affairs; they are full of lovers using every trope of erotic literature to praise their beloveds in over-the-top encomia, paramours hatching complicated schemes to achieve their desires, wily go-betweens who help smooth their way, unfaithful spouses barely avoiding

---

17. It is impossible to say where the author lived. Mazal's contention that Aristaenetus must have been part of that "humanistisch gebildeten Schicht in Konstantinopel" (1977, 5) remains purely speculative.

18. See Zanetto 1987, 196. Altogether, Aristaenetus's fifty letters contain only four brief references to the letter as medium (2.1; 2.3; 2.9; 2.17) and three more-detailed references to the act of writing (1.24; 2.5; 2.13); cf. Höschele 2012, 163–64.

capture in the midst of hair-raising and amusing infidelities—in short, the stuff of comedy, erotic poetry, and the ancient novel. We encounter, among other things, a man getting into bed with two women (1.2), a girl losing her virginity before marriage (1.6), a youth in love with his father's mistress (1.13), a prison guard cuckolded by a man incarcerated for adultery (1.20), a serving girl caught *in flagrante* with the lover of her mistress (2.7), and a young husband filled with passion for his mother-in-law (2.8). The entire collection is pervaded by a spirit of frivolity and imbued with light-hearted humor; we are invited to laugh about the erotic adventures and misdemeanors of Aristaenetus's characters. Despite its erotic topics, however, the corpus remains relatively tame in its description of amorous encounters, avoiding open obscenity and passing over the most delicate moments: it is titillatingly suggestive rather than explicit.[19] Thus, the narrator in *Ep.* 1.2 concludes his recollection of a ménage à trois by stating: "So far my story is appropriate for anyone's ear—but what follows, let me just sum it up and say that I found a rough-and-ready chamber fitting the need and did not disappoint either one." Placed toward the beginning of the collection, this erotic aposiopesis has a clear programmatic function: so far, and not further.[20]

In a similar vein, in *Ep.* 1.21 Telesippe, who grants her lover everything apart from intercourse, could be taken as an emblem of the narrative boundaries Aristaenetus set himself. "By all means touch my breasts," she tells her lover, "enjoy the sweetest kisses, and embrace me while I'm still dressed, but don't get on my nerves demanding sex, and don't expect it, since you'll only cause yourself distress and lose what you can have." It would be wrong to take this reticence as a sign of prudery: Aristaenetus evidently likes to tease his readers and to appeal to their erotic imagination by withholding a graphic account of the sexual act itself. The reader thus is in a situation similar to Telesippe's lover Architeles.[21] His longing for closure is never entirely gratified, but this is precisely what keeps him hooked, as Telesippe herself points out: "as long as you're wishing for intercourse, it's sweet, gratifying, and utterly desirable. But once it has happened, it's

---

19. Cf. Arnott 1982, 310–15.

20. As Arnott (1982, 311) has observed, Aristaenetus "prefers to draw a veil over the subsequent love-making. Or rather, a series of different veils: for even in this area of taboos he aims at variety."

21. On the significance of the names, see notes on *Ep.* 1.21.

despised; and what had long seemed the heart's most urgent desire is suddenly discarded, spit upon, ignored."

There is, however, one erotic theme whose absence strikes us as conspicuous: nowhere does Aristaenetus make mention of pederastic relationships,[22] which is particularly surprising in light of his obvious debt to Plato. As Arnott (1982, 314) poignantly puts it: "Why did 'Aristaenetus' embargo homosexuality while cheerfully tolerating marital infidelity and perhaps even incest?" He views Aristaenetus's cultural background as a possible reason for his exclusion of this topic: writing in an age when Christianity had become the official state religion, Aristaenetus might, he argues, have hesitated to portray a form of sexuality so utterly condemned by many of his contemporaries. Nothing in the collection indicates that Aristaenetus himself was Christian—quite on the contrary: given his nostalgic evocation of a pagan world,[23] it seems most likely that he was not. But whatever his personal beliefs, it is a fair assumption that Aristaenetus's omission of pederasty in some way reflects the moral climate of his time, as same-sex relationships of any kind came increasingly under attack during late antiquity, in Christian and non-Christian circles alike.[24]

THE EPISTOLARY TRADITION

In composing fictional letters, Aristaenetus inscribes himself in a long literary tradition. The epistolary genre is notoriously difficult to define, and we will not offer a comprehensive discussion of its numerous subtypes.[25] Suffice

---

22. There are some vestiges of homoeroticism in the collection (cf. Aristaenetus's description of how those "who love the sight of beauty would jostle for a chance to see [Acontius] going to his teacher's" in *Ep.* 1.10, or his characterization of a youth, who has just started to grow a beard, as "equal parts lover and beloved" in *Ep.* 1.11, or again the very suggestive relationship between groom and horseman in *Ep.* 1.8), but there is no explicit portrayal of pederasty.

23. Arnott (1982, 303) calls his oeuvre a "valedictory hymn to paganism."

24. On the change in moral attitudes and conceptions of masculinity in late antiquity, see Kuefler 2001, esp. 87–96 on *impudicitia* and pederasty. Floridi (2012) shows how, for instance, Ausonius significantly toned down the pederastic elements in a poem about a dead youth vis-à-vis his earlier models. Boswell (1980) argues that early Christianity was relatively tolerant toward homosexuality.

25. Trapp (2003, 1) gives the following definition: "A letter is a written message from one person (or set of people) to another, requiring to be set down in a tangible medium, which itself is to be physically conveyed from sender(s) to recipient(s). For-

it to say that one may roughly distinguish between "real" letters, bound to a specific occasion and composed with a pragmatic purpose (be they official or private), and multiple forms of literary epistles, including semi-private letters (such as those by Cicero and Pliny), texts of various content (e.g., didactic or scholarly) cast into epistolary form, verse epistles, and fictional letters.[26] The boundaries are, of course, blurry, and one cannot expect every letter or epistle-like text to fit neatly into one of these categories.[27] Of particular interest in our context is the last of the aforementioned types: the fictional letter. Not only are letters frequently embedded in narrative texts, especially in historiographic prose and the novel, but they also appear as important plot devices on stage.[28] Furthermore, several collections of pseudepigrapha have come down to us, that is, letters written by anonymous authors in the voice of famous historical figures (among them Aeschines, Socrates, and Euripides), some of which in fact resemble modern epistolary novels.[29]

Most closely related to Aristaenetus's literary undertaking, however, are three corpora of Greek fictional letters from the period commonly known as the Second Sophistic. The term describes an intellectual move-

---

mally, it is a piece of writing that is overtly addressed from sender(s) to recipient(s), by the use at beginning and end of one of a limited set of conventional formulae of salutation (or some allusive variation on them) which specify both parties to the transaction. One might also add, by way of further explanation, that the need for a letter as a medium of communication normally arises because the two parties are physically distant (separated) from each other, and so unable to communicate by unmediated voice or gesture; and that a letter is normally expected to be of relatively limited length." For further reflections on what constitutes a letter, see Gibson and Morrison 2007; on ancient epistolography, see also Stowers 1986; Stirewalt 1993; Morello and Morrison 2007; Ceccarelli 2013.

26. This is the classification proposed by Sykutris (1931), whose article is still an important starting point for any study of ancient epistolography.

27. With regard to Sykutris's fourth and fifth categories, for instance, Rosenmeyer (2001, 12) rightly points out that "the difference between verse and prose ... is less crucial in an epistolary context than the difference between fictive or imaginative letters and letters whose writers and receivers are not invented."

28. On Greek epistolary fiction, see the excellent study in Rosenmeyer 2001; see also Jenkins 2006 on intercepted letters in Greco-Roman literature; Olson 2010 on embedded letters in Josephus; Hodkinson, Rosenmeyer, and Bracke 2013 on epistolary narratives in Greek literature.

29. On the Greek epistolary novel, see Holzberg 1994, esp. his "Versuch einer Gattungstypologie" (1–52). On pseudepigraphic letter collections, see also Rosenmeyer 1994 and Luchner 2009.

ment during the early Roman Empire (ca. 60–230 C.E.) whose representatives immersed themselves in the rhetorical tradition and strove to assert their Greek identity by looking to the glorious past of Hellas, showcasing their knowledge of earlier literature and writing in the Classical Attic dialect.[30] Παιδεία ("education/culture") was the ideal of the time; being a πεπαιδευμένος ("cultivated individual") was not just a question of private learnedness but could also have great political significance.[31] Replete with allusions and full of rhetorical flourish, the epistolary collections by Alciphron (ca. 170–220), Claudius Aelianus (ca. 175–235), and Philostratus of Lemnos (ca. 170–ca. 244–249)[32] clearly reflect the spirit and culture of the time.

Alciphron's four books revive the world of Menandrian drama through letters penned by fishermen, farmers, parasites, and courtesans, which grant the reader glimpses into the daily lives and concerns of nonelite characters from a long bygone era.[33] His epistolary impersonation of comic stock figures and notorious hetairas moves Alciphron's oeuvre close to the realm of rhetorical *ethopoieia*, a form of school exercise that required the student to envision what a particular (historical or imaginary) person would say in a given situation, for instance, when faced with great emotional stress or when standing before an important decision.[34] "Impersonation" was one of fourteen so-called *progymnasmata* ("preliminary exercises"), which were designed to prepare future orators for more-advanced rhetorical studies; they usually took the form of short practice speeches but could, it seems, also involve the composition of letters.[35] Elevating this mode of writing to

---

30. On the Second Sophistic, see Anderson 1993; Swain 1996; Whitmarsh 2001; and Borg 2004.

31. Cf., e.g., Gleason 1995 and Schmitz 1997.

32. We know of four writers bearing the name Philostratus; most scholars identify the author of the letters with Philostratus the Elder, who is known, in particular, for his *Lives of the Sophists* and the *Life of Apollonius of Tyana*. Cf. Rosenmeyer 2001, 322, with further references.

33. As Rosenmeyer (2001, 257) remarks, "while Menander was praised for showing scenes of 'real life' to his audience, Alciphron creates for his readership a 'reality' based on the literary representations of Menander, so at a second degree of distance." On Alciphron's letters, see Anderson 1997; Rosenmeyer 2001, 255–307; Schmitz 2004; Hodkinson 2007; and König 2007. On the reception of New Comedy in Alciphron and other epistolographers, see Höschele 2014, with further references.

34. On Alciphron's letters as *ethopoieiai*, see Ureña Bracero 1993.

35. This is attested by two grammarians from the first and fifth centuries C.E.:

literary heights, Alciphron's oeuvre, however, far transcends the world of rhetorical training.

One way in which Alciphron marks his debt to comedy and highlights the artificiality of his characters is his ubiquitous use of *sprechende Namen*. As we have seen, Aristaenetus too likes to give his senders and recipients "speaking" names, but they look rather innocuous in comparison to such monstrosities as Alciphron's Cothylobrochthisus ("Cup Guzzler," 3.5) or Dipsanapausilypus ("Thirst Assuager," 3.31).[36] The fictional nature of the world evoked in Alciphron's oeuvre is, moreover, evident from the tension between the writers' social status and their literary skills. The author draws our attention to this incongruity when he has a character justify his erudition by the fact that he comes from Athens, "where there is not a single man who hasn't had a taste of these things" (3.29.3). As Schmitz has observed (2004, 98), "the Athens where everybody has part in παιδεία is not any real landscape, it is located in the nostalgic imagination of the πεπαιδευμένοι of the Second Sophistic." A similar tension is palpable throughout Aelian's collection of twenty *Rustic Letters*,[37] which invites us to picture various rural characters, including Menander's misanthrope Knemon (*Ep.* 13–16), with pen in hand. Aelian likewise reflects on the paradox of erudite country folk by sealing his work with a programmatic statement that, though voiced by a farmer to his friend, is clearly targeted at the external reader (*Ep.* 20): "If this letter sent to you sounds too smart to be supplied by the country, don't be surprised: for we are not Libyan or Lydian, but *Athenian* farmers."

While Alciphron and Aelian slip into the roles of multiple characters, men and women alike, Philostratus writes in his own voice, or rather in the voice of a fictionalized alter ego.[38] The majority of his letters are love notes of varying length (some not longer than a sentence or two) to unnamed boys and girls, though the corpus also contains messages of nonerotic content addressed to specific individuals, most notably a missive to Empress Julia Domna on matters of rhetoric (*Ep.* 73). Although we may picture Philostratus as the composer of all these texts, the collection as a whole does not present us with a coherent narratorial voice, let alone any underlying

---

Theon of Alexandria (115 Patillon) and Nikolaos (67,2–5 Felten). On the role of letters in ancient education, see Cribiore 2001, 215–19.

36. On *sprechende Namen* in Alciphron, see Schmitz 2004, 99–100.

37. On Aelian's letters, see Rosenmeyer 2001, 308–21; Hodkinson 2007 and 2013.

38. On Philostratus's letters, see Rosenmeyer 2001, 322–38; Goldhill 2009.

epistolary narrative. His *billets d'amour* for the most part offer variations on amatory *topoi* and are concerned with winning over a beloved. For the sake of erotic persuasion Philostratus resorts to any kind of argument and does not shy away from contradicting assertions phrased in other letters—though seemingly sincere confessions of love, the texts are sophistic showpieces written for the entertainment of an erudite audience.

Aristaenetus and His Epistolary Models

Most of the letters in these three corpora remain unanswered and leave it up to the reader to imagine how the various situations might have evolved. There are a few letter pairs and epistolary sequences in Alciphron and Aelian,[39] but in general the letters tend to be "soliloquies rather than dialogues" (Rosenmeyer 2001, 130). The same is true of Aristaenetus's collection, in which not a single text is accompanied by a direct reply. His work does, however, feature epistolary dialogues of another (metaliterary and intertextual) kind, for Aristaenetus significantly pays homage to those earlier epistolographers by incorporating them as correspondents into his own oeuvre[40]: *Ep.* 1.5 is sent from Alciphron to Lucian, 1.22 from Lucian to Alciphron; Philostratus appears as the author of *Ep.* 1.11, while book 2 opens with a letter from Aelian.

The absorption of Aristaenetus's literary predecessors into his epistolary universe is, in fact, prefigured by Alciphron's invention of an epistolary exchange between Menander and Glykera, which seals the fourth and last of his books (*Ep.* 4.18/19).[41] After evoking, throughout his oeuvre, a world largely based on that of New Comedy by having comic figures voice their concerns not on stage but on the written page, Alciphron intriguingly transforms the playwright into a letter writer himself. Aristaenetus, in turn, manifests his awareness of Alciphron's strong ties to New Comedy by featuring him as sender/recipient of two letters replete with Menandrian echoes.[42] Significantly, not only are *Ep.* 1.5 and 1.22 connected through their pair of correspondents (this is the only instance in the collection that a sender and recipient reappear!), but they also form, as Zanetto has seen

---

39. Rosenmeyer 2001, 315–19; Hodkinson 2007, 293–95.

40. Zanetto 1987, 197–99; Drago 2007, 22–24.

41. Rosenmeyer 2001, 301–6; Höschele 2014; for a commentary on this letter pair, see Bungarten 1967.

42. See Höschele 2014.

(1987, 198–99), a thematic diptych, insofar as each tells of a woman who cunningly regains a man's affection with the help of another female.

In *Ep.* 1.5 we hear of a married woman lured by a prospective lover to a banquet, from where she flees in panic upon noticing her husband. In order to divert his suspicions, she hands her robe, which he had seen at the party, over to a friend, who subsequently saves her from the man's fury by pretending to have borrowed the garment in question. Their trick has the desired effect: letting go of his anger, the husband even asks for his wife's forgiveness. As Arnott (1973, 203–5) has demonstrated, Aristaenetus's letter recalls Menander's *Samia* in its depiction of the raging husband. Though the plot of this comedy has little to do with the event reported by Alciphron—its main intrigue is centered on getting a youth married to the neighbor girl he had seduced—Aristaenetus repeatedly draws on the vocabulary used by Menander with reference to angry old men.[43] To name just the most conspicuous parallels: the rather exotic word that characterizes the women's deceit (βουκολέω, "bamboozle") twice appears in the *Samia* (530, 596), where it is employed by Demeas and Nikeratos in the midst of heated arguments. In addition, the conduct of the jealous husband, who leaps over the threshold (εἰσπεπήδηκεν) and screams at the top of his voice (κεκραγώς), resembles the furious behavior of Menander's Nikeratos (εἰσπεπήδηκεν, 564; κεκράξεται, 549; κέκραγε, 553; κέκραχθι, 580) upon discovering that his daughter has had a baby.

Beyond these and further verbal parallels detected by Arnott, one might, we suggest, also note a structural analogy between the two texts. In Menander's play, Demeas's concubine Chrysis passes off as hers the baby to whom Plangon, impregnated by Moschion during a festival,[44] has given birth in their fathers' absence; this pretense leads to great trouble, as Demeas ends up suspecting innocent Chrysis of having slept with his son. In Aristaenetus, on the other hand, the guilty wife clears herself of any suspicion by eliciting the help of a neighborhood friend, who passes off as "hers" the incriminating *corpus delicti*. Could this deception acted out by the two women not recall the female scheme that stands at the beginning of the *Samia*? A robe is, of course, no baby, and the women's trick in and of itself would hardly point to Menander's comedy. But a reader whose poetic

---

43. For a discussion of the parallels, see also Drago 2007, 151–53.

44. Note that the banquet to which the wife is invited in Aristaenetus also takes place during a public festival (Πανηγύρεως ἐν προαστείῳ πανδημεὶ τελουμένης ...).

memory of the *Samia* has already been triggered by its verbal echoes might very well note a similarity between the two intrigues.

Be that as it may, it is certainly no coincidence that the tale attributed to Alciphron is thus infused with Menandrian language and motifs. Significantly, the same is true of the letter addressed to Alciphron by Lucian (*Ep.* 1.22). As a composer of dialogues, this Second Sophistic author (ca. 125–180 C.E.) may be said to represent a genre related to epistolography, insofar as the ancients regarded a letter as "one half of a conversation" (Pseudo-Demetrius 223).[45] Lucian's *Dialogues of the Courtesans*, which show close similarities to Alciphron's *Letters of Hetairai*, also served as an important source of inspiration for Aristaenetus's portrayal of the erotic demi-monde.[46] Could Aristaenetus evoke Lucian's association with the genre of dialogue by having him "answer" Alciphron's story with an erotic anecdote of his own? As noted above, these are the only two letters in the collection with an identical pair of correspondents. Even if Lucian does not explicitly reply to Alciphron's message, his tale is, from its first sentence, marked as a companion piece to that of his addressee through its reference to a common acquaintance, Charisios ("you know what the boy is like"). For this seems to pick up Alciphron's aside concerning another common acquaintance, Charidemos, toward the beginning of 1.5 ("you know what a womanizer the boy is").[47] Alciphron and Lucian are thus envisioned as exchanging stories about people belonging to their mutual circle of friends; this is the closest we come in Aristaenetus to an actual epistolary *exchange*, a fact that makes the choice of dialogue-writing Lucian as one of the correspondents seem highly pointed.

On a metapoetic level, Lucian's parenthetic comment about Charisios might, as Drago (2007, 349) has observed, also appeal to the reader's literary knowledge: "you know the boy and his ways—*since you are familiar with his model*."[48] As in the case of *Ep.* 1.5, the letter's generative nucleus is

---

45. Among Lucian's texts we also find four *Saturnalian Letters* (see Slater 2013), but he is best known for his composition of literary dialogues.

46. Cf. Drago 2007 on *Ep.* 1.16, which she views as deriving from Lucian, *Dial. Court.* 3, and the textual notes below on *Ep.* 1.24 and 1.25.

47. Cf. Zanetto 1987, 198; Drago 2007, 348–49.

48. Interestingly, the words are themselves an almost verbatim quotation of a passage in Plato's *Phaedo*, where they are used of Apollodorus, one of Socrates's disciples who was present at his death (οἶσθα γάρ που τὸν ἄνδρα καὶ τὸν τρόπον αὐτοῦ, 59B).

to be found in a text of New Comedy: this time, the *Perikeiromene.*[49] Like Polemon, the lover in Menander's play, Charisios is portrayed as rash and arrogant; both are, moreover, filled with jealousy toward an imagined rival. In Menander, Polemon shaves off his beloved's hair in a fit of rage after misinterpreting an embrace between Glykera and her brother. In Aristaenetus, by way of contrast, Glykera and her slave Doris—their names are identical to those of Menander's female characters—deliberately provoke Charisios's jealousy so as to rekindle his passion. For this purpose Doris pretends that her mistress is crazy about a man named Polemon (!) and filled with hatred for Charisios, which immediately makes him seek his beloved's forgiveness. Jealousy, then, is a crucial element in both texts, yet its function in Aristaenetus's tale is opposite to that in Menander (there it sets off the crisis; here it brings about its solution). This prominent structural reversal is, we suggest, reflected in Aristaenetus's switch of names vis-à-vis his model text (turning Polemon from lover into rival)—a switch that is, moreover, paralleled by the letter's reversal of sender and addressee (Lucian to Alciphron) in relation to *Ep.* 1.5.

WHY LETTERS?

It goes without saying that it is possible to enjoy the two anecdotes told in *Ep.* 1.5 and 1.22 for their own sake; but an intertextually alert reader may find further pleasure in recognizing Aristaenetus's playful adaptation of Menandrian material and appreciate his sophisticated homage to Alciphron and Lucian: far from using the names of these two authors haphazardly, Aristaenetus attaches them to letters that mirror central aspects of their work, such as Alciphron's predilection for New Comedy or Lucian's association with dialogue. Similar observations could be made about Aristaenetus's engagement with Philostratus in *Ep.* 1.11 and Aelian in *Ep.* 2.1,[50] but the principle underlying his allusive technique should have become sufficiently clear from our preceding discussion. The question to be addressed at this point is, Why letters?

---

49. While Arnott (1973, 205–6) detects only general reminiscences of comedy in the letter, and though Magrini (1981, 154–55) views Lucian's *Dial. Court.* 8 as the letter's generative nucleus, Drago (1997, 178–86; 2007, 342–47) has persuasively argued that its main model is the *Perikeiromene.* Since she offers a detailed discussion of the parallels, we limit ourselves to a brief comparison.

50. See Drago 2007 (*ad loc.*) and our notes.

To be sure, the collection contains a few texts designed to look like actual love letters. We hear, for instance, Mousarion assure Lysias of her devotion (1.24), Euxitheos declare his love to Pythias (2.2), or Myrtale reproach Pamphilos for running after another woman (2.16). The corpus, moreover, includes various messages relating to matters of love, which are addressed to a rival (2.6) or friend (Glykera, for example, complains to Philinna about her husband [2.3], while lovesick Parthenis asks Harpedone for advice [2.5]). As mentioned above, however, there are many more texts that exhibit a mere veneer of epistolarity, and the overall scarcity of epistolary markers raises the question of why Aristaenetus opted for this genre at all. Did he, perhaps, simply follow in the footsteps of his epistolographic models without giving much weight to the generic implications of letter writing? We believe not: his choice of the epistolary form is anything but fortuitous.

A central, if not *the* defining, feature of Aristaenetus's work is his constant intertextual dialogue with earlier writers, which seems to be fueled by a fervent wish to bridge the gulf between himself and the admired authors of old. Aristaenetus's inclusion of writers from other eras as correspondents within his oeuvre gives vivid testimony to his desire to bring the literary past into his own here and now. And the medium of the letter constitutes, we submit, the ideal tool for such an undertaking.[51] As a means of communication between two persons who are physically separated, a letter serves to transport words from one locale—and one temporal moment—to another. Could the intervening distance between writer and addressee that marks any epistolary exchange not reflect the temporal, spatial, and cultural remoteness of earlier authors in relation to Aristaenetus, who attempts to overcome that distance in the act of reading and writing?[52]

Throughout Aristaenetus's collection we hear the voices of writers past whose words are inscribed into his epistles. In this context it is significant to note that the ancients attributed to letters the capacity to make the absent present. Authors frequently assert that they feel their addressees to

---

51. This and the following observations are based on Höschele 2012, 161–66.

52. In a similar vein, Höschele (2009, 148) argues that the coupling of Catullus's two translations from Sappho (*Carm.* 51) and Callimachus (*Carm.* 66) with two poetic epistles (*Carm.* 50 and 65) is not coincidental: the transportation of words across time and space through the medium of the letter parallels Catullus's transportation of words from a distant time, an alien culture, and a foreign language into his own here and now through the medium of translation.

be virtually present while writing to them. One example is from Cicero's correspondence with C. Cassius (*Fam.* 15.16.1): "It somehow happens—I don't know how—that you seem to be quasi present when I write something to you, and not just as a vision."[53] It is, we submit, precisely this mediating function, the letter's ability to evoke with such intensity the physically and temporally distant, that makes it so attractive a vehicle for an author like Aristaenetus. On a metaliterary level, the epistolary form may thus be said to embody the intertextual dialogue that stands at the core of his collection.

Stolen Mail: Aristaenetus, an Artful Thief

In the previous section, we suggested how Aristaenetus's engagement with the literary past may be figured in the very form he adopted, the epistle. The method of his dialogue with antecedent texts differs, however, from that employed by his Second Sophistic models. To be sure, like these he emulated the language of fifth- and fourth-century B.C.E. Athens. But he went further than them in the extent to which he appropriated earlier material: he not only infuses his texts with learned allusions to, and choice phrases from, the classics of the tradition, both poetry and prose; he regularly lifts big chunks—lengthy, almost-verbatim extracts—from these works, rarely with attribution. Plato and Attic comedy hold pride of place as a source of plunder (we have already seen something of what he takes from Menander), but he had also clearly read in detail and with care the learned third-century B.C.E. poet Callimachus, basing two of his letters (1.10 and 1.15, respectively) on the tales of *Acontius and Cydippe* and *Phrygius and Pieria* from book 3 of that poet's *Aetia*, and appropriating some of his exotic vocabulary.[54] Aristaenetus's epistolographic models—Alciphron, Aelian, Philostratus—also yield rich spoils to him, as do other Second Sophistic authors, such as Lucian and the Greek novelists (in particular, Achilles Tatius and Xenophon of Ephesus). Aristaenetus has consequently been disparaged as a "common burglar" and "jackdaw."[55]

---

53. On the so-called *parousia* topos in ancient letters, see Thraede 1970.

54. For the manner and detail of his thematic and lexical appropriations, see the apparatus to Pfeiffer's edition of Callimachus, frs. 67–75 (*Acontius and Cydippe*) and frs. 80–83 (*Phrygius and Pieria*); see also Arnott 1982, 308; Harder 1993; Harder 2012.

55. Arnott (1973, 202) describes Aristaenetus as a "common burglar," or again

In literary terms, however, burglary was a time-honored figure for appropriation in antiquity; its connotations could be quite positive.[56] The sneering adjective "common" here misses the mark, for Aristaenetus was, demonstrably, an artful thief. His larceny could at times be grand, in the sense of both large scale and marvelous. By way of illustration, let us examine an instance of such grand larceny: a long, near-verbatim quotation in *Ep.* 1.19. This will offer insight into our author's allusive method inasmuch as it shows both how he extracts an extended passage from a model and how he uses it most artfully to his own ends.

In the letter, a slave woman named Euphronion tells how her fellow theater artist Melissarion, though raised by an impoverished mother, managed to escape her lowly origins: her brilliant artistry as a performer (μουσουργός) opened every door, and Melissarion did her utmost to keep those doors open wide, for as the narrator puts it (1.19):

> Her company highly prized [πολύτιμον], Melissarion socialized with the richest men.
>
> It was crucial that she not get pregnant, lest the birth of a child cheapen her in the eyes of her lovers and she spoil the flower of her youth too soon in labor. The musician had heard the tale that women tell each other, that when a girl is going to be pregnant the seed doesn't come out of her at all, but rather it stays inside, held back by nature. When she heard this, it made sense to her, and she always kept it in mind. And on noticing that this had in fact happened to her, that is, that her seed had not come out, she told her mother about it, and they reported it to me, as I was more experienced in such matters. No sooner had I learned of it than I ordered her to do what I knew had to be done and quickly freed her of her anxious forebodings.

What the narrator, Euphronion, evidently knew through her greater experience was how to induce a quick abortion, whereby she freed Melissarion of her anxious forebodings. Later, however, when Melissarion fell in love with the rich and handsome Charikles (ἐπισήμου καὶ κάλλει καὶ πλούτῳ) and found that he shared her feelings, she bore him a child. He thereupon made her his lawful wife, allowing her to leave her disreputable profession.

(1974, 359) as "a jackdaw, embellishing his pages with vivid passages and phrases culled verbatim or with minimal alteration from a variety of earlier authors."

56. Theft as a figure for an author's use of the earlier tradition appears already in Callimachus, *Epigr.* 43 Pfeiffer (= 13 Gow-Page = *Anth. pal.* 12.134); cf. Bing 2009, 166–69; Hinds 1998, 22–25; McGill 2010.

Along with her new status, she adopted a new name: henceforth she has been known as Pythias.

As has long been noted, the passage above is taken with just a few minor alterations and clarifying supplements[57] almost word for word from Hippocrates, *On the Nature of the Child* (περὶ φύσιος παιδίου [7:490 Littré]).[58] Its narrative framework, however, is quite different. In *On the Nature of the Child*, the author explains how he came to see a seed (embryo) when it was in its sixth day. He was able to observe its appearance because a kinswoman of his owned a slave girl, a high-priced performer (μουσοεργὸς πολύτιμος, as in Aristaenetus), who had to avoid childbirth to maintain her value with the men she went with. When, however, the girl noticed that telltale sign of pregnancy mentioned also in the epistolographer, she informed her mistress, who in turn told Hippocrates. As a remedy, he ordered her to jump into the air, kicking up her legs so as to strike her buttocks with her heels. "And when she had made seven kicks the seed fell to the ground with a noise, and when she saw it she gazed at it and marveled. I shall tell how it looked: it was as if someone removed the shell of a raw egg so that the fluid inside showed through the inner membrane."[59]

Despite Aristaenetus's verbatim fidelity to his source, it is striking to see how artfully he adapts the Hippocratic passage, subtly altering its complexion so as to fit his own narrative: he is anything but slavish. Neither, as it turns out, is his heroine (a change that can, we think, be read metapoetically). For his μουσουργός is no longer the slave girl of the medical text but the daughter of a free, though penniless, woman, Aglais. Aristaenetus further individualizes the anonymous performer of his source by giving her a name, Melissarion. While the nameless Hippocratic slave confides the news of her pregnancy to her mistress (ἔφρασε τῇ δεσποίνῃ), Melissa-

---

57. See Arnott 1973 (198–200), who notes how the epistolographer "translates the Hippocratic Ionic as best he can into his own pseudo-Attic, with the mistakes typical of his period" (198).

58. Γυναικὸς οἰκείης μουσοεργὸς ἦν πολύτιμος, παρ' ἄνδρας φοιτέουσα, ἣν οὐκ ἔδει λαβεῖν ἐν γαστρί, ὅκως μὴ ἀτιμοτέρη ἔῃ· ἠκηκόει δὲ ἡ μουσοεργός, ὁκοῖα αἱ γυναῖκες λέγουσι πρὸς ἀλλήλας· ἐπὴν γυνὴ μέλλη λήψεσθαι ἐν γαστρί, οὐκ ἐξέρχεται ἡ γονή, ἀλλ' ἔνδον μένει· ταῦτα ἀκούσασα ξυνῆκε καὶ ἐφύλασσεν αἰεί, καί κως ᾔσθετο οὐκ ἐξιοῦσαν τὴν γονήν, καὶ ἔφρασε τῇ δεσποίνῃ, καὶ ὁ λόγος ἦλθεν ἕως ἐμέ.

59. καὶ ἐγὼ ἀκούσας ἐκελευσάμην αὐτὴν πρὸς πυγὴν πηδῆσαι, καὶ ἑπτάκις ἤδη ἐπεπήδητο, καὶ ἡ γονὴ κατερρύη ἐπὶ τὴν γῆν, καὶ ψόφος ἐγένετο, κἀκείνη δὲ ἰδοῦσα ἐθηᾶτο καὶ ἐθαύμασεν. Ὁκοῖον δὲ ἦν ἐγὼ ἐρέω, οἷον εἴ τις ᾠοῦ ὠμοῦ τὸ ἔξω λεπύριον περιέλοι, ἐν δὲ τῷ ἔνδον ὑμένι τὸ ἔνδον ὑγρὸν διαφαίνοιτο.

rion does so to her own mother (ἔφρασε τῇ μητρί).[60] She in turn informs a friend (the narrator), Melissarion's fellow showgirl, who has her best interests at heart. This contrasts starkly with the Hippocratic tale, where the slaveholder turns to a kinsman, Hippocrates, whose remedy aims only to protect the financial interests of the mistress. For Aristaenetus, Melissarion's abortion serves as an expedient, a necessary step in her pursuit of happiness, her personal journey out of poverty to riches and status.

It tells us a good deal about the epistolographer's use of his sources to see how he develops the whole story of Melissarion's rise into an upper-class milieu out of the seeds of two key terms he found in his source, μουσοεργός and πολύτιμος.[61] In Hippocrates, both appear without elaboration. We do not know what sort of μουσοεργός his anonymous slave girl is, nor in what sense she was πολύτιμος.[62] Aristaenetus, by contrast, specifies that Melissarion's activities as μουσουργός were not those of a demi-mondaine at symposia, as the term sometimes connotes;[63] rather, she performed in a larger public setting on stage (σκηνή) and was "immersed in the theater" (θεάτρου μεστὴ γεγονυῖα). Further, she became a μουσουργὸς πολύτιμος, a highly prized artist (as opposed to Hippocrates, where the same words suggest only a high-priced entertainer), by making herself εὐμουσοτέρα, "more accomplished in her artistry" than her peers (πασῶν γέγονεν εὐμουσοτέρα τῶν ὁμοτέχνων). Aristaenetus emphasizes her artistic skill (τέχνη), saying that it even transformed her appearance: "she came to look even more beautiful through the adornment of her art" (κἀκ τῆς τέχνης, οἷα φιλεῖ, κοσμηθεῖσα τὴν ὄψιν ἐδόκει βελτίων). While Hippocrates states only that his performer consorted with men (παρ' ἄνδρας φοιτέουσα), Aristaenetus changes this straightforward phrase by addition of a single word: Melissarion socialized with *the richest* men (παρ' ἄνδρας πλουσιωτάτους ἐφοίτα). These, moreover, are characterized as her "lovers" (ἐρασταί), who bestow on her ever more, and more valuable, gifts. What moves them to do so is her skill's renown (εἶτα καὶ πλείους φιλοτιμότερόν τε χαριζομένους διὰ κλέος τῆς ἐπιστήμης). Again, artistry is the key to esteem (the lovers' gifts

---

60. The above changes are also noted by Kapparis 2002, 111 n. 72.

61. Arnott (1973, 199) likewise notes the importance of these Hippocratic terms to Aristaenetus's letter.

62. In the Hippocratic text, the worry that pregnancy would make the μουσοεργός less valuable (ἀτιμοτέρη) suggests that her πολυτιμία derives only from her looks, not from musical talent as in Aristaenetus.

63. Drago 2007, 318–19.

grow ever more distinctive, φιλοτιμότερον, relative to her own growing distinction, πολύτιμος). In thus embellishing his model's simple account of a nameless performer, Aristaenetus explicates the (Hippocratic) epithet πολύτιμος, justifying its application to his μουσουργός. He thereby makes plausible Melissarion's happy ending, the heroine's blissful union with the outstandingly handsome and wealthy Charikles: each is exceptional; like has found like. Thus Melissarion transcends her origins, and Aristaenetus exceeds his Hippocratic source. Heroine and author alike break out of the (narrative) constraints that form the core of the Hippocratic text: there, the abortion tale is self-contained, functioning to maintain the status quo by permitting the μουσοεργός simply to carry on as before; here, by contrast, it enables a different conception—narrative and biological—a further chapter in the story, where Melissarion produces new life, achieves higher status, adopts another identity.

To be sure, Hippocrates's lowly slave-girl performer is still present in this story. Aristaenetus has displaced her onto the role of his narrator, Euphronion. This character's fate, like that of her Hippocratic prototype, is to remain forever a slave (ἐγὼ δ' οὖν τὸν πάντα δουλεύσω χρόνον),[64] in which capacity she toils in out-of-the-way theaters and goes with brutish lovers (ἀτόποις τε θεάτροις καὶ ἀγνώμοσιν ἐρασταῖς). Despite her lowly occupation, however, Euphronion is "more experienced" than most in medical matters, so it is no surprise that Melissarion's mother turns to this figure for help with her daughter's predicament (ὁ λόγος ἅτε πρὸς ἐμπειροτέραν ἦλθεν ὡς ἐμέ). Her expertise appears at once in her prompt appraisal of the case and prescription for a course of action: "I ordered her," she says, "to do what I knew had to be done and quickly freed her of her anxious forebodings" (καὶ ταύτῃ διαπράξασθαι ἅπερ ᾔδειν ἐγκελευσαμένη, τῆς προσδοκωμένης ἐλπίδος ἀπήλλαξα τάχιον). This statement, which caps the long quotation from *On the Nature of the Child*, implicitly points Aristaenetus's readers back to his literary model—at least those among them who, like his narrator, are "more experienced" and so familiar with his source.[65] For

---

64. Her words quote Menander's *Epitrepontes* (560), where the slave Onesimos complains ἀλλ' ἐγὼ τὸν πάντα δουλεύσω χρόνον ("But I shall serve as a slave for all time"). As Drago points out (2007, 319–20), the larger situation in Aristaenetus also resembles that in Menander's play, since Onesimos says this of himself when marveling at how the hetaira Habrotonon has hatched a plot that will, she hopes, win her freedom.

65. A second, less erudite readership is also figured in the text, namely, the broader group that has "heard the tale that women tell each other" (1.19). Their knowledge, as

Euphronion suggestively omits the Hippocratic remedy's most colorful details (the vigorous kicks to the buttocks while leaping, and the ensuing miscarriage).[66] She thereby invites us to supplement what she has left out.[67] Led thus to recall the literary paradigm, we are able to appreciate how the author embellished his source.

Such knowing play with the Hippocratic intertext clearly suggests that Aristaenetus was a learned author. His expectation, moreover, that readers understand his play suggests that he wrote for an elite reading community such as Johnson (2010) has described for the high Roman Empire—an audience of shared culture and learning, willing to apply its intelligence, readerly acumen, and care to the study of a text.[68] Does Aristaenetus's use of this source here, however, necessarily suggest that he had read deeply in the Hippocratic corpus, not to say scoured it in search of literary fodder? Does it suggest that his audience has done the same? Not necessarily, it seems. For although the anecdote of the μουσοεργὸς πολύτιμος and the termination of her pregnancy does indeed originate with Hippocrates, *On the Nature of the Child*, it turns out to have been much cited, debated, and admired—a circumstance generally ignored in Aristaenetan scholarship.

Already Soranus (fl. 98–128 c.e.) in his *Gyn.* 1.60 refers to it, mentioning both treatise and author by name, to show how it was a subject of controversy: Hippocrates's advice here to induce an abortion evidently contradicted his ban on abortion elsewhere in his work.[69] How were these

---

the text suggests, comes via popular, purely oral transmission. Contrast the suggestion of literacy in the case of Euphronion (cf. n. 67 below).

66. It may be "characteristic of this author ... to break off a story the moment before insalubrious or lubricious detail becomes necessary," as Arnott contends (1973, 199), but the meaning of the omission does not end there.

67. How much does Euphronion as a character know, and from where does she get her knowledge? Aristaenetus seems to flirt with the idea that she has read the model text herself. After all, Euphronion serves as the author of this letter; she is surely literate. The long quotation from Hippocrates appears in her mouth. Does the character cite it knowingly? A sort of holdover from the Hippocratic tale, she describes herself as ἐμπειροτέρα, "more experienced" (1.19), a term that one may be tempted to read as referring specifically to the narrator's knowledge of the Hippocratic cure.

68. For these qualities, see Johnson 2010 throughout, but especially ch. 5, "Doctors and Intellectuals: Galen's Reading Community," pp. 81–84, 91–96.

69. "And an 'expulsive' (*ekbolion*) some people say is synonymous with an abortive [*phthorion*]; others, however, say that there is a difference because an expulsive does

views to be reconciled? This question stood at the heart of a longstanding and heated dispute.[70]

Controversy aside, the passage was also singled out not just as an example of Hippocrates's acute eye and diagnostic skill but as an especially fine instance of his pleasing style and narrative art. The doctor and philosopher Galen, for instance, refers to the passage in four separate works, twice quoting the entire story verbatim (*On Semen* 4.525–526 Kühn; *On the Formation of the Fetus* 4.653–655 Kühn).[71] Each time he declares it to be by Hippocrates.[72] For Galen, what makes this passage so memorable is its combination of "accuracy of observation" (τῆς θεωρίας ἀκρίβεια) and "pleasure" (τέρψις). Here is what he says in the first of those citations when discussing the appearance of the uterus as it surrounds the seed enclosed in its membrane:

> But it is better to hear what Hippocrates says on the same subject in his work *On the Nature of the Child*; he will instruct us by the accuracy of his observation, and he will delight us, as he tempers his narrative with pleasing language, so that for a short time the seriousness of the account is relaxed and we are refreshed with enjoyment combined with profit, in order that we may thereafter with increased vigor apply ourselves more intently to the remainder of the account. And now let us listen to Hippocrates.[73]

---

not mean drugs but shaking and leaping, ... For this reason they say that Hippocrates, although prohibiting abortives, yet in his book 'On the Nature of the Child' employs leaping with the heels to the buttocks for the sake of expulsion [ἐκβολῆς χάριν τὸ πρὸς πυγὰς πηδᾶν]" (Temkin 1956, 62–63).

70. The debate is still evident in the seventh-century c.e. commentary on the Hippocratic passage by John of Alexandria: "It is customary to object at this point that it was he himself who said in the Oath 'I will not give the means to induce abortion.' How is it, then, that he orders the woman to perform the buttocks leap [κελεύει ἐπὶ πυγὴν πηδῆσαι τὴν γυναῖκα]? Numerous responses to this objection are current" (*Commentary on Hippocrates' On the Nature of the Child* 216 [*CMG* 11.1.4:146–47]). John's commentary goes on to enumerate the responses.

71. The two shorter references are in *On the Natural Faculties* 2.3 (3:163,18–20 Helmreich) and *Against Lykos* 7.3 (*CMG* 5.10.3:24,20–22).

72. In the latter passage he also weighs whether it might be by Hippocrates's student and son-in-law Polybus. In this regard as well, then, the passage was the subject of discussion.

73. Galen, *On Semen* 4.525–526 Kühn (*CMG* 5.3.1:77,28).

It is remarkable here how Galen attributes an almost therapeutic quality to the Hippocratic anecdote, one that sharpens the focus and nurtures the zeal of the reader. Immediately hereafter, Galen quotes verbatim the entire anecdote from Hippocrates as it appears also in Aristaenetus.

Lest one think that, prior to Aristaenetus, only medical writers found the Hippocratic passage appealing, we should point out that it is also quoted in full in the *Theologumena arithmeticae* (61 de Falco), attributed to Iamblichus (ca. 245–ca. 325 C.E.), though largely excerpting and incorporating the work of the mathematician Nicomachus (ca. 60–ca. 120 C.E.). Strangely, the author uses it in a part of the work on the *heptad* (i.e., sevens), so as to illustrate the universal importance of that number. To this end, he slightly alters the chronology of the Hippocratic narrative. While Hippocrates recounts "how I saw a seed that was *six* days old" (ὡς δὲ εἶδον τὴν γονὴν ἑκταίην ἐοῦσαν ἐγὼ διηγήσομαι), Iamblichus speaks of the seed's appearance when it was *seven* days old (ἡμέραις δὲ ἑπτά). Indeed, he adds to the doctor's tale that it was specifically upon hearing that it was "seven days old" (ἑβδομαίαν οὖσαν) that he ordered the slave girl to make her leaps. Hippocrates had already specified that it took *seven* leaps to expel the seed (καὶ ἑπτάκις ἤδη ἐπεπήδητο, καὶ ἡ γονὴ κατερρύη ἐπὶ τὴν γῆν). Did that detail inspire Iamblichus to change the timing, thus enabling him to render the numbers more pleasingly congruent?[74]

Be that as it may, it is clear that Aristaenetus need not have turned to the original Hippocratic treatise to read the saga of the μουσουργὸς πολύτιμος.[75] As an oft-quoted tale, it was available in a variety of works, perhaps more than have survived. Our survey of them has opened a window, revealing a whole panorama of potential sources. This circumstance in no way diminishes our assessment of the sophistication and breadth of Aristaenetus's reading; far more, it increases it. For from what we are able to glean of Aristaenetus's reading habits, we can exclude *none* of them (nothing suggests that Aristaenetus drew on a *florilegium*): our epistolographer was learned enough to plausibly have used any of these as his prototype.

Similarly, there were doubtless those among his readers who—whatever the source he was using—were able to recognize and enjoy his allu-

---

74. It is hard to account otherwise for the change, the more so as the previous chapter of the *Theologumena arithmeticae* is on the *hexad*, "sixes": Why did he not put it there?

75. His extensive verbatim quotation demonstrates conclusively that he encountered the tale through a written medium, rather than oral tradition.

sive play, both here and throughout the collection: that elite community of readers mentioned above. Yet this is only one aspect—and the least accessible one at that—of the letters' artistry. For ancient audiences as well as modern, they can hold a more general appeal. Aristaenetus tells a good tale, delighting readers with humorous incident, titillating them with risqué detail, charming them with vivid portraits of love's never-ending entanglements.

PS ON THE TRANSLATION

Ours is the first complete translation of the letters of Aristaenetus into English in nearly three hundred years.[76] The last was the elegant, though rather free work of an anonymous translator: *Letters of Love and Gallantry: Written in Greek by Aristaenetus* (1716). It was preceded by selections translated by Thomas Brown in Voiture's *Familiar and Courtly Letters* (1701)[77] and by A. Boyer in *Letters of Wit, Politicks and Morality* (1701) and followed by a verse rendering of just the first book by the playwright R. B. B. Sheridan and N. B. Halhed (1771). Since then, nothing. Time alone, then, would seem to justify, if not necessitate, a new attempt, even for so minor an author as this one. Yet Aristaenetus also deserves to reach a modern audience for his own sake. His letters are sexy, funny, learned, diverting—not necessarily at once, but by turns and recurrently. And they exude a winning passion for the Greek literary tradition (already quite ancient by his time), which Aristaenetus channels throughout his own writing, though his style also admits some later Greek peculiarities.

In our translation, accompanied here by a Greek text,[78] we, too, have aimed at a somewhat archaizing, thoroughly literary style. Readers should not be surprised if they hear echoes of earlier poetry and prose, including epistles. We have not shied, however, from leavening these with contemporary touches. Such a mixture is also evident in our inconsistent spelling of

---

76. The absence of a modern English version is particularly striking if one considers the number of translations into other modern languages from the twentieth century and after: Licht (1928) and Lesky (1951) into German; Brenous (1938) and Vieillefond (1992) into French; Conca and Zanetto (2005) and Drago (2007) into Italian; Gallé Cejudo (1999) into Spanish; Pagès (2009) into Catalan.

77. Brown enlarged his selection by several letters some years later in Brown 1707.

78. We diverge from Mazal's 1971 critical edition of the single manuscript in several places; see the list at the start of our notes, p. 103.

proper names: we Latinize the more familiar (e.g., Plato rather than Platon) but for the most part transliterate the Greek (e.g., Philokalos, not Philocalus). Throughout, we tried to create an Aristaenetus whose English is pleasing and readable—one moreover whose classical learning is no obstacle to enjoyment (we provide readers with basic help in the notes corresponding to each letter, although we do not point out every allusion[79]). Finally, we hope that our translation will help Aristaenetus find an English-speaking audience, perhaps even admirers, once again following a centuries-long absence from the scene.

PPS: Thank-You Note

Atlanta-Toronto, February 14, 2014

A collaborative translation like ours, spun out over years and between distant cities, involves pleasures comparable to those of a stimulating epistolary exchange. Ours have been enriched by the help of many friends. We would like to thank Emilia Barbiero, Lucia Floridi, and Niklas Holzberg for their astute comments and suggestions. We are indebted, too, to Patricia Rosenmeyer, who put her incomparable knowledge of the epistolographic tradition at our disposal in evaluating our typescript for the press. David Konstan, an editor of the Society of Biblical Literature's Writings from the Greco-Roman World, encouraged us to submit the volume for this series. Last but not least, our institutions, Emory University and the University of Toronto, generously provided us with research funds, which helped bring our project to fruition. We dedicate this volume to all those who have nurtured eros through the medium of the letter.

Peter Bing   Regina Höschele
Atlanta   Toronto

---

79. We note only those allusions that seem especially prominent; for a fuller list of parallel passages, see the apparatus in Mazal 1971 and the discussion in Drago 2007.

TEXT AND TRANSLATION

ΑΡΙΣΤΑΙΝΕΤΟΥ ΕΠΙΣΤΟΛΩΝ
ΒΙΒΛΙΟΝ Α΄

α΄.

Ἀρισταίνετος Φιλοκάλῳ

Λαΐδα τὴν ἐμὴν ἐρωμένην εὖ μὲν ἐδημιούργησεν ἡ φύσις, κάλλιστα δὲ πάντων ἐκόσμησεν Ἀφροδίτη, καὶ τῶν Χαρίτων συνηρίθμησε τῷ χορῷ· ὁ δὲ χρυσοῦς Ἔρως ἐπαίδευσε τὴν ποθουμένην εὐστόχως ἐπιτοξεύειν ταῖς τῶν ὀμμάτων βολαῖς. ὦ φύσεως τὸ κάλλιστον φιλοτέχνημα, ὦ γυναικῶν εὔκλεια καὶ διὰ πάντων ἔμψυχος τῆς Ἀφροδίτης εἰκών. ἐκείνη γὰρ (ἵνα κάλλος ἀφροδίσιον εἰς δύναμιν διαγράψω τοῖς λόγοις) λευκαὶ μὲν ἐπιμὶξ καὶ ὑπέρυθροι παρειαί, καὶ ταύτῃ τὸ φαιδρὸν ἐκμιμοῦνται τῶν ῥόδων· χείλη δὲ λεπτὰ καὶ ἠρέμα διῃρημένα καὶ τῶν παρειῶν ἐρυθρότερα· ὀφρύς τε μέλαινα, τὸ μέλαν ἄκρατον· τὸ δὲ μεσόφρυον ἐμμέτρως τὰς ὀφρῦς διορίζει· ῥὶς εὐθεῖα καὶ παρισουμένη τῇ λεπτότητι τῶν χειλῶν· ὀφθαλμοὶ μεγάλοι τε καὶ διαυγεῖς καὶ καθαρῷ φωτὶ διαλάμποντες· τὸ δὲ μέλαν αὐτῶν, αἱ κόραι μελάνταται, καὶ τὸ κύκλῳ λευκόν, αἱ γλῆναι λευκόταται, καὶ ἑκάτερον ὑπερβολῇ πρὸς τὸ ἕτερον ἐπιδείκνυται, καὶ τὸ λίαν ἀνόμοιον εὐδοκιμεῖ παρακείμενον. ἔνθα δὴ τὰς Χάριτας ἐγκαθιδρυμένας πάρεστι προσκυνεῖν. ἡ δὲ κόμη φυσικῶς ἐνουλισμένη ὑακινθίνῳ ἄνθει καθ᾽ Ὅμηρον ἐμφερής, καὶ ταύτην αἱ χεῖρες τημελοῦσι τῆς Ἀφροδίτης.

τράχηλος λευκός τε καὶ σύμμετρος τῷ προσώπῳ κἂν ἀκόσμητος ᾖ, δι᾽ ἁβρότητα τεθάρρηκεν ἑαυτῷ· περίκειται μέντοι λιθοκόλλητον περιδέραιον, ἐν ᾧ τοὔνομα γέγραπται τῆς καλῆς· γράμματα δ᾽ ἐστὶ τῶν λιθιδίων ἡ θέσις. ἔτι δὲ εὐμήκης ἡλικία. σχῆμα καλόν τε καὶ περίμετρον καὶ τῷ τύπῳ συνδιατιθέμενον τῶν μελῶν. ἐνδεδυμένη μὲν εὐπροσωποτάτη ἐστίν, ἐκδῦσα δὲ ὅλη πρόσωπον φαίνεται. βάδισμα τεταγμένον βραχὺ δέ, ὥσπερ κυπάριττος ἢ φοῖνιξ σειόμενος ἡσυχῇ, ἐπεὶ φύσει τὸ κάλλος ἐστὶν ὑπερήφανον. ἀλλ᾽ ἐκείνους μὲν οἷα φυτὰ κινεῖ ζεφύρου πνοή, αὐτὴν δέ πως ὑποσαλεύουσι τῶν Ἐρώτων αἱ αὖραι.

THE LETTERS OF ARISTAENETUS
BOOK 1

1.1.

Aristaenetus[1] to Philokalos[2]

Lais,[3] my beloved, was well fashioned[4] by Nature, but Aphrodite adorned her most beautifully of all and made her part of the Graces'[5] chorus. Golden Eros taught my darling[6] to take sure aim with the arrows of her eyes. O most beautiful and dearest masterpiece of Nature, O pride of the female sex and in every way the living image of Aphrodite. She has—so as to paint her intoxicating beauty in words to the best of my ability—she has white cheeks daubed with a touch of red, thus emulating the radiance of roses. Her lips are delicate, lightly parted, and redder than her cheeks. Her eyebrows are black, the blackest black, and are set apart in ideal proportion. Her nose is straight, a perfect match for the delicacy of her lips. Her eyes are large and sparkling, shining with pure light. Her pupils are darker than dark, and the whites surrounding them are brightest white; each sets off the other in its intensity, glorifying its neighbor through its exceeding difference. There indeed the Graces have settled, inviting worship. Her hair is curly by nature, comparable to the hyacinth flower as Homer describes it,[7] and its care is in Aphrodite's hands.

Her throat is white and becoming to her face, even when unadorned, confident in its plush delicacy. Nonetheless a necklace set with stones encircles it, on which the name of my beautiful girl is written; the arrangement of the stones spells out the letters. Furthermore, she is just the right size. Her clothing is lovely, well proportioned all around, and fitting the form of her limbs. Dressed, she has the loveliest face; undressed, it's as though she's all face.[8] Her step is elegant, like the motion of a cypress or a palm gently swaying,[9] for by nature beauty is majestic. But these, as befits plants, are set in motion by the wind of Zephyr,[10] whereas I imagine it's the breezes of

ταύτην ἑαυτοῖς ὡς οἷόν τε ἦν οἱ κορυφαῖοι γεγράφασι τῶν ζωγράφων. ἡνίκα οὖν
δέοι γράφειν Ἑλένην ἢ Χάριτας ἢ καὶ αὐτήν γε τὴν ἄρχουσαν τῶν Χαρίτων,
οἷον εἰς ὑπερφυὲς παράδειγμα κάλλους ἀφορῶντες ἀνασκοποῦσι τὴν εἰκόνα
Λαΐδος, κἀντεῦθεν ἀποτυποῦνται θεοπρεπῶς τὸ φιλοτεχνούμενον εἶδος. μικροῦ
με παρῆλθεν εἰπεῖν ὡς κυδωνιῶντες οἱ μαστοὶ τὴν ἀμπεχόνην ἐξωθοῦσι βιαίως.

οὕτω μέντοι σύμμετρα καὶ τρυφερὰ τῆς Λαΐδος τὰ μέλη, ὡς ὑγροφυῶς
αὐτῆς λυγίζεσθαι τὰ ὀστᾶ τῷ περιπτυσσομένῳ δοκεῖν. τοιγαροῦν ταῦτα μικροῦ
γε ὁμοίως δι᾽ ἁπαλότητα συναπομαλάττεται τῇ σαρκί, καὶ ταῖς ἐρωτικαῖς
ἀγκάλαις ὑπείκει. ἡνίκα δὲ φθέγγεται, βαβαί, ὅσαι τῆς ὁμιλίας αὐτῆς αἱ
σειρῆνες, ὅσον ἡ γλῶττα στωμύληθρος. τῶν Χαρίτων πάντως ἡ Λαῒς τὸν κεστὸν
ὑπεζώσατο, καὶ μειδιᾷ πάνυ ἐπαγωγόν. οὕτως οὖν τὴν ἐμὴν ὡραϊζομένην
καὶ τρυφῶσαν ὑπὸ πλούτου τῆς εὐπρεπείας οὐδ᾽ ἂν ὁ Μῶμος ἐν ἐλαχίστῳ
μωμήσαιτο. ἀλλὰ πόθεν ἄρα με τοιαύτης ἠξίωσεν Ἀφροδίτη; περὶ κάλλους
οὐκ ἠγωνίσατο παρ᾽ ἐμοί, Ἥρας Ἀθηνᾶς οὐκ ἔκρινα τὴν θεὸν εὐπρεπεστέραν
ὑπάρχειν, ψῆφον αὐτῇ δίκης οὐκ ἀπέδωκα μῆλον, καὶ ἁπλῶς μοι ταύτην πεφι-
λοτίμηται τὴν Ἑλένην. ὦ πότνια Ἀφροδίτη, τί σοι τῆς Λαΐδος ἕνεκα θύσω;
ἣν οἱ προσβλέποντες ἀποτροπιάζουσιν ὧδε σὺν θαύμασι προσευχόμενοι τοῖς
θεοῖς· "ἀπίτω φθόνος τοῦ κάλλους, ἀπίτω βασκανία τῆς χάριτος." τοσοῦτον
αὐτῇ περίεστιν εὐπρεπείας, ὡς τῶν προσιόντων ἀγλαΐζειν τὰς κόρας τὴν Λαΐδα.
καὶ γέροντες εὖ μάλα πρεσβῦται θαυμάζουσιν, ὡς οἱ παρ᾽ Ὁμήρῳ δημογέρον-
τες τὴν Ἑλένην, καὶ· "εἴθε," φασίν, "ἢ ταύτην ηὐτυχήσαμεν ἡβῶντες ἢ νῦν
ἠρξάμεθα τῆς ἡλικίας." οὐ νέμεσις τὸ γύναιον εἶναι διὰ στόματος τῇ Ἑλλάδι,
ἔνθ᾽ οἱ κωφοὶ διανεύουσιν ἀλλήλοις τῆς Λαΐδος τὸ κάλλος. οὐκ ἔχω ὅ τι λέγω,
οὐδὲ ὅπως παύσομαι· λήξω δὲ ὅμως, ἓν μέγιστον ἐπευχόμενος τοῖς γραφεῖσι,
τῆς Λαΐδος τὴν χάριν, ἧς δι᾽ ἔρωτα πολὺν οἶδα καὶ νῦν τὸ προσφιλὲς ὄνομα
πολλάκις εἰπών.

β΄. ΠΑΡΘΕΝΟΙ ΝΕΑΝΙΣΚΟΝ ΕΦΑΜΙΛΛΩΣ ΠΟΘΟΥΣΑΙ

Ἑσπέρᾳ τῇ προτεραίᾳ μελῳδοῦντί μοι κατά τινα στενωπὸν δύο κόραι προσῆλθον
ἀναβλέπουσαι χάριν Ἔρωτος μειδιῶσαι καὶ μόνῳ γε τῷ ἀριθμῷ λειπόμεναι τῶν
Χαρίτων· κἀμὲ διηρώτων αἱ μείρακες ἁμιλλώμεναι πρὸς ἀλλήλας ἀδόλως καὶ
ἦθος οὐ πεπλασμένον ἐμφαίνουσαι· "ἐπειδὴ μέλη προσᾴδων καλὰ τὰ δεινὰ τῶν
Ἐρώτων ἡμῖν ἐμβέβληκας βέλη, λέγε πρὸς τῆς σῆς εὐμουσίας, ἧς ἐρωτικῶς
πρὸς τοῖς ὠσὶ καὶ τὴν ψυχὴν ἐμπέπληκας ἑκατέρας ἀμφοτέρων ἡμῶν, τίνος

the Erotes[11] that dance about her. The greatest masters have painted her[12] for their own purposes as best they could. So when they need to paint a Helen,[13] or the Graces, or the Graces' queen[14] herself, they look to the image of Lais as a superb model of beauty, and from there they copy that lovingly created form in a manner fit for the gods. I almost forgot to say that her breasts, ripe as Cydonian apples,[15] virtually burst the bands that hold them. But Lais's limbs are so shapely and curvaceous that her bones seem lithely to entwine the one embracing her. Thus through their softness they are almost as pliant as her flesh, yielding to a lover's arms. And when she speaks—oh my god!—what Siren songs[16] escape her lips, how expressive her tongue.

Lais has fastened all about her the Graces' girdle,[17] and she smiles ever so seductively. So not even Blame[18] could find the slightest thing to blame with my girl in the fullness of her bloom, in the luxury of her looks. But why has Aphrodite considered me worthy of such a girl? She did not compete in a beauty contest with me as judge;[19] I did not judge the goddess more beautiful than Hera or Athena; I did not give her an apple[20] as the token of my vote, and yet she simply honored me with this Helen. O mistress Aphrodite, what offering shall I make to you in return for Lais? When people see her, they are so awestruck that they try to ward off evil by praying to the gods as follows: "May no one envy her beauty; may no one begrudge her grace!" Lais possesses such excess of beauty that she brings sparkle to the eyes of all who pass. Even the eldest of the old marvel at her, as the Trojan elders marveled at Helen in Homer,[21] and "If only," they say, "we'd had the luck to encounter her when we were young, or we were just now at the threshold of youth." There's no begrudging that the woman is on the lips of all Greece, where even the mutes nod to each other in admiration of Lais's beauty. I am dumbstruck, but unable to stop talking about her. But stop I shall nonetheless, wishing for my writings this one most crucial thing, namely, the charm of Lais[22]—my great love for her, I know, makes me utter her beloved name continually.[23]

1.2. Girls Competing for the Love of a Youth

Yesterday evening, as I was singing in an alleyway, two girls came up to me who had the grace of Eros in their look and smile. They were inferior to the Graces only in number.[1] Openly competing with each other and totally frank, the girls asked me: "Since, singing your beautiful songs, you have struck us with the dreadful arrows of the Erotes, say—by the sweetness of your music, with which you have filled not only the ears of us both but also

ἕνεκε μελῳδεῖς; ἑκατέρα γὰρ ἑαυτὴν ἐρᾶσθαί φησι. καὶ ζηλοτυποῦμεν ἤδη καὶ διὰ σὲ φιλονείκως καὶ μέχρι τριχῶν συμπλεκόμεθα πολλάκις ἀλλήλαις." "ἀμφότεραι μὲν ὁμοίως," εἶπον, "καλαί, πλὴν οὐδετέραν ποθῶ. ἄπιτε οὖν, ὦ νεάνιδες, ἀπόθεσθε τὴν ἔριν, παύσασθε ζυγομαχίας. ἄλλης ἐρῶ, πρὸς αὐτὴν βαδιοῦμαι."

"κόρη," φασίν, "ἐκ γειτόνων οὐκ ἔστιν ἐνταῦθα καλή, καὶ φὴς ἄλλης ἐρᾶν; ψεύδη προφανῶς. ὄμοσον ὡς ἡμῶν οὐδετέραν ποθεῖς." προσεγέλασα τηνικαῦτα βοῶν ὡς "εἰ μὴ θέλω, πρὸς ἀνάγκης ἐπάγετέ μοι τὸν ὅρκον;" "μόλις," ἔφησαν, "κατέβημεν καιρὸν εὔκαιρον εὑροῦσαι λαβοῦσαι, καὶ παρίστασαι διαπαίζων ἡμᾶς. οὐκ ἀφετέος εἶ, οὐδὲ καταβαλεῖς ἡμᾶς ἀπ' ἐλπίδος μεγάλης." καὶ ἅμα λέγουσαι προσεῖλκον, ἐγὼ δέ πως ἡδέως ἠναγκαζόμην. μέχρι μὲν οὖν δεῦρο τοῦ λόγου καλῶς ἂν ἔχοι καὶ πρὸς ὁντιναοῦν, τὸ δὲ ἐντεῦθεν ἐν κεφαλαίῳ τοσοῦτον λεκτέον, ὡς οὐδεμίαν λελύπηκα, θάλαμον αὐτοσχέδιον εὑρὼν ἀρκοῦντα τῇ χρείᾳ.

γ΄. ΕΤΑΙΡΑ ΚΑΙ ΝΕΟΣ ΥΠΟ ΔΕΝΔΡΩΙ ΣΥΝΕΥΩΧΗΘΕΝΤΕΣ ΑΛΛΗΛΟΙΣ

Φιλοπλάτανος Ἀνθοκόμῃ

Τῇ Λειμώνῃ χαριέντως ἐν ἐρωτικῷ συνειστιώμην παραδείσῳ καὶ μάλα πρέποντι τῷ κάλλει τῆς ἐρωμένης· ἔνθα πλάτανος μὲν ἀμφιλαφής τε καὶ σύσκιος, πνεῦμα δὲ μέτριον, καὶ πόα μαλθακὴ ὥρᾳ θέρους ἐπανθεῖν εἰωθυῖα (ἐπὶ τοῦ πεδίου κατεκλίθημεν οἷα τῶν πολυτελεστάτων δαπίδων) δένδρη τε πολλὰ τῆς ὀπώρας πλησίον, "ὄγχναι καὶ ῥοιαὶ καὶ μηλέαι ἀγλαόκαρποι," φαίη τις ἂν καθομηρίζων τῶν ὀπωρινῶν αὐτόθι Νυμφῶν τὸ χωρίον. ἦν μὲν οὖν ταῦτα καὶ ἕτερα δένδρα πλησίον, εὐανθῆ μὲν τοὺς ὄρπηκας, πάμφορα δὲ τὸν καρπόν, ὡς ἂν εὐωδέστατον παρέχοι τὸν ἐράσμιον τόπον. καὶ τούτων ἐκδρεψάμενος φύλλον ὑπεμάλαττον τοῖς δακτύλοις, εἶτα τῇ ῥινὶ προσάγων γλυκυτέρας ἐπὶ πλεῖστον εἰσέπνεον εὐοσμίας. ἄμπελοι δὲ παμμήκεις σφόδρα γε ὑψηλαὶ περιελίττονται κυπαρίττους, ὡς ἀνακλᾶν ἡμᾶς ἐπὶ πολὺ τὸν αὐχένα πρὸς θέαν τῶν κύκλῳ συναιωρουμένων βοτρύων, ὧν οἱ μὲν ὀργῶσιν, οἱ δὲ περκάζουσιν, οἱ δὲ ὄμφακες, οἱ δὲ οἰνάνθαι δοκοῦσιν. ἐπὶ τοίνυν τοὺς πεπανθέντας ὁ μὲν ἀνερριχᾶτο βεβηκὼς

our hearts, inspiring them with passion—say who is the addressee of your song? Each of us thinks that she is the one you love. We are already jealous of one another, and because of you we are often at each other's throat and in each other's hair in eager rivalry." "You are," I answered, "both equally beautiful, but I desire neither. So away with you, girls, stop quarreling, and put an end to your strife. I love someone else and will go to her."

"There is," they reply, "no beautiful girl in the neighborhood, and you claim to love another? This clearly is a lie. Swear that you desire neither one of us!" That made me laugh, and I exclaimed: "If I don't want to, what will you do, force me to swear?" "It was hard for us to find the right moment and grab the chance to come down, and you just stand here making fun of us. No, we won't let you go and deprive us of our fondest hope." Speaking thus, they pulled me toward them, and somehow sweetly I was forced to comply. So far my story is appropriate[2] for anyone's ear—but what follows, let me just sum it up and say that I found a rough-and-ready chamber fitting the need and did not disappoint either one.

1.3. A Hetaira and a Youth
Feasting Together under a Tree

Philoplatanos[1] to Anthokomes[2]

Together with Leimone,[3] I pleasurably feasted in a garden that seemed just made for love and a good match for the beauty of my darling. There was an enormous plane tree[4] providing shade; a gentle breeze; soft grass covered with flowers, as is typical during summer (reclining on the ground was like lying on the most expensive carpets); and many trees heavy with fruit: "pears, pomegranates, and apples, glorious in their yield,"[5] to use Homer's words in describing the grove of the harvest nymphs right there. These and other trees were standing nearby, their branches blooming and laden, thus infusing the lovely spot with the sweetest perfume. I picked one of their leaves and crushed it lightly between my fingers, then held it up to my nose and inhaled for quite some time an even sweeter scent. Vines of amazing length and height wound themselves around cypresses, so that we had to bend our heads far back to glimpse the clusters of grapes swaying in an arc above us, some of them already swelling with ripeness,[6] others just turning dark, others still green, and yet others appearing to be no more than blossoms. In order to gather the ripe ones, one person scaled the tree, clambering up its branches, while another, raised up off the ground on the

ἐπὶ τῶν κλάδων, ὁ δὲ ἀπὸ τῆς γῆς ἀρθεὶς ἱκανῶς ἄκρᾳ μὲν τῇ λαιᾷ σφοδρῶς εἴχετο τοῦ φυτοῦ, τῇ δεξιᾷ δὲ παρετρύγα· ὁ δὲ ἀπὸ τοῦ δένδρου χεῖρα ὤρεγε τῷ γεωργῷ ὡς ὑπεργεγηρακότι.

ἡ δὲ πηγὴ χαριεστάτη ὑπὸ τῇ πλατάνῳ ῥεῖ ὕδατος εὖ μάλα ψυχροῦ, ὥς γε τῷ ποδὶ τεκμήρασθαι, καὶ διαφανοῦς τοσοῦτον, ὥστε συνεπινηχομένων κατὰ διαυγὲς ὑδάτιον καὶ διαπλεκομένων ἐπαφροδίτως ἀλλήλοις ἅπαν ἡμῶν φανερῶς ἀποκαταφαίνεσθαι μέλος. ὅμως οὖν οἶδα πολλάκις τὴν αἴσθησιν πλανηθεὶς πρὸς ὁμοιότητα μήλων τε καὶ τῶν ἐκείνης μαστῶν· μήλου γὰρ ἀμφοῖν μεταξὺ ἐν τοῖς ὕδασι διανηχομένου τῇ χειρὶ κατεδραξάμην, τοῦτο εἶναι νομίσας τὸν κυδωνιῶντα τῆς ποθουμένης μαστόν. καλὴ μὲν οὖν, νὴ τὰς τῆς πίδακος νύμφας, καὶ καθ᾽ ἑαυτὴν ἡ πηγή, φαιδροτέρα δὲ μᾶλλον ἐδόκει τοῖς εὐωδεστέροις ἐπικοσμηθεῖσα τῶν φύλλων καὶ τοῖς μέλεσι τῆς Λειμώνης, ἥτις καίπερ ὑπερφυῶς εὐπρόσωπος οὖσα, ὅμως, ὅταν ἀπεκδύηται, δι᾽ ὑπερβολὴν τῶν ἔνδον ἀπρόσωπος εἶναι δοκεῖ. καλὴ μὲν οὖν ἡ πηγή, εὐκραὴς δὲ καὶ ἡ τοῦ ζεφύρου πνοή, τὸ χαλεπὸν παραμυθουμένη τῆς ὥρας, λεπτὸν ἅμα καὶ ὑπηνλὸν ἐνηχοῦσα καὶ τῆς εὐωδίας πολὺ συνεπαγομένη τῶν δένδρων, τοῖς μύροις ἀντέπνει τῆς γλυκυτάτης. καὶ συμμιγὴς ἦν εὐοσμία καὶ μικροῦ γε ὁμοτίμως τὴν αἴσθησιν εὐφραινόντων· βραχὺ γάρ, ἡγοῦμαι, τὸ μύρον ἐνίκα, ὅτι γε τῆς Λειμώνης ὑπῆρχε τὸ μύρον.

ἔτι δὲ τὸ ἔμπνουν τῆς αὔρας, δι᾽ ἣν καὶ τὸ πνῖγος τῆς μεσημβρίας ἠπιώτερον ἐγεγόνει, λιγυρὸν ὑπήχει τῷ μουσικῷ τῶν τεττίγων χορῷ. ἡδὺ καὶ ἀηδόνες περιπετόμεναι τὰ νάματα μελῳδοῦσιν. ἀλλὰ καὶ τῶν ἄλλων ἡδυφώνων κατηκούομεν ὀρνίθων ὥσπερ ἐμμελῶς ὁμιλούντων ἀνθρώποις. ἔτι κἀκείνους πρὸ τῶν ὀμμάτων ἔχειν δοκῶ· ὁ μὲν ἐπὶ πέτρας ἀναπαύει τὼ πόδε καθ᾽ ἕνα, ὁ δὲ ψύχει τὸ πτερόν, ὁ δὲ ἐκκαθαίρει, ὁ δὲ ᾖρέ τι ἐκ τοῦ ὕδατος, ὁ δὲ εἰς τὴν γῆν κατανένευκεν ἐπισιτίσασθαί τι ἐκεῖθεν. ἡμεῖς δὲ ὑφειμένῃ τῇ φωνῇ διελεγόμεθα περὶ τούτων, ὅπως μὴ ἀποπτήσωνται καὶ διασκεδάσωμεν τῶν ὀρνίθων τὴν θέαν.

κἀκεῖνό γε, νὴ τὰς Χάριτας, ἐπιτερπέστατον ἦν· τοῦ γὰρ ὀχετηγοῦ κατὰ τάχος ἐπὶ πρασιάς τε καὶ δένδρα τῇ σμινύῃ καθηγουμένου τῷ ῥεύματι, πόρρωθεν ὁ θεράπων φιάλας καλλίστου πόματος πλήρεις ἐπὶ τὸν ὁλκὸν ἠφίει θᾶττον φέρεσθαι κατὰ ῥοῦν, οὐ χύδην, ἀλλὰ κατὰ μίαν, ἐκ διαστήματος βραχέος διακεκριμένας ἀλλήλων· ἕκαστον δὲ τῶν ἐκπωμάτων δίκην ὁλκάδων ἐπιχαρίτως διεκπλεόντων πτόρθον Μηδικοῦ φυτοῦ ἐπεφέρετο εὔφυλλον, καὶ ἦν ταῦτα ταῖς εὐπλοούσαις ἡμῶν φιάλαις ἱστία. τοιγαροῦν αὐτοφυῶς ἠρεμαίᾳ καὶ ἀταράχῳ

tips of his toes, vigorously seized the plant with his left hand and plucked the grapes with his right. A third stretched out his hand from the tree to an exceedingly old farmer.

The spring under the plane tree, lovely as can be, runs with very cool water, as a dip of the foot reveals, and is so limpid that each of our limbs was clearly visible as we swam together in the translucent water and lovingly embraced each other.[7] Still I know I often erred in my perception, so much alike are her breasts and apples:[8] as an apple floated by in the water between the two of us, I grasped it with my hand, thinking it was the swelling breast of my beloved. Oh, by the nymphs of the fountain, that spring is beautiful all by itself, but it seemed more dazzling still adorned with the sweet-smelling leaves and Leimone's limbs. Her face is surpassing fair, and yet, when she removes her clothes, she seems almost faceless due to the perfection of what is underneath.[9] As I said, the spring was beautiful, and Zephyr's breeze was blowing gently, assuaging summer's suffocating heat; it made a soft and lulling sound, and, carrying with it a vast array of delightful scents from the trees, it competed with the perfume of my sweetheart. Mixed together the two fragrances enchanted the senses in almost equal measure—only the perfume was, I think, a little better, since it was Leimone's.

The breeze, which eased the stifling midday heat, carried the clear echo from the music of the cicada's choir.[10] Sweet too was the song of the nightingales fluttering around the water. But we also listened to the other sweet-voiced birds, which seemed to converse with us humans through their melodies. They seem to be there right before my eyes even now. Look, this one is resting its feet, first one then the other, on a stone; that one is cooling its wings, and yet a third is cleaning them; here is one that has plucked something out of the water, and still another has bent its neck down to the earth in order to pick up some food.[11] We talked about them with hushed voices, so they wouldn't fly away and leave us without this winged spectacle.

This, though, was the greatest of all delights, by the Graces: While a man running irrigation channels quickly led the water to the garden plots and trees with his mattock, our servant, from afar, put bowls filled with the most delicious beverages into the watercourse so that they would be carried more speedily by the current, not jumbled all together, but one by one, separated from each other by short intervals. Each of the drinking cups, which charmingly sailed across the water like boats, carried with it a leafy shoot of the Median plant;[12] these served as sails for our bowls on their

πνοῇ κυβερνώμεναι, καθάπερ νῆες ταχυναυτήσασαι κατὰ πρύμναν ἱσταμένου
τοῦ πνεύματος, σὺν τοῖς ἡδίστοις φόρτοις εἰς τοὺς συμπότας εὔδιον προσωρμίζον
το· ἡμεῖς δὲ ὑπουργῶς ἀνασπῶντες ἑκάστην παραθέουσαν κύλικα συνεπίνομεν
ἴσον ἴσῳ κεκραμένην μετρίως· ὁ γὰρ ἔμμετρος οἰνοχόος ἐξεπίτηδες τοσούτῳ
θερμότερον τοῦ δέοντος τὸν οἶνον συνέμισγεν ὕδατι διαπύρῳ, ὅσον ἔμελλεν ὁ
ψυχρότατος ὁλκὸς ἐπιπολάζον αὐτῷ τὸ κραθὲν ἐπιψύχειν, ὅπως ἄν, μόνης γε
τῆς ἀμέτρου θέρμης τῷ ψυχρῷ μειουμένης, τὸ σύμμετρον καταλείψοιτο.

καὶ οὕτω δὴ γέγονεν ἡμῖν ἀμφὶ Διόνυσόν τε καὶ Ἀφροδίτην ἡ πᾶσα δια
τριβή, οὓς ἐπὶ τῇ κύλικι συνάγοντες ἐθελγόμεθα. ἡ δὲ Λειμώνη τοῖς ἄνθεσιν
οἷον λειμῶνα τὴν κεφαλὴν ἐποιεῖτο. καλὸς δὲ ὁ στέφανος καὶ δεινὸς ἐπιπρέψαι
ταῖς ἐν ὥρᾳ ῥᾶστα καὶ φαιδρότερον τοῖς ῥόδοις ἀποτελέσαι τὸ ἔρευθος, ὅτ’ ἂν
εἴη τούτων καιρός. ἄπιθι τοίνυν, ὦ φιλότης, ἐκεῖσε (ἔστι δὲ τοῦ καλοῦ Φυλλί
ωνος τὸ χωρίον), καὶ τοιούτων, εὔχαρι Ἀνθοκόμη, συναπόλαυε τῇ ποθουμένῃ
Μυρτάλῃ.

δ′. ΝΕΟΣ ΣΤΟΧΑΣΤΙΚΟΣ ΤΟΥ ΤΡΟΠΟΥ ΤΩΝ ΓΥΝΑΙΚΩΝ

Φιλόχορος Πολυαίνῳ

Ἱππίας ὁ καλὸς ὁ Ἀλωπεκῆθεν ἀρτίως ἔφη πρὸς ἐμὲ γοργῶς ἀποβλέψας·
“ὁρᾷς ἐκείνην, ὦ φίλε, τὴν ἐπιβάλλουσαν τὴν χεῖρα παιδίσκῃ; ὡς εὐμήκης,
ὡς καλὴ καὶ λίαν εὐσχήμων. νὴ θεούς, ἀστεῖον τὸ γύναιον, οἷον γοῦν ἅπαξ
ἰδόντι κατὰ τάχος εἰκάσαι. δεῦρο πλησίον προσμίξωμεν καὶ πειρασώμεθα τῆς
καλῆς.” “σώφρονος,” εἶπον, “δοκεῖ μοι τὸ πρόσχημα τὸ ἁλουργὲς ἡμιφάριον,
καὶ δέδοικα μὴ προπετῶς ἐγχειρῶμεν. σκοπῶμεν οὖν ἀκριβέστερον· οἶδα γὰρ
<τοὺς εὐλαβῶς ἐγχειροῦντας> ἥκιστα εἰς τὸ κινδυνεύειν ἀφικνουμένους.”
ἐμειδίασεν ἐπιτιμητικὸν ὁ Ἱππίας, καὶ τὴν δεξιὰν ἐπιτείνας οἷος ἦν ἐπιρραπίζειν
με κατὰ κόρρης καὶ διεμέμφετο λέγων· “ἀφυὴς εἶ, νὴ τὸν Ἀπόλλωνα, καὶ ὅλος
ἀπαίδευτος Ἀφροδίτης· σώφρων γὰρ τήνδε τὴν ὥραν καὶ διὰ μέσου τοῦ ἄστεος
οὐκ ἂν οὕτω προήει κεκαλλωπισμένη τε καὶ ἱλαρὰ πρὸς τοὺς ἀπαντῶντας. οὐδὲ
τῶν μύρων ὅσον ὄζει καὶ πόρρωθεν ὑπῃσθάνῃ; οὐδὲ τοῦ κτύπου τῶν εὐήχων
ψελλίων ἀκήκοας ἥδιστον ὑποσειομένων, ὅσον ἀποτελεῖν εἰώθασιν αἱ γυναῖκες
ἐξεπίτηδες ἀνακουφίζουσαι τὴν δεξιὰν καὶ ἀκροχειρίζουσαι τὸν κόλπον,
ἐρωτικοῖς τε συμβόλοις διὰ τούτων τοὺς νέους εἰς ἑαυτὰς προσκαλούμεναι;
ἀλλὰ καὶ ἐστράφην,” ἔφη, “ἡ δὲ καὶ αὐτὴ ἀντεστράφη. ἐκ τῶν ὀνύχων τεκ

merry journey. So, naturally steered by a calm and peaceful breeze, like ships sailing fast with the wind behind their stern, they, together with their delightful cargo, happily landed close to the drinkers. We, in turn, assiduously grabbed each cup, as it ran past, and drank down the moderate blend, which contained equal parts of wine and water.[13] For the cupbearer, who knew how to mix things just right, had on purpose combined wine warmer than required with red-hot water. The heat was in proportion to the icy water that was about to cool down the mixture floating on its surface, so that, the surplus of warmth reduced by the cold, the resulting temperature would be as desired.

And in this way all our time was devoted to Dionysus and Aphrodite,[14] whom we merrily joined with cups in our hands. But Leimone used flowers to make her head resemble a very meadow. Her garland was beautiful, such as well befits women in their prime and adds a special radiance to the redness of their cheeks with its roses (when it is their season). So go there, my friend (the place belongs to the beautiful Phyllion[15]), and rejoice, my lovely Anthokomes, in such pleasures together with your beloved Myrtale.[16]

1.4. A Youth Learned in the Ways of Women

Philochoros[1] to Polyainos[2]

Fair Hippias from Alopeke[3] recently said to me with the gleam of excitement in his eye, "Do you see that woman, friend, who is resting her hand on her serving girl? How tall she is, how lovely, and what a fine figure! By the gods, the moment you see her it's pretty clear she's a woman of the world. Let's go up and try our luck with that beauty." "That purple cloak,"[4] I countered, "seems to indicate a lady, and I fear our advances might be overhasty. So let's have a closer look first. For if you're careful, you're less likely to get into trouble." Hippias sneered, and raising his hand as though to smack me in the head, he scolded me. "What a bonehead you are, by Apollo, and totally ignorant in matters of love. A *lady* would not go strolling through the middle of town at this time of day, dressed to kill and flashing everyone such fetching looks. Didn't you notice how she smells of perfume, even from afar? Didn't you hear the pleasing clatter of her bracelets, as they move with her body ever so alluringly—a typically female strategy, to send out erotic signals, deliberately raising their right hand and fingering their bosom to attract young men. When I turned to check her out," he said "she turned her head as well. You may know the lion by his claws.[5]

μαίρομαι τὸν λέοντα. ἰτέον οὖν ἐστίν, ὦ Φιλόχορε, ὅτι οὐδὲν ἡμᾶς βλάψει,
ἀλλ' ἐλπίδες καλαί. πλὴν αὐτὸ δείξει, ὁ τὸν ποταμὸν καθηγούμενος ἔφη. τὸ δὲ
προσδοκώμενον φανερὸν ὡς, εἰ θέλοιμεν, ῥᾷστα ἂν γένοιτο."

προσπελάσας οὖν καὶ προσειπὼν αὐτὴν καὶ ἀντιπροσρηθεὶς ἤρετο φάσκων·
"πρὸς τοῦ σοῦ κάλλους, ὦ γύναι, ἐπιτρέπεις ἡμῖν ὁμιλῆσαι περὶ σοῦ βραχέα
τῇ θεραπαίνῃ; οὐδὲν δὲ ὧν ἀγνοεῖς διαλεξόμεθα τῇ παιδίσκῃ, οὐδὲ ἀνάργυρον
αἰτήσομεν Ἀφροδίτην· χαριούμεθα δὲ ὅσον αὐτὴ ἂν ἐθέλοις· ἐθελήσεις δὲ οἶδ'
ὅτι τὰ μέτρια. ἐπίνευσον, ὦ καλή, † οὐ τοσοῦτον ἐλεῶ τὸ τιτθίον †." ἡ δὲ τὴν
σύννευσιν ἐνδοτικοῖς καὶ θέλουσιν ὀφθαλμοῖς ἐπιχαρίτως ἐδήλου καὶ οὐ κατει-
ρωνεύσατο τὴν ὑπόσχεσιν, ἔστη τε καὶ ἠρυθρίασε, καὶ ἀπέστειλεν ἐπαγωγόν
τινα καὶ γλυκεῖαν αὐγήν, οἷα πέφυκεν ἀπαστράπτειν ἐξ ἀπέφθου χρυσίου. τότε
δή φησιν Ἱππίας ἐπιστραφεὶς πρός με· "οὐκ ἀφυῶς ἐστοχασάμην, οἶμαι, τοῦ
τρόπου τῆς γυναικός, ἀλλὰ καὶ πέπεικα ταχύ, οὐ χρόνον μακρὸν οὐ λόγον πολὺν
ἀναλώσας. σὺ δὲ τούτων ἄπειρος ἔτι. ἀλλ' ἕπου καὶ μάνθανε, καὶ συναπόλαυ-
σον ἐρωτικῷ διδασκάλῳ· τοῦτο γὰρ τὸ μάθημα τῶν ἐρωτικῶν παρ' ὁντιναοῦν
ποιοῦμαι δεινότατος εἶναι."

ε′. ΔΟΛΟΣ ΓΥΝΑΙΚΟΣ ΚΑΙΝΟΠΡΕΠΩΣ
ΤΟΝ ΣΥΝΟΙΚΟΝ ΑΠΑΤΩΣΗΣ

Ἀλκίφρων Λουκιανῷ

Πανηγύρεως ἐν προαστείῳ πανδημεὶ τελουμένης καὶ δημοθοινίας ἀφθόνου
Χαρίδημος ἐπ' εὐωχίαν συνεκαλεῖτο τοὺς φίλους. ἔνθα καὶ γυνή τις παρῆν
(ὀνόματι γὰρ οὐδὲν δέομαι λέγειν), ἣν αὐτὸς ὁ Χαρίδημος (οἶσθα δὲ τὸν νέον
ὡς ἐρωτικός) ἐν ἀγορᾷ προϊοῦσαν ἰδὼν ἀγκιστρεύει καὶ πέπεικε παραγενέσθαι
τῷ δείπνῳ. πάντων οὖν εἰς ταὐτὸν ἀθροιζομένων τῶν δαιτυμόνων ὁ χρυσοῦς
ἑστιάτωρ εἰσῄει πρεσβύτην τινὰ συνεπαγόμενος καὶ αὐτὸν δὴ συγκεκλημέ-
νον ἡμῖν. ὃν ἐκείνη προσιόντα πόρρωθεν κατιδοῦσα ὀξέως ὑπέδυ, καὶ θᾶττον
νοήματος εἰς τὸν πλησίον οἶκον ἀπέδρα. κἀκεῖσε μεταπεμψαμένη Χαρίδημον·
"ἀγνοίᾳ," ἔφη, "μέγιστον κακὸν κατειργάσω· οὗτος ὁ πρεσβύτης ἀνήρ ἐστιν
ἐμός, καὶ τὴν ἐσθῆτα, ἣν ἐκδυσαμένη κατέλιπον ἔξω, ῥᾳδίως ἐπέγνω, καὶ
ὑποψίας, ὡς εἰκός, γέγονε πλήρης. ὅμως, ἂν ταύτην λάθρᾳ καὶ βραχέα τῶν
ὄψων ἐπιδώσῃς, αὐτὸν ἐξαπατήσω καὶ τὸν νῦν αὐτῷ κατ' ἐμοῦ διενοχλοῦντα
λογισμὸν ἑτέρωσε παρατρέψω."

We've got to go up to her, Philochoros; she won't bite, and things look very promising. We'll find out soon enough if we're in over our heads, said the man leading the way across the river.[6] It shouldn't be hard to clarify the situation if we just want to."

So he went up, said hi, and, when she said hi in turn, he asked, "By your beauty, dear lady, will you let us consult for a minute with your servant on a matter concerning you? We won't discuss anything with the girl that you don't know about, and we don't expect your love to be for free. We'll be happy to give you however much you want, though I'm sure you'll ask only what's reasonable. Just give us the nod, my beauty…."[7] She charmingly indicated her consent with a soft and willing look, and she wasn't just kidding. She stood and blushed, and flashed us a sweet, come-hither look, like the glint of pure gold. Then turning to me, Hippias said, "I guess I had her figured out just right, what sort she was, and won her over in a flash, not wasting lots of time or talk. You're still a novice in such things. But come and learn, and have some fun together with your professor in Love 101. For in the science of erotics, no one, I think, can beat the champion, me."

1.5. A WIFE DECEIVES HER HUSBAND IN AN UNHEARD-OF MANNER

Alciphron to Lucian

During a great festival of all the people outside the city, including a lavish public banquet, Charidemos[1] invited his friends over for a party. There was a woman there as well (we don't need to mention any names) whom Charidemos personally snared upon seeing her walking in the marketplace (you know what a womanizer the boy is) and persuaded to come to the dinner. So when all the guests had arrived, our brilliant host made his entrance, bringing an elderly man who had been invited together with the rest of us. As soon as the woman spied him coming from afar, she ducked out of sight at once and rushed into the next room in the blink of an eye. Sending for Charidemos, she said, "Without realizing it, you've done something really terrible. That old man is my husband, and he must easily have recognized that robe I took off and left outside; now he's bound to be just boiling with suspicion. Nonetheless, if you can secretly get it to me, together with a bit of food, I'll play a trick to divert onto someone else those suspicions now eating away at him."

τούτων οὖν ἐπιδοθέντων ἀνέζευξεν οἴκαδε, καὶ τὸν σύνοικον ἔφθη, οὐκ οἶδ᾽ ὅπως ἐκφυγοῦσα. καὶ προσλαβομένη φίλην αὑτῆς ἐκ γειτόνων οἰκοῦσαν προδιέθηκεν ὅπως ἀμφότεραι βουκολήσουσι τὸν πρεσβύτην. εἶτα ἧκεν εὐθὺς οὗτος καὶ εἰσπεπήδηκεν ἔνδον κεκραγὼς ἅμα καὶ πνέων θυμοῦ, τῆς τε γαμετῆς ὧδε τὴν ἀκολασίαν ἐβόα· "τὴν ἐμὴν εὐνὴν οὔποτε χαίρουσα καθυβρίσεις," καὶ δι᾽ ὧν ἑώρακεν ἱματίων ἀπήλεγχε τὴν μοιχείαν, καὶ ξίφος ἤδη μεμηνὼς ἐπεζήτει. τότε δὴ λοιπὸν ἡ γείτων εἰς καιρὸν ἀνεφάνη καὶ "δέχου τὴν ἐσθῆτα," φησίν, "ὦ φιλτάτη. μεγίστην οἶδά σοι χάριν. πεπλήρωκα τὴν εὐχήν. ἀλλὰ πρὸς θεῶν μηδὲν ἀλαζονικόν. μετάλαβε δὲ καὶ σὺ τῶν προτεθέντων ἡμῖν." τούτων οὕτω λεγομένων ὁ τραχὺς ἐκεῖνος ἀνένηφε γέρων, τόν τε θυμὸν ἀνεκρούετο, καὶ μετὰ τῆς ὑπονοίας εἰς τοσαύτην πραότητα συνδιέλυσε τὴν ὀργήν, ὡς τοὐναντίον ἀπολογεῖσθαι τῇ γαμετῇ· "ὦ γύναι, συγγίνωσκέ μοι," φησίν. "ἐξέστην, ὁμολογῶ· ἀλλὰ τῆς σῆς ἕνεκα σωφροσύνης θεός τις εὐμενὴς εἰς κοινὴν σωτηρίαν φιλανθρώπως ἀπέσταλκε ταύτην, καὶ ἀμφοτέρους ἀπέσωσεν εἰσδραμοῦσα."

ϛʹ. ΠΕΡΙ ΤΗΣ ΠΡΟ ΓΑΜΟΥ ΦΘΑΡΕΙΣΗΣ

Ἑρμοκράτης Εὐφορίωνι

Κόρη τις πρὸς τὴν ἑαυτῆς ἔφη τροφόν· "εἴ μοι πρότερον ἐπομόσεις ὃ δ᾽ ἂν εἴποιμι φυλάξειν ἀπόρρητον, αὐτίκα τοῦτό σοι λέξω." ὀμώμοκεν ἡ τιτθή, ἡ δὲ παῖς εὐθὺς εἴρηκεν· "οὐκέτι σοι παρθένος ἐγώ, ὥς γε πρός σε τἀληθὲς εἰρῆσθαι." εὐθὺς ἀνακέκραγεν ἡ γραῦς, ἅμα τὴν παρειὰν αἰκιζομένη καὶ σχετλιάζουσα τὸ συμβάν. ἡ δὲ κόρη φησί· "σίγα πρὸς θεῶν, ὦ Σωφρόνη· ἔχε ἡσυχῇ, μή τις τῶν ἔνδον ὠτακουστῶν ὑποκλέψῃ τὸν λόγον· οἴμοι, οὐκ ἀρτίως ὀμώμοκας μηδενὶ παντάπασιν ἐξειπεῖν; τί οὖν, ὦ φίλη, σφόδρα καὶ μεγάλως βοᾷς; νὴ τὴν Ἄρτεμιν, ὦ μῆτερ, καίτοι πρὸς τοῦ ἔρωτος φλεγομένη δεινῶς, ἐσπούδακα σωφρονεῖν καθ᾽ ὅσον ἠδυνάμην. σμικρὰ δὲ οἷά τε ἦν καὶ δίχα μοι γέγονε τὰ νοήματα. διελογιζόμην δὲ πρὸς ἐμαυτήν· 'πειθαρχήσω τῷ ἔρωτι; ἀμελήσω τοῦ πόθου;' ἀμφότερά με κρατεῖ. εἶτα πολὺ μᾶλλον ἐπὶ θάτερα πρὸς τὸν ἔρωτα κλίνω· ηὐξάνετο γὰρ τῇ μελλήσει, καὶ ὡς φυτὸν ἐν τῇ γῇ, οὕτως ἔνδον τῆς ἐμῆς ὑπερεφύετο ψυχῆς. οὕτως οὖν ἡττήθην, ὁμολογῶ, τῆς ἀνικήτου λαμπάδος."

ἔφη τοίνυν ἡ πρεσβῦτις· "χαλεπώτατον μὲν τὸ δυστύχημα, τέκνον, καὶ τὴν ἐμὴν ᾔσχυνας πολιάν· πλὴν ἐπεὶ τὸ πραχθὲν οὐκ ἂν ἄλλως ἔχοι, τὰ δεύτερα

No sooner had she gotten the things than she decamped and made for home, arriving just before her husband—how she escaped I'll never know. And teaming up with a friend who lived in the neighborhood, she got her to play along with her plan that they should both bamboozle[2] the old man. And suddenly there he was, leaping over the threshold, shouting, and breathing fire. And bawling his wife out for her shamelessness, he screeched, "You won't besmirch my marriage bed and get away with it."[3] He cited the robe he'd seen as proof of her adultery and was already reaching for a sword in his frenzy when, just in the nick of time, the neighbor woman appeared and said, "Here's your robe back, honey. Thanks so much! I accomplished my heart's desire. But don't let me go on and on about it, by the gods. Just try a sample of what they served yourself." As soon as she'd uttered these words, the hot-tempered old guy came to his senses and beat down his anger. And his rage dissolved, together with his suspicion, into utmost gentleness, so that now it was he who begged his wife for forgiveness:[4] "O woman, pardon me," he said. "I was out of my mind, I admit. Thanks to your chastity, however, some benevolent god sent this woman[5] to us in loving kindness for our common salvation. By running in, she saved us both."

1.6. On a Girl Who Lost Her Virginity before Marriage

Hermokrates to Euphorion

A girl said to her nurse, "If you swear not to breathe a word about what I'm going to say, I'll tell you right away." The nurse swore; the girl began at once. "I'll be honest with you, I'm not a virgin anymore." Instantly the nurse let out a cry, tore at her cheeks, and bewailed what had happened. But the girl said, "Be quiet, by the gods, O Sophrone![1] Keep your peace, lest anyone eavesdropping in the house overhear our conversation. O god, didn't you just swear you wouldn't tell a single soul? So why, dearest, are you screaming bloody murder? By Artemis,[2] I tried with all my might to be a good girl, Mama, even though my desire was burning out of control. But I was too weak, and my mind was torn. I debated with myself, 'Shall I bend to love's command or ignore my heart's desire?' Each argument persuaded me. But ultimately I inclined toward the one, toward love. For my hesitation itself had made it grow, and like a plant in the earth, even so it was rampant in my soul. Thus, I admit, I was overcome by the invincible flame."

And the old woman replied, "This is the worst misfortune, child, and you have disgraced my gray hair. But since what's done is done, let me

παραινῶ. πέπαυσο τούτων, καὶ μηδὲν περαιτέρω ἐξαμάρτανε, μή ποτέ σου τῆς γαστρὸς ὀγκουμένης ἐπὶ προήκοντι τῷ πράγματι καὶ τῷ χρόνῳ ἐναργῶς κατανοήσωσι τὸ τολμηθὲν οἱ τεκόντες. ἀλλ' εἴθε σοι γάμον ταχύ, πρὶν κατάφωρος γένῃ, συνεπινεύσουσιν οἱ θεοί. ἤδη δὲ τηλικαύτη γεγένησαι, καὶ αὐτίκα χρημάτων εἰς προῖκα τῷ σῷ δεήσει πατρί." "τί φής, ὦ μῆτερ; τοῦτο δέδοικα μάλιστα πάντων." "μηδὲν δείσῃς, ὦ παῖ· ἐγώ σε τηνικαῦτα διδάξω πῶς ἂν ἡ πρὸ γάμου γεγονυῖα γυνὴ παρθένος ἔτι δόξῃ τῷ νυμφίῳ."

ζ΄. ΑΛΙΕΥΣ ΑΙΤΗΘΕΙΣ ΥΠΟ ΚΟΡΗΣ ΤΗΝ ΑΥΤΗΣ ΕΣΘΗΤΑ ΦΥΛΑΞΑΙ ΜΕΧΡΙΣ ΑΝ ΑΠΟΛΟΥΣΗΤΑΙ ΤΗΙ ΘΑΛΑΤΤΗΙ, ΚΑΙ ΤΑΥΤΗΝ ΟΡΩΝ ΜΑΛΙΣΤΑ ΓΥΜΝΩΘΕΙΣΑΝ

Κυρτίων Δικτύι

Παρὰ τὴν ἀκτὴν ἑστηκότι μοι κατὰ πέτρας καὶ τῷ ἀγκίστρῳ προσπεπηγότα κάλλιστον ἰχθὺν ἀνασπῶντι, τοῦ καλάμου κυρτουμένου τῷ βάρει, προσῆλθέ τις εὐπρόσωπος κόρη, κάλλος αὐτοφυὲς καὶ ὅμοιον αὐτομάτῳ φυτῷ φέρουσα. καὶ πρὸς ἐμαυτὸν ἔφην· "ἑτέρα πολλῷ βελτίων τῆς προτέρας ἐμπέπτωκεν ἄγρα." αὕτη δέ· "τὴν ἐσθῆτα," φησί, "πρὸς τοῦ σοῦ Ποσειδῶνος, φύλαττε τὴν ἐμήν, ἄχρις ἂν τοῖς κύμασιν ἐμαυτὴν ἀπολούσω." ἥσθην ἀληθῶς καὶ σφόδρα χαίρων τὴν αἴτησιν προσηκάμην οἷα δὴ μέλλων αὐτὴν καταγυμνωθεῖσαν ὁρᾶν. ὡς οὖν ἐξεδύσατο καὶ τὸν ἔσχατον χιτωνίσκον, ὅλος ἐξέστην ἐκπλαγεὶς πρὸς τὴν λαμπρότητα τῶν μελῶν. ἐξέλαμπε γὰρ ἐκ πολλῆς τε καὶ μελαίνης κόμης λευκὸς μὲν τράχηλος, ξανθὴ δὲ παρειά· χρώματα λαμπρὰ μὲν τῇ φύσει, ἀνθηρότερα δὲ τῇ πρὸς τὸ μέλαν φιλονεικίᾳ. ἐντεῦθεν εἰσπεπήδηκεν ἔνδον καὶ παρενήχετο τῇ θαλάττῃ· ἦν γὰρ ἀτάραχον καὶ γαληναῖον τὸ κῦμα.

καὶ τῷ ἀφρῷ τοῦ περιρρέοντος κύματος ἡ χροιὰ τοῦ σώματος λευκανθίζουσα παρισοῦτο. νὴ τοὺς Ἔρωτας, εἰ μὴ πρότερον ἔτυχον τεθεαμένος αὐτήν, ᾠήθην ἄν τινα τῶν θρυλουμένων Νηρηίδων ὁρᾶν. ὡς δὲ ἱκανῶς εἶχε τῶν θαλαττίων λουτρῶν, εἶπες ἂν τὴν κόρην ἀνίσχουσαν τῶν κυμάτων ἰδών· "οὕτω τῆς θαλάττης τὴν Ἀφροδίτην εὐπρεπῶς προϊοῦσαν γράφουσιν οἱ ζωγράφοι." αὐτίκα γοῦν προσδραμὼν θοιμάτιον ἐπεδίδουν τῇ ποθουμένῃ, προσπαίζων ἅμα καὶ πειρώμενος τῆς καλῆς. ἡ δὲ (ἦν γάρ, ὡς ἔοικε, σεμνή τε καὶ βλοσυρά) ἠρυθρίασε μετ' ὀργῆς, καὶ γέγονε τὸ πρόσωπον θυμουμένη καλλίων, τὸ δὲ ὄμμα καίπερ ἀγανακτούσης ἡδύ, ὥσπερ καὶ τὸ τῶν ἄστρων πῦρ φῶς μᾶλλόν ἐστιν ἢ πῦρ. τόν τε θηρατικὸν κατέαξε κάλαμον, καὶ τοὺς ἰχθῦς προσέρριψε τῇ θαλάττῃ. ἐγὼ

suggest another course: from now on just say no, and don't repeat your mistake, lest your parents see all too clearly what you've been up to when your belly swells, as things emerge with time. But may the gods grant you a quick wedding, before you start to show. You're already the right age, and your father will soon need to use his money for a dowry anyway." "What are you saying, Mama? That's what I fear most of all." "Don't be scared, child. When the time comes, I will teach you how a girl who has become a woman before marriage may yet seem a virgin to the groom."

1.7. A Fisherman Is Asked by a Girl to Watch Her Clothes Until She Has Finished Bathing in the Sea, and He Observes Her Completely Naked

Kyrtion[1] to Diktys[1]

As I was standing on a rock by the beach, reeling in a magnificent fish caught on my hook (the rod curved forward with its weight), a good-looking girl approached me. She had the natural beauty of a wildflower. I said to myself, "Now here's a catch far better than my first." But she said, "By your god Poseidon, would you please watch my clothes until I'm done washing myself in the waves." I was truly overjoyed and more than happy to agree to her request, since it meant I was going to see her naked. So when she had stripped off even the last little shred of clothing, I was totally beside myself, amazed at the sight of her glistening limbs. For her white neck and golden cheek shone out from the thick mass of her black hair. Her coloring would have been radiant even on its own, but it bloomed all the more in rivalry with that black. Thereupon she dove into the water and swam by in the sea; it was tranquil and calm, you understand.

And in its whiteness, the color of her skin was like the foam of the wave swirling around her. By the Erotes, if I hadn't seen her before, I would have thought I was gazing on one of the murmuring Nereids.[3] When she'd had enough of her salty bath, you would have said upon seeing the girl rising up out of the waves, "This is how painters picture Aphrodite[4] gracefully emerging from the sea." I ran up at once, handed the robe to the object of my desire, and made a playful pass at this beauty. She, however, (for she was, it seems, a no-nonsense girl and stern) flushed red with anger, and her face grew even more beautiful for her rage. Despite her vexation her glance was sweet, just as the fire of stars is not so much fire but light. She snapped my fishing rod in two and hurled the fish back into the sea. I stood

δὲ ἀμήχανος παρειστήκειν, καὶ οὓς ἐθηρασάμην θρηνῶν καὶ ἣν οὐκ ἤγρευσα μειζόνως δακρύων.

η΄. ΙΠΠΟΚΟΜΟΣ ΙΠΠΕΩΣ ΕΡΩΤΙΚΟΥ

Ἐχέπωλος Μελησίππῳ

"Εὖγε τῆς εὐπρεπείας, βαβαὶ τῆς ἐλάσεως. ὡς ἀμφοτεροδέξιος οὗτος πέφυκεν ὁ ἱππότης. καὶ κάλλει διαπρέπει, καὶ ὑπερφέρει τῷ τάχει. ὡς ἔοικε, τοῦτον οὐκ ἐδάμασεν Ἔρως, ἀλλ᾽ ἔστιν αὐτὸς περιπόθητος Ἄδωνις ταῖς ἑταίραις." ταῦτά μου λέγοντος ὁ χρυσοῦς ἀκήκοεν ἱππεύς, καὶ διαμεμφόμενος ἔφη· "οὐδὲν πρὸς τὸν Διόνυσον οὐδὲ πρὸς ἐμὲ τοῦτον οἰκείως εἴρηκας τὸν λόγον. ἄριστα μόνος οἶδεν ἱππάζεσθαι πόθος. αὐτὸς ἐμὲ καὶ δι᾽ ἐμοῦ τάχιστα τὸν ἵππον ἐλαύνει, καὶ τὸν θέοντα κεντρίζει δεινῶς ὀξύτερον κατεπείγων. ἐπίδος οὖν, ἱπποκόμε, τοῖς δρόμοις, ἅμα τε ᾄδων καὶ ᾄσμασιν ἐρωτικοῖς τὸν ἔρωτα θεραπεύων." ᾖδον τοίνυν τοιόνδε πρὸς ἐκεῖνον αὐτοσχέδιον μέλος, ἐξ αὐτοῦ τὴν πρόφασιν εἰληφώς· "ἐγώ σε, δέσποτα, κατά γε τὴν ἐμὴν εἰκότως ἱπποδρόμον ἐνόμιζον ἐλεύθερον βέλους. εἰ δὲ τοσοῦτον κάλλος ἔχων ἐρᾷς, νὴ τὴν Ἀφροδίτην, ἀδικοῦσιν οἱ Ἔρωτες. ὅμως γε τοῦτό σε μὴ σφόδρα λυπείτω. καὶ τὴν ἑαυτῶν ἔτρωσαν ἐκεῖνοι μητέρα."

θ΄. ΔΟΛΟΣ ΓΥΝΑΙΚΟΣ ΔΙ᾽ ΟΥ ΘΕΡΑΠΟΝΤΩΝ ΚΑΙ ΣΥΝΟΙΚΟΥ ΠΑΡΟΝΤΩΝ ΕΦΗΨΑΤΟ ΤΟΥ ΜΟΙΧΟΥ

Στησίχορος Ἐρατοσθένει

Γυνή τις ἐν ἀγορᾷ προϊοῦσα τόν τε σύνευνον εἶχε πλησίον, καὶ ὑπὸ τῶν οἰκετῶν περιεστοιχίζετο κύκλῳ. ὡς δὲ προσιόντα τὸν ἑαυτῆς εἶδε μοιχόν, ἄφνω βουλεύεται δαιμονίως ἅμα τῇ θέᾳ, ὅπως ἂν εὐπροσώπως ἅψηται τοῦ ποθουμένου, καί τι τυχὸν καὶ λαλοῦντος ἀκούσῃ. αὐτὴ μὲν οὖν ὤλισθεν, ὡς ἐδόκει, καὶ πέπτωκεν ἐπὶ γόνυ· ὁ δὲ μοιχὸς συμπράττων ὥσπερ ἀπὸ συνθήματος τῇ γνώμῃ τῆς γυναικὸς ὀρέγει τὴν χεῖρα καὶ διανίστησι πεπτωκυῖαν λαβόμενος τῆς δεξιᾶς καὶ τοῖς ἐκείνης δακτύλοις τοὺς ἑαυτοῦ περιπλέξας, καὶ ὡς οἶμαι πρὸς τοῦ ἔρωτος ὑπέτρεμον ἀμφοτέρων αἱ χεῖρες. ὁ μὲν μοιχὸς τῆς πεπλασμένης αὐτὴν παραμυθούμενος συμφορᾶς εἶπεν ἄττα δήπου καὶ ἔβη. ἡ δέ, ὥσπερ ἀλγοῦσα, λάθρα τῷ στόματι προσάγει τὴν χεῖρα, καὶ τοὺς ἑαυτῆς πεφίληκε δακτύλους, ὧν ἐκεῖνος προσήψατο, ἔτι δὲ καὶ τοῖς ὀφθαλμοῖς ἐρωτικῶς ὑπέθηκε τούτους, δάκρυον ὑποκρίσεως ἀποματτομένη τῶν μάτην πρὸς αὐτῆς ὑποθλιβομένων βλεφάρων.

by helpless, lamenting the loss of what I'd caught and, even more so, what I'd failed to catch.

1.8. The Groom of an Amorous Horseman

Echepolos[1] to Melesippos[2]

"O what exquisite looks! My god, what horsemanship. What a sure-handed rider either way: outstanding in his beauty, unbeatable in his speed. It looks like Eros hasn't broken this one. This Adonis[3] makes even prostitutes melt." The radiant rider heard me say these things and scoldingly replied, "What you say has nothing to do with Dionysus[4] or with me. Longing, and no other, is the expert rider. For it is he that drives me on[5] and through me drives my horse to breakneck speed. And he spurs the racer mightily, pressing him to gallop faster and faster. So give your all to the race, groom, and ease desire by singing[6] songs of love." So there and then I made him the following song, which he himself inspired. "Master, I'd figured you for a horseman unscathed by the arrow of Love. But if even you, who are so beautiful, feel desire, by Aphrodite, then the Erotes are committing an injustice. However, this should not grieve you all too much: they wounded even their own mother."[7]

1.9. The Trick of a Wife by Which She Managed to Touch Her Lover in the Presence of Servants and of Her Husband

Stesichoros[1] to Eratosthenes[2]

A woman was strolling through the agora with her husband nearby and surrounded by her servants. Her lover happened to come toward her, and no sooner had she seen him than she devised a brilliant plan to touch the object of her desire while maintaining the appearance of propriety and perhaps even to hear him say something. So she pretended to slip and fell on her knee. And her lover, playing along with the woman's plan as though on cue, reached out to her, and seizing her right hand, raised her up from the fall. He entwined his fingers around hers, and both their hands were trembling, I think, with desire. The lover comforted her in her feigned suffering and, saying some sweet nothing, went on his way. She, as if in pain, secretly raised her hand to her lips, and kissed the fingers that he had touched. Then in her desire she moved them upward, deceitfully rubbing her eyes and wiping away a false tear.

ι΄. ΩΣ ΕΝ ΕΠΙΣΤΟΛΗΙ ΤΟ ΚΑΤΑ ΑΚΟΝΤΙΟΝ ΚΑΙ ΚΥΔΙΠΠΗΝ ΕΡΩΤΙΚΟΝ ΔΙΗΓΗΜΑ

Ἐρατόκλεια Διονυσιάδι

Ἀκόντιος τὴν Κυδίππην καλὸς νεανίας καλὴν ἔγημε κόρην. ὁ γὰρ παλαιὸς λόγος εὖ ἔχει, ὡς ὅμοιον ὁμοίῳ κατὰ θεῖον ἀεὶ προσπελάζει. τὴν μὲν ἅπασι τοῖς ἑαυτῆς φιλοτίμοις κεκόσμηκεν Ἀφροδίτη, μόνου τοῦ κεστοῦ φεισαμένη· καὶ τοῦτον πρὸς τὴν παρθένον εἶχεν ἐξαίρετον ἡ θεός. καὶ τοῖς ὄμμασι Χάριτες οὐ τρεῖς καθ᾽ Ἡσίοδον, ἀλλὰ δεκάδων περιχορεύει δεκάς. τὸν δὲ νέον ἐκόσμουν ὀφθαλμοὶ φαιδροὶ μὲν ὡς καλοῦ, φοβεροὶ δὲ ὡς σώφρονος, καὶ φύσεως ἔρευθος εὐανθὲς ἐπιτρέχον ταῖς παρειαῖς. οἱ δὲ φιλοθεάμονες τοῦ κάλλους εἰς διδασκά- λου προϊόντα περιεσκόπουν συνωθοῦντες ἀλλήλους, καὶ ἦν ὁρᾶν πρὸς τούτων πληθούσας μὲν ἀγορὰς στενοχωρουμένας δὲ λαύρας. καὶ πολλοί γε διὰ τοῦτο τὸ λίαν ἐρωτικὸν τοῖς ἴχνεσι τοῦ μειρακίου τοὺς ἑαυτῶν ἐφήρμοζον πόδας. οὗτος ἠράσθη Κυδίππης. ἔδει γὰρ τὸν καλὸν τοσούτους τετοξευκότα τῷ κάλλει μιᾶς ἀκίδος ἐρωτικῆς πειραθῆναί ποτε καὶ γνῶναι σαφῶς, οἷα πεπόνθασιν οἱ δι᾽ αὐτὸν τραυματίαι. ὅθεν ὁ Ἔρως οὐ μετρίως ἐνέτεινε τὴν νευράν (ὅτε καὶ τερπνὴ πέφυκεν ἡ τοξεία), ἀλλ᾽ ὅσον εἶχεν ἰσχύος προσελκύσας τὰ τόξα σφοδρότατα διαφῆκε τὸ βέλος.

τοιγαροῦν εὐθέως, ὦ κάλλιστον παιδίον Ἀκόντιε, δυοῖν θάτερον, ἢ γάμον ἢ θάνατον διελογίζου βληθείς. πλὴν αὐτὸς ὁ τρώσας ἀεί τινας παραδόξους μηχανὰς διαπλέκων ὑπέθετό σοι καινοτάτην βουλήν, τάχα που τὸ σὸν αἰδούμενος κάλλος. αὐτίκα γοῦν κατὰ τὸ Ἀρτεμίσιον ὡς ἐθεάσω προκαθημένην τὴν κόρην, τοῦ κήπου τῆς Ἀφροδίτης Κυδώνιον ἐκλεξάμενος μῆλον ἀπάτης αὐτῷ περιγέγραφηκας λόγον καὶ λάθρα διεκύλισας πρὸ τῶν τῆς θεραπαίνης ποδῶν. ἡ δὲ τὸ μέγεθος καὶ τὴν χροιὰν καταπλαγεῖσα ἀνήρπασεν, ἅμα διαποροῦσα τίς ἄρα τοῦτο τῶν παρθένων μετέωρος ἀπέβαλε τοῦ προκολπίου. "ἆρα," φησίν, "ἱερὸν πέφυκας, ὦ μῆλον; τίνα δέ σοι πέριξ ἐγκεχάρακται γράμματα; καὶ τί σημαίνειν ἐθέλεις; δέχου μῆλον, ὦ κεκτημένη, οἷον οὐ τεθέαμαι πρότερον. ὡς ὑπερμέγεθες, ὡς πυρρωπόν, ὡς ἔρυθημα φέρον τῶν ῥόδων. εὖγε τῆς εὐωδίας· ὅσον καὶ πόρρωθεν εὐφραίνει τὴν αἴσθησιν. λέγε μοι, φιλτάτη, τί τὸ περίγραμμα τοῦτο;" ἡ δὲ κόρη κομισαμένη καὶ τοῖς ὄμμασι περιθέουσα τὴν γραφὴν ἀνεγίνωσκεν ἔχουσαν ὧδε· "μὰ τὴν Ἄρτεμιν Ἀκοντίῳ γαμοῦμαι." ἔτι διερχομένη τὸν ὅρκον εἰ καὶ ἀκούσιόν τε καὶ νόθον τὸν ἐρωτικὸν λόγον ἀπέρριψεν αἰδουμένη, καὶ ἡμίφωνον καταλέ-

1.10. The Erotic Tale of Acontius and Cydippe, Set in Epistolary Form

Eratokleia[1] to Dionysias[2]

Acontius, a lovely youth, married Cydippe, a lovely girl. The old adage has it right, that by divine law like gravitates to like.[3] Aphrodite adorned her with all her own charms, except for the girdle.[4] That was the one thing the goddess kept to distinguish herself from the girl. In her eyes there were not just three dancing Graces, as in Hesiod,[5] but ten times ten. The boy had the shining eyes you'd expect in a lovely youth, but the fearful glance of one who's sensible, and the reddish bloom of Nature suffusing his cheeks. All who love the sight of beauty would jostle for a chance to see him going to his teacher's, and you could watch them crowding the marketplaces and blocking the lanes. Many indeed would follow in his very footsteps due to this excessive attraction. But he was filled with longing for Cydippe. It was just meant to be that this lovely youth, who had struck so many with the arrows of his beauty, would one day feel the sting of a single dart[6] of passion and understand clearly what those wounded on his account had suffered. For this reason, Eros did not bend his bow lightly (in which case his archery brings pleasure), but pulling it taut with all his might he shot the arrow at full force.

So from the moment you were hit, Acontius, loveliest of boys, you were pondering two possibilities, marriage or death. Whenever Eros wounds someone, he weaves some unexpected plot for them, but you—perhaps in deference to your beauty—he inspired with something truly novel. For as soon as you saw the girl sitting in the Artemisium,[7] you picked a Cydonian apple[8] from the garden of Aphrodite, inscribed its circumference with a deceptive text, and secretly rolled it in front of her servant's feet. She, struck by its size and color, snatched it up, wondering which girl might in her distraction have dropped it from the folds of her lap. "Are you sacred, O apple?" she said. "What letters are inscribed all around you? What are you trying to say? Take the apple, mistress. I've never seen another like it. What wondrous size, what fiery color, what rosy redness! And oh, what a scent! How it delights the senses even from afar! Tell me, dearest, what are the letters surrounding it?" The girl took it, and running her eyes over the text, read the words[9] it contained: "By Artemis, it is Acontius I shall wed." While still uttering the oath—unintentional and illegitimate though it was—she flung the amorous text away in shame and left half-spoken the word at its

λοιπε λέξιν τὴν ἐπ' ἐσχάτῳ κειμένην ἅτε διαμνημονεύουσαν γάμον, ὃν σεμνὴ παρθένος κἂν ἑτέρου λέγοντος ἠρυθρίασε. καὶ τοσοῦτον ἐξεφοινίχθη τὸ πρόσωπον, ὡς δοκεῖν ὅτι τῶν παρειῶν ἔνδον εἶχέ τινα ῥόδων λειμῶνα, καὶ τὸ ἐρύθημα τοῦτο μηδὲν τῶν χειλῶν αὐτῆς διαφέρειν. εἶπεν ἡ παῖς, ἀκήκοεν Ἄρτεμις· καὶ παρθένος οὖσα θεός, Ἀκόντιε, συνελάβετό σοι τοῦ γάμου.

τέως οὖν τὸν δείλαιον—ἀλλ' οὔτε θαλάττης τρικυμίας οὔτε πόθου κορυφούμενον σάλον εὐμαρὲς ἀφηγεῖσθαι· δάκρυα μόνον, οὐχ ὕπνον αἱ νύκτες ἐπῆγον τῷ μειρακίῳ· κλαίειν γὰρ αἰδούμενος τὴν ἡμέραν τὸ δάκρυον ἐταμιεύετο ταῖς νυξίν. ἐκτακεὶς δὲ τὰ μέλη καὶ δυσθυμίαις μαραινόμενος τὴν χροιὰν καὶ τὸ βλέμμα δεινῶς ὡρακιῶν ἐδεδίει τῷ τεκόντι φανῆναι καὶ εἰς ἀγρὸν ἐπὶ πάσῃ προφάσει τὸν πατέρα φεύγων ἐφοίτα. διόπερ οἱ κομψότεροι τῶν ἡλικιωτῶν Λαέρτην αὐτὸν ἐπωνόμαζον, γηπόνον τὸν νεανίσκον οἰόμενοι γεγονέναι. ἀλλ' Ἀκοντίῳ οὐκ ἀμπελῶνος ἔμελεν, οὐ σκαπάνης, μόνον δὲ φηγοῖς ὑποκαθήμενος ἢ πτελέαις ὡμίλει τοιάδε· "εἴθε, ὦ δένδρα, καὶ νοῦς ὑμῖν γένοιτο καὶ φωνή, ὅπως ἂν εἴπητε μόνον· Κυδίππη καλή.' ἢ γοῦν τοσαῦτα κατὰ τῶν φλοιῶν ἐγκεκολαμμένα φέροιτε γράμματα, ὅσα τὴν Κυδίππην ἐπονομάζει καλήν. Κυδίππη, καλήν σε καὶ εὔορκον ὁμοίως προσείπω ταχύ, μηδὲ Ἄρτεμις ἐπί σοι ποιναῖον βέλος ἀφῇ καὶ ἀνέλη· μένη δὲ τὸ πῶμα προσκείμενον τῇ φαρέτρᾳ. ὦ δυστυχὴς ἐγώ. τί δέ σοι τοῦτον ἐπῆγον τὸν φόβον; ὁπότε καί φασι τὴν θεὸν ἐπὶ πάσαις μὲν ἁμαρτάσι κινεῖσθαι δεινῶς, μάλιστα δὲ τοὺς ἀμελοῦντας τῶν ὅρκων πικρότερον τιμωρεῖσθαι. εἴθε μὲν οὖν ὡς ἀρτίως ηὐχόμην εὔορκος εἴης, εἴθε γάρ· εἰ δὲ ἀποβαίη, ὅπερ μηδὲ λέγειν καλόν, ἡ Ἄρτεμις ἔσται σοι, παρθένε, πραεῖα· οὐ σὲ γάρ, ἀλλὰ τὸν δόντα τῆς ἐπιορκίας τὴν πρόφασιν κολαστέον. μαθήσομαι μόνον ὡς μεμέληκας τῶν γραμμάτων, καὶ τοῦ σοῦ πρηστῆρος τὴν ἐμὴν ψυχὴν ἀπαλλάττων οὐχ ἧττον αἵματος ἀφειδήσω τοῦ ἡμετέρου ἤπερ ὕδατος εἰκῆ χεομένου. ἀλλ' ὦ φίλτατα δένδρα, τῶν ἡδυφώνων ὀρνίθων οἱ θῶκοι, ἆρα κἂν ἐν ὑμῖν ἐστιν οὗτος ὁ ἔρως, καὶ πίτυος τυχὸν ἠράσθη κυπάριττος ἢ ἄλλο φυτὸν ἑτέρου φυτοῦ; μὰ Δία, οὐκ οἶμαι· οὐ γὰρ ἐφυλλορροεῖτε καὶ τοὺς κλάδους ἁπλῶς ὁ πόθος κόμης ὑμᾶς καὶ ἀγλαΐας ἐψίλου, ἀλλὰ καὶ μέχρι στελέχους τε καὶ ῥιζῶν ὑπονοστήσας τῷ πυρσῷ διικνεῖτο."

τοιαῦτα μὲν τὸ παιδίον Ἀκόντιος διελέγετο πρὸς τῷ σώματι μαραινόμενος καὶ τὸν νοῦν. τῇ δὲ Κυδίππῃ πρὸς ἕτερον ηὐτρεπίζετο γάμος. καὶ πρὸ τῆς παστάδος τὸν ὑμέναιον ᾖδον αἱ μουσικώτεραι τῶν παρθένων καὶ μελιχόφωνοι (τοῦτο δὴ Σαπφοῦς τὸ ἥδιστον φθέγμα). ἀλλ' ἄφνω νενόσηκεν ἡ παῖς, καὶ πρὸς

very end, since it mentioned marriage, a word any modest virgin would blush at even if another were to utter it. And her face turned so red that a field of roses seemed to have blossomed on her cheeks, whose color was now indistinguishable from that of her lips. The girl spoke; Artemis heard. And though a virgin, the goddess joined forces with you, Acontius, in your marriage plan.

In the meantime, the poor wretch—but it is not easy to describe the wildest wave in the sea or the cresting surge of desire. The nights brought to the youth only tears, not sleep. And as he was ashamed to cry in the daytime, he ministered to his tears at night. His limbs worn away, his skin withered with unhappiness, his look terribly faint, he was afraid to encounter his father and seized on any excuse to flee to the country so as to avoid him. Consequently, the more insolent among his age-mates started calling him Laertes,[10] thinking that the youth had turned into a farmer. Acontius, however, didn't care for vineyards or for mattocks but simply sat beneath oaks or elms and spoke thus: "If only, O trees, you were to acquire a mind and a voice, just to be able to say, 'Cydippe is lovely.' Well, may you at least bear as many letters inscribed in your bark as spell out 'Cydippe is lovely.' Cydippe, if only I were soon able to call you both lovely and faithful to your oath, lest Artemis shoot and kill you with her punishing arrow. Let the lid on her quiver stay put. O miserable me, why have I exposed you to this danger, when everyone says that this goddess reacts terribly to all sinners but is especially severe in punishing those who neglect their oaths. If only, then, you were faithful to your oath, as I just wished. If only … But if that thing comes about, which is terrible even to mention, Artemis will be easy on you, maiden. For it's not you who should be punished, but he who led you to perjury. I'll just make sure that you took notice of the letters, and then, freeing my soul from the firestorm of its love for you, I'll offer up my blood as freely as though it were water carelessly spilled. O dearest trees, home to the sweet-sounding birds, do you perhaps experience love like this as well, and does the cypress ever fall in love with the pine, or any plant with another? By Zeus, I don't think so. For you would not simply shed your leaves, and Desire would not just pluck the foliage, your glory, from your branches, but it would penetrate even to the bottom of your trunk and roots with its fire."

Thus spoke the youth, Acontius, as he pined away in his body and his mind. But they were preparing a marriage for Cydippe with someone else. And in front of her chamber the maidens who were more musical and sweet voiced (to use that most lovely term of Sappho)[11] sang the wed-

ἐκφορὰν ἀντὶ νυμφαγωγίας οἱ τεκόντες ἑώρων. εἶτα παραδόξως ἀνέσφηλε, καὶ δεύτερον ὁ θάλαμος ἐκοσμεῖτο· καὶ ὥσπερ ἀπὸ συνθήματος τῆς Τύχης αὖθις ἐνόσει. τρίτον ὁμοίως ταῦτα συμβέβηκε τῇ παιδί, ὁ δὲ πατὴρ τετάρτην οὐκ ἀνέμεινε νόσον, ἀλλ' ἐπύθετο τοῦ Πυθίου, τίς ἄρα θεῶν τὸν γάμον ἐμποδίζει τῇ κόρῃ. ὁ δὲ Ἀπόλλων πάντα σαφῶς τὸν πατέρα διδάσκει, τὸν νέον, τὸ μῆλον, τὸν ὅρκον, καὶ τῆς Ἀρτέμιδος τὸν θυμόν· καὶ παραινεῖ θᾶττον εὔορκον ἀποφῆναι τὴν κόρην. "ἄλλως τε," φησί, "Κυδίππην Ἀκοντίῳ συνάπτων οὐ μόλιβδον ἂν συνεπιμίξαις ἀργύρῳ, ἀλλ' ἑκατέρωθεν ὁ γάμος ἔσται χρυσοῦς."

ταῦτα μὲν ἔχρησεν ὁ μαντῷος θεός, ὁ δὲ ὅρκος ἅμα τῷ χρησμῷ συνεπληροῦτο τοῖς γάμοις. αἱ δὲ τῆς παιδὸς ἡλικιώτιδες ἐνεργὸν ὑμέναιον ᾖδον οὐκ ἀναβαλλόμενον ἔτι οὐδὲ διακοπτόμενον νόσῳ. καὶ ἡ διδάσκαλος ὑπέβλεπε τὴν ἀπᾴδουσαν καὶ εἰς τὸ μέλος ἱκανῶς ἐνεβίβαζε χειρονομοῦσα τὸν τρόπον. ἕτερος δὲ τοῖς ᾄσμασιν ἐπεκρότει, καὶ ἡ δεξιὰ τοῖς δακτύλοις ὑπεσταλμένοις ὑποκειμένην τὴν ἀριστερὰν ἔπληττεν εἰς τὸ κοῖλον, ἵν' ὦσιν αἱ χεῖρες εὔφωνοι συμπληττόμεναι τρόπον κυμβάλων. ἅπαντα δ' οὖν ὅμως βραδύνειν ἐδόκει τῷ Ἀκοντίῳ, καὶ οὔτε ἡμέραν ἐκείνης ἐνόμισε μακροτέραν ἑωρακέναι οὔτε νύκτα βραχυτέραν. Τῆς νυκτὸς ἐκείνης Ἀκόντιος οὐκ ἂν ἠλλάξατο τὸν Μίδου χρυσόν, οὐδὲ τὸν Ταντάλου πλοῦτον ἰσοστάσιον ἡγεῖτο τῇ κόρῃ. καὶ σύμψηφοι πάντες ἐμοί, ὅσοι μὴ καθάπαξ τῶν ἐρωτικῶν ἀμαθεῖς· τὸν γὰρ ἀνέραστον οὐκ ἀπεικὸς ἀντίδοξον εἶναι. ὃς δ' οὖν τῇ παρθένῳ βραχέα νυκτομαχήσας ἐρωτικῶς, τό γε λοιπὸν εἰρηναίων ἀπέλαυεν ἡδονῶν. ἐκαίοντο δὲ κατὰ δώματα δαΐδες ἐκ λιβανωτοῦ συγκείμεναι, ὥστε ἅμα καίεσθαι καὶ θυμιᾶσθαι καὶ παρέχειν τὸ φῶς μετ' εὐωδίας. πάλαι τοίνυν αἱ παρθένοι συναριθμουμένης αὐταῖς τῆς Κυδίππης ἐπλεονέκτουν σφόδρα τῶν γυναικῶν, τὸν κολοφῶνα φέρουσαι τῆς εὐπρεπείας· νυνὶ δὲ τῆς νύμφης ἐν γυναιξὶ ταττομένης μειονεκτοῦσιν αἱ κόραι· τοσοῦτον ἡ φύσις ἁπανταχοῦ τὸ λαμπρὸν αὐτῆς ἐκορυφώσατο κάλλος. ὥσπερ δὲ χρυσόπολις ἡ πόα τῷ χρυσῷ μειρακίῳ συνήπτετο προσφυῶς. ἄμφω δὲ λαμπροῖς ὄμμασιν οἷον ἀστέρες ἀνταυγοῦντες ἀλλήλοις φαιδρότερον τῆς ἀλλήλων ἀπέλαυον ἀγλαΐας.

ding song. But the girl fell ill at once, and her parents faced the prospect of holding a funeral rather than a bridal procession. Then, unexpectedly, she recovered from her illness, and they were decking out the wedding chamber yet again. But as though by the plan of Destiny she fell ill once more. When the same thing happened yet a third time to the girl, her father did not wait for the fourth illness but inquired of the Pythian god[12] which deity was standing in the way of his daughter's marriage. But Apollo explained everything most clearly to the father, regarding the youth, the apple, the oath, and Artemis's wrath. He admonished that the girl quickly fulfill her oath. "Besides," he said, "by joining Cydippe and Acontius you would not mix lead with silver, but on each side the marriage will be golden."[13]

Thus the mantic god prophesied, and the oath was fulfilled together with the prophecy through the wedding celebrations. And the girl's agemates sang the hymenaion,[14] this time for real, without further delay or interruption by illness. And when anyone sang off-key, the chorus leader gave her a sharp look and got her back in tune by signaling the rhythm with her hand.[15] Another beat time to the songs,[16] pounding his right hand into the hollow of his left, with his fingers slightly curved, so that his hands made a pleasing sound as they struck each other like cymbals. To Acontius, however, all this just seemed to slow things down, and he thought he'd never seen a longer day or shorter night. Acontius would not have exchanged that night for all the gold of Midas,[17] nor did he consider the wealth of Tantalus of equal value to his girl. And anyone who is not an utter ignoramus in matters of love would agree with me, for it would not be surprising for someone inexperienced in love to think otherwise. Anyhow, he had to engage the girl in a brief nocturnal combat in bed but afterward enjoyed purely peaceful pleasures. Throughout the house there were torches burning, made of incense, so as to burn and give off scent at the same time, providing light together with a pleasing smell. As long as Cydippe belonged to their group, the maidens had always had a strong advantage over the women, since they had with them the pinnacle of beauty. But now that the girl was numbered among the women, the maidens no longer had the edge. So strongly did Nature make her shining beauty excel. Just like the golden plant Chrysopolis,[18] she clung tightly to her golden lad. The two of them, their eyes shining like stars, reflected back the other's light with yet greater brightness and so rejoiced in their mutual radiance.

ια΄. ΓΥΝΗ ΠΟΘΟΥΣΑ ΜΕΙΡΑΚΙΟΝ ΠΥΝΘΑΝΕΤΑΙ ΤΗΣ ΔΟΥΛΗΣ ΕΙ ΚΑΛΟΣ Ο ΠΟΘΟΥΜΕΝΟΣ

Φιλόστρατος Εὐαγόρᾳ

Παιδίσκην ἑαυτῆς ὧδέ πως ἤρετό τις γυνή· "πρὸς τῶν Χαρίτων, ὁποῖον δοκῶ σοι νεανίσκον ποθεῖν; ἐγὼ μὲν γὰρ οἶμαι καλόν· ἀλλ᾽ ἐρῶσα τυχὸν σφάλλομαι περὶ τὴν κρίσιν τοῦ ποθουμένου καὶ ἔρωτι πλανῶμαι τὴν ὄψιν. λέγε δή μοι κἀκεῖνο, τί φασιν αἱ καθορῶσαι τοῦτον γυναῖκες; πότερον αὐτὸν ἐπαινοῦσι τοῦ κάλλους, ἢ ψέγουσιν ἀποστραφεῖσαι τὴν θέαν;" ἡ δὲ μαστροπεύουσα πρὸς τὴν κεκτημένην φησί· "νὴ τὴν Ἄρτεμιν, ἐγὼ πολλῶν ἀκήκοα γυναικῶν αὐτήκοος γινομένη πλησίον ἐπιφθεγγομένων τοιάδε τῷ νέῳ· ʽἰδοὺ μειράκιον εὐπρεπές, ἰδοὺ κάλλος ἀπηκριβωμένον τῇ φύσει· τοιούτους ἔδει πλάττεσθαι τοὺς Ἔρωτας μᾶλλον ἢ κατὰ Ἀλκιβιάδου μορφήν. κάλλος γε καλόν, νὴ τὰς φίλας Ὥρας. χαρίεις ὁ νεανίας ἐπὶ κάλλει μέγα φρονῶν, οὐ μέντοι εἰς ὑπερηφάνειαν, ἀλλ᾽ εἰς τὸ ἁβρὸν καὶ μεγαλοπρεπές. ἱκανὸν πρὸς ἔρωτα καὶ μόνον τὸ ἐπίγρυπον τοῦ νεανίσκου, ἱκανὴ δὲ καὶ ἡ κόμη, καλὴ μὲν καθ᾽ ἑαυτὴν οὖσα, ἔτι δὲ καλλίων περικειμένη μὲν τῷ μετώπῳ, συγκατιοῦσα δὲ τῷ ἰούλῳ παρὰ τὸ οὖς. τὸ δὲ χλανιδίσκιον βαβαὶ τῶν χρωμάτων· οὐ γὰρ ἐφ᾽ ἑνὸς μένει χρώματος, ἀλλὰ τρέπεται καὶ μετανθεῖ. οὗτος ἡμῖν εὐκταῖος ἐραστής, ἡβάσκων ἀμφὶ πρώτην ὑπήνην. εὐδαίμων ἡ τὸν νέον εὐτυχοῦσα ἐπίσης ἐραστὴν ὁμοῦ καὶ ἐρώμενον. μακαρία ἡ συγκοιμωμένη τούτῳ, χλιδῶσα κατ᾽ εὐνὴν καὶ ἐντρυφῶσα τῷ κάλλει. εὐμενεστέροις ὄμμασιν ἐκείνην αἱ Χάριτες εἶδον.' καὶ πᾶσαί μοι δοκοῦσιν ἐρᾶν αὐτίκα τοῦ μειρακίου." ἤσθη ταῖς μαρτυρίαις καὶ ὑφ᾽ ἡδονῆς παντοδαπὰ χρώματα παρ᾽ ἕκαστον λόγον ἠφίει, καὶ (τὸ λεγόμενον δὴ τοῦτο) ἐδόκει τῇ κεφαλῇ ψαύειν τοῦ οὐρανοῦ. καὶ τότε πεπίστευκε τὸν νέον εἶναι καλόν· αὐταὶ γὰρ ἑαυτὰς αἱ γυναῖκες τότε δὴ κρίνουσιν εἶναι καλάς, ὅταν ἰδών τις ἐπαινέσῃ, ὅταν ἐρασθεὶς θαυμάσῃ.

ιβ΄. ΝΕΟΣ ΠΡΟΣΚΑΛΟΥΜΕΝΟΣ ΠΑΝΤΑΣ ΤΗΣ ΦΙΛΗΣ ΔΟΚΙΜΑΣΑΙ ΤΟ ΚΑΛΛΟΣ

Εὐήμερος Λευκίππῳ

Τίς ἄρα τεθέαται τῆς ἕω τὰ κάλλη, τίς δὲ ταῖς ἑσπερίαις ὡμίληκε γυναιξίν; ἡκέτωσαν οἱ πανταχόθεν ἐρωτικοὶ φιλογύναικες πρὸς κρίσιν τῆς ἐμῆς καλλι-

1.11. A Woman in Love with a Boy Asks Her Maid Whether the Object of Her Desire Is Beautiful

Philostratus to Euagoras[1]

A woman questioned her maid in the following manner: "By the Graces, what do you think of the boy I'm in love with? I, for my part, consider him beautiful. But as I'm in love, I may be mistaken in how I judge my heart's desire, and due to that love I may not see him straight. So tell me, what do the women say when they behold him? Do they praise his good looks, or do they turn away and mock what they see?" And pandering to her mistress the maid replied, "By Artemis, with these very ears I've overheard many a woman speak like this about the youth: 'Look, what a pretty boy! Look, what beauty perfectly wrought by Nature! They should model Erotes after *him* rather than Alcibiades.[2] He makes beauty beautiful, by the dear Seasons.[3] The boy is charmingly confident of his good looks, not to the point of arrogance, but in a refined and pleasing manner. The youth's hooked nose alone would be enough to make you love him; his hair would be enough, beautiful in itself, but lovelier still as it falls about his face joining the down of his cheeks at the ear.[4] And my, the colors of his cloak! They never stay the same but change and take on a different hue.[5] This is the lover of our dreams, a lad with his beard just darkening his lip. Lucky is she who gets this boy as her prize, equal parts lover and beloved.[6] Blessed the one who sleeps with him, luxuriating in bed and indulging in his beauty. The Graces have looked on her with more gracious eyes.' To me they all seem smitten with the boy the moment they set eyes on him." The mistress was delighted with this testimonial and, overjoyed, changed color at every word her maid spoke; indeed, her head seemed to touch the sky,[7] as the saying goes. So at last she was convinced the youth was beautiful. For even when it comes to themselves, women judge they are beautiful only when another sees and praises them, admires and falls in love with them.

1.12. A Youth Invites One and All to Come Examine the Beauty of His Beloved

Euhemeros[1] to Leukippos[2]

Who has glimpsed the beauties of the East, and who has encountered the women of the West? Let all amorous lovers of women from all over the

κοίτης, καὶ σὺν ἀληθείᾳ λεγόντων, εἴ που τοιοῦτον ἱστορήκασιν ἀξιοθέατον κάλλος. ὅπου γὰρ ἄν τις αὐτῇ τοὺς ὀφθαλμοὺς ἐπιβάλῃ, πανταχοῦ κάλλος αὐτῷ συναντᾶται καὶ κάλλους ἐφάπτεται. ταύτης ὁ Μῶμος ἀποσφαλεὶς ἄχθεται καὶ στένει καὶ ἀπορεῖ παραδόξως. τεθαύμακα τὴν ἡλικίαν, τὴν χάριν, καὶ μέχρι τοῦ ποδὸς διῆλθε τὸ θαῦμα· φύσει γὰρ ὁ ποὺς εὔπλαστος ὢν καὶ τὰς ἀκοσμήτους οἶδε κοσμεῖν. ἐφήδομαι τοῖς τρόποις εὖ μάλα συμπρέπουσι τῇ μορφῇ· ἑταίρας μὲν γὰρ ἡ Πυθιὰς εἴληχε βίον, ἁπλότητα δὲ σύμφυτον ἔχει καὶ ἄμεμπτον ἦθος. ἅπαντα τῆς τάξεως τοῦ βίου βελτίω, καὶ αὐτόν με μάλιστα ἤρηκε τῷ ἀκάκῳ. δῶρον δ᾽ ὅ τις δῷ ἐπαινεῖ, οὐχ ὥσπερ ἑταίρα πᾶν τὸ διδόμενον σμικρὸν ἡγουμένη. καὶ ὥσπερ κολοιὸς ἀεὶ παρὰ κολοιὸν ἱζάνομεν ἄμφω.

τί δεῖ περαιτέρω προβαίνειν, ἔνθα δὴ τὰ τερπνὰ τῆς Ἀφροδίτης ἀπόρρητα; λεκτέον δὲ μόνον ὡς ἀντιλέγει τοσοῦτον, ὅσον ἐν τῷ βραδύνειν ἐρεθίσαι. Ὁ μὲν οὖν τράχηλος αὐτῆς ἀμβροσίας ὄδωδε, καὶ τὸ ἆσθμα ἡδύ· εἰ δὲ μήλων ἢ ῥόδων πόμασι συμμιγέντων ἀπόζει, φιλήσας ἐρεῖς. τοῖς δὲ στέρνοις τῆς καλῆς ἐπιθεὶς τὴν κεφαλὴν ἠγρύπνουν, αὐτὸ καταφιλῶν τὸ πήδημα τῆς καρδίας. οὔκουν τῶν ἀφροδισίων, ὡς ἔφη τις, εἰς τὸ τῆς ἡδονῆς τέλος ὁδός ἐστιν μία. ἀναφρόδιτοι γὰρ αἱ δυσειδεῖς γυναῖκες, καὶ ἡδονῆς ἐν ἐκείναις οὐκ ἀρχὴν οὐ τέλος εὕροι τις ἄν. ἐπεὶ κἂν τοῖς ἐδέσμασιν ἓν τέλος ὁ κόρος· ἀλλὰ τὰ μὲν τρέφει καὶ τέρπει, τὰ δὲ παντελῶς ἀνατρέπει. διὰ ταύτην ἡμέρα μοι πᾶσα λευκὴ καὶ τῶν ἐν φαρέτρᾳ λογιζομένων εἰς εὐτυχίαν οὐχ ἧττον. ᾀδόντων μὲν οὖν ἀκήκοα πολλάκις ὡς πέφυκεν ἀποδημία τὸν πόθον ἐκλύειν, καὶ παροιμιαζόμενοι δέ φασι "τοσοῦτον φίλος, ὅσον ὁρᾷ τις ἐναντίον." ἐγὼ δὲ ὄμνυμι τὰς χάριτας Πυθιάδος ὡς οὐδὲ ἀποδημῶν ἀπεστάτουν τῆς πρὸς ἐκείνην φιλίας. οὐδὲν οὖν ἧττον ἐπανῆλθον ἐρῶν, μᾶλλον διαλιπὼν καὶ μειζόνως ᾐσθόμην τοῦ πόθου, καὶ χάριν οἶδα τῇ Τύχῃ, ὅτι μοι λήθην οὐκ ἐνέθηκε τῆς φιλτάτης. ἔφη δ᾽ ἄν τις ἐρωτικὸς ποιητὴς καθομηρίζων ἡμᾶς "ἀσπάσιοι λέκτροιο παλαιοῦ θεσμὸν ἵκοντο."

world come to judge my gorgeous bedmate, and let them declare truthfully whether they've ever found such a remarkable beauty. For whatever part of her you cast your eyes on, your gaze meets beauty everywhere—beauty upon beauty. Blame,[3] unable to get her in his clutches, is peeved, groans, and is unexpectedly at a loss. I'm awestruck at her stature, her grace, and my admiration reaches right down to her feet. For a naturally well-made foot can adorn even those who lack adornment otherwise. I also love her manners, which are perfectly suited to her looks. For my Pythias may live the life of a hetaira, but she has a natural honesty, a blameless character. Everything about her is better than her status, and above all it was her innocence that took me captive. Whatever gift you give her she praises, and she doesn't turn her nose up at every present as hetairas do. Like birds of a feather we snuggle together.[4]

Must I go on and reveal the secret joys of Aphrodite? No, let me just say that she resists only to the point that by delaying she excites an even greater passion. Her neck smells of ambrosia, and her breath is sweet. Whether it smells of apples or of roses mixed together in a drink, you'll be able to tell once you've kissed her. I like to lie awake with my head on my darling's chest and press kisses where I feel her heartbeat. So in matters of love, as they say, there truly is only one way to satisfy one's desires. For ugly women don't inspire love, and you won't find in them lust's spark, or its fulfillment. When it comes to food, as well, the overriding goal is to get your fill. But some foods nourish and give pleasure, while others only disgust. Because of her, every day is a joy to me, and my ledger is filled with happiness.[5] I have often heard singers sing of how absence naturally eradicates desire, and the proverb says, "Out of sight, out of mind."[6] But I swear by the charms of my Pythias that I never stopped loving her, even when I was away. And I came back, loving her no less; rather, in being separated I felt an even stronger desire for her. And I'm grateful to Tyche[7] that she did not make me forget my beloved. An erotic poet might say of us in the manner of Homer, "Happily they returned to the bond of their ancient marriage bed."[8]

ιγ΄. ΠΑΙΣ ΕΠΟΘΕΙ ΤΗΝ ΤΟΥ ΦΥΣΑΝΤΟΣ ΠΑΛΛΑΚΗΝ.
ΙΑΤΡΟΣ ΔΙΕΓΝΩ ΤΟΝ ΕΡΩΤΑ ΤΥΧΗΙ ΠΛΕΟΝ Η ΤΕΧΝΗΙ
ΧΡΗΣΑΜΕΝΟΣ, ΚΑΙ ΜΕΘΟΔΩΙ ΠΕΙΘΕΙ ΤΟΝ ΠΑΤΕΡΑ
ΤΩΙ ΠΑΙΔΙ ΠΑΡΑΧΩΡΗΣΑΙ ΤΗΣ ΠΑΛΛΑΚΙΔΟΣ

Εὐτυχόβουλος Ἀκεστοδώρῳ

Τῷ μακρῷ καὶ τοῦτο, φίλτατε, κατέμαθον χρόνῳ, ὡς καὶ τέχναι πᾶσαι προσ-
δέονται τύχης, καὶ τύχη διακοσμεῖται ταῖς ἐπιστήμαις. αἱ μὲν γὰρ ἀτελεῖς
μὴ συνεργοῦντος τοῦ θείου, ἡ δὲ μᾶλλον εὐδοκιμεῖ τὰς ἑαυτῆς ἀφορμὰς τοῖς
ἐπιστήμοσι δωρουμένη. ἐπεὶ τοίνυν μακρόν γε τὸ προοίμιον, εὖ οἶδα, τῷ
ποθοῦντι θᾶττον ἀκοῦσαι, ἤδη λέξω τὸ συμβάν, μηδὲν ἔτι μελλήσας. Χαρικλῆς
ὁ τοῦ βελτίστου Πολυκλέους υἱὸς παλλακίδος τοῦ τεκόντος πόθῳ κλινοπετὴς
ἦν, σώματος μὲν ἀφανῆ πλαττόμενος ἀλγηδόνα, ψυχῆς δὲ ταῖς ἀληθείαις
αἰτιώμενος νόσον. ὁ γοῦν πατήρ, οἷα πατὴρ ἀγαθὸς καὶ σφόδρα φιλόπαις,
αὐτίκα Πανάκειον μεταπέμπεται τὸν ὄντως ἐπώνυμον ἰατρόν, ὃς τοὺς μὲν
δακτύλους τῷ σφυγμῷ προσαρμόζων, τὸν δὲ νοῦν μετάρσιον ἄγων τῇ τέχνῃ,
καὶ τοῖς ὄμμασι τὸ διαγνωστικὸν ὑποφαίνων κίνημα τῆς διανοίας οὐδὲν ὅλως
ἀρρώστημα κατενόει γνώριμον ἰατροῖς. ἐπὶ πολὺ μὲν οὖν ὁ τοιοῦτος ἰατρὸς
ἀμήχανος ἦν· τῆς δὲ ποθουμένης ἐκ ταὐτομάτου παριούσης διὰ τοῦ μειρακίου,
ἀθρόον ὁ σφυγμὸς ἄτακτον ἥλατο, καὶ τὸ βλέμμα ταραχῶδες ἐδόκει, καὶ οὐδὲν
ἄμεινον τὸ πρόσωπον διέκειτο τῆς χειρός. καὶ διχόθεν ὁ Πανάκειος διέγνω τὸ
πάθος, καὶ ὅπερ ἁπλῶς ἐκ τέχνης οὐχ εἷλεν, ἐκ τύχης μᾶλλον εἶχε λαβών, καὶ
τὸ δῶρον τῆς προνοίας εἰς καιρὸν ἐταμιεύετο τῇ σιωπῇ.

καὶ πρῶτος ἦν αὐτῷ τῆς ἐπισκέψεως ἡγούμενος ὅδε ὁ τρόπος. αὖθις δὲ παρα-
γενόμενος διεκελεύετο πᾶσαν τῆς οἰκίας κόρην τε καὶ γυναῖκα διὰ τοῦ κάμνον-
τος παριέναι, καὶ μὴ χύδην, ἀλλὰ κατὰ μίαν, ἐκ διαστήματος βραχέος διακρι-
νομένας ἀλλήλων. καὶ τούτου γιγνομένου αὐτὸς μὲν τὴν ὑποκάρπιον ἀρτηρίαν
τοῖς δακτύλοις ἡρμοκὼς ἐπεσκόπει, τὸν ἀκριβῆ γνώμονα τῶν Ἀσκληπιαδῶν
καὶ μάντιν ἀψευδῆ τῶν ἐμφυομένων ἡμῖν διαθέσεων· ὁ δὲ τῷ πόθῳ κλινή-
ρης πρὸς μὲν τὰς ἄλλας ἀτάραχος ἦν, τῆς δὲ παλλακῆς, ἧς εἶχεν ἐρωτικῶς,
ἐκφανείσης, εὐθὺς καὶ τὸ βλέμμα πάλιν καὶ τὸν σφυγμὸν ἀλλοιότερος ἦν. ὁ δὲ
σοφὸς καὶ λίαν εὐτυχὴς ἰατρὸς ἔτι μᾶλλον τὴν ἀπόδειξιν τῆς νόσου παρ᾽ ἑαυτῷ
βεβαιότερον ἐπιστοῦτο, τὸ τρίτον τῷ σωτῆρι φάσκων. προφασισάμενος γὰρ
κατασκευῆς αὐτῷ φαρμάκων δεῖσθαι τὸ πάθος, ἀπεχώρει τέως ὑπισχνούμενος

1.13. A Youth Desired His Father's Mistress. A Doctor Found Out about His Love More by Accident Than by Art and Skillfully Persuades the Father to Yield His Mistress to the Youth

Eutychoboulos[1] to Akestodoros[2]

In the fullness of time I have learned among other things, dear friend, that all arts require some luck, and luck is enriched by knowledge. For the arts are futile without divine aid, while luck is most glorious when it bestows its resources upon those who are knowledgeable. Since I know well that this prelude is rather long for those anxious to hear the story, I'll tell you what happened and won't delay any longer. Charikles, son of the most excellent Polykles, was sick in bed with desire for his father's mistress. He pretended he was suffering from some unseen physical ailment, though in truth he knew the origin of his disease lay in his soul. So the father, like the good and child-loving father he was, sent for a doctor fittingly named Panacea.[3] He took the boy's pulse, letting his mind fly aloft into the highest regions of his art, and in his eyes you could see how his thoughts moved in search of a diagnosis. But he was unable to identify any illness known to medicine. For a long time, even a doctor of his caliber was perplexed. But when the youth's object of desire happened to pass nearby, at once his pulse started to beat erratically and his gaze seemed troubled, the face showing the same signs of distress as the hand. And from either symptom, Panacea deduced the malady, and what he didn't grasp simply from his art, he understood rather through happenstance. This gift of Providence he stored up in silence for the right moment.

During his first visit, then, this was the method of investigation he pursued. But upon coming again, he bid every girl and woman in the house to walk by the bed of the invalid, not all in a bunch, but one at a time, a brief interval between each. And as this was happening, Panacea himself observed the boy's pulse as he held his wrist, the most accurate guide for those following in Asclepius's footsteps,[4] and truthful prophet of our inner states. The lovesick boy showed no signs of distress with the other women, but when the mistress appeared, with whom he was in love, his expression and pulse immediately changed again. The wise and most fortunate doctor found his diagnosis of the illness borne out with even more certainty, concluding that his third visit would be the charm. Pretending that he needed to prepare some remedies for the illness, he went away for a while, promis-

τῇ ὑστεραίᾳ ταῦτα κομίζειν, ἅμα τε τὸν νοσοῦντα χρησταῖς παραθαρρύνων ἐλπίσι καὶ δυσφοροῦντα ψυχαγωγῶν τὸν πατέρα.

ὡς δὲ κατὰ καιρὸν ἐπηγγελμένον παρῆν, ὁ μὲν πατὴρ καὶ πάντες οἱ λοιποὶ σωτῆρα τὸν ἄνδρα προσεῖπον, καὶ φιλοφρόνως ἠσπάζοντο προσιόντες· ὁ δὲ χαλεπαίνων ἐβόα, καὶ δυσανασχετῶν αὐστηρῶς τὴν θεραπείαν ἀπέγνω. τοῦ δὲ Πολυκλέους λιπαροῦντος ἅμα καὶ πυνθανομένου τῆς ἀπογνώσεως τὴν αἰτίαν, ἠγανάκτει σφοδρότερον κεκραγώς, καὶ ἀπαλλάττεσθαι τὴν ταχίστην ἠξίου. ἀλλ' ὁ πατὴρ ἔτι μᾶλλον ἱκέτευε, τά τε στήθη φιλῶν καὶ τῶν γονάτων ἁπτόμενος. τότε δῆθεν πρὸς ἀνάγκης ὧδε σὺν ὀργῇ τὴν αἰτίαν ἐξεῖπε· "τῆς ἐμῆς γαμετῆς οὗτος ἐκτόπως ἐρᾷ καὶ παρανόμῳ τήκεται πόθῳ, καὶ ζηλοτυπῶ τὸν ἄνθρωπον ἤδη καὶ οὐ φέρω θέαν ἀπειλουμένου μοιχοῦ." ὁ τοίνυν Πολυκλῆς τοῦ παιδὸς ᾐσχύνθη τὴν νόσον ἀκούων, καὶ τὸν Πανάκειον ἠρυθρία, πλὴν ὅλως τῆς φύσεως γεγονὼς οὐκ ἀπώκνησε περὶ τῆς αὐτοῦ γυναικὸς τὸν ἰατρὸν ἱκετεύειν, ἀναγκαίαν τινὰ σωτηρίαν οὐ μοιχείαν τὸ πρᾶγμα καλῶν. ἔτι δὲ τοιαῦτα δεομένου τοῦ Πολυκλέους ὁ Πανάκειος διωλύγιον κατεβόα φάσκων οἷάπερ εἰκὸς ἦν φθέγγεσθαι δεινοπαθοῦντα τὸν αἰτούμενον ἐξ ἰατροῦ μεταβαλεῖν εἰς μαστροπὸν καὶ μοιχείας τῆς ἑαυτοῦ γαμετῆς <συλλαβεῖν>, εἰ μὴ φανερῶς οὕτως τοῖς ῥήμασιν.

ἐπεὶ δὲ πάλιν ἐνέκειτο Πολυκλῆς ἀντιβολῶν τὸν ἄνδρα, καὶ πάλιν σωτηρίαν οὐ μοιχείαν ἐκάλει τὸ πρᾶγμα, ὁ συλλογιστικὸς ἰατρὸς ὡς ἐν ὑποθέσει τὸ συμβὰν ἀληθῶς ἀντεπάγων ἤρετο Πολυκλέα· "τί οὖν, πρὸς Διός, οὐδ' ἂν ὁ παῖς τῆς σῆς ἤρα παλλακίδος, ἐκαρτέρεις αὐτῷ ποθοῦντι ταύτην ἐκδοῦναι;" ἐκείνου δὲ φήσαντος "πάνυ γε, νὴ τὸν Δία," ὁ σοφὸς ἔφη Πανάκειος· "οὐκοῦν σαυτόν, ὦ Πολύκλεις, ἱκέτευε, καὶ παραμυθοῦ τὰ εἰκότα. τῆς σῆς γὰρ οὗτος παλλακίδος ἐρᾷ. εἰ δὲ δίκαιον ἐμὲ τὴν ὁμόζυγα παραδιδόναι τῷ τυχόντι διὰ σωτηρίαν, ὡς ἔφης, πολύ γε μᾶλλον δικαιότερόν σε τῷ παιδὶ κινδυνεύοντι παραχωρῆσαι τῆς παλλακίδος." εἶπεν εὐμεθόδως, συνελογίσατο δυνατῶς, καὶ πέπεικε τὸν τεκόντα τοῖς οἰκείοις πειθαρχῆσαι δικαίοις. πρότερον μέντοι Πολυκλῆς ἑαυτῷ προσεφθέγγετο λέγων· "χαλεπὴ μὲν ἡ αἴτησις· δύο κακῶν εἰς αἵρεσιν προκειμένων τὸ μετριώτερον αἱρετέον."

ing to bring them along the next day, but also raising the invalid's hopes with words of comfort and reassuring his distressed father.

When he came back at the appointed hour, the father and all the rest rushed forward to greet him as their savior and welcome him cordially. But the doctor cried out in anger and, as though unable to bear the cruelty of it, declared that he wouldn't continue the treatment. And when Polykles pleaded with him, wanting to know why he wouldn't go on, the doctor started to rage and rant all the more, deciding to leave without delay. But the father's pleas grew even more impassioned; he pressed kisses onto the doctor's chest, grasped him by the knees. Then bowing, finally, to necessity, Panacea angrily declared the cause of the illness: "This boy here is insanely in love with my wife and pines for her with illicit desire. The thought alone sends me into a jealous rage against, against this ... man, and I can't bear the sight of the would-be adulterer." Now Polykles was ashamed when he heard what his son was sick with and blushed in front of Panacea. Still, totally following paternal instinct, he did not waver from asking the doctor even for his own wife, claiming that it was not adultery, but a life-saving necessity. Even as Polykles beseeched him, Panacea threw a fit, screaming just what you'd expect of a man who'd been asked to turn from a doctor into a pimp and to assist in the adultery of his own wife, even if that had not been stated in such explicit terms.

But when Polykles pressed him again with his entreaties, once more saying that the issue was salvation, not adultery, the doctor following the laws of logic countered with a hypothetical situation (which was in fact the truth), and asked Polykles, "Well, then, by Zeus, if your son was in love with your mistress, could you bear to give her up to satisfy his desire?" The father replied, "Of course, by Zeus," and the wise doctor said, "Then turn to yourself for help, and assuage yourself with the conventional excuses. For this boy here is in love with your mistress. And if it is right for me to give my wife to any comer for the sake of curing him, as you say, then it is all the more right for you to grant your mistress to your son when his life's in danger." Thus he spoke with irrefutable method, reaching powerful conclusions, and convincing the father to yield to his own just arguments. But before going along with it, Polykles grumbled to himself, "That's a tough demand. But when there's a choice between two evils, one must pick the lesser of the two."

ιδ′. ΠΟΡΝΙΔΙΟΝ ΠΡΟΣ ΝΕΟΥΣ ΑΙΣΜΑΣΙΝ ΟΥΚ ΑΡΓΥΡΙΩΙ ΠΡΟΤΡΕΠΟΜΕΝΟΥΣ ΑΥΤΗΝ

Φιλοχρημάτιον Εὐμούσῳ

Οὔτε αὐλὸς ἑταίραν οἶδε προτρέπειν οὔτε λύρα τις ἐφέλκεται πόρνας ἀργυρίου χωρίς· κέρδει μόνον δουλεύομεν, οὐ θελγόμεθα μελῳδίαις. τί οὖν μάτην, ὦ νέοι, διαρρήγνυσθε τὰς γνάθους ἐμφυσῶντες τῇ σύριγγι; οὐδὲν ὑμᾶς ὀνήσει τὰ κιθαρίσματα· τί πράγματα παρέχετε ταῖς χορδαῖς; τί δὲ καὶ ᾄδοντες ἔφητε· "οὐκ ἐπιθυμεῖς, ὦ παρθένε, γενέσθαι γυνή; μέχρι τίνος παρθένος καὶ κόρη, τὰ τῶν ἀνοήτων ὀνόματα;" ἢ ταῦτα μὲν ἴστε που πάντως ὡς ἀνάργυρον οὐδὲν ταῖς ἑταίραις ἐστὶ πιθανόν, ᾠήθητε δέ με ῥᾳδίως ἐξαπατᾶν ὡς ἐρωτικῶν ἀγύμναστον παῖδα καὶ παντελῶς ἀμύητον Ἀφροδίτης, καὶ προχειρότερον ἑλεῖν ἢ λύκος λιπαρὰν ἄρνα καθεύδουσαν; ἀλλ' ἔγωγε παλαιᾷ συνοῦσα πορνοδιδασκάλῳ τῇ ἀδελφῇ καὶ τοῖς ἐκείνης ἐρασταῖς κατὰ πρόφασιν ὁμιλοῦσα οὐδὲν ἔδοξα δυσμαθής, ἀλλὰ τὸν ἑταιρικὸν ἤδη μεμελέτηκα βίον καὶ παρατέθηγμαι τὸν νοῦν καὶ γέγονα ξυρὸν εἰς ἀκόνην καὶ ἀργυρίῳ τῶν νέων τὸν ἔρωτα δοκιμάζω· χρυσίου γὰρ μεῖζον τεκμήριον τοῦ κομιδῇ φιλεῖν οὐκ οἶδα ἕτερον. τοιγαροῦν τινες ἅμα προϊούσας ὁρῶντες Κρωβύλου ζεῦγος ἀστεϊζόμενοι πολλάκις ἐπιφωνοῦσιν ἡμᾶς. νὴ τὰς Χάριτας, ἀκήκοα πολλάκις αὐτῆς εἰκότως ἐκεῖνο μάλιστα τοῖς φίλοις λεγούσης· "ὑμεῖς μὲν ὀρέγεσθε κάλλους, ἐγὼ δὲ χρημάτων ἐρῶ. οὐκοῦν ἀνεπιφθόνως τοὺς ἀλλήλων θεραπεύσωμεν πόθους." κἀγὼ τὸν νόμον ἀποδέχομαι καὶ ζηλῶ. τούτῳ πείθεσθε τῶν περιττῶν ὀργάνων ἀφέμενοι. τό γε ἡμέτερον οὐ κωλύσει· ἀλλ' ἐὰν ἀργύριον ᾖ, πάντα θεῖ κἀλαύνεται.

ιε′. ΔΥΟ ΠΟΛΕΙΣ ΚΑΤ' ΑΛΛΗΛΩΝ ΔΙΕΚΕΙΝΤΟ ΠΟΛΕΜΙΩΣ· ΜΙΑΣ ΤΟΥΤΩΝ ΒΑΣΙΛΕΥΣ ΗΡΑΣΘΗ ΚΟΡΗΣ ΕΚ ΤΗΣ ΕΝΑΝΤΙΑΣ ΠΟΛΕΩΣ, [ΩΣ] ΕΠΑΦΡΟΔΙΤΩΣ ΕΚΜΑΝΕΙΣΗΣ ΑΥΤΩΙ, ΚΑΙ ΓΑΜΟΥ ΤΥΧΩΝ ΕΝ ΑΜΟΙΒΗΣ ΜΕΡΕΙ ΠΡΟΣ ΤΟΥΣ ΠΟΛΙΤΑΣ ΕΣΠΕΙΣΑΤΟ ΤΗΣ ΦΙΛΤΑΤΗΣ

Ἀφροδίσιος Λυσιμάχῳ

Οὐδέν, ὡς ἔγωμαι, πιθανώτερον πέφυκεν οὐδ' ἀνυσιμώτερον Ἀφροδίτης. ἴσασι δὲ οἱ βεβλημένοι, καὶ τούτων ἡμῖν ἀντίψηφος οὐδὲ εἷς. αὕτη καὶ πόλεμον

1.14. A Prostitute to Youths Who Want to Win Her Over with Songs, Not Money

Philochremation[1] to Eumousos[2]

You can't win over a hetaira by playing a flute, nor can you attract prostitutes with a lyre if you don't have money. We are slaves only to profit and are not bewitched by melodies. So why, boys, do you break your jaws with blowing on the pipes?[3] Kithara music won't help you. Why trouble the strings? Why do you sing the words "Aren't you yearning, girl, to become a woman? How long do you intend to be called virgin or child, names only a fool would want?" Or do you actually *know* that without cash absolutely nothing at all can persuade a hetaira, yet still you think you can easily fool me as though I were a child inexperienced in erotic things and totally uninitiated in the mysteries of Aphrodite, an easier prey than a tender lamb in its sleep for a wolf? But I used to hang out with my older sister, who instructed me in the erotic trade, and when I mingled with her lovers under some pretext or other, they did not think me a slow learner. On the contrary, even back then I applied myself to the life of the hetaira, sharpened my mind, and became a veritable razor on the whetstone.[4] I judge a young man's love by his dough. For I know no better proof of devotion than money. Some people, when they see the two of us promenading together, often call out in jest, "Hey, the dynamic duo of Krobylos."[5] By the Graces, here's what I'd hear her tell her lovers, and right she was: "You pursue beauty; I'm in love with money. So let's not be stingy in tending to each others' desires." I, for my part, accept this custom and try to keep it. So you should follow it, too, and discard your useless instruments. As for me, nothing will stand in the way. When there's money, there's smooth sailing into every port.

1.15. Two Cities Were Waging War. the King of One Was Smitten with a Girl from the Enemy City, While She Too Was Madly in Love with Him, and upon Being Joined with Her He in Turn Made Peace with His Darling's Fellow Citizens

Aphrodisios[1] to Lysimachos[2]

Nothing, I think, is more persuasive and efficient than Aphrodite. Those who have been wounded by her know this all too well, and none would

διαλύει καὶ δυσμενεῖς παρασκευάζει βεβαιότατα σπένδεσθαι πρὸς ἀλλήλους. ἀμέλει τοι πολλάκις μετὰ στρατηγοὺς ἀρίστους καὶ μεγάλα στρατόπεδα καὶ πολλὴν τοῦ πολέμου συσκευὴν ὁ βραχὺς ἐκεῖνος τοξότης μικρᾶς ἀκίδος βολῇ καὶ αὐτὸν δήπου τὸν Ἄρη περιττὸν ἀποφαίνει, πραότητα μὲν πορίζων, <ἀγριότητα δὲ ἐξορίζων>. ἔνθα τις ὁπλίτην μὲν ἰδών, εἰ καὶ δύσμαχον, προυβάλλετο τὴν ἀσπίδα σὺν εὐτολμίᾳ κατιθύνων τὸ δόρυ, Ἔρωτος δὲ φανέντος γέγονε ῥίψασπις εὐθὺς ὁ τέως θρασύς, καὶ τὴν δεξιὰν ἀκονιτὶ προσανατείνας ὡμολόγει τὴν ἧτταν, τῆς τε μάχης ὑπανεχώρει, μετατρέπων τὰ νῶτα παιδαρίῳ τοξότῃ, μηδέ γ᾽ οὖν μαλθακὸς αἰχμητὴς εἶναι δι᾽ ἐκεῖνον τολμήσας.

Μίλητος τοίνυν καὶ Μυοῦς αἱ πόλεις ἐπὶ μήκιστον χρόνον πρὸς ἀλλήλας ἀνεπίμικτοι διετέλουν, πλὴν ὅσον ἐς Μίλητον οἱ τῆς ἑτέρας ὑπόσπονδοι βραχὺ προσεφοίτων, καιρὸν ἔχοντες καὶ μέτρον τῆς αὐτόθι τιμωμένης Ἀρτέμιδος τὴν πανήγυριν καὶ σμικρὰν ἀνακωχὴν ἑκάτεροι τὴν ἑορτὴν ἐποιοῦντο. τούτους Ἀφροδίτη κατελεοῦσα διήλλαξεν, ἀφορμὴν εἰς σύμβασιν μηχανησαμένη τοιάνδε. κόρη γάρ τις τοὔνομα Πιερία, φύσει τε καλὴ κἀκ τῆς Ἀφροδίτης ἐπισημότερον κοσμηθεῖσα, ἐκ τοῦ Μυοῦντος ἐγκαίρως ἐπεδήμησε τῇ Μιλήτῳ. καὶ τῆς θεοῦ τὸ πᾶν διεπούσης μετὰ τοῦ πλήθους εἰς Ἀρτέμιδος ἐχώρουν, ἡ μὲν παρθένος ταῖς Χάρισιν ἀγλαϊζομένη, Φρύγιος δὲ ὁ τοῦ ἄστεος βασιλεὺς πρὸς τῶν Ἐρώτων κατατοξευόμενος τὴν ψυχὴν ἐπὶ τῇ κόρῃ τὴν πρώτην αὐτίκα φανείσῃ. καὶ θᾶττον ἄμφω συνῆλθον εἰς εὐνήν, ἵνα καὶ πρὸς εἰρήνην ὅτι τάχιστα συναφθῶσιν αἱ πόλεις.

ἔφη δ᾽ οὖν ὁ νυμφίος ἐρασμίως ἐναφροδισιάσας τῇ κόρῃ καὶ σπεύδων αὐτῇ πρέπουσαν ἀμοιβὴν ἀποδοῦναι· "εἴθε γὰρ θαρροῦσα λέξειας, ὦ καλή, τί ἄν σοι χαριέστατα γένοιτο παρ᾽ ἐμοῦ. καὶ διπλασίαν ἡδέως τὴν αἴτησιν ἀποπληρώσω." τοιαῦτα μὲν ὁ δίκαιος ἐραστής· σὲ δέ, ὦ πασῶν ὑπερφέρουσα γυναικῶν καὶ κάλλει καὶ γνώμῃ, τῆς ἔμφρονος οὐ παρήγαγεν εὐβουλίας οὐχ ὅρμος, οὐχ ἑλικτῆρες, οὐ πυλεὼν ὁ πολύτιμος, οὐ περιδέραιον, οὐ Λύδιός τε καὶ ποδήρης χιτών, οὐ πορφυρίδες, οὐ θεράπαιναι τῆς Καρίας οὐδὲ Λυδῶν ὑπερφυῶς ἱστουργοῦσαι γυναῖκες, οἷς ἅπασιν ἀτεχνῶς ἀγάλλεσθαι τὸ θῆλυ πέφυκε γένος, ἀλλ᾽ εἰς γῆν ἑώρας τὸ πρόσωπον, ὥσπερ τι συννοουμένη. εἶτα ἔφης ἐπιχαρίτως πεφοινιγμένη τὰς παρειὰς καὶ τὸ πρόσωπον ἐξ αἰδοῦς ἀποκλίνασα καὶ πῇ μὲν τῆς ἀμπεχόνης ἄκροις δακτύλοις ἐφαπτομένη τῶν κροσσῶν, πῇ δὲ περιστρέφουσα τοῦ ζωνίου τὸ ἄκρον, ἔστι δὲ ὅτε καὶ τοὔδαφος περιχαράττουσα τῷ ποδί (ταῦτα δὴ τὰ τῶν αἰδουμένων ἐν διαπορήσει κινήματα), ἔφης οὖν μόλις ἠρεμαίᾳ φωνῇ· "ἐπίνευσον, ὦ βασιλεῦ, ἐμέ τε καὶ τοὺς ἐμοὺς συγγενεῖς εἰς τήνδε τὴν εὐδαίμονα πόλιν ὅταν ἐθέλοιμεν ἐπ᾽ ἀδείας ἰέναι."

contradict us. She puts a stop to war and causes enemies to make the most enduring peace. Even when the most cunning generals take the field with their mighty armies all equipped for war, that little archer with his tiny dart often shows that Ares is beside the point; his gift is gentleness instead. Say someone spots a warrior, fearsome as can be, and hoists his shield against him with confident daring, thrusting out his spear. But let Eros appear on the scene, and like a coward he immediately casts away his shield,[3] bold as he may have been before; he offers his hand without a fight, acknowledging his defeat, then turns and flees the combat with the boy archer. Under his power, the warrior doesn't even dare to fight half-heartedly.

Even so had the cities of Miletus and Myus[4] been estranged for the longest time, except for once a year—when, protected by a short truce, the inhabitants of the latter city would seize the opportunity to visit Miletus for the celebrations in honor of Artemis, who is worshiped there, each side taking the festival as a brief respite from arms. Out of pity for them, Aphrodite reconciled the warring parties by devising the following pretext for their reunion. A girl named Pieria,[5] a natural beauty, rendered even more radiant by Aphrodite, opportunely came from Myus to Miletus. As the goddess was seeing to everything, both the virgin, splendidly adorned by the Graces, and Phrygios, king of the city, marched with the crowd to Artemis's temple. No sooner, however, did the girl appear before him than the king was pierced through the heart by the Erotes. In no time the two of them went to bed together, so that their cities too could be joined in peace as quickly as possible.

Having made passionate love to the girl and eager to offer her a suitable favor in return, the bridegroom said: "Pluck up your courage, my lovely one, and tell me what I could give that would most delight you. I will gladly give you twice what you request." Thus the just lover. But you, excelling all women in beauty and judgment, were not led astray from prudent counsel, neither by a necklace, nor earrings, nor a precious crown, nor a chain, nor a sweeping Lydian robe, nor purple fabrics, nor by Karian[6] handmaids or marvelous weaving women from Lydia, all those things that the female sex is utterly crazy about—no, you cast your glance down to the earth, as though deliberating something. Then you said, your cheeks charmingly ablush, tilting your head in modesty, now fingering the tassels of your shawl, now fiddling with the trim on your belt, and sometimes tracing figures in the ground with your foot (for such are the gestures that betray embarrassment in the shy)—so in a hushed and gentle voice you said: "Grant, O king, that I and my kinsmen may come without fear to this blessed city whenever we wish."

ὁ δὲ Φρύγιος τῆς φιλοπάτριδος γυναικὸς ὅλον κατενόησε τὸν σκοπόν, ὡς διὰ τούτων ἐκείνη σπονδὰς πρὸς Μιλησίους πραγματεύεται τῇ πατρίδι, κατένευσέ τε βασιλικῶς, καὶ τὸ σπουδασθὲν ἐκύρωσε τῇ φιλτάτῃ, πιστότερον ἢ κατὰ θυσίαν ἐμπεδώσας ἐξ ἔρωτος τοῖς ἀστυγείτοσι τὴν εἰρήνην· φύσει γὰρ εὐδιάλλακτον ἄνθρωπος, ὅταν εὐτυχῇ· αἱ γὰρ εὐπραξίαι δειναὶ τὰς ὀργὰς ὑφαρπάζειν καὶ τοῖς εὐτυχήμασι τὰ ἐγκλήματα διαλύειν. οὕτως οὖν ἐκφανῶς δεδήλωκας, ὦ Πιερία, τὴν Ἀφροδίτην ἱκανὴν εἶναι παιδεύειν ῥήτορας οὐκ ὀλίγου ἀμείνους καὶ τοῦ Νέστορος τοῦ Πυλίου· πολλοὶ γὰρ πολλάκις ἑκατέρωθεν τῶν πόλεων σοφώτατοι πρέσβεις ἐξ ἑτέρας εἰς ἑτέραν ὑπὲρ εἰρήνης εἰσιόντες διὰ κενῆς ὅμως κατηφεῖς τε καὶ ἀσχάλλοντες ἄπρακτον ἀνέλυον τὴν πορείαν· ἐντεῦθεν τοιοῦτος εἰκότως παρὰ ταῖς Ἴωσι πάτριος ἐπεκράτησε λόγος· "εἴθε με παραπλησίως ὁ σύνοικος τιμήσειε τὴν ὁμόζυγα, ὥσπερ ὁ Φρύγιος τὴν καλὴν τετίμηκε Πιερίαν."

ις΄. ΗΡΑ ΤΙΣ ΑΠΟΡΡΗΤΟΝ ΕΧΩΝ ΤΟΝ ΠΟΘΟΝ. ΕΙΤΑ ΤΥΧΩΝ ΕΚ ΠΕΡΙΧΑΡΕΙΑΣ ΓΕΓΡΑΦΗΚΕ ΦΙΛΩΙ

Λαμπρίας Φιλιππίδῃ

Ἔρωτι περιπεσὼν ἀπορρήτῳ κατ' ἐμαυτὸν ἔφασκον ἀπορῶν· "οὐδεὶς ἕτερος ἐπίσταται τῆς ἐμῆς καρδίας τὸ βέλος, εἰ μὴ σύ γε πάντως ὁ τρώσας καὶ ἡ ταῦτά σε καλῶς παιδεύσασα μήτηρ. οὐ δύναμαι γὰρ οὐδενὶ τοὐμὸν ἀφηγήσασθαι πάθος. πέφυκε δὲ τοῖς ποθοῦσιν ἔτι μᾶλλον ἐπαύξειν ὁ λαθραῖος ἅμα καὶ σιγώμενος ἔρως· ἅπας γάρ, δι' ὁτιοῦν ἀχθόμενος τὴν ψυχήν, τὸ λυποῦν ἐκλαλῶν ἐπικουφίζει τῇ διανοίᾳ τὸ βάρος. ὡς ταύτην, Ἔρως, βέβληκας τὴν ψυχήν, οὕτως ἴσῃ βολῇ τὴν ἐμὴν κατατόξευσον ἐρωμένην, μᾶλλον πραοτέρως, ἵνα μὴ ταῖς ἀλγηδόσιν αὐτῆς ἀμαυρώσῃς τὸ κάλλος."

... μηνύομαι ταχύ· ἔνδον εἰσπορεύομαι πρὸς ἐκείνην. λόγου μεταδίδωσιν ἡ φιλτάτη, καὶ συμπαραθεῖ τοῖς ῥήμασι χάρις καὶ τῶν μύρων αὐτῆς εὐοσμία καὶ πως αἰδουμένης τὸ βλέμμα δεινῶς ἐκμαῖνον τὸν ὀρθῶς ἐρῶντα· εἶδον χεῖρας ἄκρας καὶ πόδας, τὰ λαμπρὰ τοῦ κάλλους γνωρίσματα, καὶ πρόσωπον εἶδον εὐπρόσωπον· τὸ δέ τι καὶ τῶν στέρνων ἀμεληθὲν τεθεώρηκα. πλὴν οὐ τεθάρρηκα τὸν πόθον ἐκφῆναι, ἐντὸς δὲ μόλις τῶν χειλῶν ὑποστένω· "σὺ τοίνυν, ὁ Ἔρως (δύνασαι γάρ), αὐτὴν παρασκεύασον πρώτην αἰτῆσαι καὶ προτρέψαι καὶ καθηγήσασθαι πρὸς εὐνήν." ταῦτα μὲν οὖν ἔφην ἀρτίως τῷ κρατίστῳ προσευχόμενος Ἔρωτι, ὁ δὲ ἀκήκοεν εὐμενῶς καὶ πεπλήρωκε τὴν εὐχήν. καὶ τῆς ἐμῆς

Phrygios grasped the entire scope of what this woman, so devoted to her country, was asking for—that she thus wanted to procure peace with the Milesians for her fatherland—and like a true king he nodded his agreement; he granted his beloved's wish, fixing the peace with his neighbors more securely through the bond of love than he would have through a sacrifice. For by nature man is easily reconciled when he enjoys good fortune. Luck and success have the power to dispel anger and dissolve accusation. Thus you have clearly shown, O Pieria, that Aphrodite can train orators far more eloquent than even Pylian Nestor.[7] Indeed, many a most wise ambassador from either side had often come to the other's town to sue for peace, and yet downcast and grieved had had to break off his journey empty-handed. This is probably the origin of the ancestral saying among Ionian women: "If only my spouse would honor me, his wife, in the same manner as Phrygios honored the beautiful Pieria."

1.16. A Man Was in Love Yet Did Not Dare to Speak of His Desire. On Achieving His Goal, He Was Overjoyed and Wrote to a Friend about It

Lamprias to Philippides

Fallen prey to a secret love, I said to myself in my helplessness, "No one else knows about the wound in my heart except you, of course, who inflicted it, and your mother,[1] who taught you so well. I cannot tell a soul about my suffering. And a passion kept secret and silent naturally grows even stronger in the one filled with desire. For anyone who talks about his pain—no matter what it is that vexes his heart—can lighten his burden by giving it voice. But with that same arrow with which you have wounded my soul, shoot my beloved as well—but strike her more gently, lest you make her beauty wither with pain."

[...] Soon I was shown[2] into the house and came before her. And as my beloved conversed with me, grace attended her words, as did the scent of her perfume and modest glance, which drives a true lover completely out of his mind. I beheld her fingertips and feet, those unmistakable marks of beauty, and gazed at her captivating face. Because of her carelessness, I even caught a glimpse of her breasts. Still I did not dare reveal my desire, but in a moan that barely passed my lips I said, "Please, Eros, since you have the power, make her be the first to act, to urge me on, and lead me into bed." No sooner had I said these words in supplication to mighty Eros

αὐτὴ λαβομένη χειρὸς ἐμάλαττε τοὺς δακτύλους ἐκ τῶν ἁρμῶν ἠρέμα χαλῶσα,
καὶ προσεγέλασεν ἡδύ, καὶ ἦν σφόδρα βουλομένης τὸ βλέμμα, πάλαι μὲν
σεμνόν, νῦν δὲ γέγονεν ἐξαίφνης ἐρωτικόν. τοιγαροῦν ἐκβακχευθεῖσα τῷ ἔρωτι
ἀνέκλασέ τε πρὸς ἑαυτὴν τὸν αὐχένα, καὶ πεφίληκεν οὕτω προσφῦσα μανικῶς,
ὥστε μόλις ἀποσπάσαι τὰ χείλη, καὶ κατατέτριφέ μου τὸ στόμα. τῶν δὲ χειλῶν
αὐτῆς ὑπανοιχθέντων ἀτμὸς εὐώδης καὶ τῶν ἔξωθεν οὐκ ἐλαττούμενος μύρων
εἰς τὴν ψυχὴν ἐπωχετεύετο τὴν ἐμήν· τὰ δ' ἄλλα (οἶδας γὰρ ὁποῖα τὰ λοιπά)
νόει μοι κατὰ σαυτόν, ὦ φιλότης, οὐδὲν περιττοῦ δεόμενος λόγου. λέξω μέντοι
τοιοῦτον, ὡς πρὸς ἀλλήλους ἐφιλονεικοῦμεν δι' ὅλης τῆς νυκτός, ἁμιλλώμενοι
τίς φανεῖται θατέρου μᾶλλον ἐρῶν· κἂν τοῖς ἀφροδισίοις κολακικῶς ὁμιλούντων
ἡμιτελεῖς ὑφ' ἡδονῆς ὠλίσθαινον λόγοι.

ιζ'. Ο ΤΗΣ ΚΑΚΟΗΘΟΥΣ ΕΡΩΝ

Ξενοπείθης Δημαρέτῳ

Ὦ δυστρόπου γυναικός, ὦ βαρβάρων ἠθῶν, ὦ ψυχῆς ἀνημέρου μηδὲ ἴσα θηρίοις τιθασευομένης τὴν φύσιν. ἔγνων ἑταίρας, ἐνέτυχον θεραπαίναις, ὁμοζύγων
πεπείραμαι διαφόρων, καὶ θνητὸς ὢν πολλάκις καὐτὸς ὑπηρέτηκα <τῷ> θεῷ
(ὁ γὰρ Ἔρως ὡς ὕδωρ ἀνὰ τοὺς κήπους ἀμαρεῦον ἄγει με πολυτρόπως), καὶ
<πολλὰ> πολλαχοῦ κατὰ γυναικῶν, ὡς ἐπήβολος, ὡς ἐπιτυχής, ἔστησα τρό-
παια, προσφόρως ἑκάστη τὰς ἐρωτικὰς μεθόδους προσάγων. ἀλλὰ τῆς Δάφ-
νιδος ἡττήθην, ὁμολογῶ, καὶ νῦν πρῶτον εἰς γύναιον ἠπόρηκε Ξενοπείθης·
κύρβις γὰρ ἑταιρικῶν ἐστι κακῶν. ἐρῶσα καρτερεῖ, ὑπεραίρεται ποθουμένη,
οὐκ ἐνδίδωσι κολακείαις, κέρδους ὑπερορᾷ, οἰκείῳ μόνῳ δουλεύει σκοπῷ, καὶ
πάντα δεύτερα ποιεῖται τοῦ δοκοῦντος αὐτῇ. ὁ δὲ γέλως αὐτῆς, εἴ ποτε συμ-
βαίη, ἐπ' ἄκρων κάθηται τῶν χειλῶν. ἐγὼ δὲ παρήνεσα τῇ βαρβάρῳ λέγων·
"μὴ σκυθρώπαζε καλή γε οὖσα, μηδὲ τὰς ὀφρῦς ἄναγε· εἰ γὰρ φοβερὰ γένοιο,
ἧττον ἔσῃ καλή." ἀλλ' οὐδὲν αὐτῇ τῶν ἐμῶν ἐμέλησε λόγων. ὄνος λύρας. οὐδὲ
γρῦ τῆς ἐμῆς συμβουλῆς ἐπαΐειν δοκεῖ. πλὴν οὐκ ἀπογνωστέον ταῦτά ἐστι
τοῖς ἀνδρειοτέροις τῶν ἐραστῶν· ῥανὶς γὰρ ὕδατος ἐνδελεχῶς ἐπιστάζουσα καὶ
πέτραν οἶδε κοιλαίνειν. συχνότερον οὖν τὸ δέλεαρ αὐτῇ προσακτέον, κἂν αὖθις
τὸ ἄγκιστρον καταπίῃ, πάλιν ἀσπαλιεύσω, καὶ τό γε τρίτον αὖθις ἀνακρούσω
τὴν γένυν· οὐ γάρ με νικήσει ἡ δυσμεταχείριστος οὖσα, οὐδὲ ἀπαγορεύσω τὴν

than with kind intent he heard my prayer and made my wish come true. And taking my hand she massaged my fingers, gently easing their tension right from the joint. She smiled at me sweetly, and her previously solemn gaze turned suddenly seductive and full of desire. In a frenzy of passion she pulled me over by the neck and kissed me, pressing her lips to mine with such wild abandon that she could barely get them off—even now my mouth is sore. As her lips parted slightly, her breath, no less fragrant than the perfume she was wearing, streamed into my soul. As for the rest[3] (for you know exactly what came next), you can just imagine it yourself, my friend; you don't need further description. Yet I'll say this much: we vied with each other all night long in competition as to which would seem to love the other more. And as we exchanged sweet nothings in our games of love, our half-formed words were garbled with pleasure.

1.17. THE LOVER OF A WICKED WOMAN

Xenopeithes[1] to Demaretos[2]

What an insufferable bitch! What savage ways! What a brutal heart, harder to tame than a wild beast! I have known hetairas, had encounters with serving girls, tried my luck with married women galore. As a mortal, I have put my own body at the service of the god, frequently (for like water through gardens Eros has channeled me through many furrows); I have set up trophies in many places to commemorate my conquests, using the right strategy against each on the battlefield of love.[3] But Daphnis has crushed me, I admit, and now for the first time Xenopeithes can't figure out how to handle a woman. For she's a walking inventory of female vices. When in love, she keeps herself in check, and being loved she just responds with scorn; she does not give in to flattery, disdains profit, serves only her own aims, and puts all things second to her own interest. Her laughter, if ever you get to hear it, barely escapes her lips. I have tried to advise this barbarian, saying, "Pretty as you are, you shouldn't scowl and knit your brows. For if you terrify, you'll seem less beautiful." But she doesn't give a damn for what I say. Well, does the ass appreciate the lyre?[4] Not one syllable of my advice will she accept, it seems. But the determined lover must not give up. A steady drip will wear down even stone.[5] Just give her the bait more often. If she gulps down the hook a second time, I'll just make another cast; the third time around I'll reel the hook back in.[6] Though she is hard to handle, she won't defeat me, nor will I renounce my angler's art, even if the woman

ἐμὴν ἀγκιστρείαν, εἰ καὶ δυσθήρατος ἡ γυνή. ἐπεὶ καὶ τοῦτο ἔρωτος ἴδιον, τὸ
λιπαρὲς καὶ φιλόπονον· χρόνῳ δὲ καὶ Ἀτρεῖδαι τῆς κλεινῆς ἐκράτησαν Τροίας.
συνεπιλαβοῦ τοίνυν, ὦ φίλε· καὶ σὺ γὰρ ὁμοίως ἐκοινώνεις μοι τοῦ πόθου, καὶ
τρικυμίας τὸν τρόπον τῆς ἀστάτου σαλεύεις. κοινὴ γὰρ ναῦς, κοινὸς κίνδυνος, ὁ
παροιμιώδης διετάξατο λόγος.

ιη′. ΕΤΑΙΡΑ ΜΟΝΟΙΣ ΚΑΛΟΙΣ ΤΕ
ΚΑΙ ΝΕΑΝΙΑΙΣ <ΕΥΠΕΙΘΗΣ>

Καλλικοίτη Μειρακιοφίλη

Ὑπερευδαιμονεῖς ἔρωτα φιλόκαλον εὐτυχοῦσα καὶ μηδενὶ παρὰ τὸ ἥδιστον
δουλεύοντα πλούτῳ. ἀεὶ γοῦν τοῖς ἐν ἡλικίᾳ προστρέχεις, οἷα ποθεινοῖς
ἐρασταῖς συνήδεσθαι βουλομένη, καὶ τοῖς ἀκμάζουσι χαίρεις, καὶ μειρακίοις
ὡραϊζομένοις εὐφραίνῃ συνοῦσα, καὶ λίαν ἐρωτικῶς διάκεισαι τῶν καλῶν,
καὶ διατελεῖς ἀμελὴς ἀκόμψων, ἐπιμελὴς εὐπρεπῶν. ὥσπερ οὖν αἱ Λάκαιναι
σκύλακες εὖ μεταθεῖς τε καὶ ἰχνεύεις ὅπῃ δ᾽ ἂν αἴσθῃ τινὸς τῆς σῆς ἀμέλει
θήρας ἀξίου· τοὺς δὲ πρεσβύτας παντελῶς ἀτερπεῖς καὶ πόρρωθεν ἀποφεύγεις,
κἄν τις γέρων προτείνοι Ταντάλου θησαυρούς, οὐχ ἱκανὸν ταῦτα παραμύθιον
κρίνεις πρὸς ἀναφρόδιτον πολιὰν μὴ οὐχὶ ἐπ᾽ ἔσχατον ἐλθεῖν σε τῆς ἀηδίας
ὁρῶσαν μὲν ὄψιν πρεσβυτέραν καὶ οὐκ ἐν ὥρᾳ, ἑπομένων δὲ τῶν ἄλλων ταύτῃ,
ἃ καὶ λόγοις ἀκούειν οὐκ ἐπιτερπές, μὴ ὅτι δὴ ἔργοις ἀνάγκης ἀεὶ προσκει-
μένης μεταχειρίζεσθαι. ἐντεῦθεν ἐπὶ πάσης προφάσεως τοὺς ἐν ἡλικίᾳ ποθεῖς·
ἥλικα γὰρ δὴ καὶ ὁ παλαιὸς λόγος τέρπειν τὸν ἥλικα· ἢ γάρ, οἶμαι, χρόνου
ἰσότης ἐπὶ ἴσας ἡδονὰς ἄγουσα δι᾽ ὁμοιότητα φιλίαν παρέχεται. καὶ ὃ μέν τις
τῶν νέων, ὅτι σιμός, ἐπίχαρις παρὰ σοὶ κληθεὶς ἐπαινεῖται, τοῦ δὲ τὸ γρυπὸν
βασιλικὸν ἔφης, τὸν δὲ διὰ μέσου τούτων ἐρεῖς ἐμμετρότατα ἔχειν, μέλανας
δὲ ἀνδρικοὺς ὀνομάζεις, λευκοὺς δὲ θεῶν παῖδας προσείρηκας. μελιχλώρους δὲ
οἴει τοὔνομα τίνος ἄλλου ποίημα εἶναι ἢ τοῦ ἐνόντος σοι πόθου, ὑποκοριζομένου
τε καὶ φέροντος εὐχερῶς τὴν ὠχρότητα, εἰ μόνον ἐπὶ ὥρᾳ προσῇ; καὶ ἑνὶ λόγῳ
πάσας προφάσεις προφασίζῃ, καὶ πάσας φωνὰς ἀναφθέγγῃ, ὥστε διὰ φιλερα-
στίας μηδέν᾽ ἀποβαλεῖν τῶν ἀνθούντων ἐν ὥρᾳ, ὥσπερ τοὺς φιλοίνους ὁρῶμεν
πάντα οἶνον ἐπὶ πάσης προφάσεως ἀσπαζομένους. τὸ δὲ τῆς οἰνοποσίας, ὦ φίλε

is tough to catch. For these too are typical of love: tenacity and endless toil. With time the sons of Atreus[7] too defeated glorious Troy. So lend me a hand, dear friend, for you too have a share in this passion and are churned up like a mighty, roiling wave. We're all in the same boat, facing a common danger, as the proverb has it.

1.18. A Hetaira Who Is Only Responsive to Good-Looking Men and Young Ones

Kallikoite[1] to Meirakiophile[2]

How very fortunate you are: graced with a desire that rejoices in beauty and is not a slave to any form of wealth averse to what is most delightful. At least you always gravitate toward those who are in their prime, as though you want your share of pleasure, along with attractive lovers. You enjoy those in the flower of their youth and relish being in the company of boys just reaching ripeness. You're all too wild about the pretty ones. You don't give a thought to the unrefined; all you can think of is the gorgeous type. So like Laconian hounds,[3] you swiftly pursue them and follow their scent wherever you notice one that's indeed worthy of the chase. The old ones, however, with not an ounce of charm, you flee even from afar. And if some old geezer offers you the riches of Tantalus, you don't consider that consolation enough for his unappealing white hair. No, that would not prevent you from being utterly disgusted at the sight of his aged, sagging face.[4] Add to this all the other things that are unpleasant even to hear about, let alone actually touch due to ever-pressing compulsion. Therefore you always find an excuse for liking the young ones. As the old saying goes, youth enjoys youth.[5] And a like age, I believe, brings like pleasures, generating love through likeness. Say one of the youths is snub-nosed: you praise him with the name Prince Charming; another is hook-nosed: you call him regal; and if he's in between, you'll dub him "The Golden Mean"; swarthy ones you pronounce manly; the fair-skinned you address as the gods' own children. Who else do you think came up with the title "honey-hued," if not your heart's desire, which is always ready with a euphemism and glosses over sickly pallor, as long as it's coupled with youth? In a word, you find every possible excuse with which to excuse them and sound each note that language offers, just so that, in your devotion to lovers, you won't have to reject a single one in the bloom of youth. We see the same among wine addicts: they'll embrace each and every bottle with open arms, excusing

Διόνυσε, κἂν ἐφ᾽ ἡμῖν αὐταῖς θεωρήσαιμεν, ἀλλοτρίου παραδείγματος μηδὲν δεηθεῖσαι.

ιθ΄. ΜΟΥΣΟΥΡΓΟΝ ΕΤΑΙΡΑΝ ΤΙΣ ΑΠΕΣΤΗΣΕΝ ΕΡΑΣΤΗΣ ΠΑΙΔΟΣ ΑΥΤΩΙ ΠΑΡ᾽ ΕΚΕΙΝΗΣ ΟΜΟΙΟΤΑΤΟΥ ΤΕΧΘΕΝΤΟΣ

Εὐφρόνιον Θελξινόη

Μελισσάριον τὴν Ἀγλαΐδος, νὴ τὴν Ἥραν, εὐμενέσιν ὀφθαλμοῖς εἴπερ ποτὲ καὶ νῦν εἶδεν ἡ Τύχη, καὶ τῆς σκηνῆς ἀπαλλαγεῖσα παγκάλως ἐπὶ τὸ σεμνὸν μετήλλαχε προσηγορίαν ἅμα καὶ σχῆμα. ἐγὼ δὲ (ἀλλὰ φθόνος ἐκποδὼν εἴη τῆς ἐλευθερίας), ἐγὼ δ᾽ οὖν τὸν πάντα δουλεύσω χρόνον ἀτόποις τε θεάτροις καὶ ἀγνώμοσιν ἐρασταῖς. αὕτη μουσουργὸς ἦν ὑπὸ μητρὶ πενιχρᾷ τὰ πρῶτα πονήρως τρεφομένη, προϊοῦσα δὲ πασῶν γέγονεν εὐμουσοτέρα τῶν ὁμοτέχνων, καὶ θαρσαλέως ἐχρῆτο τῇ τέχνῃ, ἅτε λοιπὸν θεάτρου μεστὴ γεγονυῖα. πρότερον μὲν γὰρ ὡς εἰκὸς ἐγελᾶτο, εἶτα λαμπρῶς ἐθαυμάζετο, τὰ δ᾽ οὖν τελευταῖα καὶ δεινῶς ἐφθονεῖτο· οὐπώποτε γὰρ κατὰ μνήμην ἐμὴν ἐκβέβηκε τῆς σκηνῆς. κἀκ τῆς τέχνης, οἷα φιλεῖ, κοσμηθεῖσα τὴν ὄψιν ἐδόκει βελτίων, καὶ τοὺς ἐραστὰς εἶχε θερμοτέρους, εἶτα καὶ πλείους φιλοτιμότερόν τε χαριζομένους διὰ κλέος τῆς ἐπιστήμης. πολύτιμον τὸ Μελισσάριον παρ᾽ ἄνδρας πλουσιωτάτους ἐφοίτα.

ἣν οὐκ ἔδει λαβεῖν ἐν γαστρί, ὅπως μὴ διὰ παιδογονίαν ἀτιμοτέρα γένοιτο τοῖς συνοῦσι, τῆς ἀκμῆς τὸ ἄνθος ἄωρον ἀποβαλοῦσα τοῖς πόνοις. ἀκηκόει δὲ ἡ μουσουργὸς ὁποῖα γυναῖκες λέγουσι πρὸς ἀλλήλας, ὡς ἐπειδὰν ἐν γαστρὶ γυνὴ λήψεσθαι μέλλοι, οὐκ ἐξέρχεται οἱ παντάπασιν ἡ γονή, ἀλλ᾽ ἔνδον ἐμμένει κεκρατημένη τῇ φύσει. ταῦτα τοίνυν ἀκούσασα ξυνῆκεν ἐμφρόνως καὶ διεφύλαττεν ἀεὶ τὸ ῥηθέν· καὶ ὡς ᾔσθετο τὸ συμβὰν οὕτως, οὐκ ἐξιοῦσάν οἱ τὴν γονήν, ἔφρασε τῇ μητρί, καὶ ὁ λόγος ἅτε πρὸς ἐμπειροτέραν ἦλθεν ὡς ἐμέ. κἀγὼ μαθοῦσα καὶ ταύτῃ διαπράξασθαι ἅπερ ᾔδειν ἐγκελευσαμένη, τῆς προσδοκωμένης ἐλπίδος ἀπήλλαξα τάχιον.

ὡς δὲ Χαρικλέους ἠράσθη νέου τινὸς ἐπισήμου καὶ κάλλει καὶ πλούτῳ καὶ ἀντερῶντος οὐχ ἧττον ἐκείνης, παιδοποιεῖν ἐξ ἐκείνου προσηύχετο πᾶσι τοῖς γενεθλίοις θεοῖς. καὶ δὴ συνείληφεν ἀσφαλῶς, εἶτα τῆς Εἰλειθυίας ἐγκαίρως

even the worst.[6] And when it comes to drinking wine, dear Dionysus, we can simply look among ourselves;[7] no further example required.

1.19. A Lover Liberates a Musician Hetaira from Her Profession Because the Child She Gave Birth To Bears Such a Close Resemblance to Him

Euphronion[1] to Thelxinoe[2]

By Hera,[3] if Fortune ever looked with friendly eyes on Melissarion,[4] daughter of Aglais, she has done so now. For not only did the girl escape the performing life in the most marvelous way, she also changed her name and appearance into something respectable. I, on the other hand (may I never be jealous of her freedom!), am enslaved forever to back-alley arenas and unfeeling lovers. She herself had been a musician[5] miserably reared by an impoverished mother. But with time she surpassed her fellow musicians and became a confident practitioner of her art, as she was in any case immersed in the theater world. As you might expect, she was ridiculed at first, then passionately admired, while ultimately she became the source of terrible envy. As far as I recall, she was never booed off the stage. No, as it happens, she came to look even more beautiful through the adornment of her art. Her lovers grew more passionate and numerous, giving her ever more precious gifts in response to her artistic fame. Her company highly prized, Melissarion socialized with the richest men.[6]

It was crucial that she not get pregnant, lest the birth of a child cheapen her in the eyes of her lovers and she spoil the flower of her youth too soon in labor. The musician had heard the tale that women tell each other, that when a girl is going to be pregnant the seed doesn't come out of her at all, but rather it stays inside, held back by nature. When she heard this, it made sense to her, and she always kept it in mind. And on noticing that this had in fact happened to her, that is, that her seed had not come out, she told her mother about it, and they reported it to me, as I was more experienced in such matters. No sooner had I learned of it than I ordered her to do what I knew had to be done[7] and quickly freed her of her anxious forebodings.

But when she fell in love with Charikles, a young man outstanding for his beauty and wealth, and who reciprocated her feelings in equal measure, she prayed to all the gods of birth to make her pregnant by him. And sure enough she conceived, and with Eileithyia[8] coming to her aid at the crucial

ἐφισταμένης τίκτει παιδίον ἀστεῖον, νὴ τὰς Χάριτας, καὶ τῷ φύσαντι γνησίως
ἐξεικονισμένον τῇ φύσει. ἡ μὲν οὖν μήτηρ ἕρμαιον αὑτῇ καὶ εὐτύχημα λογί-
ζεται τοῦτο, καὶ τὸν υἱὸν ἐπωνόμακεν Εὐτυχίδην· ὑπερηγάπα δὲ τὸ βρέφος,
στέργουσα διαφόρως ὡς υἱόν, ὡς εὐπρεπές, ὡς ποθούμενον παιδίον καὶ λίαν
ἐμφερὲς ὡραιοτάτῳ πατρί. εὑρήσεις γάρ τινα ῥοπὴν εὐνοίας παρὰ τοῖς γεγεννη-
κόσιν εὐτυχοῦντας τοὺς εὐειδεστέρους τῶν παίδων, καὶ δυοῖν ὄντοιν ἢ καὶ πλει-
όνων ἡδίων τοῖς γονεῦσιν ὁ καλλίων. ὁ δὲ Χαρικλῆς οὕτως εὐθὺς διετέθη πρὸς
τὸ τεχθὲν φιλοστόργως, ὥστε ἀδικώτατον κρίνειν ἑταίραν ἔτι καλεῖσθαι τὴν
ἐρώτιον τοιοῦτον τεκοῦσαν. τοιγαροῦν αὐτίκα τῆς αἰσχρᾶς αὐτὴν ἀπέστησεν
ἐργασίας καὶ ἐπ᾽ ἀρότῳ παίδων γνησίων τὴν ἐρωμένην ἠγάγετο γαμετήν. καὶ
πολλαπλασιάζει τὸν πόθον ... τῆς σχέσεως τοῦ παιδαρίου.

ὅθεν εἰκότως ἐκ περιχαρείας τῇ μητρὶ τὸ βλέμμα φαιδρόν, καὶ οὐδὲ τεκούσῃ
<τὸ κάλλος> ἀπήνθησεν. ἀρτίως οὖν περιβαλομένη σεμνὴν ἐφεστρίδα γέγονα
παρὰ τῇ Πυθιάδι (τοῦτο γὰρ μετακέκληκεν ἑαυτήν) καὶ πάντων ἀγαθῶν συν-
ηδόμην αὐτῇ. τὸ δὲ παιδίον κλαυθμυριζόμενον ἰδοῦσα πεφίληκα, θερμῶς μὲν
ὡς καλόν, ἀπαλῶς δὲ ὡς τρυφερώτερον καὶ τῶν ῥόδων, οἷσπερ ἔοικε τὴν χροιάν.
ἐκπλήττομαι, νὴ τὼ θεώ, πῶς ἀθρόως ἅπαντα μεταβέβληκεν ἡ γυνή. καὶ
πάρεστι θαυμάζειν ἐκείνης βλέμμα προσηνές, μέτριον ἦθος, μειδίασμα σεμνόν,
κόμην ἀφελῶς πεπλοκισμένην, καλύπτραν ἐπ᾽ αὐτῆς εὖ μάλα σεμνήν, βραχυ-
λογίαν ἐν ἠρεμαίᾳ φωνῇ. εἶδον καὶ ἀμφιδέας καὶ περισκελίδας, οὐ τὰς περιέρ-
γους ἐκείνας, ὦ φίλη, ἀλλ᾽ ἔργον ὄντως ἐλευθέρᾳ πρεπῶδες. τοιοῦτον ἐν αὐτῇ
καὶ περιαυχένιον καὶ τὸν ἄλλον κόσμον ἴδοι τις ἄν. προϊοῦσάν τε φασι νεύειν
τε κάτω καὶ τεταγμένα βαδίζειν· σχῆμα δὲ συμπρέπον τῇ σωφροσύνῃ· καὶ
εἴποις ἂν ὡς ἀεὶ τοιαύτη γέγονεν ἐκ παιδός. ἅπαντα γοῦν ἐν ταῖς γυναικωνίτισι
καὶ ταῖς ταλασίαις πρὸς ἀλλήλας ὁμιλοῦσι γυναῖκες. ἄπιθι τοίνυν, Θελξινόη,
καὶ σὺ παρ᾽ ἐκείνην ἐκ γειτόνων οἰκοῦσαν, μεταμφιασαμένη μέντοι κοσμίως
ἡμιφάριον ἁλουργές. φυλάττου δέ, γλυκυτάτη, μὴ μεταξὺ παρελκομένη τῇ
συνηθείᾳ Μελισσάριον τὴν νῦν Πυθιάδα προσείπῃς· ὃ μικροῦ πέπονθα, νὴ τὴν
Διώνην, εἰ μὴ Γλυκέρα παροῦσα λάθρᾳ με ταχὺ διένυξε τῷ ἀγκῶνι.

moment, she gave birth to a boy, who, by the Graces, was pretty and the spitting image of his father. The mother considered this a godsend and a great stroke of luck, and so she called him Lucky. She loved the baby beyond measure, treasuring him above all else as her son, as her pretty one, as the child of her dreams, and as the virtual replica of his handsome father. For you will find that, on the scale of parental affection, those children who are better looking outweigh the others, and that if there are two or more, the prettier one is dearer to the parents. And Charikles was at once so enamored of his offspring that he considered it the greatest injustice for his beloved, the mother of such a child, to still be called hetaira. So he liberated her at once from that shameful profession and made his beloved his wife, so as to plant in her the seed of legitimate children. And his desire for her increased many times over by having this child.

Given her great joy at this, it was understandable that the look in the mother's eyes grew radiant, and her beauty did not wither from the ordeal of birth. Not long ago I put on a respectable robe and went to see Pythias (for that is what she changed her name to), and the two of us rejoiced in all her good fortune. And when I saw the child crying, I gave him kisses—warm ones, since he was such a pretty fellow, and tender ones, because his skin was more delicate than roses. I was amazed, yes, by the two goddesses,[9] at the woman's sudden and total transformation. Her gentle gaze, her composed manner, her serene smile, her hair artlessly plaited, the veil so modestly covering her, her restrained speech and quiet voice—all these were admirable. I also noticed her bracelets and anklets, and they were not the gaudy kind, my dear, but pieces truly fit for a free woman. You would find her necklace and all the rest of her jewelry no different. They say that she bows her head chastely as she strolls along and that she walks with a measured step. Her whole demeanor radiates modesty. And you would say she has always been that way, ever since she was a child. All these things the women discuss among themselves while spinning wool in their quarters. Go visit her yourself now, Thelxinoe, as she lives in your neighborhood, but put on something proper, like a purple cape.[10] But be careful, dearest, not to call her Melissarion out of habit rather than Pythias. That would nearly have happened to me, by Dione,[11] if Glykera had not been there and discretely jabbed me with her elbow.

κ′. ΦΡΟΥΡΑΡΧΟΣ ΜΟΙΧΕΥΘΕΙΣΗΣ ΑΥΤΟΥ ΤΗΣ ΓΑΜΕΤΗΣ ΥΠΟ ΤΙΝΟΣ ΕΜΒΕΒΛΗΜΕΝΟΥ ΜΟΙΧΟΥ

Φυλακίδης Φρουρίωνι

Ἥλω τις νεανίας μοιχός, καὶ δεσμώτης ἐφυλάττετο παρ' ἐμοῦ. ἐγὼ τοῦτον εὐπρεπῆ καὶ νεανίσκον ὁρῶν πρὸς ἔλεον ἐπεκάμφθην, καὶ τῶν δεσμῶν ἀπολύσας ἄδετον ἁπλῶς καὶ σχεδὸν ἄφρουρον κατὰ τὴν εἰρκτὴν διαφῆκα. ὁ δέ μοι δίκαιον μισθὸν τῆς φιλανθρωπίας διδοὺς τὴν σύνοικον ἐμοίχευσε τὴν ἐμήν. τοιοῦτον οὐδὲ τὸν κλέπτην Εὐρύβατον τετολμηκέναι φασίν. ἐκεῖνον μὲν γὰρ ἁλόντα φυλάττεσθαι, φίλον δὲ γενόμενον τοῖς ἐπὶ τοῦ δεσμωτηρίου τὸν τρόπον ἐπιδείκνυσθαι τῆς κλοπῆς· ἦσαν ἐγκεντρίδες αὐτοῖς καὶ σπογγίαι· ταύτας λαβὼν ἀνερριχᾶτο τὸν τοῖχον, ἀλλ' οὐ τὴν καλὴν ἀνήρπασε γαμετήν. τοῦτο ἔκπυστον καὶ περιβόητον ὡς παράδοξον καὶ παγγέλοιον γέγονε τὸ κακόν, καί με, νὴ τὴν Δίκην, ὑπὲρ τὴν μοιχείαν ὁ γέλως λυπεῖ, ὅτι δεσμοφύλαξ ἅμα καὶ φρούραρχος ὢν τὴν ἐμὴν ἔνδον οὖσαν οὐκ ἐφύλαξα γαμετήν.

κα′. ΠΕΡΙ ΓΥΝΑΙΚΟΣ ΠΑΝΤΑ ΠΛΗΝ ΜΙΞΕΩΣ ΕΠΙΤΡΕΠΟΥΣΗΣ ΤΩΙ ΕΡΑΣΤΗΙ

Ἀριστομένης Μυρωνίδῃ

Καινόν γε τὸ κακόν, ὦ Μυρωνίδη· τοιοῦτον ἔρωτος οὐδ' ἀκήκοα τρόπον. τῆς Τελεσίππης ὁ Φαλερεὺς Ἀρχιτέλης ἐρᾷ, ἡ δὲ πεισθεῖσα μόλις ὁμιλῆσαι τῷ μειρακίῳ παράδοξον αὐτῷ προδιώρισε μέτρον· "ἅπτου," φησί, "τῶν μαστῶν, ἡδίστων ἀπόλαυε φιλημάτων, καὶ προσαγκαλίζου περιβεβληκυῖάν με τὴν ἐσθῆτα, γάμον δὲ μήτε πολυπραγμόνει μήτε προσδόκα, ἐπεὶ σαυτὸν ἀνιάσεις καὶ τῶν ἐπιτετραμμένων ἐκπίπτων." "ἔστω, δεδόχθω," ἐξ ἀπορίας ἔφησεν Ἀρχιτέλης· "εἰ γὰρ οὕτω σοι φίλον, ὦ Τελεσίππη, οὐδ' ἐμοὶ ἐχθρόν. ἀλλὰ καὶ χάριν," εἶπεν, "εἴσομαι τῇ Τύχῃ καὶ ψιλοῦ ῥήματος ἀπολαύων ἢ καὶ μόνης ἀξιούμενος θέας. ἐβουλόμην δέ, εἴ γε σοί, φιλτάτη, δοκεῖ, γνῶναι τί δή ποτέ μοι παντελῶς ἀπέγνως τὴν μῖξιν;" "ὅτι," ἔφη, "ἐλπιζόμενός ἐστιν ὁ γάμος ἡδύς, εὔχαρις καὶ λίαν εὔκταιος· γεγονὼς περιεφρονήθη, καὶ τὸ πάλαι σπουδαζόμενον ἐξαίφνης ἀπέρριπται καὶ περιπτυόμενον ἀμελεῖται. αἱ γὰρ ἐπιθυμίαι τῶν νέων

1.20. A Prison Guard Whose Wife Commits Adultery with an Imprisoned Adulterer

Phylakides[1] to Phrourion[2]

A youthful adulterer was arrested, and I had the job of guarding the prisoner. On seeing how handsome he was and how young, I was inclined to pity him, and so removing his shackles I let him just go about unchained and virtually unguarded in the prison. But he gave me my just deserts for this kindliness by seducing my wife. Not even the notorious thief Eurybatos[3] is known to have dared anything like this: according to the tale, he'd been caught and imprisoned but then made friends with the prison guards and gave them a demonstration of his burglar's art. They had some climbing spurs and sponges. Grabbing these, he climbed right up and over the wall. But *he* didn't snatch a lovely bride. This, my disaster, became well known, the talk of the town, because it was so surprising, so utterly ridiculous. More than the adultery, though, it's the laughter that pains me. After all, I'm a jailor and prison guard, who failed to secure his wife though she was right inside the walls.

1.21. About a Woman Who Grants Her Lover Everything except Intercourse

Aristomenes to Myronides

Here's a strange dilemma, O Myronides. I've never heard of a love like this. Architeles of Phaleron[1] is crazy about Telesippe. But after the youth had gone to great lengths to convince her to meet him, she set surprising limits. "By all means touch my breasts," she said, "enjoy the sweetest kisses, and embrace me while I'm still dressed, but don't get on my nerves demanding sex, and don't expect it, since you'll only cause yourself distress and lose what you can have." "Let it be so. Agreed," said Architeles, helpless. "If that's your pleasure, O Telesippe, I won't fight it. Rather, I'll be grateful to Fortune that I can enjoy your naked speech and am deemed worthy just to behold you. But if it's all right with you, dearest, I'd like to know why on earth you categorically refuse to have sex with me." "Because," she replied, "as long as you're wishing for intercourse, it's sweet, gratifying, and utterly desirable. But once it has happened, it's despised; and what had long seemed the heart's most urgent desire is suddenly discarded, spit upon,

ταχεῖαι καὶ αὐταὶ πολλάκις ἑαυταῖς ἐναντίαι." τοιαύτης ὁ δύσερως ἀνέχεται γυναικός, τοσοῦτον δεδυστύχηκεν Ἀρχιτέλης. καὶ σύνεστι ποθουμένη καθάπερ εὐνοῦχος τὰ ἐρωτικὰ περιεργαζόμενος καὶ λιχνεύων, μᾶλλον δὲ τῶν ἐρώντων εὐνούχων ὁ μέλεος ἀργότερα δυστυχεῖ.

κβ΄. ΔΟΛΟΣ ΠΡΟΑΓΩΓΟΥ

Λουκιανὸς Ἀλκίφρονι

Γλυκέρα Χαρίσιον ἐπόθει, καὶ νῦν δὲ ποθεῖ· μὴ φέρουσα δὲ τὴν ἀγερωχίαν τοῦ μειρακίου (οἶσθα γὰρ τὸν νέον καὶ τὸν τρόπον αὐτοῦ) ἤθελε πρὸς μῖσος αὐτῇ μεταβληθῆναι τὸ φίλτρον. αἴτιον δὲ ἦν τοῦ βούλεσθαι μισεῖν τὸ λίαν φιλεῖν. αὕτη οὖν συμβουλεύεται τῇ Δωρίδι· ἄβρα δὲ καὶ μαστροπὸς τῆς Γλυκέρας ἡ Δωρίς. ὅτε τοίνυν ἱκανῶς αὐταῖς εἶχε τὸ σκέμμα, ἡ προαγωγὸς ὡς ἐφ᾽ ἕτερόν τι προῆλθεν. ταύτην ὁ Χαρίσιος ἰδὼν "χαίροις," εἶπε, "φιλτάτη." ἡ δέ· "καὶ πόθεν ἂν ἐμοί," φησί, "γένοιτο χαίρειν;" ὁ δ᾽ οὖν νεανίας ἐπύθετο· "τί δ᾽ ἔστι, πρὸς θεῶν; νεώτερόν τι συμβέβηκεν;" ἡ δὲ μαστροπὸς ἀπεκρίθη δεδακρυμένη δῆθεν πικρῶς· "ἡ Γλυκέρα τοῦ βδελυροῦ Πολέμωνος ἐκτόπως ἐρᾷ, σὲ δέ, εἰ καὶ παράδοξον ἐρῶ, μισεῖ μῖσος ἐξαίσιον." "ἆρα λέγεις ἀληθῆ;" καταπλαγεὶς ἤρετο πάλιν ὁ νέος πολλὰ χρώματα ἀφιείς. "καὶ μάλα," φησίν, "ἀληθινά," ἡ Δωρίς. "ἐμὲ γοῦν ἔπληξεν ἀφειδῶς, ἵνα σου μόνην ἐπὶ στόματος ἠρεμὶ τὴν προσηγορίαν ἐνέγκω."

ἐνταῦθα Χαρίσιος ἐλέγχεται μᾶλλον ἐρῶν ἢ ποθούμενος· πολλοὶ γὰρ ὧν κατεφρόνουν ἐπ᾽ ἐξουσίας ὑπὸ τοῦ ζηλοτυπεῖν ἠράσθησαν ἐκφανῶς. τὴν οὖν πολλὴν ἀλαζονείαν ἀφεὶς φθέγγεται ταπεινόν τε καὶ σκυθρωπὸν καὶ τεθνηκὼς ἀθυμίᾳ· εἴωθε γὰρ ἡ βαρύτης, ἐὰν ἀμελεῖσθαι δοκῇ, καταβάλλεσθαι. ἐδάκρυέ τε ἀστακτὶ μεταστραφεὶς ἐπὶ θάτερα καὶ τῇδε κἀκεῖσε τὸ πρόσωπον ἐξωθῶν <ὡς> ἀποπέμπεσθαι τὰ δάκρυα τῶν παρειῶν. "τί δὴ οὖν ἄκων," φησίν, "λελύπηκα τὸ Γλυκέριον; ἑκὼν γὰρ οὐκ ἄν ποτε κατ᾽ ἐκείνης ἐπλημμέλουν ἐγώ. ταῦτα, νὴ τοὺς Ἔρωτας, ἐβουλόμην σοῦ γε παρούσης πυθέσθαι τῆς Γλυκέρας, καὶ γνῶναι εἴ τι τυχὸν δίκαιον ἐγκαλεῖ, καὶ τὸ λυποῦν εἴπερ τι ἔστι θεραπεῦσαι. πλὴν ἥμαρτον, ὁμολογῶ· οὐδὲν ἀντιτείνω· ἆρ᾽ οὖν οὐκ ἂν δέξαιτό με καὶ παραιτούμενον συγγνώμην ἔχειν;" ἐπένευσε μόλις καὶ ἀμφισβητήσιμον ἡ Δωρίς, ἐφ᾽ ἑκάτερα παρακινοῦσα τὸ βλέμμα. ὁ δὲ δυσανασχετῶν ἐπανήρετο· "οὐδ᾽ ἂν ἱκετεύων προσπέσω;" "εἰκός γε, ὦ φίλτατε· οὐδέν, οἶμαι, κωλύει

ignored. For a young man's cravings are short-lived and often change into their opposite."[2] That's the kind of woman our unhappy lover has to put up with; that's the misfortune Architeles has to bear. When he's with the object of his desire, he's like a eunuch, engaging in futile exertions and lusting in vain. No, the poor wretch is even worse off than eunuchs in love.

1.22. THE BAWD'S DECEIT

Lucian to Alciphron

Glykera[1] pined for Charisios[2] and does so even now. But unable to stand the youth's arrogance (you know what the boy is like[3]), she wished her affection would change into its opposite. Indeed, it was her excessive love that made her want to hate. So she discussed this with Doris, her favorite slave and procuress. When they had worked out a scheme, the procuress set off as though on some other business. But when Charisios saw her, he said, "Good day, hon." And she replied, "What could be good about it for me?" Whereupon the youth asked, "What's the matter, by the gods? Has something bad happened?" And the bawd answered him, weeping bitterly, "Glykera is crazy about that loathsome Polemon. But you (absurd though it may seem) she hates with the most violent hate." "Is that the truth?" the boy demanded in turn, thunderstruck and growing pale. "The whole truth and nothing but the truth," replied Doris. "She beats me mercilessly, if I ever so much as bring up your name, no matter how softly."

Then and there it was established beyond all doubt that Charisios loved more than he was loved. For many men disdain what they can readily have[4]—but throw in a bit of jealousy, and they'll desire it passionately. So casting aside his former boastfulness, he began to speak humbly, gloomily, and as though fatally disheartened. For pride ignored is typically in for a fall. He turned away and cried his eyes out, tossing his face from side to side so as to shake the tears from his cheeks. "How," he wailed, "could I have grieved my sweet little Glykera against my will? For I could never have wronged her willingly. That, by the Loves, is what I'd like to ask her in your presence and find out if she justly accuses me of something, and whether there's any way I can alleviate her suffering. I wronged her, I admit it. I don't deny the charges. But would she not let me come and beg for her forgiveness?" Doris nodded ever so slightly and ambiguously, shifting her eyes this way and that. But he, barely able to stand it, implored again, "Not even if I groveled at her feet in supplication?" "Possibly, my

συκάζειν τῆς ἐρωμένης τὸν τρόπον, ὅπως ἔχει συμβάσεως περὶ σέ." τότε δὴ χαίρων δεδράμηκεν ὁ Χαρίσιος οἴκαδε τῆς ἑταίρας, ὁ καλός, ὁ τριπόθητος, ἐφ' ἱκετείας τραπόμενος καὶ περιτυχὼν αὐτίκα προσπίπτει. ἡ Γλυκέρα μὲν τέως τὸν τράχηλον ἐθαύμαζε τοῦ ποθουμένου, εἶτα τὸ πρόσωπον ἡδέως ἀνερείδουσα τῇ χειρί, ἀνέστησέ τε καὶ λάθρα τὴν ἑαυτῆς πεφίληκε δεξιάν, ᾗ προσήψατο τοῦ μειρακίου, καὶ πρὸς τὸν νέον ξυνέβη ταχύ· οὐ γὰρ ἐπέτρεπεν ὁ μανικῶς ἐγκείμενος ἔρως δόξαι γοῦν σμικρὸν ἀπωθεῖσθαι τὸν φίλον. ἡ δὲ μαστροπὸς λαθραίως μειδιῶσα διένευσε τῇ Γλυκέρα, ἐδήλου δέ πως τὸ νεῦμα· "ἐγώ σοι μόνη τὸν ὑπερήφανον ὑπέταξα τοῖς ποσίν."

κγ'. ΕΡΩΤΙΚΟΣ ΚΥΒΕΥΤΗΣ ΠΕΡΙ ΑΜΦΟΤΕΡΑ ΔΥΣΤΥΧΗΣ

Μονόχωρος Φιλοκύβῳ

Δύο δεινοῖς ἅμα περιπέπτωκα, φίλε, καὶ πρὸς ἓν τούτων μόλις ὁποτερονοῦν διαρκῶν ἐξ ἐπιμέτρου θάτερον ἔχω, καὶ διπλάσια δυστυχῶ. καὶ τὸ μὲν κακόν, τὸ δὲ οὐκ ἄμεινον· ἐμὲ γὰρ κατανάλωσαν ἄπληστος ἑταίρα καὶ πεσσοὶ πίπτοντες ἀτυχῶς μὲν ἐμοί, εὐβολώτερον δὲ τοῖς ἐναντίοις. ἀλλὰ καὶ τοῖς ἀντερῶσιν ἀστραγαλίζων ἢ κυβεύων συγχέομαι τὸν νοῦν τοῦ ἔρωτος μεμηνότος, κἀντεῦθεν περὶ τὰς ποικίλας μεταστάσεις τῶν ψήφων πολλὰ παραλογιζόμενος ἐμαυτὸν καὶ τῶν καταδεεστέρων ἡττῶμαι τὴν παιδιάν. πολλάκις γὰρ μετέωρος ἐκ τοῦ πόθου ταῖς ἡμετέραις βολαῖς ἀντὶ τῶν ἐμῶν τὰς ἐκείνων διατίθημι ψήφους. εἶτα πρὸς τὴν ἐρωμένην ἀπιὼν ἐκεῖ δευτέραν ἧτταν ὑπομένω καὶ χείρονα τῆς προτέρας· οἱ γὰρ εὐτυχεῖς ἀντερασταί, ἅτε δή με τὰ τοσαῦτα νενικηκότες, φιλοτιμότερον δωροῦνται τῇ ποθουμένῃ, καὶ προκρίνονταί μοι τοῖς δώροις, κᾆτα τῶν ἐμῶν ἐμὲ πολεμοῦντες μεταπεττεύουσί μοι τῆς φιλίας <τὸν> κύβον. οὕτω τοίνυν ἑκάτερον τῶν κακῶν διὰ θάτερον γέγονε δυστυχέστερον.

κδ'. Η ΤΩΝ ΕΡΑΣΤΩΝ ΕΝΑ ΠΡΟΚΡΙΝΟΥΣΑ ΜΟΝΟΝ

Μουσάριον Λυσίᾳ τῷ φιλτάτῳ

Ἄρτι παρ' ἐμοὶ συναθροισθέντες ἑσπέρας οἱ κορυφαῖοι τῶν ἐμῶν ἐραστῶν τὸ μὲν πρῶτον ἐσίγων, καὶ ἄλλος ἄλλον τῶν πλησίον προώθει, κελεύων διεξελθεῖν πρὸς ἐμὲ τὰ μελετηθέντα πᾶσι κοινῇ· ὁ δ' οὖν θρασύτερος προσχήματι μὲν

dear. No reason, I think, that you couldn't question your beloved as to how she might be reconciled with you." Overjoyed, Charisios then dashed to the home of the hetaira—he, the dazzling object of desire, now turned to begging—and the second he arrived he fell at her feet. Glykera gazed for a while in admiration at her beloved's neck, then tenderly lifted his head with her hand, made him stand up, and secretly kissed the hand with which she had clasped the youth, and in no time she came to terms with the boy. For her frenzied desire would not permit her even for one moment to seem like she was pushing away her beloved. The bawd nodded to Glykera with a secret smile, and her nod seemed to say, "I alone managed to bring this haughty fellow to heel."

1.23. One Unlucky in Love and at Dice

Monochoros[1] to Philokybos[2]

I fell victim to two dreadful things at once, dear friend, and though I can just about cope with one of these at a time, the addition of the second tips the scales, and I end up suffering a double misfortune. The one is bad, the other no better. I've been wrecked by an insatiable hetaira and by unlucky throws of the dice, unlucky for me but beneficial to my adversaries: when I play knucklebones or dice with rivals in love, my brain gets befuddled in the frenzy of desire; as a result I confuse the various moves of the pieces in the game and am beaten by players who are less competent than I. For often, in a transport of desire, I throw the dice but move their pieces, not my own. And then, when I go off to my beloved, I suffer a second defeat there, worse than the first. For my rivals, lucky in the winnings they extract from my pocket, are able to give more precious gifts to my darling, and she prefers them for those gifts. Fighting me with my own resources, they prevent me from ever getting lucky in the game of love. And so each of the two misfortunes magnifies the other.

1.24. A Woman Who Prefers Just One of Her Many Lovers

Mousarion[1] to Her Beloved Lysias[2]

Not long ago, as the most outstanding among my lovers were assembled one evening at my place, not one of them could utter a word at first, but each kept trying to press his neighbor forward, urging him to explain to

συμβουλῆς, σὲ δὲ ταῖς ἀληθείαις ζηλοτυπῶν διεμέμφετό με τοιάδε· "πασῶν
τῶν ἐπὶ σκηνῆς ὑπερφέρουσα τῷ κάλλει ἑκάστης αὐτῶν ἀπολείπῃ τῷ κέρδει·
παρὸν γάρ σοι χρηματίζεσθαι παρ' ἡμῶν, ὧν ὑπερορᾷς, προῖκα δὲ μόνῳ τῷ
Λυσίᾳ τὴν σὴν ἐκδέδωκας ὥραν, καὶ οὐδὲ καλῷ μειρακίῳ· οὕτω γὰρ ἂν ἦν
φορητὸν ἑνὸς ἄγαν εὐπρεποῦς ἡττᾶσθαι τοσούτους, σοὶ δ' ἂν τυχὸν συνέγνω
τις ἐρωτικὸν κάλλος ἄμαχον προκρινούσῃ χρημάτων. πυκνὰ γοῦν ὅμως τοῦτον
παρ' ἡμῖν ἐπαινοῦσα ἐκκεκώφηκας ἡμῶν τὰ ὦτα καὶ ἐμπέπληκας τοῦ Λυσίου,
ὥστε καὶ ἀνεγρομένους ἐξ ὕπνου οἴεσθαι τοῦ νέου τὴν προσηγορίαν ἀκούειν. οὐ
πόθος τοίνυν ἐστίν, οὔ, παραπληξία δὲ μᾶλλον νομίζεταί μοι δεινή. πλὴν τουτί
σε μόνον αἰτοῦμεν, λέγε σαφέστερον, εἰ τοῦτον ἔχειν ἀντὶ πάντων ἐθέλεις· οὐ
γὰρ ἀντιστατοῦμεν τῷ ποθουμένῳ."

τοιαῦτα μὲν οὖν ᾖδον ἐκεῖνοι σχεδὸν εἰς ἀλεκτρυόνων ᾠδάς, ἅπερ εἰ βουλη-
θείην ἑξῆς ἀπαγγεῖλαι, καταδύσειν μοι δοκῶ τὸν ἥλιον ἐπὶ τῷ μήκει τοῦ λόγου·
τὰ δὲ πολλὰ τῶν λεχθέντων τῷ μὲν δεξιῷ τοῖν ὤτοιν ἠκροασάμην, θατέρου
δὲ παραχρῆμα ἐξερρύη. τοσοῦτον δὲ ἀπεκρίθην· "αὐτὸς ὑμῶν προτέταχε τὸν
Λυσίαν ὁ Ἔρως, ὃς οὐ νύκτωρ, οὐ μεθ' ἡμέραν διαλείπει τὴν ἐμὴν καταφλέ-
γων καρδίαν." μάνθανε καὶ τοῦτο, γλυκύτατε. ἐπεὶ σὺν ἐπιτιμήσει βοῶντες
ἐπύθοντό μου· "καὶ τίς ἀναφρόδιτον βδελυρὸν ἄκομψον τοιόνδε ποθεῖ;" εἶπον
ἠθικῶς ἄγαν μετὰ τῶν χειρῶν ὑποκινοῦσα σὺν τοῖς ὤμοις τὸ βλέμμα· "τίς; ἐγώ.
ἔρρωσθε τοίνυν," ἔφην ἀναστᾶσα, "καὶ σύγγνωτέ μοι ποθούσῃ. ἐμὲ γὰρ οὐδὲν
θάλπει κέρδος, ἀλλ' ὃ θέλω· θέλω δὲ Λυσίαν." σὺ δ' οὖν, ὦ ἐμὸν δεσποτίδιον,
εὐθὺς εὐθύς· τὸ ταχὺ γὰρ ἐπαφρόδιτον. μηδὲν μελλήσας ἧκέ μοι φίλημά τι
μόνον ἀποκομίζων, κἀγὼ τῶν ὤτων λαβομένη τρίς σε φιλήσω, καὶ τοιοῦτον
καλόν ... ναί, πρὸς τῆς Ἀφροδίτης, ᾗ νῦν τεθύκαμεν. γνώσομαι δ' <εὐκαίρως
θύσασα> τὴν θυσίαν, ἐάν σε πρὸς ἡμᾶς ἡ θεὸς ἐπικλίνῃ. προσείρησό μοι, ψυχὴ
Λυσία, θᾶττον ἤδη, ἐπεὶ καὶ τὸν χρόνον τοῦτον, ὃν ἐπιστέλλω σοι, χρονίζεις.
πρὸς σὲ πάντες ἐκεῖνοι σάτυροι, οὐκ ἄνθρωποι, καὶ παρ' οὐδὲν τίθεμαι τούτους.

κε'. ΕΤΑΙΡΑ ΜΕΜΦΕΤΑΙ ΤΗΙ ΑΔΕΛΦΗΙ
ΥΠΕΛΘΟΥΣΗΙ ΑΥΤΗΣ ΤΟΝ ΦΙΛΟΝ

Φιλαινὶς Πετάλῃ

Χθὲς ἐπὶ πότον ὑπὸ Παμφίλου κληθεῖσα Θελξινόην μετεπεμπόμην τὴν ἀδελφήν·
ἐλάνθανον δὲ οὐ τὸ τυχὸν ἐμαυτῇ προξενοῦσα, ὡς ἔργῳ γέγονε δῆλον. πρῶτον
μὲν ἦλθε περιεργότερον κοσμηθεῖσα καὶ στίλψασα τὰς παρειὰς ἐντρίμματι, καὶ

me what was on everybody's mind. So the boldest, on the pretext of giving me good counsel, but actually out of jealousy toward you, scolded me as follows: "Though you excel all other girls on the stage in beauty, you don't come close to them in profits. You could earn a fortune from us, whom you disdain, but you squander your youth on Lysias alone, and he's not even good-looking. For it would be bearable if the whole bunch of us was bested by a real hunk, and one could perhaps forgive you for preferring the irresistible appeal of looks over money. All the same, you've deafened us with your constant praise of him and stuffed our ears with the boy's name, so that now the moment we wake up we imagine we hear 'Lysias.' You're not in love; no, I'd say you're totally deranged. There's only one thing we ask. Tell us clearly if you prefer him over all of us. We wouldn't want to stand in the way of the one you love."[3]

That was the song they sang almost till cockcrow, and if I wanted to recount each detail, I think I'd still be talking when the sun went down. Most of what they said went in one ear and right out the other. But this was my reply: "Eros himself has set Lysias before the rest of you, he who kindles the fire in my heart both night and day." And listen to this too, sweetheart. When, with cries of reproach, they asked, "Who could love such a charmless, repulsive, plain-looking sort?" I replied with a vivid gesture of the hands, a shrug, and a killing look. "You want to know who? Me! Goodbye," I said, standing up, "and forgive a person in love. No profit warms my heart, only what I desire. And what I desire is Lysias." Please, then, my sweet master, come now, right now. Speed is a sure sign of love. Don't delay. Just come, and bring me a single kiss. And I will grab your ears and give you three in turn. And so beautiful …[4] Yes, by Aphrodite, to whom I've just made sacrifice. I'll know the sacrifice was successful if the goddess leads you to me. A quick farewell, then, Lysias, my soul, since the very time I take to write this letter delays your coming. Compared with you, all the others are satyrs,[5] not men. I don't give a damn for them.

1.25. A Hetaira Complains That Her Sister Has Been Endearing Herself to Her Lover

Philainis[1] to Petale[2]

Yesterday when I was invited for a drink by Pamphilos,[3] I sent for my sister Thelxinoe.[4] Little did I know that I was thus fated to procure a rival for myself, as events revealed. First of all, she came dressed to kill. She had polished

πρὸς ἔσοπτρον ὡς εἰκὸς διαπλεξαμένη καὶ εὐθετίσασα τὰς κόμας ἀφῆκε τοῦ
αὐχένος ὅρμους πολυτελεῖς, ἀγλαΐσματα δέρης, ἄλλην τε πολλὴν περιέκειτο
φλυαρίαν ὑπομάζιόν τε καὶ ἀμφωλένια, καὶ οὐδὲ τῶν περικρανίων ἠμέλησε
κόσμων. τὸ δὲ ταραντινίδιον, ἐξ οὗ διαφανῶς ἡ ὥρα διέλαμπεν. θαμὰ δὲ καὶ
τὴν πτέρναν αὐτὴ πρὸς ἑαυτὴν ἐπιστρεφομένη διεσκοπεῖτο, πολλάκις δ᾽ ἅμα τε
ἑαυτὴν ἐθεώρει καὶ εἴ τις αὐτὴν ἄλλος θεᾶται. ἔπειτα παρακαθέζεται μέση ἐμοῦ
τε καὶ Παμφίλου, ἵνα χωρὶς ἡμᾶς διαλάβῃ, καὶ προσπαίζουσα τῷ μειρακίῳ εἰς
ἑαυτὴν ἐκείνου μετάγει τὸ βλέμμα, καὶ τῶν ἐκπωμάτων πρὸς αὐτὸν ἀντίδοσιν
ἐποιεῖτο. ὁ δὲ ῥᾳδίως ἠνείχετο, ἅτε νέος ἐρωτικός, καὶ οἴνου πολλοῦ διαθερ-
μαίνοντος αὐτοῦ τὴν ψυχήν, καὶ τοῦτον δὴ τὸν τρόπον ὥσπερ ἐκ στομάτων
ὑπεφίλουν ἀλλήλους καταπίνοντες τὰ φιλήματα, καὶ τὸν οἶνον τοῖς χείλεσι
κεκραμένον μέχρι καὶ αὐτῆς παρέπεμπον τῆς καρδίας.

Πάμφιλος δὲ μήλου μικρὸν ἀποδακὼν εὐστόχως ἠκόντισεν εἰς τὸν κόλπον
ἐκείνης, ἡ δὲ φιλήσασα μεταξὺ τῶν μαστῶν ὑπὸ τῷ περιδέσμῳ, ὃν περιε-
στερνίσατο, παρέβυσε. τούτοις οὖν ἐδακνόμην. τί δὲ οὐκ ἤμελλον, ζήλην ἐμοὶ
καθορῶσα τὴν ἐμὴν ἀδελφήν, ἣν ταῖς ἐμαῖς ἀνέτρεφον ἀγκάλαις; τοιαῦτά μοι
παρ᾽ αὐτῆς τὰ τροφεῖα· οὕτω με νῦν ἀντιπελαργοῦσα δικαίαν ἀποδίδωσι χάριν.
καίτοι πολλάκις ὧδε παρ᾽ ἕκαστον αὐτὴν ἐμεμφόμην· "κατ᾽ ἀδελφῆς ταῦτα,
Θελξινόη; μή, Θελξινόη." ἀλλὰ τί μακρηγορῶ; ἀπῆλθεν ἡ βάσκανος οὕτως
ἀνέδην σφετερισαμένη τὸν νέον. ἀδικεῖ με τοίνυν Θελξινόη. μαρτύρομαι τὴν
Ἀφροδίτην καὶ σέ, ὦ Πετάλη, κοινὴν ὑπάρχουσαν φίλην, ὡς αὐτὴ πανταχοῦ
τῶν κακῶν προκατάρχει. ἀδικῶμεν οὖν ἀλλήλας. εὑρήσω κἀγὼ τοιοῦτον πρὸς
ἑτέραν ἀλώπεκα (καὶ τοῦτο δεδόχθω) <ἀλωπεκίζουσα> ἢ σίδηρος ἐλαυνέσθω
σιδήρῳ· οὐ γὰρ ἀπορήσω τρεῖς ἀνθ᾽ ἑνὸς <τὴν> ἄπληστον ἀφελέσθαι.

κϛ΄. ΠΡΟΣ ΟΡΧΗΣΤΡΙΔΑ

Σπεύσιππος Παναρέτῃ

Πάλαι μέν μοι προδιέγραψε τὴν <σὴν> χάριν ἡ φήμη, πάντων ἀνὰ στόμα
ταύτην φερόντων, νῦν δὲ παρέστηκε πρῶτον. ἦ καὶ πλέον ἄγαμαί σε τοῦ κάλλους, ὅσῳ γε μᾶλλον ἢ κατὰ φήμην ὁρῶ. τίς οὐ τεθαύμακεν ὀρχουμένην; τίς ἰδὼν
οὐκ ἠράσθη; Πολύμνιαν, Ἀφροδίτην ἔχουσιν οἱ θεοί· ἐκείνας ἡμῖν, ὡς ἐφικτόν,

up her cheeks with rouge and had probably sat in front of the mirror plaiting and carefully arranging her hair. She fastened rich jewelry around her neck, finery for the throat, put on plenty of other trinkets, a breast-band and bracelets, and took care to deck out her head as well. I won't even mention her diaphanous Tarentine tunic,[5] which let her ripe beauty shine through clear as day. She often turned on her heel to inspect her looks, frequently gazing at herself and at the same time checking to see if anyone else was looking at her. Then she positioned herself right between me and Pamphilos so as to keep us apart and, by bantering with the youth, turned his eye her way; and what is more, she exchanged cups with him. He went along with it all too happily, young and prone to passion as he is, and with all that wine heating up his soul. And so they secretly locked lips as though their mouths were touching when in fact they were drinking liquid kisses, and they let the wine, steeped in the taste of their own lips, penetrate to their very hearts.

Pamphilos bit off a piece of apple and, excellent marksman that he was, propelled it straight into her bosom; she, for her part, kissed it and tucked it between her breasts, under the band that she had fastened about her chest. I was really stung by this. And how not, seeing my sister, whom I had nurtured in my own arms, acting as my rival? This is how she pays back the favor! That's how she returns my love and gives me the thanks I am due? And all despite my repeated scolding: "You're doing this to your sister, Thelxinoe? Thelxinoe, don't!" But why go on? The jealous bitch took off, after she had so recklessly gotten the young man in her clutches. So Thelxinoe is wronging me. May Aphrodite be my witness, and you, Petale, our mutual friend, that she's the one entirely to blame for this fight. All right, let's hurt each other, then. I will outfox this fox (that's a done deal) and strike back with her own weapons. It won't be hard to steal three guys from that voracious vixen for the one she took.

1.26. To a Dancer

Speusippos[1] to Panarete[2]

Long ago Fame had already sketched out for me a preview of your grace—it is, after all, on everyone's lips—but now it is there before my eyes for the first time. And even as vision outdoes hearsay, so the actual sight of your beauty stuns me all the more. Who has not marveled at your dancing? Who, upon seeing you, did not fall head over heels in love? Polymnia[3] and Aphrodite belong to the gods. You mimic them for us, as far as it is pos-

ὑποκρίνει παρ' αὐτῶν κοσμουμένη. ὀνομάσω <σε> ῥήτορα, προσείπω ζωγρά-
φον; καὶ πράγματα γράφεις καὶ λόγους παντοδαποὺς ὑποφαίνεις καὶ φύσεως
ἁπάσης ἐναργὴς ὑπάρχεις εἰκών, ἀντὶ χρωμάτων καὶ γλώττης χειρὶ πολυσχήμῳ
καὶ ποικίλοις ἤθεσι κεχρημένη, καὶ οἷά τις Φάριος Πρωτεὺς ἄλλοτε πρὸς ἄλλα
μεταβεβλῆσθαι δοκεῖς πρὸς τὴν εὔμουσον τῶν ὑπορχημάτων ᾠδήν. ὁ δὲ δῆμος
ἀνέστηκέ τε ὀρθὸς ὑπὸ θαύματος, καὶ φωνὰς ἀμοιβαίας ἀφίησιν ἐμμελῶς,
καὶ τὼ χεῖρε κινεῖ καὶ τὴν ἐσθῆτα σοβεῖ· ἔπειτα συγκαθήμενοι διηγεῖται καθ'
ἕκαστον ἄλλος ἄλλῳ κινήματα πολυτρόπου σιγῆς, καὶ πᾶς θεατὴς ὑφ' ἡδονῆς
χειρονόμος εἶναι πειρᾶται. ἕνα δὲ μόνον προσφυῶς μιμουμένη τὸν Καράμαλλον
τὸν πάνυ, ἁπάντων ἔχεις τὴν μίμησιν ἀκριβῆ. ὅθεν οὐκ ἀνάξιον οὐδὲ τὸν εὖ
μάλα σπουδαῖον παραπολαύειν τῆς σῆς θυμηδίας· ἀνάπαυλα γὰρ τῆς σπουδῆς
ἐνίοτε γίνεται ἡ παιδιά.

πολλὰς τοίνυν ἅτε ταχὺς τῆς πολιτείας ἱππεὺς διελήλυθα πόλεις, καὶ πρός
γε τῇ νέᾳ τὴν πρεσβυτέραν ἱστόρηκα Ῥώμην, καὶ τοιαύτην ἐν οὐδετέρᾳ τεθέαμαι. εὐδαίμονες οὖν οἱ Παναρέτην εὐτυχοῦντες οὕτως ὑπερφέρουσαν καὶ τέχνῃ
καὶ κάλλει.

κζ'. Η ΤΟΝ ΕΡΑΣΤΗΝ ΑΙΝΙΤΤΟΜΕΝΗ ΜΑΤΗΝ
ΠΕΡΙ ΑΥΤΗΝ ΠΟΝΟΥΝΤΑ

Κλέαρχος Ἀμυνάνδρῳ

Νέου τινὸς ἐξεπίτηδες διὰ γυναικὸς παριόντος ἑσπέρας ἔφη τις ἄλλη πρὸς
ἐκείνην παρισταμένη πλησίον, ἅμα νύττουσα τῷ ἀγκῶνι· "πρὸς τῆς Ἀφροδίτης,
ὦ φίλη, σὲ ποθῶν οὑτοσὶ προσάδων παρέρχεται καὶ μορφῆς οὐκ ἀφυῶς ἔχων. ὡς
εὐπάρυφον τὸ θερίστριον καὶ ποικίλον ταῖς ἀπὸ κερκίδος γραφαῖς, ὡς εὔμουσος
τὴν φωνήν. ἔοικέ μοι καὶ περὶ καλὴν ἀσχολεῖσθαι τὴν κόμην· ἐπεὶ καὶ τοῦτό
γε τοῦ ἔρωτος ἴδιον καὶ μάλα μέντοι καλόν, τὸ σφόδρα πείθειν τοὺς ἐρῶντας
ἐπιμελῶς ἄγαν διακοσμεῖσθαι, καὶ εἰ πρότερον ἀτεχνῶς ἑαυτῶν κατημέλουν."
"νὴ τοὺς Ἔρωτας," εἶπεν, "ἀποστρέφομαι δὲ τὸν νέον καίπερ ὄντα καλόν, ὅτι
φυσῶν αὐτὸς ἑαυτὸν οἴεται μόνος ἀξιέραστος <εἶναι> ταῖς γυναιξὶ καὶ πρε-
πόντως τῷ κάλλει ποθεῖσθαι· καί που καὶ Φίλωνα τυχὸν ἐπωνόμακεν ἑαυτόν,
φρονῶν ἐπὶ τῇ ὥρᾳ θαυμάσιον ὅσον, καὶ πολλῷ τῷ ὀφθαλμῷ βλέπει καὶ φρο-

sible, the very goddesses who have decked you out with all their charms. Shall I call you an orator or label you a painter? You depict actions, express all sorts of stories, are the vivid image of all nature; instead of the painter's brush or speaker's tongue, you use your versatile hands and diverse poses, and like a kind of Pharian Proteus[4] you seem to morph now into this form, now into that, following the inspired melody of the dance. The spectators spring to their feet in awe, raise their voices in tuneful responsion, wave their hands, and set their garments swaying. Then, as they sit together, each recounts to the other point by point how you move in variegated silence, and every spectator in his delight attempts to be a pantomime. Though clearly your art reflects just a single model, the one and only Karamallos,[5] all life is truthfully mirrored in your repertoire. Thus even a respectable person may share in the joys you offer, for play can provide the occasional respite from his earnest tasks.

I have made my way through many a town as a public courier,[6] been acquainted with the new Rome[7] and the old, yet I have never seen such a woman in either one. Happy, then, are those with the good fortune to have encountered Panarete, so excellent in art, so peerless in beauty.

1.27. A WOMAN MOCKING A LOVER COURTING HER IN VAIN

Klearchos[1] to Amynandros[2]

One evening, as a young man was deliberately promenading in front of a woman, one of her comrades approached and, giving her a nudge, said: "By Aphrodite, my dear, this fellow walking by here and serenading you is in love with you—and he's not exactly ugly. Just look at that nice purple border adorning his robe, how colorfully it is embroidered, and then the marvelous sound of his voice! I think he also takes great pains to make his hair appear beautiful. For this too is typical of desire (and indeed a beautiful part of it) that it irresistibly goads those in love to pay close attention to their appearance, even if before they simply let themselves go." "By the Erotes," she replied, "I'm not in the least interested in that youth, pretty as he may be, because he's all puffed up and thinks that he alone deserves a woman's love and that it's only right that they desire him due to his good looks. And, who knows, considering how incredibly smug he is about his beauty,[3] maybe he even gave himself the name Philon;[4] he shoots around that haughty glance and his brows are full of arrogance. I cannot stand a

νήματος ἐμπέπληκε τὴν ὀφρῦν. μισῶ γοῦν ἐραστὴν παρευδοκιμεῖν εὐμορφίᾳ τὴν ἐρωμένην ἀξιοῦντα, οἰόμενόν τε κάλλος ὑπὲρ κάλλους χαρίζεσθαι, μέγιστον ἀντὶ βραχέος. ὅρα δὲ πῶς ἠθικῶς τὸν ὑπερήφανον διαπαίζω· καὶ σφόδρα τοῖς αἰνίγμασι τέρπῃ.

ποθεῖ μέ τις ἐρωτομανής, καὶ οὐδὲ νεύματος ἀξιοῦται, καὶ πολλὰ τὸν ἐμὸν στενωπὸν διέρχεται μάτην· ᾄδει δὲ ἄλλως καὶ τοῖς ἐμοῖς ὠσὶν ἀπιθάνως καὶ ἀμουσότερα Λειβηθρίων, οὐδὲ ἐρυθριᾷ περιττῶς ἐκπεριτρέχων διαύλους. ἐγώ, νὴ τὼ θεώ, τοὐναντίον ἀντ᾽ ἐκείνου λοιπὸν ἐγκαλύπτομαι." ἔφασκε δὲ ταῦτα ἄλλα τε πολλὰ θρυπτομένη καὶ δὴ καὶ τὸ σκέλος ὑπογυμνοῦσα, ἵνα δείξῃ τῷ νέῳ κνήμην ἰθυτενῆ καὶ πόδα λεπτόν τε καὶ εὔρυθμον· ἕτερα δὲ τοῦ σώματος ἐγύμνωσε μέρη τὰ δυνατά, ὅπως ἂν πολλαχόθεν τὸ μειράκιον ἐρεθίσῃ. ὁ δέ φησιν αἰσθόμενος τῶν λεχθέντων (ἐψιθύρισε γὰρ ἐκείνη τοσοῦτον, ὥστε τὸν νέον ἀκοῦσαι)· "οἷα βούλει καὶ ὁσάκις ἂν θέλῃς εἰπέ· οὐ γὰρ ἐμὲ γελᾷς, ἡ καλή, ἀλλὰ τὸν Ἔρωτα παίζεις. ἐλπὶς ἄρα τὸν τοξότην ἐκεῖνον τοιοῦτον ἐπαφεῖναί σοι βέλος, ἵνα τούτων προκαλινδουμένη τῶν ποδῶν ἱκετεύῃς ἐμὲ τὸ σὸν ἀκέσασθαι πάθος."

ἡ δὲ διαμωκωμένη καὶ ὑποβλέπουσα λοξόν, τοῖς δακτύλοις τῆς δεξιᾶς ἠθικῶς οἷα γυνὴ τὸ μετακάρπιον ἐπικροτοῦσα τῆς εὐωνύμου χειρὸς ὑπεροπτικῶς ἀπεκρίθη· "ἐγώ, τάλαν; μή, ὦ Χάριτες, γένοιτο. κεναῖς ἐλπίσιν ἐπείσθης. οἴει μᾶλλον <εἶναι> καλός, καὶ τούτου γε χάριν τοιοῦτον ἐπῆλθέ σοι προσδοκᾶν, ἕως ἂν παραγένηται τυχὸν ὁ σὸς ἔκδικος Ἔρως. παράμενε προσάδων, ἐπαγρυπνῶν, μηδὲν διανύων, μόνον δὲ κλυδωνιζόμενος ἐκ τοῦ πόθου, ἔνθα, φασίν, ἄνεμος οὔτε μένειν οὔτε πλεῖν ἐᾷ. οὔτε οὖν ἑκτέον ἐστί σοι τῶν ἡμετέρων τινός, οὐ μαστῶν, οὐ περιβολῆς, οὐ φιλημάτων· οὐδὲ μὴν ἀπαλλακτέον, οἶμαι, τοῦ πόθου."

κη΄. ΝΕΟΣ ΑΔΗΜΟΝΕΙ ΠΡΟΣ ΤΗΝ ΤΗΣ ΕΡΩΜΕΝΗΣ ΠΑΛΙΜΒΟΛΟΝ ΓΝΩΜΗΝ

Νικόστρατος Τιμοκράτει

Τίς ἄρα περὶ ἐμὲ τῆς Κοχλίδος ὁ τρόπος; τί δὲ μηχανωμένη ἄλλοτε πρὸς ἄλλον ἀθρόως μεταβαίνει σκοπόν; ἐκλύομαι, νὴ τοὺς θεούς, ὑπὸ τῆς ἀπορίας. ἀπεῖπον τὸν νοῦν ἀνελίττων, ἀπεῖπον τοῖς λογισμοῖς πολλὰ κατ᾽ ἐμαυτὸν ἀπορῶν. οὐδὲν

lover who deems himself superior to his beloved when it comes to looks, believing that he is just trading beauty for beauty—and indeed a lot for a little.[5] But watch how I give that snob a teasing taste of his own medicine—you'll really enjoy how I make fun of him.

"Imagine, there's this love-crazed guy who is absolutely wild about me, but to me he's not even worth a nod; he often parades up and down my alley, all for nothing. He sings his serenade in vain, making no impression on my ears and sounding worse than the tone-deaf Libethrians,[6] and he doesn't even blush to engage in a race he cannot win. Unlike him, I want to hide myself in shame, by the two goddesses."[7] She said many such things in her coyness, even as she exposed her leg in order to show the youth its straight form together with her delicate, well-proportioned foot. She also bared further parts of her body, as far as she could, so as to worry the young man from various angles. On hearing her words (for she had whispered so loud that the youth could not miss it), he said: "Say what you will and as much as you want. For it's not me you are deriding, my pretty one, you are mocking Eros. So there's a good chance this archer will shoot you with an arrow of the kind that will have you squirming at my feet and beseeching me to cure you of your suffering."

She, however, had nothing but scorn for the fellow and looked at him askance, tapping the palm of her left hand with the fingers of her right just like a woman, and replied contemptuously: "I, you poor fool? God forbid, by the Graces! You're a victim of vain hopes. You consider yourself pretty, and for this reason you got it into your head to wait until your vengeful Eros might happen to come by. Go on, then, with your serenades, lie awake at night, accomplishing nothing, just tossed about on the waves of passion, where, as the saying goes, the wind permits you neither to drop anchor nor to sail.[8] You shall not have anything that's mine, neither my breasts, nor my embraces, nor my kisses. Yet even so, I think, you won't be freed of your desire."

1.28. A Young Man Is Dismayed
at the Fickleness of His Beloved

Nikostratos[1] to Timokrates[2]

So, how in the world am I to explain Kochlis's behavior toward me? What's in her head when she, ever so suddenly, shifts her sights from this to that? By the gods, the uncertainty has quite unhinged me! I've given up racking

εὗρον παντελῶς διαγνῶναι, καθάπερ ἐν λευκῷ λίθῳ στάθμην λευκὴν διατείνων. τίς γὰρ ἀστάτῳ δύναιτο ἂν ἐπιστῆσαι σκοπῷ; ὥστε, μὰ τοὺς θεούς, οὐκ ἔχω ὅτι χρήσωμαι ταύτῃ. ἐπώνυμος ἄρα τῆς σκολιότητος ἡ Κοχλίς. αὐτὸς ἐρῶν ἐκείνης ἐξήγησαί μοι τὴν ἀστάθμητον γνώμην· εἰ δὲ καὶ σὺ πρὸς αὐτὴν ἀπορεῖς δυσξύμβολον οὖσαν, μὴ κατόκνει, φίλτατε, πυθέσθαι τῆς σῆς <φίλης τῆς> σφοδροτάτης. τοτὲ μὲν ἐρώσης ἅπαντα πράττει, καί μοι τὸν πόθον ὑφάπτει πολύν, καὶ ὅλον με ταῖς ἐλπίσιν ἐπαίρει· τοτὲ δὲ πάλιν, ὡς εὐμεταβολωτέρα κοθόρνου, ἀναίνεται σοβαρῶς ὃν ἀρτίως ἐπόθει, καὶ πᾶσαν αὖθις ἀναλύει μου τὴν ἐλπίδα, καὶ τὴν ἐμὴν οὕτω ψυχὴν ἤθεσιν ἐξ ὑπογυίου παλιμβόλοις ἱστὸν ἀπέδειξε Πηνελόπης.

τί πράξω; τίς γένωμαι; φεῦ τῶν ἀφορήτων κακῶν, παπαὶ τῶν ἀμέτρως κατεβλακευμένων ἠθῶν. ὡς ἄγαν ἐπιθρυπτομένη τὴν λαμπρὰν ἑαυτῆς ἡμαύρωσε χάριν. ταύτην κἂν νουθετῇς, κἂν ἱκετεύῃς, παρὰ κωφὸν ᾄδειν δοκεῖς. ὅθεν καὶ ἄκοντά με λοιπὸν τοσοῦτον ἐραστὴν ἀποτρέπει καὶ δυσαπότρεπτον γεγονότα. τοιγαροῦν οὐκέτι πρὸς ταύτην, ὦ Τιμόκρατες, κοινωνῶ σοι τοῦ πόθου, ἐπεὶ τοῦτό γέ ἐστιν ἀνδρὸς τὰ δυνατὰ ἀκριβῶς διαγνῶναι καὶ μηκέτι ματαίαν ἐπάγεσθαι λύπην. φθόνος δὲ μηδεὶς τῆς ἄλλης ἡμῶν ἐπικρατήσῃ φιλίας, ἀλλὰ συνενέγκαι σοι τῆς Κοχλίδος ἐκ μεταβολῆς ἐκείνης ὁ τρόπος, καὶ γένοιο φίλος μακρῷ γε μᾶλλον εὐτυχέστερος ἐμοῦ.

my brain; I've abandoned trying continually to puzzle it out by means of reason. I've found no solution at all: it's like trying to measure a white surface with a white tape measure.[3] And anyhow, who can hit a moving target? By the gods, then, I don't know what to make of her. Evidently Kochlis is named for her crookedness.[4] Since you're in love with her yourself, do explain to me her fickleness. But if you too are at your wits' end with this incomprehensible woman, don't hesitate, my friend, to ask the temperamental bitch herself. At times she acts all amorous, sets my passion ablaze, and makes me fly with hope. Then—changeable as a slipper where one size fits all[5]—she turns up her nose at the one she has just desired, unravels once more my entire hope, and thus, with her ways suddenly changing, she uses my soul like Penelope her loom.[6]

What should I do? What will become of me? Ah, what unbearable sufferings; oh, what a character, thoughtless beyond bounds! How her high and mighty attitude has killed the sparkle of her radiant charm! Whether you chide her or beseech her—whatever your tune, it falls on deaf ears. That's how she's managed to drive me away, once and for all, though against my will—me, a lover so passionate and hard to shake off. So from now on you can have my share of desire for this woman, O Timokrates; it's all yours. For it's a man's job to recognize exactly what is possible and no longer to bring upon himself unnecessary grief. No other jealousy shall affect our friendship, but Kochlis's character in all its inconsistency shall be your joy—may you be a far more fortunate lover than I am.

ΑΡΙΣΤΑΙΝΕΤΟΥ ΕΠΙΣΤΟΛΩΝ
ΒΙΒΛΙΟΝ Β′

α′. ΠΡΟΣ ΕΤΑΙΡΑΝ ΥΠΕΡ ΦΙΛΟΥ ΠΡΕΣΒΕΥΤΙΚΗ

Αἰλιανὸς Καλύκῃ

Τὴν παροῦσαν ἐπιστολὴν ἱκετηρίαν ὑπὲρ Χαριδήμου ποιοῦμαι. ἀλλ', ὦ φίλη
Πειθοῖ, παροῦσα συνεργὸς ποίει κατορθοῦν ἀνυσίμως, οὓς ἂν ἐπιστείλαιμι
λόγους. ταῦτα μὲν δή, φασίν, εὔχθω. οὗτος δ' οὖν ἐρᾷ σου, Καλύκη, καὶ τῷ σῷ
φλέγεται γλυκυτάτῳ πυρί, καὶ τεθνήξεται θᾶττον ἐκ τριχὸς κρεμάμενος καὶ
σκιᾶς εἴδωλον γεγονώς, εἰ μὴ τὴν παροῦσαν θεραπείαν ἐπινεύσεις τῷ μειρακίῳ.
Ἄπολλον ἀποτρόπαιε, μὴ φόνου τις, ὦ γύναι, τὸ σὸν αἰτιάσηται κάλλος, μηδὲ
ταῖς σαῖς χάρισιν ἐπικωμάσωσιν Ἐρινύες. ἐγκαλεῖς, εὖ οἶδα, τῷ νέῳ· ἔπταισεν
ὁμολογουμένως· νέος ὢν ἔπταισεν, ἱκανὴν δέδωκε δίκην, μὴ θάνατος ἔστω τοῦ
πλημμελήσαντος ἡ ζημία. λογίζου, πρὸς θεῶν, καὶ μιμοῦ τὴν σὴν Ἀφροδίτην,
ὡς ἐφικτὸν γυναικί. πυρὸς ἄρχει, τόξα διέπει, ἀλλὰ καὶ Χάριτες ἕπονται τῇ
θεῷ· σὺ δὲ ὀφθεῖσα φλέγεις καὶ ὁμιλοῦσα τιτρώσκεις. ἐπίθες <οὖν> ταχὺ καὶ
τὰς Χάριτας τῷ πληγέντι. φέρεις μὲν πῦρ, ἔχεις δὲ ὕδωρ· τὴν σὴν αὐτῇ φλόγα
κατάσβεσον πρὸς βραχύ.

ταῦτα μὲν οὖν ἱκετεύων φημί. ἃ δὲ παραινεῖν ἔχω σοι, λεκτέα λοιπόν.
χαριέστατον οἶδα τὸ σμικρὸν ὑποκνίζειν τοὺς νέους· τοῦτο γὰρ τῶν ἀφροδισίων
προαναστέλλει τὸν κόρον, καὶ τὰς ἑταίρας ὑποδείκνυσιν ἀεὶ ποθεινὰς τοῖς
ἐρασταῖς. ἀλλ' εἰ τοῦτο γένοιτο πέρα τῆς χρείας, ἀποκάμνουσιν οἱ ποθοῦντες.
οὕτως οὖν ὁ μὲν ὠργίσθη, ὁ δὲ ἐπέβαλεν ἄλλῃ τὰ ὄμματα. ὀξύς ἐστιν ὁ Ἔρως
καὶ ἐλθεῖν καὶ ἀναπτῆναι· ἐλπίσας πτεροῦται καὶ ἀπελπίσας ταχὺ πτερορρυεῖν
εἴωθεν ἀπογνωσθείς. διὸ καὶ μέγα τῶν ἑταιρουσῶν ἐστι σόφισμα ἀεὶ τὸ παρὸν

THE LETTERS OF ARISTAENETUS
BOOK 2

2.1. MESSAGE TO A HETAIRA ON BEHALF OF A FRIEND

Aelian to Kalyke[1]

I am writing the present letter as a plea for Charidemos. Please, Persuasion, be present as my coauthor; grant efficacy and success to the words I shall send.[2] Let this be my prayer, as they say. This fellow is in love with you, Kalyke, and he is burning for you with the sweetest flame. Soon he'll be a dead man—his life is hanging by a thread; he has become a shadow's shade[3]—unless you bestow on him that cure that lies in your hands. By Apollo, who wards off evil, let no one accuse your beauty, woman, of murder, nor let your charms attract the Furies' deadly revels.[4] I know well that you have grounds for complaint against the young man. Admittedly, he made a mistake, a youthful mistake, and he's been punished enough. Don't exact the death penalty for his offense. Think about it, by the gods, and imitate your own Aphrodite, as much as a mortal woman can. She is master of the fire, wields the bow, yet it is the Graces who form this goddess's retinue. Whoever sees you starts to burn; whoever chats with you suffers wounds. Quick, apply some Graces to the injured party. You bear fire, but you have water at hand as well. Extinguish your flame yourself without delay.

This I say as a suppliant. But what I'm urging you to do, I shall say in what follows. I know that it's a thrill to torment young guys a bit, as it prevents them from getting weary of love; it makes hetairas appear forever desirable to their lovers. But if this happens more than is necessary, lovers get sick of it. Some of them grow angry; others start turning their eyes elsewhere. Eros is speedy, both coming and flying away. When he's hopeful, he sprouts feathers, but when his hopes are dashed, he sheds them in despair. Therefore it's a great trick among those in the hetaira trade

τῆς ἀπολαύσεως ὑπερτιθεμένας ταῖς ἐλπίσι διακρατεῖν τοὺς ἐραστάς. ἤδη μὲν
οὖν πολλαὶ τὸν νέον ὑπῆλθον ἑταῖραι προτρέπουσαι πιθανῶς, καὶ δὴ τοῦτον
ἔφθη τις ἂν πανουργότερον λαβοῦσα, εἰ μὴ τὸ μειράκιον ἀπηύχετο παντελῶς
ἐναφροδισιάσαι τινὶ μετὰ σέ. χρῆσαι τοίνυν τοῖς μὲν ὑποκρινομένοις φιλεῖν
ἑταιρικῶς, τοῖς δὲ γνησίοις ἐρασταῖς φιλικώτερον. πείθου μοι καὶ τῆς ἀμετρίας
ἀπόσχου. ὅρα μὴ κατὰ τὴν παροιμίαν ἀπορρήξωμεν πάνυ τείναντες τὸ καλώ-
διον, μηδὲ λάθῃς λοιπὸν εἰς ἀγερωχίαν μεταβαλοῦσα τὸ φρόνημα. οἶσθα δὲ
ὅσον Ἔρως ἀντιστρατεύειν τοῖς ὑπερηφανοῦσι φιλεῖ. ἄλλως τε ὀπώραν πωλεῖς,
ἡ καλή· ἔστι δὲ ἡ σὴ ὀπώρα ἡδίων τῆς ἀπὸ τῶν δένδρων. δικαία δ' ἂν εἴης
ἀπ' αὐτοῦ γε τοῦ ἔργου συνεῖναι, ὅτι οὐ δεῖ τηρεῖν ὀπώραν. δίδου τοῖς σοῖς
ὀπωρώναις τὴν ὥραν τρυγᾶν. μετ' ὀλίγον ἔσῃ γεράνδρυον· οἱ δὲ τῶν καλῶν
σωμάτων ἐρασταὶ τῇ τοῦ φαινομένου κάλλους ἀκμῇ παραμετροῦσι τὸν ἔρωτα.

καὶ ἑτέρως δὲ μάνθανε· οὐ γάρ σε καὶ διαφόρως ἐπεκδιδάσκειν ὀκνήσω.
γυνὴ ἔοικε λειμῶνι, καὶ ὅπερ ἐκείνῳ τὰ ἄνθη, τοῦτό γε ταύτῃ τὸ κάλλος. ἕως
μὲν οὖν <ἔαρ ἀκμάζει>, ἡ κόμη τῷ λειμῶνι ἐπακμάζει καὶ ἡ χροιὰ τῶν ἀνθέων,
ἦρος δὲ παρακμάσαντος πέπαυται μὲν τὰ ἄνθη τοῦ <λειμῶνος>, ὁ δὲ λειμὼν
γεγήρακε. γυναικός τε αὖ πάλιν εἰ τὸ εἶδος παρέλθῃ καὶ τὸ κάλλος παραδράμῃ,
τίς ἔτι καταλείπεται εὐφροσύνη; ἀνανθεῖ γὰρ καὶ ἀπηνθηκότι σώματι οὐ
πέφυκε προσιζάνειν ὁ Ἔρως· οὗ δ' ἂν εὐανθές τε καὶ εὐῶδες ᾖ, ἐνταῦθα καὶ
ἐνιζάνει καὶ μένει. ἀλλὰ τί μακρὸν ἀποτέτακα λόγον, δελφῖνα διδάσκων νήχε-
σθαι; μεθαρμοσαμένη τοίνυν, ὦ καλλίστη γυναικῶν, τὴν ψυχὴν καλλίονα τοῦ
σώματος ἀπόφηναι, ἵν' ἔξῇ λέγειν· "ὦ κάλλους φιλανθρώπου." τὸ δ' οὖν ῥόδον,
κἂν μή τις αὐτῷ χρήσηται, μαραίνεται. ἆρ' ἐπένευσας, ὦ φιλτάτη; πάντως
δήπου, τὸν σὸν εὐμετάβολόν τε καὶ εὐπαράκλητον ἐπίσταμαι τρόπον. ἥκω
τοίνυν καὶ προσάξω τὸν νέον πλουσίως ἐπικηρυκευόμενον δι' ἐμοῦ. τὸ γὰρ πρὸς
ἑταίρας κηρύκειον ἐκ τοῦ Βαβυλωνίου χρυσοῦ χαρακτηρίζεσθαι πέφυκεν. ἀλλὰ
τῶν προτέρων τε συγγνώμην καὶ τῶνδε χάριν ἔχουσα εὐμενὴς τό γε λοιπὸν εἴης
τῷ σῷ Χαριδήμῳ.

always to defer the moment of fulfillment and so to have power over their lovers by means of their hopes. And many a hetaira has already cozied up to him, coaxing him persuasively, and one of them with greater cunning would have snatched him up ahead of you, if the youth had not foresworn making love with anyone else. Treat according to the rules of your trade those who only feign love, but be more affectionate toward those who love truly. Take my advice, and don't do anything extreme. Watch out lest, as the proverb says, we snap the string by stretching it too tight.[5] And watch out too lest your pride turn to arrogance before you even know it. You know how hard Eros typically hits back at the haughty. In any case, you're trading in fruit, my pretty. And your crop is sweeter than what grows on trees. From your line of work, you're bound to understand that you can't store fruit indefinitely. Let your clients pluck it when it's ripe. In a little while you'll be a shriveled stump. The intensity of desire among lovers of beautiful bodies stands in direct relation to how close that outward beauty is to its peak.

Or think of it differently, for I won't hesitate to instruct you in a variety of ways: A woman is like a meadow; her beauty resembles its flowers. As long as spring is at its height, the grasses of the meadow and the color of its blossoms are at their best. But when springtime is over, the blossoms fade, the meadow has grown old. When a woman's appearance slips away and her beauty passes its prime, what joy is left? For by nature Eros does not go near a body that has lost its bloom and withered. But where things are flowering and fragrant, that is where Eros settles and remains. But why do I make a long speech, as though teaching a dolphin to swim? Change your ways, O loveliest of women, and make your soul appear more beautiful than your body, so that one can say, "What a kindhearted beauty!" The rose, after all, withers away if it's not plucked. Do you agree, dearest? I imagine you do, since I know you have an obliging and a pliant character. I am coming, therefore, to bring you the young man, richly equipped by me as a herald. For in dealing with hetairas, a herald's staff ought to be sheathed in Babylonian gold.[6] But forgiving him for what's past, and being grateful for what's present, may you look kindly on your Charidemos forever after.

β'. ΗΡΑΣΘΗ ΤΙΣ ΚΟΡΗΣ, ΗΝ ΕΠΙΠΡΟΣΕΥΧΟΜΕΝΟΣ ΕΙΔΕ, ΚΑΙ ΤΑΥΤΗΙ ΠΡΟΣΠΕΠΟΝΘΩΣ ΕΠΙΣΤΕΛΛΕΙ

Εὐξίθεος Πυθιάδι

Ἐν τοῖς ἱεροῖς, ἔνθα τῶν παθῶν ἀπαλλαγὴν αἰτούμεθα τοὺς θεούς, δεινοτάτοις περιπέπτωκα πόνοις. ἔτι γὰρ ὑψοῦ προσανατείνων τὼ χεῖρε καὶ τὴν ἱκετείαν κατ' ἐμαυτὸν λαλῶν οὐκ οἶδ' ὅπως ἐξαίφνης ὑπὸ τοῦ Ἔρωτος ἐρραπίσθην. καὶ μετεστράφην πρός σέ, καὶ ἅμα τῇ θέᾳ τῷ σῷ τετόξευμαι κάλλει· ὡς γὰρ εἶδον, οὐχ οἷός τε ἦν τοὺς ὀφθαλμοὺς ἄλλοσε μεταφέρειν, σὺ δέ με θεωροῦντά σε κατιδοῦσα (τοῦτο δὴ τὸ σύνηθες ὑμῖν ταῖς ἐλευθέραις) ἠρέμα παρεκαλύψω, μετακλίνασα δ' οὖν τὴν δέρην ἐπὶ θάτερα προβέβληκας τοῦ προσώπου τὴν χεῖρα, παραφαίνουσα τῆς παρειᾶς ὀλίγον. δοῦλόν με θέλεις ἔχειν; ὡς ἐθελόδουλον ἔχε· φίλος γὰρ Πυθιάδος τίς, εἰ μή γε Ζεὺς ταῦρος ἢ χρυσὸς ἢ κύκνος γενόμενος διὰ σέ; ἀλλ' εἴθε μετὰ τῆς εὐπρεπείας ἐπαινέσομαί σε τῆς περὶ ἐμὲ προθυμίας, καὶ μὴ τρόπος ἀπειθὴς ἀνασοβήσῃ ὃν εὖ μάλα τεθήρακεν ἡ μορφή. ταύτην οὖν τὴν προσευχήν, ὦ θεοί, εἰ δοκεῖ, διανύσατε· ὄμνυμι δέ σοι, φιλτάτη, τίνα μέντοι θεῶν; ἢ βούλει μᾶλλον, <οὓς> ἐπηυξάμην ἀρτίως θεούς; ὡς ἄχρις ἂν ἐμοῦ δεσπόζειν ἐθέλοις (βουληθείης δὲ μέχρι παντός), ἐρωτικός σοι διατελέσω θεράπων.

γ'. ΓΑΜΕΤΗ ΡΗΤΟΡΟΣ ΑΜΙΞΙΑΣ ΑΙΤΙΑΤΑΙ ΤΟΝ ΑΝΔΡΑ

Γλυκέρα Φιλίννῃ

Οὐκ εὐτυχῶς, Φίλιννα, Στρεψιάδῃ τῷ σοφῷ ῥήτορι συνεζύγην· οὗτος γὰρ ἑκάστοτε παρὰ τὸν καιρὸν τῆς εὐνῆς πόρρω τῶν νυκτῶν πλάττεται περὶ πραγμάτων σκοπεῖσθαι, καὶ ἃς ἐδιδάχθη δίκας τηνικαῦτα προφασίζεται μελετᾶν, σχηματιζόμενος δὲ ὑπόκρισιν ἠρέμα τὼ χεῖρε κινεῖ καὶ ἄττα δήπου πρὸς ἑαυτὸν ψιθυρίζει. τί οὖν οὗτος ἔγημε κόρην καὶ λίαν ἀκμάζουσαν, μηδὲν δεόμενος γυναικός; ἢ ἵνα μοι τῶν πραγμάτων μεταδοίη, καὶ νύκτωρ αὐτῷ συνεπιζητήσω τοὺς νόμους; ἀλλ' εἴγε δικῶν γυμναστήριον τὴν ἡμῶν ποιεῖται παστάδα, ἐγὼ καὶ νεόνυμφος οὖσα ἀποκοιτήσω λοιπὸν καὶ καθευδήσω χωρίς. κἂν ἐπιμείνῃ

2.2. A Boy Fell in Love with a Girl Whom He Saw While Praying, and He Writes to Her in His Suffering

Euxitheos[1] to Pythias[2]

In the sanctuary, where we pray to the gods for relief from suffering, I fell victim to the most terrible pain. Even as my arms were still outstretched in prayer,[3] and I was supplicating the gods on my own behalf,[4] suddenly (god alone knows how) I was struck by Eros. I turned around toward you, and no sooner did I see you than I was pierced by the arrows of your beauty. The moment I beheld you, I could not tear my eyes away. And you, when you noticed my gaze, gently covered your face (for that is the custom among free women) and, turning your neck away from me, raised a hand before your head, so that only a bit of cheek remained visible. Do you want to have me as your slave?[5] I'd be that willingly. For who could be your lover, Pythias, if not Zeus, transformed[6] for your sake into a bull, or into gold, or into a swan? If only I could praise not just your beauty but your kindness toward me. Don't let hard-heartedness put to flight one whom your good looks have lured into the net. O gods, answer this prayer of mine, if it seems good to you. By which divinity, dearest, should I swear my oath to you? Or do you prefer those to whom I addressed my prayers just now? As long as you wish to be my master (and may you wish to be so for all time), I will continue to be your love slave.

2.3. The Wife of an Orator Accuses Her Husband of Avoiding Her Bed

Glykera to Philinna

Unlucky me, Philinna, to have married that learned orator Strepsiades. For whenever it's bedtime, he pretends to ponder legal matters deep into the night and then (of all times!) makes excuses about having to practice arguments he's learned by heart; and striking the pose of someone delivering a speech, he gesticulates in slow motion and whispers god knows what to himself. So why did this guy marry a girl—one in full flower, I might add—if he doesn't really need a woman? Was it so he could fill me in—on his cases? So I could conduct nocturnal research with him—on the laws? But if he turns our bedroom into a place for workouts in the penal code, I, though newly wed, will henceforth spend my nights elsewhere and sleep

πρὸς μὲν ἀλλότρια πράγματα κεχηνώς, μόνης δὲ τῆς κοινῆς ὑποθέσεως ἀμελῶν, ἕτερος ῥήτωρ τῆς ἐμῆς ἐπιμελήσεται δίκης. ἆρα κατάδηλον ὃ βούλομαι λέγειν; πάντως δήπου, ἐπεὶ ταῦτα γράφω συντόμως ἐκ τούτων συνιέναι καὶ τὰ λείποντα δυναμένη. ταῦτά μοι νόει καλῶς, ὦ γύναιον δηλαδὴ συμπαθὲς γυναικί, κἂν αἰδουμένη τὴν χρείαν οὐ μάλα σαφῶς ἐπιστέλλω, καὶ πειρῶ τὸ λυποῦν εἰς δύναμιν θεραπεύειν. σὲ γὰρ τὴν καλὴν προμνήστριαν χρή, καὶ ἄλλως ἐμὴν αὐτανεψιὰν οὖσαν, μὴ μόνον τὴν ἀρχὴν ἐσπουδακέναι τῷ γάμῳ, ἀλλὰ καὶ νῦν αὐτὸν σαλεύοντα διορθοῦσθαι. ἐγὼ γὰρ τὸν λύκον τῶν ὤτων ἔχω, ὃν οὔτε κατέχειν ἐπὶ πολὺ δυνατόν, οὔτε μὴν ἀκίνδυνον ἀφεῖναι, μή με δικορράφος ὢν ἀναίτιον αἰτιάσηται.

δ′. Ο ΤΗΙ ΔΟΥΛΗΙ ΠΡΟΣΚΑΡΤΕΡΩΝ ΤΕΩΣ ΑΣΧΟΛΟΥΜΕΝΗΙ

Ἑρμότιμος Ἀριστάρχῳ

Χθὲς ἐν τῷ στενωπῷ τὸ σύνηθες ὑπεσύριττον τῇ Δωρίδι. ἡ δὲ ὑπερκύψασα μόλις, ὡς λαμπρὸν ἀνέτειλεν ἄστρον, καὶ ἠρέμα φθεγγομένη φησίν· "ᾐσθόμην τοῦ συνθήματος, ὦ φιλότης· ἀλλὰ πρὸς τὴν κάθοδον ἀμηχανῶ. οὑμὸς πάρεστι δεσπότης· οὐ καταβέβηκεν οὗτος, ἵνα σοι τυχόν, γλυκύτατε, περιτύχω. μεῖνον, ἀνάμεινον· καταβήσομαι θᾶττον, καὶ τῆς βραχείας μελλήσεως ἕνεκα μειζόνως σε θεραπεύσω. καρτέρει πρὸς θεῶν. μὴ λίαν ἀθυμῶν τὴν παροῦσαν ἀπείπῃς ἑσπέραν, μηδὲ λύπει τὸν ἐνοικοῦντά μοι πόθον, ἵνα μὴ καὶ πυρωδεστέραν ὑφάψῃς τὴν φλόγα." τούτοις παραθαρρύνουσα, τοιαῦτα ψυχαγωγοῦσα καὶ ὥσπερ βέλη τοὺς λόγους ἀφεῖσα πέπεικεν, εἰ δέοι, καὶ μέχρι μέσων ἀναμεῖναι νυκτῶν. ὅμως ὑδροφορῆσαι πιθανῶς προφασισαμένη κατέβη ταχύ, ἐπὶ λαιοῦ τοῖν ὤμοιν κομίζουσα τὴν κάλπιν. καί μοι καὶ οὕτως ἀνεφάνη καλή, ὥσπερ εἰ χρυσοῦν τινα περιέκειτο κόσμον. ἡ δὲ κόμη, βαβαὶ τῆς ἀγλαΐας· ὡς τετανόθριξ ἡ παῖς. τῶν μὲν οὖν ὀφρύων ἐμμέτρως ἀνέσταλται, τοῦ δὲ αὐχένος ἐπιχαρίτως καθήπλωται καὶ τοῖν ὤμοιν· αἱ δὲ παρειαὶ τὸν ἀπὸ τῶν ὀμμάτων ἵμερον ὑποδέχονται, ὃν φιλῆσαι μὲν ἥδιστον, ἀπαγγεῖλαι δὲ οὐ ῥάδιον. ἔφη δ' οὖν· "ἕως ἀλλήλους ἔχομεν, μὴ παραναλώσωμεν ἣν δίδωσιν ἡμῖν ὁ καιρὸς ὀξύρροπον ἐξουσίαν." ἅσμενοι τοίνυν περιπλακέντες ἀλλήλοις ἐρασμιώτερον τὰ ἐπὶ τούτοις ἐδρῶμεν· ἥδιον γὰρ καὶ σφόδρα ποθεινὸς μετὰ δή τινα συμβᾶσαν δυσκολίαν τοῖς ἐρῶσιν ὁ γάμος.

apart. And if he persists, has eyes only for other affairs, and neglects our common cause alone, well, then another orator can handle my case, if you know what I mean.... No doubt you do, as I'm writing to someone who can understand my shorthand and read between the lines. Give it some good thought—woman to woman, you're clearly sympathetic—even if, out of shame, my letter doesn't express my needs outright; and do try to find a cure for my affliction as best you can. For it's not enough that you, my pretty matchmaker and cousin to boot, have busied yourself setting up my marriage; no, you've also got to set it straight again, now that it's reeling. For I am grasping a wolf by its ears,[1] and I cannot hold him long or let him loose without danger, lest (innocent though I am) that wretched shyster try to sue me.

2.4. A Man Patiently Waits for a Servant Girl While She Is Busy Working

Hermotimos to Aristarchos

Yesterday, in the alleyway, I whistled the usual signal to Doris.[1] When she managed, after great effort, to pop her head out the window, like a bright star rising,[2] she whispered: "I heard your signal, darling, but I see no way to get down to you. My master is here: he hasn't gone out so I could possibly meet you, sweetie. Wait, please wait. I'll come down soon and will tend to you all the more lovingly for this brief delay. By the gods, do persevere. Don't lose hope and give up on the present evening, and don't vex the desire that dwells inside me, lest you kindle an even hotter flame." Thus encouraging and beguiling, she aimed her words like arrows, persuading me to wait even till the dead of night, if need be. But on the clever pretext of having to fetch water, she came down soon, bearing a pitcher on her left shoulder. But she might as well have been adorned with golden jewelry, so lovely did she appear to me. Her hair—oh, what splendor! It simply stretches on forever. Pulled back harmoniously from her brows, it spreads over her neck and shoulders with such charm. Her cheeks reflect back the desire emanating from her eyes, most pleasurable to kiss, yet hard to describe.[3] "For as long as we're together," she said, "don't let us squander the fleeting chance the moment grants us." Happily, then, we embraced, and with greater passion we did what came next.[4] For after certain difficulties lovers find it all the sweeter and more desirable to have sex.

ε'. ΠΑΡΘΕΝΟΣ ΕΡΩΣΑ ΚΙΘΑΡΩΙΔΟΥ

Παρθενὶς Ἀρπεδόνῃ

Εὖγε τῆς φωνῆς, εὖγε τῆς λύρας. ὡς ἄμφω μουσικώτατα συνηχεῖ, καὶ πρόσχορ-
δος ἡ γλῶττα τοῖς κρούμασι. Μουσῶν τε καὶ Χαρίτων ἡ κρᾶσις, μάλα τοῦτο
ἀληθές. πλῆρες δὲ μουσικῆς ἐννοίας τὸ βλέμμα καὶ διασκέψεως τῶν μελῶν. τὸ
δὲ πρόσωπον τοῦ νέου χαριέντως ἀτενίζοντος εἰς ἐμὲ ὑπὲρ τὰ μέλη καταθέλγει
μου τὴν ψυχήν. εἰ μὴ τοιοῦτος ἦν Ἀχιλλεύς, ὃν ἔμαθον ἐκ τῶν οἴκοι πινάκων,
οὐκ ἦν ἄρα ὄντως καλός· εἰ μὴ τοιαῦτα κεκιθάρικεν, οὐκ ἦν μουσικὸς τοῦ Χεί-
ρωνος ζηλωτής. εἴθε ποθήσειεν ἐμὲ καὶ ἀντιφιλοῦντα θεάσομαι. τολμηρὸν ἔφην·
τίς γὰρ ἂν τούτῳ δόξειε καλή, εἰ μὴ φιλανθρώποις αὐτὴν ὄμμασιν ἴδοι; ὡς ἡδὺ
τὸ γειτόνημα, νὴ τὰς Μούσας. ἀλλὰ πικρὰς ὀδύνας μεταξύ πως ᾐσθόμην. πυκνὰ
παλλομένης ἐφάπτομαι τῆς καρδίας, καὶ δεινῶς ἐκπηδᾷ καὶ φλέγεσθαί μοι
δοκεῖ. τοτὲ μὲν οὖν εἰς τὰ γόνατα ἡ κεφαλὴ βρίθει, τοτὲ δὲ εἰς ὦμον ἐγκλίνει·
θεωροῦσα δὲ τὸν καλὸν αἰδοῦμαι, φοβοῦμαι, ὑφ' ἡδονῆς πνευστιῶ. ὦ γλυκύ-
τατον πῦρ· τί ποτε ἄρα μοι πεφοίτηκεν ἔνδον; ὡς ἐγὼ θαμὰ ἀνιῶμαι, καὶ οὐκ
οἶδα, ἐφ' ᾧ τοῦτό γε πάσχω. ἐκβόσκεται γάρ μέ τις ἀνερμήνευτος ὀδύνη, καὶ
δακρύων ἀνεπίσχετοι πηγαὶ καταρρέουσι τῶν παρειῶν·

ποικίλα τῆς διανοίας ὑπεκπηδᾷ μοι κινήματα, καθάπερ αἴγλη τις ἡλίου
πάλλεται συχνὰ περὶ τοῖχον ἐξ ὕδατος ἀνταυγοῦσα κατὰ σκαφίδος ἢ λέβη-
τος κεχυμένου καὶ ἀστάτῳ φορᾷ τὴν εὐκίνητον συστροφὴν ἀπεικονίζεται τῶν
ὑδάτων. ἢ τοῦτο μᾶλλον, ὅνπερ φασίν, ἔρως; Ἔρωτος ὁ πυρσὸς καὶ μέχρι τοῦ
ἥπατος διελήλυθεν εἰσρυείς. καὶ τί δὴ καταλιπὼν ἐκεῖνος ὁ δᾳδοῦχος θεὸς τὰς
ἐπιτηδείας αὐτῷ καὶ συνήθεις ἀμύητον βιάζεται κόρην, καὶ πολεμεῖ παιδισκάριον ἄωρον Ἀφροδίτης, ἔτι θαλαμευόμενον, ἔτι φρουρουμένην, καὶ μόλις
ὑπὸ φύλαξιν ἔσθ' ὅπη προκύπτουσαν τῆς οἰκίας; εὐδαίμων παρθένος, ἥτις
ἄνευ φροντίδων ἐρωτικῶν ζῇ, μόνης ἐπιμελὴς τῆς ταλασίας. αἰσχύνομαι τὸ
πάθος, ἐγκαλύπτομαι τὴν νόσον, δέδοικα σύμβουλον προσλαβέσθαι· ταῖς γὰρ
ἐμαῖς θεραπαινίσιν οὐ μάλα θαρρῶ. ὦ τῆς ἀπορίας, δι' ἣν περιπατῶ τρίβουσα
τὰς χεῖρας, ὅτε καὶ τὸ πάθος ἐπείγει. καὶ οὔτε θεραπείαν οὔτε λήθην αὐτοῦ
βραχεῖαν ἔνεστί μοι λαμβάνειν· κατάντικρυς μὲν γὰρ ὁ νέος ὁ γλυκὺς πολέμιος
ἥδιστα μελῳδεῖ, ἐγὼ δὲ οὐδὲ βουλὴν πρὸς τὸ πρακτέον οἵα τέ εἰμι παντελῶς
ἐξευρεῖν. πῶς γὰρ ἡ δειλαία, περὶ πράγματος σκοπουμένη, οὗ καὶ τὴν φύσιν

2.5. A Girl in Love with a Cithara Player

Parthenis[1] to Harpedone[2]

Ah, what a voice! Ah, what a lyre! How the two of them resound most musically, and how attuned his tongue is to the chords! Truly it mingles the Muses with the Graces. His gaze exudes musical understanding and hard-won skill in singing.[3] And when he looks at me sweetly, the youth's face puts an even greater spell on my soul than his songs. If Achilles[4] did not resemble him—that hero whom I learned about from the pictures at home—then he was not truly beautiful. If he couldn't play the lyre like that, then Chiron's pupil[5] must have been tone-deaf. Oh, if only he longed for me as well, and I could see him love me back. No, I've said too much. For could any girl seem beautiful to him if she were not already the object of his kind regard? How sweet it is to live next door to him, by the Muses. But in the midst of such sweetness I've also, I suppose, felt bitter pangs. I clasp my ever-pounding chest, and the heart within leaps terribly and seems to me ablaze. At times my head grows heavy, sinking to my knees; at times it simply droops toward my shoulder.[6] He's so beautiful, I blush to look at him, I shrink in fear, I'm breathless with pleasure. O sweetest flame! What in the world has gotten into me? I'm in continual distress, and I don't know why I'm suffering like this. An incomprehensible pain is eating away at me, and unstoppable streams of tears are flooding my cheeks.

My thoughts leap now this way, now that, as a ray of sunshine flickers on a wall when water newly poured into a pail or basin casts its reflection, and with its restless motion it mirrors water's graceful twists and turns.[7] Or is this maybe what they call love? The blazing fire of love has invaded deep into my guts. Why has the torch-bearing god[8] left his usual lady friends? Why is he coercing a girl who knows nothing of his mysteries? Why does he wage war against a child unripe for Aphrodite, one still shut away at home, still watched, and barely even able to peek out of the house for all the guards? Happy the girl who lives without the cares of love, whose only concern is her spindle. I'm ashamed of my suffering, I cover up my illness, I'm afraid of seeking anyone's advice. I don't trust my handmaids. I don't know what to do, and so I wander about wringing my hands, as my anguish urges me on. I can't find a remedy; I can't even stop thinking about it for a moment. For right across from me that youth, my sweet enemy, is singing the loveliest songs, while I am utterly unable even to form a plan for what to do. For how could a wretched girl like me find a solution, when trying to

ἠγνόηκα καὶ τοὺς τρόπους, ἅτε ἀνομίλητος μὲν παιδείας ἐρωτικῆς, ἀνομίλητος δὲ συνουσίας;

ἐρρέτω αἰδώς, ἐρρέτω σωφροσύνη, ἐρρέτω καὶ τὸ σεμνὸν τῆς ὀδυνηρᾶς ἐμοὶ παρθενίας. ὑπαισθάνομαι τῆς φύσεως βουλομένης, ἧ νόμων ὡς ἔοικεν οὐδὲν μέλει. μικρὸν ἀπερυθριάσω καὶ τὴν ἐμὴν ἴσως ἐκ τῆς περιωδυνίας ἀνακτῶμαι ψυχήν. ἡδέως μάλα ἔπταρον μεταξὺ γράφουσα. ἆρα ὁ νέος, τοὐμὸν μέλημα, διεμνημόνευσέ μου; εἴθε καὶ δι' ἑαυτῶν ἤδη, καὶ μὴ μόνων τῶν ὀφθαλμῶν, ἀλλὰ καὶ δι' ὅλων ἀπολαύσομεν τῶν σωμάτων. σὺ τοίνυν, Ἀρπεδόνη (πρὸς σὲ γὰρ ἐξεπίτηδες, ὡς ἔχω πάθους, ἀπήγγειλα τὴν ὑπόπικρον τῶν βελῶν ἡδονήν), ἧκέ μοι σύμβουλος περὶ τούτων, προφασισαμένη στήμονα τυχὸν ἢ κρόκην ἢ γοῦν ἄλλο τι τῶν μάλιστα γυναιξὶν ἀνηκόντων. ἔρρωσο, καὶ πρὸς τοῦ Ἔρωτος, ὃν ἐπόμνυσθαι πρῶτον μεμάθηκα παρ' αὐτοῦ, μυστήριά σοι ταῦτα γεγράφθω.

ϛ'. ΝΕΟΣ ΥΠ' ΑΝΤΕΡΑΣΤΟΥ ΤΗΣ ΦΙΛΗΣ ΠΑΡΕΚΒΕΒΛΗΜΕΝΟΣ

... <Φορμίωνι>

Ὡς ἐρώμενος αὐθαδέστερον ὑπεραίρῃ καὶ πεφρόνηκας μέγα καὶ σοβαρώτερος γέγονας τὴν ὀφρύν, ἀεροβατεῖς δὲ μετάρσιος ταῖς φαντασίαις καὶ ὑπερορᾷς ἡμῶν τῶν βαδιζόντων χαμαί, καὶ ὡς αὐλητρίδος υἱὸς ἐξαίρεις τὰς γνάθους, καὶ γίνεταί σοι μεῖζον τὸ φύσημα τοῦ φυσήματος τῆς μητρός. πόθεν δὲ ποθεῖσθαι οὕτω ταχὺ καὶ ῥᾳδίως ἐπείσθης; ἢ μᾶλλον, ὦ θαυμάσιε Φορμίων, ὡς ἀξιέραστον ἔχων τὴν ὄψιν; τοιαύτην ἔχοι κἀκείνη ἀξία γε οὖσα· καὶ ὄναισθέ γε δικαίως ἀλλήλων ἐπὶ μήκιστον χρόνον, καὶ γένοιτο παιδίον ὑμῖν ὅμοιον τῷ πατρί. εὗρεν οὖν ἡ μάχαιρα κολεὸν ἄξιον ἑαυτῆς. νενίκηκάς με τὴν ἐμὴν ἐρωμένην λαβών, δι' ἐμοῦ τε παριὼν ἐξεπίτηδες οὐκ ἀγελαστὶ τονθορύζεις, ἀλλ' ἡδέως ἐπεγγελᾷς ὑβριστήν τινα γέλωτα, καὶ ἀλαζονευόμενος τὼ χεῖρε σοβεῖς, καὶ χαίρων ἐπιτωθάζεις ἐμοί, μέγα δὲ καγχάζεις ὅτι με τῆς φίλης ἐκβέβληκας κατὰ κράτος. ἀλλ' ἔγωγέ σοι ἥδιστον ἐπιχαίρω, ὅτι σε νῦν ἔνδον εἰσβέβληκα παρ' ἐκείνην, καὶ ἥτταν ὑπέστην ἐγὼ τῆς σῆς, φασί, Καδμείας νίκης ἀμείνω· φανερὸν γὰρ ὡς ἐν πονηραῖς ἁμίλλαις ἀθλιώτερος ὁ νικήσας.

figure out a thing whose nature and ways I don't know, unschooled as I am in love, unschooled in sex?

Away with shame; away, good sense; away, the painful pride of maidenhood![9] What I feel is nature's will, which pays no heed, it seems, to laws. For a time, I shall forget how to blush and maybe save my soul from its dreadful suffering. Ha, sweet coincidence: I sneezed while writing. Did the youth, my darling, remember me in his thoughts? Oh, if only we could enjoy each other already, and not only with our eyes, but in the flesh. Now, Harpedone (since I've told you on purpose of the slightly bitter pleasure of love's arrows), come be my advisor in these things, giving as your excuse that you're out trying to find some thread, perhaps, or yarn,[10] or something else that women really need for work. Farewell, and by Eros, the very god who taught me to invoke his name in oaths, don't breathe a word about what I've written; protect it as you would the mysteries.[11]

2.6. A Young Man Supplanted in His Girlfriend's Affection by a Rival

… \<to Phormion\>

Just because you're the one she loves, you go around giving yourself airs, you think you're so great, and your frown itself has started to frown; your thoughts are sky-high,[1] and you look down on us who walk on the ground below; and son of a flute girl that you are, you thrust out your cheeks, inflating them further than your mother ever could. But how did you manage to convince yourself with such speed and ease that you are desirable? Or do you think you have a face that kindles the flame of love, O wondrous Phormion? May her face be a match for yours;[2] it would serve her right. May you enjoy the fruits of each other's company for a long, long time,[3] and may your child be the spitting image of its father.[4] I guess the sword has found the sheath it deserves.[5] You were the winner in snatching away my beloved, and walking by me deliberately, you don't just mutter something with a smirk—no, you exult over me with a laugh that's full of hubris, you wave your arms about triumphantly, you gleefully mock me, and you laugh out loud because you kicked me out by force from my beloved. But believe me, I've got the last laugh, because I kicked you now into her clutches, and my defeat is better than your so-called Cadmeian victory.[6] For it's clear that when you compete for a rotten prize, the winner is the bigger loser.

ζ΄. ΠΕΡΙ ΔΟΥΛΗΣ ΦΙΛΟΥΣΗΣ ΤΟΝ ΠΡΟΣΦΘΕΙΡΟΜΕΝΟΝ ΤΗΙ ΚΕΚΤΗΜΕΝΗΙ

Τερψίων Πολυκλεῖ

Θεράπαινά τις παρθένος τοῦ μοιχοῦ τῆς δεσποίνης ἠράσθη· διακονουμένη γὰρ ἀμφοῖν τὰ δοκοῦντα ταύτην ἔλαχε τοῦ ἔρωτος ἀφορμήν. πολλάκις οὖν αὐτῶν ἐρωτικῶς ὁμιλούντων ἀλλήλοις ἠκροᾶτο, πλησίον ὡς φύλαξ παρισταμένη καὶ προορῶσα μή τις ἐξαίφνης ἀναφανείη κατάσκοπος. καί που καὶ συμπλεχθέντας αὐτοὺς εἶδεν ἡ κόρη, καὶ δι᾽ ἀκοῆς τε καὶ θέας ὤλισθεν Ἔρως ἐπὶ τὴν ἐκείνης ψυχὴν αὐτῇ λαμπάδι καὶ τόξοις. καὶ πρὸς τὴν τύχην ἐσχετλίαζεν ἡ παιδίσκη, ὅτι δὴ καὶ αὐτὸς δεδούλωται τῆς δουλείας ὁ ἔρως· οὐ γὰρ εἶχε παρρησίαν τῶν αὐτῶν μετασχεῖν τῇ δεσποίνῃ, ἀλλὰ μόνου τοῦ ἔρωτος ἐκοινώνει τῇ κεκτημένῃ. τί οὖν ἡ κόρη; οὐ γὰρ ἀμήχανον αὐτὴν ἀφῆκεν ὁ Ἔρως. ἀποσταλεῖσα προσκαλέσασθαι τὸν μοιχὸν ἔφη πρὸς ἐκεῖνον ἁπλῶς, μηδὲν ποικίλλουσα· "εἰ βούλει, φίλτατε, ἐμὲ συμπράττειν καὶ διακονεῖσθαί σοι πάλιν προθύμως—ἀλλὰ τί σοι λέξω; τὸν ἐμὸν ὡς ἐρωτικὸς ἤδη νενόηκας πόθον. ἆρα δοκῶ σοι καλὴ καὶ μετὰ τὴν σὴν εὐμορφίαν ἀρέσκω σοι; τί φής; ποιήσεις ἤδη; ποιήσεις, οἶδα ἐγώ."

ὁ δ᾽ οὖν νέος (καλὴ γὰρ ἦν καὶ παρθένος) ἅμα ἔπος ἅμα ἔργον ἄσμενος αὐτίκα μάλα τὴν αἴτησιν τῆς κόρης ἐπλήρου, περικρατῶν ὀμφάκια τοῦ στέρνου τὰ μῆλα καὶ φιλημάτων ἀπολαύων ἅμα γνησίων· φιλήματα γὰρ ἕωλα μὲν τὰ τῶν γυναικῶν, ἄπιστα δὲ τὰ τῶν ἑταίρων, ἀψευδῆ δὲ τὰ τῶν παρθένων, ἐοικότα τοῖς σφετέροις ἤθεσι. μέμικται δὲ ἁπαλῷ μὲν ἱδρῶτι, θερμῷ δὲ καὶ πολλῷ τῷ τοῦ πνεύματος ῥεύματι {τὸ δὲ ἆσθμα πυκνόν}. ἐγγὺς μὲν <γὰρ> τοῦ στόματος ἡ καρδία, ἡ δὲ ψυχὴ τῶν θυρῶν· εἰ δὲ τὴν χεῖρα τῷ στέρνῳ προσαγάγῃς, ὄψει τὸ πήδημα. ταῦτα μὲν οὖν ἐκεῖνοι· ἡ δὲ κεκτημένη πανούργως ἐπέστη τοῖς τελουμένοις, ἠρέμα βαδίζουσα καὶ κτύπου χωρίς, καὶ ζηλοτυποῦσα τὴν παιδίσκην τῆς κόμης ἐξεῖλκεν. ἡ δὲ στένουσά φησιν· "μὴ γὰρ ἡ τύχη σὺν τῷ σώματι κατεδούλωσε τὴν ψυχήν. ἐπιτεθύμηκα· ἔξεστι γάρ. παῦσαι πρὸς θεῶν. ὡς ἐρῶσαν δίκαιόν σε μᾶλλον ὑπεραλγῆσαι ποθούσης. μὴ τοίνυν ἀτιμάσῃς, ὦ δέσποινα, τὸν ἐμόν τε καὶ σὸν δεσπότην Ἔρωτα, ἵνα μὴ ταῖς σαῖς ἐπιθυμίαις ὀνειδίζουσα λάθοις. καὶ σὺ γὰρ ἐκείνῳ δουλεύεις, κἀγώ τε καὶ σὺ τὸν αὐτὸν ἕλκομεν ζυγόν." ταῦτα μὲν ἡ παῖς, ἡ δὲ κεκτημένη πρὸς τὸν νέον λάθρα φησί, τῆς δεξιᾶς αὐτοῦ λαβομένη, "Σικελὸς ὀμφακίζει, Ἐμπεδόκλεις,

2.7. ABOUT A SLAVE GIRL ENAMORED
WITH HER MISTRESS'S LOVER

Terpsion[1] to Polykles[2]

A serving girl fell in love with her lady's paramour. It was while rendering both of them the service that was expected that she experienced the onset of desire. Often she overheard them exchange amorous whispers as she stood nearby as a guard and kept watch lest someone suddenly appear. And the girl likely saw them entwined in each other's arms, so it was through what she heard and beheld that Eros slipped into her soul with his torch and arrows. The girl lamented her fate, because a slave's desire is itself enslaved. For she was not free to partake in the same joys as her mistress; the only thing they had in common was their longing. So what did the girl do? Eros had not left her helpless. Upon being sent to invite the lover for a rendezvous, she said to him simply and without embellishing, "If you want me to be a willing ally and servant to you in the future, darling—but why beat around the bush? As a connoisseur of desire, you've already noticed my passion. Do I seem pretty to you, and do my looks please you, even if they don't equal your own? What do you say? Are you willing to do it already? You are willing, I'm sure."

No sooner said than done—the youth, seeing as the girl was pretty and a virgin, gladly fulfilled her request without delay. He seized the unripe apples of her chest and enjoyed kisses that were genuine. For a matron's kisses are already stale, a hetaira's treacherous, those of a virgin without guile, each reflecting their respective character. Hers are mingled with dewy sweat, and her breath comes hot and in full stream. For her heart is close to her mouth, the soul to its portals. If you put your hand on her chest, you'll see how it leaps. And so it was with them. But the mistress deviously discovered them as they performed the rites of love. She crept quietly without a sound, and filled with jealous rage she dragged the girl off by the hair. But she, sobbing, said, "Fate did not enslave my soul along with my body. I felt desire. No law against that. Stop, by the gods. The right thing would be if you, as a lover, rather felt pain for one in love. Do not, O mistress, dishonor Eros, who is my master as well as yours, lest you belittle your own desires without realizing it. For you too are his slave; you and I are laboring under the same yoke." Thus the girl. The mistress, however, spoke aside to the youth, taking hold of his right hand: "You are a veritable Empedocles, a Sicilian filching unripe grapes[3] by plucking a girl before her

παρατρυγῶν παιδισκάριον <ἄωρον> καὶ τοῦ φιλήματος ἀμαθές. παρθένος γάρ,
ἅτε τῆς Ἀφροδίτης ἀμύητος ἔτι, τὴν συνουσίαν ἀτερπής ἐστι καὶ δύσκοιτος,
ἀγνοοῦσα τὴν ἐπὶ τῆς εὐνῆς κολακείαν. γυνὴ δέ, οἵαπερ ἐγώ, τῶν ἀφροδισίων
ἱκανὴν ἔχουσα πεῖραν, ὁμοίως ἑαυτήν τε καὶ τὸν ποθοῦντα λίαν εὐφραίνει, καὶ
γυνὴ μὲν καταφιλεῖ, παρθένος δὲ καταφιλεῖται. καὶ τοῦτο μὲν ἔγνως· εἰ δὲ
τὰ νῦν ἐπιλέλησαι, δεῦρο, φίλτατε, κἀγώ σε ἥδιστα δίς τε καὶ τρὶς τῶν ἐμῶν
ἀναμνήσω."

η΄. ΠΕΝΘΕΡΑΣ ΕΡΑΣΤΗΣ ΕΓΚΡΑΤΩΣ
ΑΠΟΜΑΧΕΤΑΙ ΠΡΟΣ ΤΟΝ ΠΟΘΟΝ

Θεοκλῆς Ὑπερείδῃ

Ἤρων τῆς Ἀριγνώτης, παρθένου καλῆς. ταύτην μοι νομίμως κατενεγύησαν οἱ
τεκόντες, καὶ ἦν ὄντως ἐπαφρόδιτος ὁ γάμος· ἐρωμένης γὰρ ἀπέλαυον γαμετῆς.
καὶ τὴν συνάφειαν ἡγούμην βεβαίαν, γινώσκων ὡς ἀσφαλέστερος καθίστα-
ται γάμος ἐκ πόθου τινὸς τὴν πρόφασιν εὐτυχήσας. ἀλλ᾽ ὁ βάσκανος Ἔρως
ἐνήλλαξέ μου τὸν πόθον, καὶ τῆς πενθερᾶς ἀντ᾽ ἐκείνης ἐρῶ. τί οὖν πράξω; πῶς
ἀναιδῶς πρὸς ἐρωμένην, πῶς ἐπιεικῶς πρὸς πενθερὰν ἐκλαλήσω; αὕτη με τὸν
κηδεστὴν ἐξ εὐνοίας παῖδα καλεῖ. πῶς οὖν διαλέξομαι γυναικί, ἣν πολλάκις
μητέρα προσεῖπον; τοιγαροῦν κἂν τύχω κἂν ἀποτύχω, διχόθεν ἐγὼ δυστυχής·
ὑμεῖς τοίνυν, ὦ θεοί, ἀποτρόπαιοί γε ὄντες τὸ δυσσεβὲς ἀποτρέψετε. θυγατρὶ
καὶ τεκούσῃ μήποτε συμμιγείην.

θ΄. ΝΕΟΣ ΠΡΟΣ ΕΠΙΟΡΚΟΝ ΕΡΩΜΕΝΗΝ ΔΕΔΙΩΣ, ΜΗ ΤΙ
ΠΡΟΣ ΤΗΣ ΕΠΙΟΡΚΙΑΣ ΕΚΕΙΝΗ ΠΕΙΣΕΤΑΙ ΧΑΛΕΠΟΝ

Διονυσόδωρος Ἀμπελίδι

Σὺ μὲν ἴσως οἴει βαρύνεσθαί με δεινῶς, ὅτι δή με τοσοῦτον ἐρῶντα κατέλι-
πες. ἐμοὶ δὲ τούτου, νὴ τὸ σὸν πρόσωπον, βραχεῖα φροντὶς πρὸς ἕτερόν γε
μεῖζον κακόν, ἐπείπερ ὡς ἁπλουστάτη καὶ νέα περιφρονοῦσα τηλικοῦτον ὅρκον
παρέβης. ἀλλὰ τοὐμὸν μέρος ἀνυπεύθυνος εἴης τοῖς ὁρκίοις θεοῖς, εἰ καὶ σὺ
ποθοῦντα μὴ στέργεις, μηδὲ συνθήκας ἔγνως ἐνωμότους φυλάττειν. ἀλλ᾽ ἔγωγε
δέδοικα (εἰρήσεται γάρ, κἂν ἀπεύχωμαι), μή τινά σοι ποινὴν ἀντεπαγάγωσιν

time, who doesn't even know how to kiss yet. For a virgin, still uninitiated in the rites of Aphrodite, gives no joy in sex and is a useless bedmate, ignorant as she is of the flattery that delights between the sheets. But a woman like me, who has enough experience in the games of Aphrodite, brings tremendous pleasure to herself and her lover alike. A woman, after all, knows how to kiss; a girl, only to be kissed. But you've come to understand that, I suppose. Yet if you've forgotten now, come here, darling, and I'll remind you very sweetly two or three times over of what I've got to offer."

2.8. A MAN IN LOVE WITH HIS MOTHER-IN-LAW STRUGGLES MIGHTILY TO FIGHT OFF THE URGE

Theokles[1] to Hypereides[2]

I was in love with Arignote,[3] a beautiful girl. Her parents betrothed her to me as the law required, and it was truly a match made in heaven. For I got to enjoy a bride who was my beloved. And I considered our union secure, knowing that a marriage stands on a sturdier foundation if it has the good fortune to be born out of desire. But spiteful Eros replaced my passion with another; instead of her, I love my mother-in-law. So what should I do? How will I speak freely to her as to a beloved, how with the respect owed to a mother-in-law? Me, her in-law, she affectionately calls son. So how should I talk to a woman whom I have often addressed as mother? Whether I get her or not, either way I am wretched. You then, O gods, in that you can ward off evil, prevent this impiety. May I never sleep with both a daughter and her mother!

2.9. A YOUTH TO HIS PERJURED BELOVED, FEARING THAT SOMETHING BAD MIGHT HAPPEN TO HER BECAUSE OF HER PERJURY

Dionysodoros[1] to Ampelis[2]

Perhaps you think I'm utterly crushed because you abandoned me, who loved you so. But this barely matters to me, yes, by that pretty face of yours, compared with the greater evil that, naïve and youthful as you are, you held so weighty an oath in contempt and trampled it. Still I, for my part, hope you are not held accountable by the oath-enforcing gods, even if you do not cherish your lover and did not know how to keep a sworn pact. I'm afraid, though (god forbid it happen, but I've got to say it), that the gods

οἱ θεοί. καὶ ἀνιαρότερον ἔσται μοι τοῦτο ἢ τῆς σῆς διαπεπτωκέναι φιλίας. ἐμὸν <τὸ> ἀτύχημα τοῦτο· σὲ δὲ τὸ παράπαν οὐ ψέγω· τοιγαροῦν ἱκετεύων ὑπὲρ σοῦ τὴν Δίκην οὔποτ' ἄν, ὦ φιλτάτη, παυσαίμην, μηδαμῶς αὐτὴν εἰς τιμωρίαν τῶν ἡμαρτημένων ἐλθεῖν, ἀλλὰ καὶ αὖθις ἀδικούσης, εἴ γέ σοι τοῦτο φίλον, ἀνέχεσθαι πάλιν καὶ συγγνώμην ἀπονέμειν τῇ σῇ πρέπουσαν ἡλικίᾳ· ἀνεκτὸν γὰρ ἐμοὶ τὸν ἐμὸν ἔρωτα φέρειν καὶ μή σε μοχθηρόν τι πεπονθυῖαν ὁρᾶν. ἔρρωσο. κἂν ἀδικῇς, οἱ θεοὶ συγγνώμονες εἶεν. τίς ἂν οὖν, πρὸς Διός, εὐφημότερον ἐπέστειλεν ἀδικούμενος;

ι′. ΖΩΓΡΑΦΟΣ ΕΙΚΟΝΟΣ ΚΟΡΗΣ ΠΑΡ' ΑΥΤΟΥ ΓΕΓΡΑΜΜΕΝΗΣ ΕΡΩΝ

Φιλοπίναξ Χρωματίωνι

Καλὴν γέγραφα κόρην, καὶ τῆς ἐμῆς ἡράσθην γραφῆς. ἡ τέχνη τὸν πόθον, οὐκ Ἀφροδίτης τὸ βέλος· ἐκ τῆς ἐμῆς ἐγὼ κατατοξεύομαι δεξιᾶς. ὡς ἀτυχής, <ὃς> οὐ γέγονα τὴν γραφικὴν ἀφυής· οὐ γὰρ αἰσχρᾶς εἰκόνος ἡράσθην. νῦν δὲ ὅσον μέ τις ἀποθαυμάζει τῆς τέχνης, τοσοῦτον κατοικτείρει τοῦ πόθου· οὐ γὰρ ἂν ἧττον δόξαιμι κακοδαίμων ἐραστὴς ἢ σοφὸς εἶναι τεχνίτης. ἀλλὰ τί λίαν ὀδύρομαι καὶ τὴν ἐμὴν καταμέμφομαι δεξιάν; ἐκ τῶν πινάκων ἐπίσταμαι Φαίδραν, Νάρκισσον, Πασιφάην· τῇ μὲν οὐκ ἀεὶ παρῆν ὁ τῆς Ἀμαζόνος, ἡ δὲ καθόλου παρὰ φύσιν ἐπόθει, ὁ δὲ κυνηγέτης, εἰ τῇ πηγῇ προσῆγε τὴν χεῖρα, διεχέχυτο ἂν ὁ ποθούμενος καὶ παρέρρει τῶν δακτύλων· ἡ μὲν γὰρ πηγὴ γράφει τὸν Νάρκισσον, ἡ δὲ γραφὴ καὶ τὴν πηγὴν καὶ τὸν Νάρκισσον οἷον διψῶντα τοῦ κάλλους. ἐμοὶ δὲ ὅσον ἐθέλω, πάρεστιν ἡ φιλτάτη, καὶ κόρη τὸ φαινόμενον εὐπρεπής, κἂν τὴν χεῖρα προσάξω, ἀσύγχυτος ἐπιμένει βεβαίως, καὶ τῆς οἰκείας μορφῆς οὐκ ἐξίσταται.

ἡδὺ προσγελᾷ καὶ μικρὸν ὑποκέχηνε, καὶ εἴποις ἂν ὡς ἐπ' ἄκρων τῶν χειλῶν προκύπτει τις λόγος καὶ ὅσον οὔπω τοῦ στόματος ἐκπηδᾷ. ἐγὼ δὲ καὶ τὴν ἀκοὴν προσεπέλασα πολλάκις ὠτακουστῶν, τί ποτε ἄρα βούλεται ψιθυρίζειν, ἀποτυχὼν δὲ τοῦ λόγου πεφίληκα τὸ στόμα, τῶν παρειῶν τὰς κάλυκας, τῶν βλεφάρων τὴν χάριν, καὶ ὁμιλεῖν ἐρωτικῶς προτρέπω τὴν κόρην. ἡ δὲ καθάπερ ἑταίρα τὸν ἐραστὴν ὑποκνίζουσα σιωπᾷ. ἐπέθηκα τῇ κλίνῃ, ἠγκαλισάμην, ἐπιβέβληκα τῷ στήθει, ἵνα τυχὸν τὸν ἔνδον ἔρωτα θεραπεύσῃ, καὶ πλέον ἐπιμέμηνα τῇ γραφῇ. αἰσθάνομαι πάλιν τῆς παραπληξίας, καὶ κινδυνεύω τὴν ἐμὴν προσαπολέσαι ψυχὴν δι' ἄψυχον ἐρωμένην. χείλη μὲν φαίνει

will punish you for it. And this will cause me greater grief than having fallen from your grace. That is my tragedy. But I don't blame you for it in the least. Therefore, dearest, I will not stop supplicating Dike[3] on your behalf never to take vengeance on your sins but, even if it pleases you to transgress again, to put up with it once more and grant forgiveness appropriate to your youth. For I can bear my love, if I don't have to see you suffer some hardship. Farewell. And if you stray, may the gods be forgiving. By Zeus, has ever a lover wronged written so kind a note?

2.10. A Painter in Love with the Image of a Girl That He Himself Has Painted

Philopinax[1] to Chromation[2]

I painted a beautiful girl—and fell in love with my own painting. Art, not Aphrodite's arrow, filled me with longing. I was shot by my own hand! O miserable me—to be born with a talent for painting! After all, I would not have fallen in love with an ugly picture. Now people pity me for my desire as much as they admire me for my art: my wretchedness in love appears to match my brilliance in painting. But why am I lamenting so excessively and blaming my right hand? From pictures I know Phaedra, Narcissus, and Pasiphae.[3] The first did not always have the Amazon's son at her side; the latter burned with a desire that was *completely* unnatural; and the hunter—whenever his hand reached out for the spring, his beloved would dissolve and slip away from his fingers. For the spring bears the image of Narcissus, even as the painting bears that of both spring and Narcissus: like someone dying of thirst for his own beauty.[4] I, however, can be with my darling as much as I want, the girl is good looking, and when my hand reaches out for her, she stays, steadfast and unshaken, without losing her own shape.

    She smiles at me sweetly, her lips slightly parted, and one could say that a word crouches at their very tip,[5] ready to jump out of her mouth at any given moment. I have often moved my ear closer so as to hear what she might want to whisper. But unable to catch what she is saying, I kiss her mouth, her blossoming cheeks, her eyes full of grace, and try to persuade the girl to make love to me. She, however, remains silent, like a hetaira who wants to tease her lover a little.[6] I put her on my bed, embrace her, throw myself upon her chest, hoping that she might, perhaps, cure the love inside me, but I am all the more maddened by my desire for this painting. Then, again, I become aware of my insanity, and I am at risk of losing my life for

ὡραῖα, ἀλλ' οὐκ ἀποδίδωσι τὸν καρπὸν τοῦ φιλῆσαι. τί δὲ ὄφελος κόμης καλῆς
μὲν φαινομένης, κόμης δὲ οὐκ οὔσης; κἀγὼ μὲν δακρύω καὶ ποτνιῶμαι, ἡ δὲ
εἰκὼν φαιδρὸν ἀποβλέπει. ἀλλ' εἴθε μοι τοιαύτην ἔμψυχον, ὦ χρυσόπτεροι
παῖδες Ἀφροδίτης, δοίητε φίλην, ὅπως ἂν ἐκ τῶν τῆς τέχνης ἔργων ἴδω κρείσ-
σονα τέχνης, ὡραϊζομένην ἐν ζῶντι κάλλει, καὶ προσαρμόζων ἡδέως τῇ φύσει
τὴν ἐμαυτοῦ τέχνην ἄμφω θεάσωμαι συμφωνούσας ἀλλήλαις.

ια'. ΝΕΟΣ ΓΑΜΕΤΗΣ ΤΕ ΚΑΙ ΦΙΛΗΣ ΟΜΟΙΩΣ ΕΡΩΝ

Ἀπολλογένης Σωσίᾳ

Ἐβουλόμην, εἴπερ οἷόν τε ἦν, τοὺς ἐρωτικοὺς ἅπαντας διερωτῆσαι καθ' ἕκαστον,
εἴ τις αὐτῶν ἐπαμφοτερίζων ὑφ' ἕνα καιρὸν δυοῖν περιπέπτωκε φίλτροις. ἐγὼ
γὰρ ἑταίρας ἐρῶν πρὸς ἀπαλλαγὴν τοῦ πόθου (οὕτω γὰρ ᾤμην) συνεζύγην
σώφρονι γαμετῇ· καὶ νῦν τῆς τε πόρνης οὐδὲν ἧττον ἐρῶ, καὶ ὁ τῆς ὁμοζύγου
προσετέθη μοι πόθος, καὶ θατέρᾳ συνὼν οὐκ ἀμνημονῶ τῆς ἑτέρας, τὴν εἰκόνα
ταύτης ἐπὶ τῆς ψυχῆς ἀναπλάττων. ἔοικα γοῦν κυβερνήτῃ ὑπὸ δυοῖν πνευμά-
των ἀπειλημμένῳ, τοῦ μὲν ἔνθεν, τοῦ δὲ ἔνθεν ἑστηκότος καὶ περὶ τῆς νεὼς
μαχομένων, ἐπὶ τἀναντία μὲν τὴν θάλασσαν ὠθούντων, ἐπ' ἀμφότερα δὲ τὴν
μίαν ναῦν ἐλαυνόντων. ἀλλ' εἴθε, καθάπερ οἱ Ἔρωτες τῇ ἐμῇ συνομιλοῦντες
ἐνδιαιτῶνται ψυχῇ, οὕτω ζηλοτυπίας χωρὶς αἱ γυναῖκες συνῴκουν ἀλλήλαις.

ιβ'. ΕΥΠΟΡΟΣ ΠΕΝΙΧΡΑΝ ΑΥΘΑΙΡΕΤΩΣ ΓΗΜΑΣ, ΙΝΑ
ΜΗΔΕΝ ΑΛΑΖΟΝΙΚΟΝ ΕΚ ΠΛΟΥΣΙΑΣ ΥΠΟΜΕΙΝΗΙ

Εὐβουλίδης Ἡγησιστράτῳ

Δυστρόπου γυναικὸς οὐδὲ πενία δεδύνηται μᾶλλον ἐξημερῶσαι τὴν γνώμην,
οὐδὲ βραχὺ γοῦν αὐτὴν παρασκευάσαι τοῦ ἀνδρὸς κατήκοον εἶναι. ἐγὼ γὰρ
πενιχρὰν ἐξεπίτηδες ἠγαγόμην, ὅπως εὐπόρου γαμετῆς μηδὲν ὑποστήσωμαι
σοβαρόν. καὶ ἤρων αὐτῆς αὐτίκα, τὸ πρῶτον τῆς ἀπορίας αὐτὴν ἐποικτείρων.
καὶ τῆς τύχης ἐνόμιζον αὐτὴν ἐλεεῖν, οὐκ ᾔδειν δὲ ὅτι τοιοῦτος ἔλεος ἔρωτός
ἐστιν ἀρχή. ἐκ γὰρ ἐλέου τὰ πολλὰ φύεται πόθος. ἀλλ' ἡ τοσοῦτον ἐξ ἀρχῆς τὴν
τύχην ἐνδεὴς πάσης ὁμοζύγου πλουσίας φρύαγμα καὶ τῦφον πολλῷ τῷ μέσῳ
παρῆλθεν· ἔστι δὲ καὶ τὸν τρόπον καὶ τοὔνομα Δεινομάχη, καὶ τὼ χεῖρε μόγις
ἀπέχεται, καὶ ὥσπερ δέσποινα δεινὴ κεκράτηκέ μου πικρῶς, οὔτε γοῦν ὡς

a lifeless beloved. The look of her lips is lovely, but they are fruitless to kiss. What good is hair dazzling in appearance, when it is hair that doesn't exist? I weep and implore, but her image just gazes at me cheerily. O golden-winged children of Aphrodite, if only you could give me such a girl alive, so that, thanks to the works of my art, I might see her greater than art, abloom with living beauty; and so that I might delight in setting the product of my skill beside that of nature and contemplate each in perfect harmony with the other.

2.11. A Youth Is in Love with Both His Wife and His Girlfriend

Apollogenes to Sosias[1]

I would like, if I could, to ask all specialists in love, one by one, if any of them ever played a double game, yielding to two passions at once. For I, in love with a hetaira, got married to a sensible girl, so as to rid myself of my desire (or so I thought). Now, however, I don't love my girlfriend any less; I desire my wife as well. When I'm with the one, I can't get the other out of my head, as I keep forming her image in my mind. I'm like the pilot of a ship in the grip of two winds, one sweeping in from this direction, one from that, as though fighting over the ship. They whip the waves against each other and drive the solitary ship in two directions. If only the women could live together without jealousy, even as these two Loves dwell side by side in my soul in pleasing conversation.

2.12. A Wealthy Man Deliberately Marries a Poor Girl So as Not to Have to Put Up with the Arrogance of a Rich Woman

Euboulides[1] to Hegesistratos[2]

Not even poverty can tame the mind-set of a nasty woman, nor can it even for a moment make her obedient to her husband. Take me, for instance. I deliberately married a poor girl so that I would not have to put up with the arrogance of a rich wife. I loved her from the start, though at first I had pitied her for her poverty. I thought that I felt sorry for her hard luck but didn't know that such pity is the wellspring of love. For desire is often born from pity.[3] Yet although she was so lacking in good fortune initially, she surpassed every wealthy wife by far in insolence and vanity. She is truly a Deinomache[4] in both character and name, always on the verge of raising

εὔπορον τιμῶσα, οὔτε μὴν ὡς σύνοικον αἰδουμένη. ταῦτά μοι τῆς γαμετῆς ἐστιν
ἡ προίξ. ναὶ μὰ Δία (ὑπεμνήσθην γάρ) θαυμαστὸν ἐπηνέγκατό μοι κἀκεῖνο·
ἐπεντρυφᾷ πολυτελῶς, καθάπερ ἐπειγομένη πένητά με καταστῆσαι ταχύ·
οὐδεὶς γὰρ ἐξαρκεῖ πλοῦτος αὐτῇ, οὐδ᾿ ἂν ἐκ ποταμῶν ἐπιρρέῃ. ἐγὼ δὲ θοἰ-
μάτιον αὐτῇ δεικνύς, ὅπερ ἂν τύχω φορῶν, κωμικῶς τὴν ἄσωτον ὑπαινίττομαι
φάσκων· "ὦ γύναι, λίαν σπαθᾷς." ἀλλ᾿ οὐδεπώποτε τῶν ἐμῶν πεφρόντικε
λόγων, ὀδυνᾷ δέ με τὸν ἀγαπῶντα μάλιστα ἀναισθήτου γυναικὸς ἀτιμία.
τοσοῦτόν ἐστι δύσχρηστον τὸ κακόν. καὶ πέρας ἓν μόνον ἐμοὶ τούτου δοκεῖ, τὴν
βάρβαρον ἐς κόρακας ἐκπέμψασθαι τῆς οἰκίας, πρίν τι σκαιότερον ὑπομείνω·
φύσει γὰρ αἱ γυναῖκες, ἐπὰν τούτων οἱ συνοικοῦντες ἀνέχωνται, βαρύτερον
ἐπεμβαίνουσιν. ἀπίτω τοίνυν ἡ θηριώδης. ἔστω, δεδόχθω, οὐδὲν ἀμφιβάλλω.
κατάδηλος ἡ γυνή· ἄρκτου παρούσης, φασίν, οὐκ ἐπιζητήσω τὰ ἴχνη.

ιγ΄. ΕΤΑΙΡΑΣ ΑΠΟΛΟΓΙΑ ΠΡΟΣ ΥΠΟΚΝΙΖΟΜΕΝΟΝ ΦΙΛΟΝ

Χελιδόνιον Φιλωνίδῃ

Μάτην ὑποκνίζῃ, γλυκύτατε, μάτην ᾠήθης με ποθεῖν ἕτερον μετὰ σέ. οὕτως
ἵλεως εἴη μοι Ἀφροδίτη· ὅσον ἡμῶν ἐκδεδήμηκας χρόνον, τὸν ἔρωτα βεβαίως
ἀνεπίληστον διετήρουν ἀεί. καί τοι με καθεύδουσαν ἀφεὶς Μέγαράδε προσ-
έπτης, ἐγὼ δ᾿ ἀφυπνισθεῖσα πρὸς ἐμαυτὴν ἐβόων τοῦτο· "οὐκ ἔστι Φιλωνίδης,
ἀλλὰ Θησεύς." κοιμωμένην καταλιπὼν ᾤχου. Ἀριάδνην με πᾶσαι καλοῦσι· σὺ
δὲ Θησεὺς ἐμοὶ καὶ Διόνυσος. οὐκ ἐβόμβει σοι τὰ ὦτα, ὅτε σοῦ μετὰ δακρύων
ἐμεμνήμην; εἰ μέντοι εἰδείης, ὅτι καὶ νυκτηγετοῦσα διεμνημόνευον, καὶ
<τὴν> σὴν ἐπιστολὴν ὡς αὐτοχειρίᾳ μάλιστα γεγραμμένην μέσην ὑπέθηκα
τοῖς μαστοῖς, τὴν ἐπὶ σοὶ διεκπηδῶσαν παραμυθουμένη καρδίαν, ἐντεῦθεν ἂν
ἤδη χίλια παρασκευάζου φιλήματα. οἶδα, οἶδα, πόθεν εἰκότως τὴν ἀπάτην
ὑπέστης. ὡς ἑταίρα διὰ κέρδος ὁμιλοῦσα τοῖς νέοις ὑποκρίνομαι τῶν συνόντων
ἐρᾶν, ὅπως ἂν μείζονα τούτοις ἐρεθίσω τὸν πόθον. ἵνα γὰρ μὴ πολλάκις σοι
διενοχλῶ, παρ᾿ ἑτέρου τι λαβεῖν ἀνάγκη. σὺ δέ μοι καταμέμφῃ, τὴν ὑπόκρισιν

her hand against me, and like a terrible tyrant she harshly lords it over me, showing me not the slightest honor for my wealth nor the least respect as her husband. Such is the dowry I got for this bride. And by Zeus, as I'm thinking of it just now, she also brought me another fabulous thing: she indulges in the most costly luxuries, as though all she could think of was to make me a beggar as fast as she can. No amount of wealth is enough for her, not even if it streamed into her coffers with the force of a great river. As for me, I show her the threadbare coat I'm wearing and, as in the comedy, hint at her hopeless extravagance with the words "O woman, you are laying it on too thick!"[5] But she never pays the slightest heed to my words, and it is the disrespect of this insensitive woman that pains me most in my love for her. So unbearable is my misfortune. The only way to end it, it seems, is to kick the barbarian out of the house and straight to hell before I suffer even worse things at her hands. If once you put up with their insolence, it is women's nature to trample you even deeper into the dirt. Away with the bitch, then. Let it be thus, it's decided; no more delay. That woman stands revealed for what she is. The bear is in the room, as they say; no need to look for its tracks.[6]

2.13. A Hetaira's Defense to Her Somewhat Angry Lover

Chelidonion[1] to Philonides[2]

There's no cause for you to be angry, sweetheart; there's no cause for you to think that I want someone other than you. So help me Aphrodite, as long as you were out of town, away from me, I single-mindedly protected our love and kept it safe. For all that, you left me while I was sleeping and flew off to Megara,[3] and I, as I awoke, cried out to myself, "He's not Philonides; he's Theseus!" You hurried off, leaving behind a sleeping woman. All the girls now call me Ariadne. But to me you are both Theseus and Dionysus. Didn't your ears ring when I thought of you through my tears? If only you knew how I lay awake, forever thinking about you, how I held your letter between my breasts, trying to still the heart that was beating for you—a letter written in your own hand—if only you knew that, then you would make ready a thousand kisses for express delivery—stamped urgent. I know, I know why you probably suspect that I deceived you. To make a living as a hetaira, I keep the company of young men and pretend to love those I am with in order to increase their desire. At times I need to look to someone else for income so I won't bother you too often. You blame me because you don't

ἀγνοήσας. μὴ σύγε, δέομαι καὶ ἱκετεύω, καὶ κατασπένδω δάκρυα τῶν γραμμάτων. ὅμως ἥμαρτον, ὁμολογῶ, εἴ σοι φίλον ἁπλῶς ὁμολογούσης ἀκοῦσαι.
καὶ ἢν βούλει δίκην ἐπίθες, πλὴν τοῦ διαλῦσαι τὴν ἡμετέραν φιλίαν· τοῦτον
γὰρ μόνον οὐ φέρω τῆς τιμωρίας <τὸν> τρόπον, οὐ μὰ τὴν σὴν φαρέτραν, ἐξ
ἧς ἥδιστά με τοξεύεις. φυλάξομαι δὲ τοῦ λοιποῦ, ἵνα σε μηδὲν ἀνιάσω· οὐκέτι
γάρ σε ὡς ἐμόν, ἀλλὰ καὶ ὡς ἐμαυτήν, ὦ Φιλωνίδη, φιλῶ. ταῦτα γέγραφα, νὴ
τοὺς Ἔρωτας, ἀσθμαίνουσα καὶ δεδακρυμένη καὶ καθ᾽ ἕκαστον ὧν ἐπέστελλον
ἀναστενάζουσα.

ιδ′. ΦΙΛΙΑΣ ΑΝΑΚΛΗΣΙΣ

Μέλιττα Νικοχάρητι

Εἰ μὴ τὴν καθ᾽ ἡμῶν βασκανίαν ταχὺς ἀπεσόβησεν Ἔρως, καὶ Ἀφροδίτη
θᾶττον ἀμφοτέροις ἀλεξίκακος ἀνεφάνη, καλοῦ παιδὸς καλὴ μήτηρ, μέχρι
παντὸς ἂν ἡμᾶς ἐχώριζον ἀπ᾽ ἀλλήλων ἄσπονδος μάχη καὶ ἀδιάλλακτος ἔρις.
μάτην ἐπέχαιρον οἱ βασκαίνοντες ἡμῖν τῆς φιλίας, καὶ εἰς κενὸν αὐτοῖς ἀπέβη
τῆς ἐπιβουλῆς ὁ σκοπός. ὅθεν, ὦ φίλτατε, μὰ τὸν φίλιον Ἔρωτα τὸν ἐμόν τε
καὶ σόν, χθὲς ἐπὶ τὸ σὸν δωμάτιον εἰσιοῦσα θᾶττον ἢ βάδην ἔκλαον ὑφ᾽ ἡδονῆς,
κατησπαζόμην τε ἀπλήστως τὸν ἀφροδίσιον οἶκον, καὶ τῶν τοίχων ἐφαπτομένη
τοὺς δακτύλους ἐφίλουν ὑπερχαίρουσα καὶ μειδιῶσα γλυκύ. μεταξὺ δέ πως
προσαπιστοῦσα, πρὸς ἐμαυτὴν ἔφασκον· "ἆρα ἐγρήγορα, ἢ πλανῶσί με τῶν
ὀνειράτων εἰκόνες;" ὑπὸ τοῦ σφόδρα γὰρ ἐπιθυμεῖν ἐλάμβανέ με τις ἀπιστία.
σὺ δὲ ὡς τὸ σὸν ἑώρακας Μελισσάριον, ὥσπερ εἰς σύμβολον χρονίου θεάμα-
τος μεθ᾽ ἡδονῆς τὸν δάκτυλον ἀνατείνας, ἀσμένως αὐτὸν περιέστρεφες ἠθικῶς.
πολλὴ οὖν χάρις τοῖς φιλίοις θεοῖς, ὅτι δὴ πάλιν ἡμῖν ἀνανεοῦνται τὸν πόθον·
μᾶλλον δὲ νῦν χαριεστέρου καὶ μείζονος αἰσθάνομαι τούτου· ἀεὶ γάρ πως ἡδίους
αἱ τῶν ἐρώντων μεθ᾽ ὕβριν κολακεῖαι δοκοῦσιν.

ιε′. ΓΑΜΕΤΗ ΚΑΙ ΧΗΡΑ ΓΕΓΟΝΑΣΙ ΦΙΛΑΙ ΚΑΙ
ΠΟΘΟΥΣΙΝ, Η ΜΕΝ ΤΗΣ ΧΗΡΑΣ ΤΟΝ ΔΟΥΛΟΝ,
Η ΔΕ ΤΗΣ ΕΤΕΡΑΣ ΤΟΝ ΑΝΔΡΑ

Χρυσὶς Μυρρίνῃ

Τοὺς ἀλλήλων, ὦ φιλτάτη, συνεπιστάμεθα πόθους. σὺ μὲν τὸν ἐμὸν ἄνδρα
ποθεῖς, ἐγὼ δὲ τοῦ σοῦ θεράποντος ἐκθύμως ἐρῶ. τί οὖν πρακτέον; πῶς ἂν

grasp that it's all a show. Don't, I beg, I entreat you with an offering of my tears on this letter. Nevertheless, it was wrong of me, I admit, if it pleases you to hear this frank admission. Inflict whatever penalty you want, just don't break our bond. That is the only kind of punishment I can't bear, no, by that quiver of yours,[4] from which you shoot me with the sweetest arrows. I will take care in the future not to grieve you. For dear Philonides, I no longer love you as my own but as myself. I have written these words, by the Erotes, gasping for breath, drenched with tears, and groaning aloud with each syllable I set down.

2.14. LOVE RENEWED

Melitta[1] to Nikochares[2]

If Eros had not swiftly driven away the spite against us, and if Aphrodite, charming mother of a charming son, had not even more quickly appeared to both of us as a guard against evil, then a truceless war and irreconcilable strife would have kept us apart for all time. But those begrudging our love rejoiced in vain and missed the mark in their plot against us. That's why, by the Eros of your love and mine, I did not merely walk, I flew into your home and cried with joy, pressing insatiable kisses on the beloved house. After touching the walls, I kissed my fingers, overjoyed and smiling sweetly. All the while I could scarcely believe it and said to myself, "Am I awake, or are dream visions deceiving me?" For a certain incredulousness took hold of me, because I just wanted it so much. But when you saw your Melissarion,[3] you stretched your finger out in joy and waved it happily and expressively around—a sign of how you'd longed to see me.[4] A million thanks to the gods of love, since they renewed our passion for each other. I feel it now has grown even more pleasing and stronger. For the tenderness of lovers somehow always seems sweeter after suffering an outrage.

2.15. A WIFE AND A WIDOW BECOME FRIENDS, AND THE FORMER LONGS FOR THE WIDOW'S SLAVE, WHILE THE LATTER YEARNS FOR HER FRIEND'S HUSBAND

Chrysis[1] to Myrrhine[2]

We know of each other's desires, dearest. You want my husband, and I am passionately in love with your servant. What's to be done? How can we

εὐμηχάνως ἑκάστη τὸν ἑαυτῆς ἔρωτα θεραπεύσῃ; ἐδεήθην <τῆς Ἀφροδίτης>,
εὖ ἴσθι, τῆς θεραπείας τὴν ἔννοιαν ἐμβαλεῖν, καὶ ταύτην ἐξ ἀφανοῦς ἡ δαίμων
προσέπνευσέ μοι τὴν γνώμην, ἣν οὕτω πράττειν παρεγγυῶ σοι, Μυρρίνη. τὸν
σὸν μὲν οἰκέτην, ἐμὸν <δὲ> δεσπότην ἐρωτικὸν δόκει οὖν θυμουμένη ἅμα καὶ
τύπτουσα τῆς οἰκίας ἐκπέμπειν, ἀλλὰ πρὸς θεῶν πεφεισμένως καὶ τῷ παρόντι
μοι πόθῳ τὴν μάστιγα συμμετροῦσα· ὁ δ' οὖν οἰκέτης, Εὔκτητος ὁ καλός,
πάντως ἅτε πρὸς φίλην τῆς κεκτημένης φεύξεται παρ' ἐμέ, κἀγὼ τὸν ἄνδρα
ὡς ὑπὲρ τοῦ θεράποντος τὴν δέσποιναν ἱκετεύσοντα τὴν ταχίστην ἐξαποστέλλω
πρὸς σέ, οἷον μετὰ δεήσεως αὐτὸν ἐξωθοῦσα. τοῦτον δὴ τὸν τρόπον ἑκατέρα
τὸν ἑαυτῆς δεξαμένη ἐρώμενον οὐκ ἀμελήσει τοῦ Ἔρωτος ὑφηγουμένου ἐπὶ
σχολῆς ἅμα καὶ ῥαστώνης χρήσασθαι τῷ παραπεπτωκότι καιρῷ. ἀλλ' ἐπὶ μήκιστον ἐμφοροῦ τῆς ἐπιθυμίας τῇ συγκοιμήσει, καί μοι συνεπεκτείνουσα τῶν
ἀφροδισίων τὴν τέρψιν. ἔρρωσο, καὶ πέπαυσό μοι θρηνοῦσα τοῦ συζύγου τὴν
ἄωρον τελευτήν, φίλον ἀντ' ἐκείνου τὸν ἐμὸν σύνοικον εὐτυχοῦσα.

ις'. ΠΟΡΝΗ ΠΡΟΣ ΝΕΟΝ ΑΛΛΗΝ
ΑΥΤΗΣ ΠΡΟΚΡΙΝΟΝΤΑ ΦΙΛΗΝ

Μυρτάλη Παμφίλῳ

Ἐμὲ <τὴν> ποθοῦσαν περιφρονεῖς καὶ περὶ ἐλαχίστου ποιῇ, ἐμὲ τὴν ἐρῶσαν
ὑστέραν ἔχεις καὶ πάρεδρον ἡδονήν, καὶ πολλάκις τὴν ἡμετέραν οἰκίαν ὡς οὐδὲ
ἰδών ποτε παρέρχῃ. θρύπτῃ, Πάμφιλε, πρὸς ἐμέ, καὶ καλῶς, ὅτι μὴ ἀπέκλεισα
ἐλθόντα "ἔνδον ἕτερος" εἰποῦσα, ἀλλ' εἰσεδεχόμην ἀποφασίστως. τότε δ' ἂν
σε καιόμενον εἶδον καὶ ἀντιμεμηνότα. ἐγὼ διέφθειρά σε ὑπεραγαπῶσα καὶ
τοῦτο διεμφανίζουσα. ὑπερόπται γὰρ αἰσθόμενοι γίγνεσθε. μία μόνη δικαίως
ἐσπούδασταί σοι Θαΐς· καλὴ γὰρ ὅτι <μάτην> ποθεῖται. ἐκείνην διώκεις, ὅτι
σε πόρρωθεν ἀποφεύγει· τῶν γὰρ μὴ ῥαδίων ἐφίεσθε· καὶ ὅτε πολλὰ διδοὺς
μάτην ἱκετεύων τὴν σὴν ἀποκάμῃς, ἐμὲ λοιπὸν τὴν ἐξ ἀπορίας ἐπιζητεῖς.
καίτοι γε τεττάρων ὀβολῶν ἀξία Θαΐς, εἰ πάνυ πολλοῦ. ἐγὼ τοίνυν ἡ λαικὰς
τῶν κακῶν ἐμαυτὴν αἰτιῶμαι· πολλάκις γὰρ ἐπομοσαμένη τὴν ἄτοπον ταύτην

find a good way for each of us to attend to her desire? Just so you know, I begged Aphrodite to inspire me with a helpful idea, and here's the plan the goddess conjured up in my mind out of nowhere; I recommend you carry it out as follows, Myrrhine. You must seem to be angry with your slave, the master of my heart, and throw him out of your house with a beating. But by the gods, do it sparingly, and measure the whip's force according to the desire dwelling within me. The handsome Euktetos,[3] your servant, will certainly flee straight over to me as the friend of his mistress; I, in turn, will straightway dispatch my husband to you so that he can plead with his lady on your servant's behalf. I'll virtually push him out of the house with my entreaties. In this way, each of us will get to be with her beloved and surely won't neglect to use, at her leisure and ease, the opportunity that has presented itself to her under the guidance of Eros. But please indulge your heart's desire by making love for as long as you can, since in that way you also prolong my erotic pleasures. Farewell! Stop lamenting the untimely death of your husband, and be glad to get the man I live with as your lover instead.

2.16. A Prostitute to a Youth Who Prefers Another Lover over Her

Myrtale[1] to Pamphilos[2]

I love you, yet you despise me, and I'm not worth a damn to you; you consider my love for you second rate and our pleasure just a sideline; often you pass by my house as though you have never even seen it.[3] You give yourself airs toward me, Pamphilos, and that's really nice, since I never shut you out[4] when you came, saying, "Someone else is here"; no, I welcomed you, was always ready for you. If I had behaved differently, then I would have seen you inflamed with desire and crazy with passion in turn. I ruined you by loving you too much and showing it.[5] Once you notice something like that, you men become disdainful. It's only right that Thais[6] is the sole object of your desire. She's attractive precisely because you yearn for her in vain. You pursue her because she flees you even from afar.[7] For you guys go after what is hard to get. And after you've grown tired of begging that love of yours and showering her with gifts, not knowing where else to turn you seek me out as a stand-in. This, although Thais is barely worth four cents,[8] and that would be saying a lot. Stupid bitch that I am, I blame myself for my sufferings. For often I swore to break off

διαλῦσαι φιλίαν, ἡνίκα σε πάλιν ἑώρων, αὐτίκα μανικῶς προσεπήδων καθάπαξ ἐπιλελησμένη τῶν ὅρκων, καὶ λίαν ἐκκεχυμένως ἠγάπων, ἐφίλουν τε ἡδέως, καὶ σφοδρῶς ἄγαν ὑπελάμβανον ταῖς ἀγκάλαις, καὶ τιτθολαβεῖν ἐπέτρεπον. σὺ μὲν οὖν οἴει με τὸν αὐτὸν ἀεὶ τρόπον ἕξειν ὡς εὐπειθῆ καὶ ἑτοιμότατα προκειμένην· ἀλλ' ἔγωγε μὰ τοὺς Ἔρωτας—μαθήσῃ δὲ τῇ πείρᾳ. καὶ τί χρή με περιττὸν ἀποτελέσαι τὸν ὅρκον, παρὸν τοῖς ἔργοις ἐμαυτὴν ἐμπεδῶσαι καὶ περὶ τῶν δοκούντων ἀποδεῖξαι βεβαίαν; ἔρρωσο, καὶ πρὸς τῶν Θαΐδος μαστῶν καὶ φιλημάτων μηδὲ αὖθις <με> παρενόχλει.

ιζ'. ΜΟΙΧΟΣ ΕΠΙΜΟΝΟΣ ΚΑΙ ΠΡΟΣ ΣΩΦΡΟΝΑ

Ἐπιμενίδης Ἀριγνώτῃ

Φιλανθρώπως, ὦ γύναι, παραγγέλλεις, καὶ φειδομένης ἄγαν ὁ λόγος· ἔφης γάρ· "μέχρι τίνος, ὦ μειράκιον, παραμένεις, μηδένα διαλεῖπον καιρόν; σύνοικον ἔχω· μὴ μάτην τὸν ἐμὸν ῥύπαινε βίον. ἄπιθι, τὴν σὴν ὁδὸν διανύον, πρὶν ὑπ' ἐκείνου φωραθῇς καὶ δι' ἐμὲ τοιοῦτος τεθνήξεται νεανίας." ἀλλ' εἰ τοιαῦτά μοι παραινεῖς, οὐπώποτε ἠράσθης ἀφ' ὧν λέγεις, οὐδὲ κατεῖδες ἐρῶντα· σφόδρα γοῦν ἀπειρότερον διαλέγῃ. οὐκ ἔστιν αἰδήμων ἐραστής, κἂν προπηλακιζόμενος τύχῃ, οὐδὲ δειλός, κἂν δέοι τεθνάναι. πρὸς κῦμα, πρὸς πνεῦμα πλεῖν οὐδὲν αὐτῷ διαφέρει. τούτοις μᾶλλον τιμᾶται Ἀφροδίτη ἢ λιβανωτῷ καὶ θυσίαις. ἐκείνων οὖν ἀπόσχου τῶν λόγων· λῆροι γάρ εἰσι καὶ φλήναφοι παντελῶς. ἐγὼ τοίνυν ἐρωτικὸς ἀνέκπληκτος μηδὲν ὀρρωδῶν τὴν ἀνδρείαν μιμήσομαι τῶν Λακώνων· παρ' ἐκείνοις γὰρ αἱ μητέρες πρὸς τοὺς παῖδας ἔφασκον, ἐμοὶ δὲ παρακελεύεται κάλλιον ἡ ψυχή· "ἢ ταύτην ἢ ἐπὶ ταύτης," καὶ διὰ <τὸ> σὸν κάλλος ἢ γάμον ἀσμένως ἢ τάφον αἱροῦμαι. ἔστωσαν ἢ τρὶς ἓξ ἢ τρεῖς κύβοι νῦν οἱ πεπτωκότες. μὴ τοίνυν, ὦ καλλίστη γυναικῶν, ὑπολάβῃς τὰ γεγραμμένα μόνης χειρὸς εἶναι καὶ γλώττης ἁπλῶς· ἁμαρτήσῃ γὰρ τῆς ἀληθείας πολύ. ἔλεγχός ἐστι ταῦτα ψυχῆς ἐρώσης, κἀκείνη διὰ τούτων τὸ συμβὰν κατεμήνυσε πάθος.

this monstrous love. But when I saw you again, at once I leaped up like a madwoman having completely forgotten my oaths, I overflowed with love for you, I kissed you with rapture, I took you into my arms all too passionately, and I allowed you to fondle my titties. You think I'll always be available to you in the same way, easily persuaded and more than willing. But I, by the Erotes—well, just you try and see. Why should I finish this superfluous oath when I can prove myself steadfast through deeds and show that I am unwavering in my decisions. Farewell, and by the breasts and kisses of Thais, don't bother me again.

2.17. A Seducer Who Refuses to Give Up Even When Faced with an Honest Woman

Epimenides[1] to Arignote[2]

You mean well in warning me, woman, and your words show that you are all too merciful. For you said, "How long, O youth, will you persist, trying to seize every possible opportunity? I already live with someone.[3] Don't stain my life. Away with you, just keep on walking, before he discovers you and a youth of such qualities is killed[4] on my account." But if this is how you advise me, then judging from what you say you've never been in love or even seen a lover. You speak like someone utterly inexperienced. A lover is not timid, even if treated like dirt, nor is he cowardly, even in the face of death. No matter if he has to sail against wave and wind. Aphrodite derives more honor through this than through frankincense or sacrifice. So refrain from such speeches. They're nothing but drivel and nonsense. As a lover, I will be steadfast, fear nothing, emulate the bravery of the Spartans. For among them, mothers always told their sons, "With it, or on it"[5]—a choice to which my soul exhorts me too, though even more beautifully, since on account of your beauty, I choose either marriage with delight or death.[6] Let the dice's cast come up either all or nothing.[7] O loveliest of women, don't consider this letter a token merely of my hand or tongue. That would be far from the mark. It is proof, rather, of a loving soul, which through these words revealed the passion that befell it.

ιη΄. ΠΕΡΙ ΠΡΟΑΓΩΓΟΥ ΠΡΟΣ ΕΡΑΣΤΗΝ
ΜΑΓΓΑΝΕΙΑΝ ΠΛΑΣΑΜΕΝΟΥ

Μαντίθεος Ἀγλαοφῶντι

Γυνὴ τοὔνομα Θελξινόη προσχήματι σώφρονος ἐπὶ τοὺς ὀφθαλμοὺς καθέλκουσα
τὴν ἀμπεχόνην κἀκεῖθεν κομιδῇ στενὸν ὑποβλέπουσα, ἐλάνθανε κακοτεχνοῦσα
τοὺς νέους· καὶ γὰρ κυνὶ προσέοικε λύκος, ἀγριώτατος ἡμερωτάτῳ. ταύτης
ὁ Πάμφιλος οὐκ οἶδα ὅπως πολυπραγμονήσας τὸ βλέμμα ἐκ πρώτης θέας
ἠράσθη ταχύ· δεξάμενος γὰρ τοῦ κάλλους τὴν ἀπορροὴν διὰ τῶν ὀμμάτων
ἐρωτικῶς διεθερμάνθη, καὶ ὥσπερ βοῦς μυωπισθεὶς ἐταράττετο. ὤκνει δὲ τὸν
πόθον δηλῶσαι, τὴν ἐμφαινομένην σεμνότητα δεδιώς. συνῆκε τοῦ μειρακίου
τὴν ὑπόνοιαν ἡ γυνὴ ὡς πολλὴν ἔχουσα τοῦ πράγματος ἐμπειρίαν. ... ὁ γὰρ
ἄνθρωπος οὐχ ὡς προαγωγὸς τῷ ποθοῦντι προσῆλθεν, ἀλλά τις εἶναι τῶν περιέργων ἐδόκει· καὶ πολλὰ τερατευσάμενος ἐπηγγείλατο μόνος αὐτὴν δαιμονίως
καταδουλῶσαι τῷ νέῳ. καὶ χρυσοῦς αὐτὸν πρότερον εἰσπραξάμενος οὐκ ὀλίγους
ὑπὸ τὼ πόδε τοῦ ποθοῦντος ἤγαγεν ἀρρήτῳ λόγῳ τὴν ἄνθρωπον, ὥσπερ αὐτὸς
ὑποδεικνὺς τὴν γυναῖκα προσιοῦσαν ἐνεανιεύετο λέγων.

ἡ δὲ τὴν ὑπόκρισιν αὐτοῦ πιστουμένη τὸ μὲν πρῶτον οἷον ὑπόσεμνος συνε-
δείπνησεν ἐγκεκαλυμμένη, καὶ σμικρὸν τῶν ἀργυρίδων ἀπεγεύετο, μέχρι καὶ
αὐτὰς καταπέπωκε τὰς χρυσίδας. ἔπειτα τέως ἀντερᾶν ὡμολόγει νῦν πρῶτον
ἔρωτος πειρασθεῖσα, καὶ ἦν πάντα μιμηλῶς ἐρώσης τὰ δρώμενα παρ' ἐκείνης·
καὶ πολλάκις παρεδάκρυε τῷ μειρακίῳ, νῦν μὲν ἀποστένουσα τὸν πόθον, νῦν δὲ
πικρῶς ὀλοφυρομένη ἣν ἐζημίωται σωφροσύνην, καὶ ὁ Κρὴς ἐδόκει τὴν θάλατταν
ἀγνοεῖν. ὁ δὲ σχηματισάμενος μαγγανείαν παρ' ἕκαστον ἑαυτὸν ἀπεθαύμαζεν,
εἰς σύμβολον παραδόξου νίκης ἀνατείνων τὴν χεῖρα. ταῦτα μὲν οὖν γέγονε δίς
τε καὶ τρὶς καὶ σφόδρα πολλάκις. ὡς δὲ λοιπὸν τὸν ἀθλίως ἐρώμενον ἐψίλωσαν
τῶν χρημάτων καὶ κατέστησαν παττάλου γυμνότερον, ἀπέλιπον αὐτὸν ἐν
πενίᾳ δήπου μυρίᾳ, καὶ περιπεφρονήκασι παντελῶς.

ὁ μὲν οὖν ἐραστὴς περιώδυνος ἐκ τοῦ πόθου τὸν φιλτροποιὸν ἱκέτευε
πάλιν κατ' ἐκείνης ἀνακινῆσαι τὰς ἴυγγας· ἔτι γὰρ οὕτως ἡγεῖτο κεκρατημέ-
νος τῇ χλεύῃ. ὁ δέ φησιν· "ὦ τάν, εἴς γε τὰ τοιαῦτα πρόσκαιρος ἡμῶν ἐστιν ἡ

2.18. About a Pimp Who Poses as a
Magician to Deceive a Lover

Mantitheos[1] to Aglaophon[2]

A woman named Thelxinoe[3] practiced her deceptive arts on clueless lovers by pulling her shawl right down to her eyes in feigned modesty and casting furtive glances out from underneath. After all, a wolf resembles a dog; the most savage of beasts, the gentlest.[4] But Pamphilos, somehow unable to restrain the curiosity of his gaze, instantly fell in love with her at first sight. As her beauty flooded his eyes, he was filled with passion's fire[5] and was rattled like a cow pricked by the gadfly. He hesitated to reveal his desire, as he feared her seemingly stern demeanor. Having much experience in such matters, the woman grasped the boy's intent. [...][6] For the man did not approach the lover as a pimp, but rather as though he was one involved in esoteric arts. Having told him all sorts of marvelous tales, he proclaimed that through his divine powers he would single-handedly make her the young man's slave. After extracting from him several pieces of gold, he used a secret spell to draw the woman to her lover's feet—something he affirmed with youthful pride, pointing to her approach. And the woman played along with his act with perfect credibility.

At first, still veiled and somewhat somber, she shared the meal with him, just picking at the food brought out on silver dishes. No sooner was it served on golden ones, however, than she seemed to devour everything, plates and all. Then at last she admitted that she requited his desire, and that now for the first time she had tasted true love, and her whole performance mimicked a woman in the grip of passion. She gushed tears before the young man, now bemoaning her desire, now lamenting that modesty for which she had strived—all just an act, like a Cretan who claims he's unacquainted with the sea.[7] But the man who had pretended to be a conjurer marveled at his own prowess with each advance and raised his hands in joy at his unexpected triumph. All this happened twice, thrice, and many times over. When at last they had plucked the wretched lover bare of all his money and set him out more naked than a pole, they abandoned him to abundant poverty, showering him with contempt.

But the lover, sick with desire, begged the spellbinder to set in motion once again his magic wheel[8] to get the girl. That's how thoroughly ensnared he still was in their deceptive game. But the man replied, "Poor guy, my art in such matters requires perfect timing. And besides, you have already

τέχνη, ἄλλως τε καὶ ἀπολέλαυκας ἱκανῶς." τούτοις ἀμφότεροι φενακίσαντες τὸν νέον ἀπῆλθον, ἣ μὲν πλασαμένη σώφρονος ἤθη, ὃ δὲ καθάπερ ἐπὶ σκηνῆς ὑποκρινάμενος τῶν περιέργων τὸ σχῆμα καὶ δαιμόνων προσηγορίας συνείρων πλασματώδεις τέ τινας ὑποφθεγγόμενος ἐπικλήσεις καὶ ψιθυρίζων ἀπατηλῶν γοητευμάτων λόγους φρικώδεις, ἔνθα δῆθεν αὐτὸς ὑποτρέμων παρεστῶτι πλησίον μὴ δεδιέναι παρεκελεύετο τῷ μειρακίῳ.

ιθ′. ΓΥΝΗ ΠΡΟΠΑΡΑΣΚΕΥΑΖΟΥΣΑ ΠΡΟΑΓΩΓΟΝ ΑΥΤΗΙ ΤΗΝ ΘΕΡΑΠΑΙΝΙΔΑ ΓΕΝΕΣΘΑΙ

Ἀρχίλοχος Τερπάνδρῳ

Ὅρα, πρὸς Διός, ὅπως γυνή τις ἠρέμα προτρέπει μαστροπὸν αὐτῆς γενέσθαι τὴν δούλην. ἔφη γάρ· "ἢ φαντασίαν εἶδον, ὦ παιδίσκη, καθ' ὕπνον, οἶα φιλεῖ, ἢ πρὸ θυρῶν ἀκήκοα νέων κωμαστῶν ὑπὲρ ἐμοῦ <ἀγωνιζο>μένων ἀωρὶ νύκτωρ, οὐκ ὄναρ, ἀλλ' ὕπαρ. ἐλεύθεροι γὰρ οἱ στενωποί· παίζειν καὶ γελᾶν καὶ ᾄδειν τῷ θέλοντι ἔξεστιν. νὴ τὰς Μούσας, εὐστόμως ᾖδον, ἴσα καὶ Σειρῆνες γλυκεῖαν ἀφιέντες φωνήν." "ἀληθῆ," φησὶν ἡ παῖς, "ἀκήκοας, ὦ κεκτημένη· σὲ γὰρ τις νέος καταβόστρυχος ἔτι ἐν ἁπαλῇ τῇ ὑπήνῃ πάλαι ποθεῖ, Ἱπποθάλης μὲν ὄνομα, ἱκανὸς δὲ καὶ ἀπὸ μόνου τοῦ κάλλους γινώσκεσθαι. καὶ πολλάκις μοι διείλεκται περὶ σοῦ, καὶ 'βούλομαι,' ἔφη, 'τὴν σὴν δέσποιναν προσειπεῖν,' ἀλλ' ἐδεδίειν προσαγγεῖλαι τὸν λόγον." αὐτίκα γοῦν ἡ κεκτημένη τὴν θεράπαιναν ἐπανήρετο· "τὸ βούλημα ἤκουσας, ὦ φιλτάτη;" "ναί," φησὶν ἡ παιδίσκη. ἡ δέ· "ὡς ἐμοῦ γε μήπω μαθούσης," ἔφη, "παρίτω πάλιν προσᾴδων, κἂν ἐρωτικός μοι δοκοίη, χαριοῦμαι τῷ μειρακίῳ." ἦλθεν, ἐφάνη τὴν κεφαλὴν ῥόδοις ἀνθίσας, ἐμμελέστερον ᾖδεν, ἐκρίθη καλός, καὶ ἀλλήλων συναπέλαυον ἄμφω οὐ μόνον στέρνῳ στέρνον ἁρμόζοντες, ἀλλὰ καὶ φιλήμασιν ἐπισυνάπτοντες τὰς ψυχάς· τοῦτο γὰρ φίλημα δύναται, καὶ τοῦτό ἐστιν ὃ βούλεται· σπεύδουσιν αἱ ψυχαὶ διὰ τῶν στομάτων πρὸς ἀλλήλας καὶ περὶ τὰ χείλη συναντῶσιν, καὶ ἡ μῖξις αὕτη γλυκεῖα γίνεται τῶν ψυχῶν.

enjoyed its benefits enough." Having thus cheated the young man, they both took off. The woman had presented the appearance of a modest character; the man, like an actor on stage, had played the role of one involved in the esoteric arts, stringing together invocations of deities, muttering invented epithets, and whispering the shivery words of deceptive charms. All the while, though trembling himself, he bid the young man at his side to have no fear.

2.19. A Woman Arranges for Her Maid
to Be Her Go-Between

Archilochus to Terpander[1]

Consider, by Zeus, how a woman got her slave to pimp for her, without drawing attention to her plan. For she said, "Either, my girl, I saw a dream vision in my sleep—a common thing—or I heard youthful revelers fighting over me before my door in the dead of night[2]—not in a dream but wide awake.[3] For the alleyways are open to all, and whoever wants to can amuse themselves, laugh, and sing. And by the Muses, they sang delightfully, projecting a sweet tone like the Sirens."[4] "You heard them, mistress, sure enough," answered the girl, "for a youth, his hair still flowing down his neck and a delicate beard just coming in, has long yearned for you. Hippothales is his name; you'd know him at once just by his good looks.[5] He's often talked to me about you, and said, 'I'd like to speak with your mistress,' but I've been afraid to pass his words along to you." So at once the mistress asked her maid, "You heard his wish, dearest?" "Yes," said the girl. And the lady replied, "Let him come by again and serenade me, as though I'd no idea, and if he seems attractive, I'll grant the boy my favors." He came, appeared with his head crowned by roses, sang even more tunefully than before, and was judged beautiful. So they took delight in each other, not only pressing breast against breast, but through their kisses weaving their souls together. That, after all, is what a kiss can do; that is what it wants. For souls hasten toward each other through the mouth and meet around the lips. And so this sweet mingling of souls comes about.[6]

κ΄. ΠΕΡΙ ΓΥΝΑΙΚΟΣ ΑΥΣΤΗΡΩΣ ΑΠΩΘΟΥΜΕΝΗΣ ΝΕΟΝ ΔΙΑ ΤΗΝ ΜΕΤΑ ΚΟΡΟΝ ΤΩΝ ΕΡΑΣΤΩΝ ΥΠΕΡΟΨΙΑΝ

Ὠκεάνειος Ἀριστοβούλῳ

Νέος ἐρωτικός, ὄνομα Λύκων, ἀνήνυτα προσκαρτερῶν καὶ θυραυλῶν γυναικὶ μέμφεται δεινῶς ἀπωθούσῃ· ὃ μὲν γὰρ ἱκετεύων ἔφασκε ταῦτα δὴ τὰ μυριόλεκτα καὶ συνήθη πρὸς τὰ παιδικὰ τοῖς ἐρῶσιν, "οὐκ ἐπικάμπτῃ πρὸς ἔλεον ὁρῶσα μειράκιον; οὐ συναλγεῖς μοι ποθοῦντι; ἔχε με κατὰ κράτος ἑλοῦσα τὸν πᾶσι καὶ πάσαις ἀνάλωτον." ἡ δὲ τὴν ἀπὸ Σκυθῶν ὧδε ῥῆσιν ἐρεῖ· "ἐμοὶ προσλαλῶν εἰς πῦρ ξαίνεις, γύργαθον φυσᾷς, σπόγγῳ πάτταλον κρούεις, καὶ τὰ λοιπὰ τῶν ἀμηχάνων ποιεῖς." τέλος ἐξ ἀπορίας ὁ νεανίσκος ἐξωργίσθη, καὶ ἀναφλεχθεὶς τῷ θυμῷ τὸν λαιμὸν ὀγκούμενος ἐφύσα τε καὶ τραχύτατα διελοιδορεῖτο τῇ ποθουμένῃ· "ὡς φιλόνεικος," εἶπεν, "ὑπάρχεις καὶ λίαν γυνή, ὡς ἀτεράμων, ὦ γῆ καὶ θεοί. θαυμαστὸν οὖν πῶς ἡ τοιάδε ψυχὴ οὐκ ἐτέχθη μᾶλλον θηρίον."

ἡ δὲ τῇ λαιᾷ χειρὶ βραχὺ τὴν παρειὰν ἐπικλίνασα, τῇ δὲ λαγόνι τὴν δεξιὰν ἐμβαλοῦσα ἠθικῶς ἅμα "τὸν λόγον ἀμυνοῦμαι," φησίν. "κλᾶταί σου μᾶλλον ἡ γλῶττα, καὶ φληναφᾶν μόνον ἐθέλεις. πλὴν ὁποῖον εἴρηκας ἄκουε. ἐν ταῖς ἀκρωρείαις περιπλανώμενα τὰ θηρία σπανίως ἐπιτίθεται τοῖς ἀνθρώποις, ἐξ ὑμῶν δὲ ζωγρηθήτω, καὶ παραθηγόμενα τοῖς κυνηγεσίοις μανθάνει καὶ θυμὸν ἀγριαίνειν· ὡσαύτως δὲ καὶ ἡμᾶς ἐκδιδάσκετε οἷον θηριοτροφοῦντες μηδαμῶς ἐλεεῖν, ἀλλὰ σκληρῶς ἀπαυθαδιάζεσθαι τοὺς νέους. ὅτε μὲν γὰρ αὐτοὶ ποθεῖτε, ἀστρώτους καὶ χαμαιπετεῖς κοιμήσεις ἐπὶ θύραις ποιεῖσθε, καὶ λιπαρῶς ἱκετεύετε μόνου ῥήματος τυχεῖν ἀξιοῦντες, καὶ δακρύοντες κατόμνυσθε τοὺς θεούς, ἐπ᾽ ἄκρου τοῦ χείλους ἔχοντες τὸν ὅρκον. ὡς γὰρ λύκοι τοὺς ἄρνας ἀγαπῶσιν, οὕτω τὰ γύναια ποθοῦσιν οἱ νέοι, καὶ λυκοφιλία τούτων ὁ πόθος. ἡνίκα δὲ μέχρι κόρου τὸν ἑαυτῶν ἀποπληρώσετε πόθον, καὶ τὰς πρότερον ὑμῶν ἐρωμένας ἐκ μεταβολῆς ἐραστρίας ποιήσετε, μεγαλαυχεῖτε λοιπὸν καὶ καταγελᾶτε τῆς ὥρας, μυσαττόμενοι τὰς ἀθλίας, καὶ βδελύττεσθε ταῖς ἀρτίως περιποθήτοις προσπτύοντες ἡδοναῖς· ἐφήμερα γὰρ ὑμῖν τὰ δάκρυα καὶ ὥσπερ ἱδρὼς ἀπομάττεται. τοὺς δὲ ὅρκους αὐτοὶ φατε μὴ προσπελάζειν τοῖς ὠσὶ τῶν

2.20. About a Woman Who Harshly Rebuffs a Youth Since She Knows That Lovers Turn Arrogant After Getting What They Want

Okeaneios[1] to Aristoboulos[2]

An amorous youth named Lykon[3] was getting nowhere keeping vigil before his lady's door, despite all his efforts. He complained bitterly about the woman who had rebuffed him, begging her with entreaties that have been uttered countless times before and that lovers customarily address to the objects of their desire. "Are you not moved to pity at the sight of me, a mere youth? Don't you sympathize with my desire for you? Keep me now that you've taken me by force—me, who'd never been captured by man or woman." But she replied in the rude manner of a Scythian,[4] "When you try to speak with me, you are just flogging fire, blowing into a net, hammering nails with a sponge, attempting every possible impossibility." Finally the youth grew enraged at his helplessness, and inflamed with ire he puffed out his swelling neck and cruelly railed against his beloved. "What a belligerent bitch you are, and just like a woman! How merciless, by Earth and the gods. It's a wonder that such a soul was not born a beast."

But she, lightly leaning her cheek onto her left hand, and setting the other expressively on her hip, replied, "I reject your words. Your tongue's twisted, and you only want to talk drivel. But I can give as good as I get; just listen: Animals ranging across mountain peaks rarely attack people. But just catch such a beast alive, and it will learn to make its heart savage, provoked by the hunt. In the same way, just like those who raise wild beasts, you teach us never to take pity but to harden our hearts and spurn young lovers. When you want a girl, you camp out on the ground before her door without a blanket;[5] you make grandiose entreaties, hoping even for a single word in response; you tearfully swear by the gods, an oath forever ready on the tip of your tongue.[6] For as wolves love sheep, so youths hunger after women;[7] their desire is wolfish ardor. But once you've sated your appetite and gotten more than your fill, making those you previously wanted want you in turn, then you go around boasting and making fun of those beauties; you can't stand being around the poor wretches, you pour contempt on them, you spit on the joys that you'd just been so keen for. For your tears are fleeting; you wipe them off like sweat. You yourself say that your oaths don't reach the ears of the gods.[8] So Lykon, wolf that you are, away with you and your gaping mouth[9]—it will have to stay unfilled.

θεῶν. λύκος οὖν χανών, ὦ Λύκων, ἄπιθι διὰ κενῆς, καὶ μηκέτι κάλει θηρία τὰς φυλαττομένας αὐτοῖς περιπεσεῖν τοῖς θηρίοις."

κα′. Ο ΣΥΜΒΑΛΩΝ ΤΗΝ ΕΑΥΤΟΥ ΦΙΛΗΝ ΠΡΟΣ ΤΑΣ ΑΛΛΑΣ ΓΥΝΑΙΚΑΣ

Ἁβροκόμης Δελφίδι ἐρωμένῃ

Περίεργος διατελῶ πρὸς τὰ γύναια πανταχῇ, μὰ Δία, οὐχ ἵνα τούτων ἅψαιμι (μὴ οὕτω χαλεπῶς ἀκούσῃς τοῦ λόγου), ἀλλ᾽ ὅπως παράθεσιν ἀκριβῆ σου τε κἀκείνων ποιήσωμαι, τῆς ἐν πάσαις διαπρεπούσης τῷ κάλλει, καὶ παραλλήλους κατ᾽ ἐμαυτὸν ἐννοούμενος ἀντικρίνω· καὶ νὴ τὸν Ἔρωτα τὸν εὐτυχῶς εἰς τὴν ἐμὴν τετοξευκότα ψυχήν, πάσας ἐν πᾶσι νενίκηκας, ὡς ἔπος <εἰπεῖν>, τῷ σχήματι, τῷ κάλλει, ταῖς χάρισιν· αἱ γὰρ χάριτές σου παντελῶς ἄδολοι καὶ ἀληθῶς κατὰ τὴν παροιμίαν γυμναί· καὶ φύσεως αὐτόσκευον ἔρευθος ἐπιτρέχει ταῖς παρειαῖς, ὀφρὺς μέλαινα κατὰ λευκοῦ τοῦ μετώπου· οὔτε στεφανοῦσθαί σοι τὴν κεφαλὴν ἀναγκαῖον, ἅτε τῆς κόμης ἀποχρώσης αὐτῇ· καὶ ὅσον τὸ ῥόδον φαιδρότερον τῆς ἄλλης πέφυκε πόας καὶ λίαν καθ᾽ ἑαυτὴν εὐδοκιμούσης, τοσοῦτον καὶ τῶν ἐπισήμων γυναικῶν ὑπερφέρεις. τοιγαροῦν, ὦ μέλισσα ἐμή, ἁρπάζεις τὰ πάντων ὄμματα καὶ προσέλκεις καινότερον τρόπον, οἷον οὔτε ἰχθὺν ἁλιεὺς εἵλκυσεν, οὔτε ὄρνιν θηρευτὴς οὔτε κυνηγέτης νεβρόν. ἀλλ᾽ ἐκεῖνα μὲν ἢ ἀπὸ δελεάτων ἢ τῶν ἰξῶν ἄγουσιν ἢ ὅπως ποτέ· σὺ δὲ ἀπὸ τῶν ὀμμάτων τῇ θέᾳ γαννυμένους ἄγεις ἡμᾶς. ἀλλ᾽ ὦ Δελφίδιον ἐμόν τε πρόκριτον ἀγαθόν, ζώης ἐπὶ μήκιστον, εὖ ζώης· ἐπὶ σοὶ γὰρ ἐγὼ φλέγομαι μόνῃ, καὶ τοῖς θεοῖς ἐπεύχομαι πᾶσι μηδαμῶς ἔχειν περὶ τὴν ὀρθῶς φανεῖσάν μοι κρίσιν ἑτεροῖον τὸν νοῦν. εἴθε τοίνυν, ἐμὸν γάνος, σὺ μὲν ταύτην ἐκ τῆς φύσεως ἔχοις τὴν νίκην, ἐγὼ δὲ μέχρι παντὸς τὸ χρυσοῦν τῶν Ἐρώτων εὐτυχήσαιμι βέλος. σὺ οὖν αὐτὸ μὴ πειρῶ τῆς ἐμῆς ἀφελέσθαι καρδίας· οὔτε γὰρ αὐτὴ δύνασαι οὔτε ἐγὼ βούλομαι· οὐ γὰρ ἀποθύμιον ἔχω τὸν πόθον. ἔστω τοίνυν ἔργον ἓν μόνον ἐπιδέξιον ἐμοὶ φιλεῖν Δελφίδα καὶ ὑπὸ ταύτης φιλεῖσθαι, καὶ λαλεῖν τῇ καλῇ καὶ ἀκούειν λαλούσης.

κβ′. ΠΕΡΙ ΤΗΣ ΕΥΜΕΘΟΔΩΣ ΤΟΝ ΜΟΙΧΟΝ ΑΠΟΛΥΟΥΣΗΣ

Χαρμίδης Εὐδήμῳ

Γυναικὸς ἔτι προσεμβατεύοντα τὸν μοιχὸν ἔνδον ἐχούσης, οὕτω συμβὰν ὁ ταύτης ἀνὴρ ἐξ ἀλλοδαπῆς ἀφιγμένος ἔκοπτε τὴν θύραν ἅμα βοῶν. ἡ δὲ

And henceforth, don't refer to those as beasts who just want to avoid falling prey to beasts."

2.21. A Man Compares His Beloved
with Other Women

Habrokomes[1] to His Beloved Delphis

I am in a state of permanent curiosity about the female sex, by Zeus, not because I want to sleep with them (don't misunderstand my words), but so as to make an accurate comparison between you and the rest—you who surpass all women in beauty—picturing you all side by side and judging one against the other.[2] And by Eros, whose arrow happily has pierced my soul, you've triumphed over all in every category, so to speak, in stature, beauty, charms. For your charms are utterly honest and truly naked, as the proverb says.[3] An artless blush naturally suffuses your cheeks, and a dark brow sits on your white forehead. There's no need for you to wear a crown, as your own hair is adornment enough for your head.[4] And just as a rose outshines all other plants, admired though they may be in themselves, so too do you leave other dazzling women far behind.[5] You, my honey, catch the eyes of all men and draw them to you in a novel way, as no angler has ever caught a fish, no fowler a bird, no hunter a fawn. For those are caught either with bait or birdlime, or in some other way. You, however, take us captive with your eyes, whenever we happily catch sight of you.[6] But my little Delphis, my treasured favorite, may you have a long and happy life. For I burn only for you, and I pray to all the gods, may I never change my mind, never alter that judgment that appears right to me. May you, my delight, maintain that victory granted you by nature, and may I forever rejoice in the golden arrow of the Erotes. So don't you try to pull it out of my heart. You couldn't do it, and I wouldn't want it. For this yearning is my heart's desire. Let this, therefore, be my one rightful pursuit, to love Delphis and to be loved by her, to chat with this lovely girl and to listen to her chatting.[7]

2.22. About a Woman Who Cleverly Sets Her Lover Free

Charmides[1] to Eudemos[2]

At the very moment when a woman had her lover within, still mounted on top of her, it so happened that her husband unexpectedly returned from

τοῦ κτύπου καὶ τῆς βοῆς αἰσθομένη ἐξανέστη τῆς εὐνῆς καὶ τὴν στρωμνὴν ἐνετάραξε, παντελῶς συγχέουσα τὸ ἔρεισμα τοῦ δευτέρου σώματος, ὅτι κατηγόρει μηνύματα συζυγίας. εἶτά φησι παραθαρρύνουσα τὸν μοιχόν· "εἰ νῦν τῷ συνοίκῳ δεσμώτην σε προσαγάγω, μηδὲν δείσῃς μηδ' ὑποπτήξῃς, ὦ φίλε." συνέδησε τοῦτον, ἀνέῳγε τὴν θύραν, ὡς ἐπὶ τοιχωρύχον ἐκάλει τὸν ἄνδρα, φάσκουσα· "τοῦτον κατέλαβον, ἄνερ, ἐγχειροῦντα συλαγωγῆσαι τὸν ἡμέτερον οἶκον." ὁ δὲ θυμωθεὶς ὥρμηκεν εὐθέως αὐτὸν ἀνελεῖν, ἀλλ' ἡ γυνὴ διεκώλυε παραινοῦσα μᾶλλον τὸν κακοῦργον ἕωθεν παραδοθῆναι τοῖς ἕνδεκα· "εἰ δέ γε δέδοικας, ἄνερ, ἐγὼ συναγρυπνοῦσα τοῦτον φυ<λάξω> ...

abroad. He started beating on the door and shouting. No sooner had she heard the knocking and the cries than she leaped from the bed and rumpled the sheets, thus completely obscuring the traces of the second body, since these provided damning proof of their intercourse. Thereupon she reassured her lover with the following words: "If I lead you now before my husband as a prisoner, don't be afraid or start to tremble, darling." So she tied him up, opened the door, and called to her husband for help as though with a burglar, saying, "I caught this one here, husband, as he was trying to plunder our house." And her husband, enraged, rushed to kill him right away. But the woman held him back, counseling instead that the scoundrel be handed over to the Eleven[3] the next morning. "But if you're afraid, husband, I will stay awake and guard him." ...

NOTES

LIST OF CHANGES AND CORRECTIONS TO MAZAL'S TEXT

Epistle	Mazal	This Edition
1.1.5	κάλλιστος	κάλλιστον
1.10.69	γὰρ	γάρ
1.13.64	τι	τί
1.15.21	Ἀρροδίτη	Ἀφροδίτη
1.16.28	αὐχὲνα	αὐχένα
1.17.15	παρήνεσα	παρήνεσα
1.17.24	αὐτῆς	αὖθις (emendavit Höschele)
1.22.23	ἐπί	ἐπὶ
1.24.15	οἴσεθαι	οἴεσθαι
1.25.7	πολλὴν	πολλὴν
2.13.1	ποθείν	ποθεῖν
2.15.11	Εὔκτιτος (Hercher 1873)	Εὔκτητος (editions before Hercher)
2.20.2	ἀπειθούσῃ	ἀπωθούσῃ (Zanetto in Conca and Zanetto 2005)

NOTES TO THE TRANSLATION

The following notes offer short interpretive introductions to each letter, explain the correspondents' names (where relevant), and try to give non-specialists the necessary background information to read the texts with pleasure.

Letter 1.1

As outlined in the introduction (pp. xii–xiii), the name of the collection's author was probably inferred from this first letter. But even if the historical author was not called Aristaenetus, it is nonetheless plausible that he speaks here through this character, since the letter sets the tone for the whole collection. Aristaenetus addresses Philokalos, the "Lover of Beauty"—evidently not just a single individual but a flattering designation for all readers whose interests lead them to take up this volume. Appropriately, the subject of the first letter is Lais, a well-known paragon of beauty, whose perfect looks are extensively described and praised. But Lais is more than just a woman: Aristaenetus makes it clear that he is evoking her through his letter; that is, she is a literary construct that owes its existence to the author's verbal powers, and as such she serves as an emblem of the work itself (see Höschele 2012, 167–76). When at the end of this letter Aristaenetus prays that his writings be granted the one most crucial gift, namely, to possess the charm of Lais, his words may also be understood as a prayer by the author "Aristaenetus" for his compendium of letters in its entirety.

1. **Aristaenetus:** "Best Praising."
2. **Philokalos:** "Lover of Beauty."
3. **Lais:** Name of a famous Corinthian hetaira of the late fifth century B.C.E., who came to embody the ideals of beauty, charm, and sexual allure.
4. **well fashioned:** The Greek term, δημιουργεῖν, refers to the act of creation by either a divine force or an artist.
5. **Graces:** Goddesses of charm and beauty, usually represented in a group of three.
6. **Eros taught my darling:** Eros appears as an archer already in fifth-century B.C.E. art and literature (see, e.g., Euripides, *Hipp.* 530–532). Here his archery is metaphorical, referring to the power of the beloved's gaze.
7. **as Homer describes it:** A reference to Homer, *Od.* 6.231; 23.158, passages in which Athena rejuvenates Odysseus before his encounters with Nausicaa and Penelope, respectively ("she made his hair curly, just like the hyacinth's blossom"). But whereas in Homer the hero needs a divine makeover, the beloved's hair in Aristaenetus naturally resembles a hyacinth's curl.
8. **Dressed, she has the loveliest face…:** This reverses what is said in Plato's *Charmides* (154d), where someone comments that the youth would be completely "without face" if stripped naked. *Epistle* 1.3 (see n. 9) also refers to this passage, but without reversal.

9. **like the motion of a cypress or a palm:** In Homer's *Odyssey* (6.162), Odysseus compares the Phaeacian princess, Nausicaa, to the young shoot of a palm, and Theocritus likens Helen to a cypress at *Id.* 18.30.

10. **Zephyr:** The west wind, often associated with the mild breezes of spring.

11. **Erotes:** Cupids (i.e., gods of love), often represented as winged boys or youths.

12. **The greatest masters have painted her:** Athenaeus 13.588e tells how artists flocked to Lais simply to paint her breasts.

13. **Helen:** The mythic ideal of human beauty, for whose sake the Trojan War was fought. She was the wife of Menelaus but given by Aphrodite to the Trojan prince, Paris, as a bribe for his vote in a beauty contest between herself, Hera, and Athena.

14. **the Graces' queen:** Aphrodite.

15. **Cydonian apples:** Quinces, a favored fruit in erotic contexts since the lyric poet Ibycus (*PMG* 286). The fruit came to be associated with the Cretan town Cydonia.

16. **Siren songs:** The sirens, who first appear in Homer, *Od.* 12.39–54, 153–200, were mythical singers whose song irresistibly lured passing sailors to their death.

17. **the Graces' girdle:** At *Il.* 14.214–215, Homer describes the girdle (κεστός) of Aphrodite, which gives its wearer irresistible sex appeal. As Aphrodite and the Graces are closely linked right from the start of this letter, the fact that the girdle here belongs to the Graces is not in opposition to the *Iliad* passage.

18. **Blame:** Personified Blame (Μῶμος) appears as early as Hesiod, *Theog.* 214, where he is a child of Night, and frequently thereafter (see Callimachus, *Hymn Apoll.* 113). The idea that Blame himself would find nothing to blame was proverbial (see Plato, *Rep.* 487a).

19. **a beauty contest with me as judge:** This begins an elaborate reference to the judgment of Paris (see note 13 above).

20. **I did not give her an apple:** The apple has a long history in erotic literature as a token of love. Here, however, it may refer to the fruit thrown by Discord (*Eris*) into the divine assembly at the wedding of Peleus and Thetis and inscribed "to the fairest." This led to the argument between Hera, Aphrodite, and Athena, which ultimately resulted in the Judgment of Paris.

21. **as the Trojan elders marveled at Helen in Homer:** The elders admire Helen at Homer, *Il.* 3.154–160, when she joins them on the Trojan wall during the *teichoskopia*.

22. **the charm of Lais:** "Charm," χάρις, is not only a quality to be praised in a beautiful woman but also a term used by ancient critics to denote the so-called elegant style (see Demetrius, *On Style* 128–189). The Hellenistic epigrammatist Meleager already plays with this ambiguity (see *Anth. pal.* 5.148, 149).

23. **utter her beloved name continually:** For the programmatic injunction to repeat over and over the name of the beloved, see Meleager, *Anth. pal.* 5.136.

Letter 1.2

This letter presents a witty rewriting of the Judgment of Paris: the speaker is asked by two girls to choose the fairest, and, unable to make a decision, he ends up in bed with both of them. However, he teasingly breaks off his narrative at the most titillating point, refusing to give any details about his ménage à trois.

1. **inferior to the Graces only in number:** The number of the Graces is three (see Hesiod, *Theog.* 907).
2. **so far my story is appropriate:** Direct quotation of a passage in Plato, *Symp.* 217e, where Alcibiades is telling of his vain attempts to seduce Socrates. In reusing this phrase, Aristaenetus highlights that the speaker of this letter is not as strong-minded as the Athenian philosopher and succumbs to the temptation. Aposiopesis is a common device in erotic contexts (see most famously Ovid's *cetera quis nescit?* or "who would not know what followed?" in *Am.* 1.5.25).

Letter 1.3

The narrator's name, Philoplatanos, means "He Who Loves the Plane Tree." It may also play on the personal name Plato (Πλάτων), as this letter very clearly evokes the setting of the *Phaedrus* (229b–230b), a *locus amoenus* where the characters sit beside a stream in the shade of a plane tree (πλάτανος) conversing about love in the midday heat. The addressee's name, Anthokomes, likewise suggests the lush vegetation of the scene described in the letter.

1. **Philoplatanos:** "He Who Loves the Plane Tree."
2. **Anthokomes:** "Blossoming Hair."

3. **Leimone:** The narrator's beloved has a speaking name, signifying "meadow," a term used already in early Greek literature to connote the female genitalia (see Euripides, *Cycl.* 171; see also *Ep.* 2.1). Toward the end of the letter, he plays on the identification of that name with the setting.

4. **an enormous plane tree:** See the introduction to this letter.

5. **"pears, pomegranates, and apples, glorious in their yield":** The speaker quotes Homer, *Od.* 7.115, a line from the famous description of the garden of the Phaeacian king Alkinoos. The passage is one of the *loci classici* for *loca amoena*, and the speaker explicitly marks the reference by saying that it comes from Homer. The line also appears at Homer, *Od.* 11.589, in the description of the torture faced by Tantalus in the underworld, who is never able to reach the luscious fruit that hangs just above his head or drink the refreshing water in which he stands. It may be that our author implicitly contrasts this torture with his depiction of how delightful refreshments (apples and drinks) come floating right up to the lovers for their enjoyment.

6. **some of them already swelling with ripeness:** The description of grape clusters in varying states of ripeness appears already in that same scene from the *Odyssey* cited above (7.122–126). Here, however, Aristaenetus approaches the passage through the filter of one of his favorite models, the imperial author Philostratus the Elder, who had adapted the Homeric lines in his ecphrasis of a painting at *Imag.* 2.17.8.

7. **The spring under the plane tree…:** Aristaenetus describes the cool water of the spring in almost the same terms as that in Plato, *Phaedr.* 230b–c.

8. **so much alike are her breasts and apples:** Starting with Old Comedy (e.g., Crates, fr. 43 Kassel-Austin; Aristophanes, *Ach.* 1199; *Lys.* 155), it was a commonplace of ancient erotic literature to compare female breasts with apples.

9. **she seems almost faceless due to the perfection of what is underneath:** The compliment is a close adaption of Plato, *Charm.* 154d, which Aristaenetus inverted in *Ep.* 1.1 (see n. 8).

10. **the clear echo from the music of the cicada's choir:** Carrying on the frequent reference to Plato's *Phaedrus*, this is an almost verbatim quotation (230c). As early as Hesiod (*W. D.* 582–584), the cicada is associated with song and summer heat.

11. **this one is resting its feet…:** Again, an almost verbatim quotation of the Elder Philostratus, *Imag.* 1.9.2, from the description of a marsh. For birds in a *locus amoenus*, see already the description of Calypso's grove at Homer, *Od.* 5.65–67.

12. the Median plant: The lemon.

13. the moderate blend, which contained equal parts of wine and water: This is in fact a fairly strong mixture. Ancient authors make various recommendations: Hesiod, for instance, soberly suggests three parts water to one of wine (*W. D.* 592–596); Alcaeus calls for a stronger mix of two parts wine to one of water (fr. 346 Lobel-Page); Anacreon describes a two-to-one proportion of water to wine as moderate (*PMG* 356a–b).

14. all our time was devoted to Dionysus and Aphrodite: These gods stand metonymically for wine and love. The line is a quote from Plato, *Symp.* 177e.

15. Phyllion: A speaking name suggesting the Greek word for "leaf," φύλλον.

16. Myrtale: This female name evokes the myrtle, the sacred tree of Aphrodite.

LETTER 1.4

Philochoros describes how his friend Hippias taught him to recognize a hetaira at first sight. The erotodidactic character of the letter, in which Philochoros passes on to Polyainos what he learned from Hippias, squares well with its position toward the beginning of the collection, as it indirectly initiates the reader into the art of love and makes the reader familiar with the type of woman that plays a major role in the corpus.

1. Philochoros: "Lover of Dances."

2. Polyainos: "The One of Much Praise."

3. from Alopeke: An Attic deme, whose name reflects Hippias's fox-like character (from ἀλώπηξ, "fox").

4. purple cloak: Purple was made from a precious dye extracted from a sea snail and typically associated with upper-class clothing.

5. You may know the lion by his claws: A well-attested proverb, indicating that it is possible to make inferences about the whole from a small detail. According to an ancient anecdote, the fifth-century artist Phidias could judge the size of a sculpted lion from the size of one of its claws (see Lucian, *Hermot.* 54).

6. said the man leading the way across the river: A proverb taken from Plato, *Theaet.* 200e. As a scholium to the Platonic text explains, someone asked a guide if the river they were about to cross was deep, to which the latter replied αὐτὸ δείξει ("the matter itself will reveal it"; i.e., "we will see").

7. my beauty…: The rest of the sentence in Greek is corrupt.

LETTER 1.5

The names of the correspondents—Alciphron and Lucian—pay homage to two of Aristaenetus's literary predecessors, who likewise composed fictive letters or dialogues. As Zanetto (1987, 198) has shown, *Ep.* 1.5 forms a thematic diptych with 1.22, which (in a reversal of sender and addressee) is written by Lucian to Alciphron: each text tells of a woman who cunningly regains a man's affection with the help of another female. Both letters contain clear Menandrian echoes, which may attest to Aristaenetus's awareness of how closely Alciphron modeled his letters on New Comedy (see the introduction, pp. xxii–xxv).

1. **Charidemos:** "The One Who Pleases the People."
2. **bamboozle:** The Greek word (βουκολέω) appears twice in Menander's *Samia* (530, 596); see the introduction (pp. xxiii–xxiv) for further details of Aristaenetus's evocation of this play here.
3. **You won't besmirch ... away with it:** An almost verbatim quotation of the words that Rhenaia addresses to Anthia in Xenophon, *Eph.* 5.5.3, when she finds her marriage bed threatened by her husband's love for the girl.
4. **begged his wife for forgiveness:** In *Ep.* 1.22, the companion piece to our letter, the man is likewise tricked into begging for forgiveness.
5. **some benevolent god sent this woman:** The husband interprets the neighbor's sudden appearance as a kind of *deus ex machina*, which highlights the theatrical aspects of the scenario.

LETTER 1.6

The letter tells of a girl who confides in her nurse after engaging in premarital sex. The situation is strongly reminiscent of Euripides's *Hippolytus*, where Phaedra, torn between reason and desire, seeks help from her nurse, to whom she confesses her illicit love for her stepson. As in the play, the nurse initially reacts with shock but then takes a more pragmatic approach and offers her help.

1. **Sophrone:** The nurse's name, from σώφρων ("prudent, reasonable"), stands in contrast to the girl's behavior (see below, where she says that she tried σωφρονεῖν, "to be prudent").
2. **By Artemis:** As a virgin goddess Artemis stands for the virtue that the girl has lost.

LETTER 1.7

The fisherman Kyrtion describes a tantalizing yet ultimately frustrating erotic encounter with a bathing beauty. The scene recalls stories of mortal men (e.g., Tiresias and Aktaion) seeing a goddess at her bath (the girl is, in fact, twice compared to a divinity), which typically results in brutal punishment. In this case, however, the paradigm is brought down to earth when the girl reacts only with mock anger, taking light-hearted, sexually suggestive vengeance on the fisherman for his transgression. According to Alciphron, fishermen are especially susceptible to the allure of Aphrodite due to their intimate connection to the sea, from which the goddess of love was born (see Alciphron, *Ep.* 1.22).

1. **Kyrtion:** "Lobster Pot."
2. **Diktys:** "Net Man."
3. **Nereids:** Daughters of the sea god Nereus and the sea nymph Doris.
4. **how painters picture Aphrodite:** This evokes the motif of Aphrodite Anadyomene, most famously embodied in the painting by the fourth-century B.C.E. artist Apelles.

LETTER 1.8

This letter reproduces the conversation between a horseman and his groom about the omnipotence of Love. Though seemingly untouched by desire, the horseman in fact owes his mastery in riding to Eros, who spurs him on. Moved by his predicament, the groom composes a song to alleviate his master's longing and possibly his own for the rider.

1. **Echepolos:** "The One Who Has Colts."
2. **Melesippos:** "Horse Attendant."
3. **Adonis:** A youth famed for his beauty and loved by Aphrodite.
4. **nothing to do with Dionysus:** An ancient proverb. The precise origin of the proverb is unclear, but it probably refers to the prevalence of non-Dionysian themes in Attic tragedy, a genre performed at festivals in honor of this god.
5. **it is he that drives me on:** The idea that Desire motivates a person toward outstanding accomplishments probably derives from Plato's *Symposium.*
6. **ease desire by singing:** This motif prominently features in Theocritus, *Id.* 11, a poem about the love-struck Cyclops Polyphemus, whose story serves

as an example for the dictum that there is no remedy (φάρμακον) against love but the Muses (see *Id.* 11.1–3).

7. even their own mother: Aphrodite was, for instance, struck with desire for Adonis and Anchises.

LETTER 1.9

The letter tells of a woman who devises a way to touch and even exchange a few words with her lover in the presence of her spouse. It is an irony of this text that the addressee is called Eratosthenes, since this was the name of a famous adulterer caught *in flagrante* and murdered by the angry husband (see Lysias, *On the Murder of Eratosthenes*). Are we therefore to imagine that by reading this anecdote with its portrayal of successful deceit in the service of adultery the historical Eratosthenes was encouraged to enter into a liaison that was not just dangerous but fatal?

1. **Stesichoros:** "Producer of Choruses."
2. **Eratosthenes:** "Love Strong."

LETTER 1.10

The narrative of Acontius and Cydippe is closely modeled on the famous account in Callimachus's *Aetia* (frs. 67–75 Pfeiffer) and has in fact played a crucial role in reconstructing the fragmentary original. Its place within a collection of epistles is particularly appropriate because the story hinges on an object cunningly turned into a sort of letter: an apple inscribed with an oath by Acontius, to which Cydippe inadvertently binds herself when she reads out loud the apple's message: "By Artemis, it is Acontius I shall wed" (see Rosenmeyer 1996; 2001, 110–30). It is notable that Eratokleia is the first female epistolary narrator within the collection, and she seems to show a special sympathy for Acontius, addressing him directly as "loveliest of boys." The name of the letter's actual addressee, Dionysias, may be relevant inasmuch as Callimachus specifies that Cydippe comes from Naxos, the island of Dionysus (fr. 67.5 Pfeiffer).

1. **Eratokleia:** "Famous in Love."
2. **Dionysias:** "The Dionysian One."
3. **the old adage…:** the dictum first appears in Homer, *Od.* 17.218, where it is used as an insult against the swineherd Eumaios and Odysseus in his

disguise as a beggar. The introduction of the maxim is modeled on Plato, *Symp.* 195b (ὁ γὰρ παλαιὸς λόγος εὖ ἔχει).

4. **the girdle:** See *Ep.* 1.1 note 17.

5. **as in Hesiod:** See Hesiod, *Theog.* 907.

6. **dart:** The Greek word ἀκίς is possibly a pun on the name of Acontius (Arnott 1982, 47). Note that the verb ἀκοντίζειν ("to hurl") is used of throwing an apple in *Ep.* 1.25. See also Ovid, *Her.* 21.209–210: "I was wondering why you were called Acontius; well, you have such sharpness (*acumen*) as to cause a wound from afar."

7. **Artemisium:** Callimachus specifies that the encounter between Acontius and Cydippe occurred during a festival of Artemis at Delos.

8. **Cydonian apple:** See *Ep.* 1.1 note 15.

9. **read the words:** In antiquity people commonly read aloud. By uttering the words inscribed on the apple in the temple of Artemis, Cydippe involuntarily binds herself to an oath.

10. **Laertes:** The name of Odysseus's father, who in his grief for the absent son withdrew to the countryside.

11. **sweet voiced (to use that most lovely term of Sappho):** The word μελλιχόφωνος appears in Sappho (fr. 71.6 Voigt). This reference to the Archaic poetess, who was famed for her composition of epithalamia (wedding songs), is particularly fitting in a nuptial context. The explicit citation of Sappho closely echoes that in Philostratus, *Imag.* 2.1.3, though also correcting it. For while Philostratus in his description of a maiden chorus quotes the Sapphic word as μελίφωνος, a term not attested in extant Sapphic verse, Aristaenetus writes μελλιχόφωνος, which we know Sappho used in one of her poems (he seems to mark the superiority of his quotation by employing the superlative ἥδιστον φθέγμα, "most lovely term," instead of Philostratus's ἡδὺ πρόσφθεγμα, "lovely epithet"). The author's engagement here with Philostratus anticipates further allusions to the same work later in this letter.

12. **Pythian god:** Apollo, who had a famous oracle in Delphi.

13. **not mix lead with silver...:** This dictum looks back to the beginning, where it is said that like gravitates to like.

14. **hymenaion:** A song addressed to the wedding god Hymenaios.

15. **when anyone sang off-key, the chorus leader gave her a sharp look...:** This passage closely imitates Philostratus, *Imag.* 2.1.3, again (see note 11 above). By saying that this time the female chorus was singing "for real" (ἐνεργόν), Aristaenetus may be setting off his description from Philostratus's ecphrasis of a painting.

16. **Another beat time to the songs:** Aristaenetus quotes Philostratus again almost verbatim, this time from the ecphrasis *Komos* (*Imag.* 1.2.5). He signals that he is using *another* passage from that author relative to the one in the previous sentence (see note 15 above) by saying that "*another* [ἕτερος] beat time to the songs."

17. **Midas:** The Phrygian king who turned everything into gold by his touch.

18. **Chrysopolis:** A plant believed to soak up melted gold if it is genuine.

LETTER 1.11

This letter portrays a woman who needs to have her beloved's attractiveness confirmed by hearing of it from others. Significantly, the letter writer is named Philostratus after one of Aristaenetus's main models (the same kind of homage can be found in *Ep.* 1.5, 1.22, and 2.1, where Lucian, Alciphron, and Aelian appear as correspondents). The Philostratean coloring is emphasized by clear echoes of *Imag.* 1.10 in the speech of the maid who reports that she has heard the youth praised by others.

1. **Euagoras:** "The Good Speaker."

2. **Alcibiades:** A fifth-century B.C.E. politician, famed for his beauty and ostentatious wealth. According to Pliny (*Nat. Hist.* 36.28), a statue of Eros was modeled after him. The reading of the text, however, is not certain ('Ερωτας is an emendation), and it has been suggested that we read Ἑρμᾶς ("herms") instead, since Clement of Alexandria (*Protr.* 41.26) attests that Alcibiades served as model for these statues at Athens. Herms were stone pillars topped by a bust and, frequently, equipped with genitals; put up at crossroads and boundaries, they served an apotropaic function. In 415 B.C.E. a great scandal was caused by the mutilation of the herms at Athens, in which Alcibiades might have been involved.

3. **Seasons:** Three daughters of Zeus, who represent the peak of physical ripeness and beauty (ὥρα).

4. **his hair would be enough, beautiful in itself...:** This passage is closely modeled on Philostratus, *Imag.* 1.10.3, which describes Amphion as the beloved of Hermes (this intertext might speak in favor of the reading Ἑρμᾶς above; see also note 5 below).

5. **And my, the colors of his cloak! ...:** Another close imitation of Philostratus, *Imag.* 1.10.3, where Amphion's cloak is also described as seeming to change color. There, the narrator tries to explain the garment's magical

quality by suggesting that it may have come from Hermes. Here, the origin of that quality is not explained functionally; rather, it simply points to the origin of the description in Philostratus—who happens to be presented as the letter writer.

6. **equal parts lover and beloved:** The boy stands at the threshold between adolescence and manhood (his facial hair is just coming in), during which phase he is equally attractive to women (as ἐραστής) and men (as ἐρώμενος).

7. **her head seemed to touch the sky:** An expression denoting extreme joy, possibly also used in the same sense in Sappho (52 Voigt) and Horace (*Carm.* 1.1.36).

LETTER 1.12

The speaker praises his beloved Pythias, who is not only stunningly beautiful but also blameless of character, even though she leads a hetaira's life. The type of the good hetaira, as represented by Pythias, is contrasted in *Ep.* 1.14 with the type of the greedy one. Thematically, this letter forms a diptych with the previous epistle in that it presents a man inviting confirmation of his beloved's beauty, while *Ep.* 1.11 presents a female in that role.

1. **Euhemeros:** "Good Day."

2. **Leukippos:** "White Horse" (see note 5 below).

3. **Blame:** See *Ep.* 1.1 note 18.

4. **Like birds of a feather:** Literally, "we both sit next to each other, as a jackdaw always sits next to a jackdaw."

5. **my ledger is filled with happiness:** Literally, "the days are no less happy than those reckoned up in a quiver." This refers to the proverbial Scythian custom of marking each day as happy or unhappy by putting either a white or a black pebble into a quiver. When a person dies, the pebbles are counted up so as to determine whether their life has been fortunate or not (see Phylarchus, *FGrHist* 81 F 83). The names of sender and addressee might allude to this custom and underline the profound happiness of the speaker (Euhemeros, "Good Day," and Leukippos, "*White* Horse").

6. **out of sight, out of mind:** Literally, "a friend for as long as one sees him face to face."

7. **Tyche:** Goddess of fortune.

8. **in the manner of Homer…:** See Homer, *Od.* 23.296, of Odysseus and Penelope, who are reunited after twenty years apart.

LETTER 1.13

This novella-like story is based on a widespread motif in which a wise doctor is able to diagnose and cure the love sickness of a son enamored with his father's mistress or wife. Aristaenetus's version seems especially close to a tale told in a number of ancient sources (e.g., Valerius Maximus 5.7 ext.1; Plutarch, *Demetr.* 38) about the love of Antiochus I, son of Seleucus I, for his stepmother Stratonike. In this case, the son's desperate longing is finally recognized and healed by the famous doctor Erasistratus, who cunningly gets the father to give up his wife for his son's sake, using precisely the same trick as Panacea in this letter.

1. **Eutychoboulos:** "The Fortunate Planner."
2. **Akestodoros:** "The Cure Giver."
3. **Panacea:** "All-Healer," also the name of a goddess, the daughter of the divine doctor Asclepius (see note 4 below).
4. **Asclepius's footsteps:** Asclepius was son of Apollo and the nymph Koronis. He was the model of all future doctors (often called Asklepiadai, "sons of Asclepius").

LETTER 1.14

A hetaira addresses a young man serenading her, declaring that she is interested not in music but in money. The song in front of the beloved's door (*paraklausithyron*) is a widespread topos in ancient erotic poetry; Aristaenetus adds an amusing twist by featuring the woman's less-than-enthusiastic reaction (for similar complaints on the part of females, see Alciphron 4.9 and 4.15). In the letter's second half the speaker describes her introduction to the erotic trade by an elder, more experienced female (in this case her sister), again a common motif.

1. **Philochremation:** "Money Lover."
2. **Eumousos:** "Skilled in Music."
3. **break your jaws…:** Allusion to the legendary invention of the flute by Athena. While playing the newly made instrument, the goddess saw her reflection in the water and, shocked by the disfigurement of her face, she threw away the flute.
4. **a veritable razor on the whetstone:** A proverb that can be applied to people achieving what they want (*CPG* 2:249).

5. **the dynamic duo of Krobylos:** A proverb of obscure origin. It is said to relate to a pimp named Krobylos and the two hetairas working for him (see Zenobius 26).

LETTER 1.15

Like the story of Acontius and Cydippe in *Ep.* 1.10, the tale told in this letter appears to be a reworking of an episode from book 3 of Callimachus's *Aetia* (frs. 80–83 Pfeiffer). Once again we hear of a man falling in love with a girl during a religious festival in honor of Artemis. Pieria's selfless behavior—all she wants from the king is peace for her city, not fabulous riches for herself—stands in stark contrast to the mercenary demands of the hetaira Philochremation portrayed in the previous letter.

1. **Aphrodisios:** "Love Struck."
2. **Lysimachos:** "Battle Dissolver."
3. **casts away his shield:** The iambic poet Archilochus famously presented himself as a ῥίψασπις (one who throws away his shield in battle; see 5 West), which invited later poets to claim the same act of cowardice for themselves (see Alcaeus 428 Lobel-Page; Horace, *Odes* 2.7).
4. **Miletus and Myus:** Two Ionian cities.
5. **Pieria:** The name is appropriate for a woman of great persuasive power, as this is a standing epithet of the Muses, who are described as daughters of Pieria, their natal mountain in Macedonia. There may be added point to the name of Pieria, as she is a kind of antitype to the mercenary hetaira of the previous letter, who rejects the arts of the Muses.
6. **Lydian ... Karian:** Lydia and Karia were regions in Asia Minor.
7. **Pylian Nestor:** Homeric hero and elder statesman of the expedition to Troy, he is often portrayed as giving lengthy and elaborate speeches.

LETTER 1.16

The speaker of this letter recalls how he secretly yearned for a woman (who remains unnamed) and suffered long in silence, until daring to ask Eros for help, twice: first when alone, then in the presence of his beloved, who, miraculously overcome by desire and acting just as the speaker wished, made the first move. Now no longer reticent about his passion, Lamprias tells all to his addressee Philippides, or not quite all, as he breaks off his narrative suggestively so as to leave the rest to the imagination of his friend,

and of the reader. The impulse to talk about one's love—here described as therapeutic—is one that animates a good part of Aristaenetus's collection.

1. **except you ... and your mother:** Eros and Aphrodite.
2. **with pain." [...] Soon I was shown:** There seems to be a lacuna in the text.
3. **the rest:** Euphemistic description for sex, often used in the context of an erotic aposiopesis (see *Ep.* 1.2 note 2).

LETTER 1.17

The speaker of this letter, Xenopeithes, is humorously unable to live up to his name, "the charmer of strangers," in dealing with the hetaira Daphnis. Given all his previous amatory conquests about which he boasts (he seems also familiar with every erotic metaphor and cliché), Xenopeithes is left baffled and indignant at her indifference. In his frustration, he presents the woman as the embodiment of all vice, though her only fault is resisting his desire. Yet with redoubled determination he resolves mid-letter to persevere, enlisting his addressee, Demaretos, likewise a suitor of Daphnis, to do the same. It is interesting to observe that the situation in *Ep.* 1.28 is very similar to the one portrayed here, though with one important difference: there the speaker ultimately decides to give up, telling his addressee and rival that he may keep on trying if he wants.

1. **Xenopeithes:** "Charmer of Strangers."
2. **Demaretos:** "Prayed for by the People."
3. **on the battlefield of love:** The imagery of love as war not only appears in the idea of setting up trophies of conquest but also comes up later in the text when the speaker compares his ongoing amatory attempts to the long siege of Troy.
4. **does the ass appreciate the lyre:** A proverb characterizing someone who is unable to appreciate the excellence of what is being offered to them.
5. **A steady drip...:** For the use of this proverb in erotic contexts, see, for example, Ovid, *Ars* 1.476.
6. **reel the hook back in:** We read αὖθις for the nonsensical αὐτῆς of the transmitted text. The scribe probably did not know that γένυς could mean the edge of a fishing hook (see Oppian, *Hal.* 3.539) and thus supposed that the reference must be to "her jaw."
7. **sons of Atreus:** Agamemnon and Menelaus, who took ten years to finally

conquer Troy (see note 3 above). The reference to the two brothers united in their siege anticipates the speaker's plea to his friend Demaretos for help in overcoming the resistance of Daphnis.

LETTER 1.18

The letter's speaker, Kallikoite, addresses a young fellow hetaira with the speaking name of Meirakiophile, who is exclusively interested in young lovers and does not care for riches. Is there maybe an implicit critique of her friend for neglecting a large and potentially lucrative market in older suitors, or is Kallikoite jealous of Meirakiophile's ability to entice younger customers? A large part of the text consists of extended quotations from Plato: the pederastic behavior described by the Greek philosopher is here transferred to a heterosexual context, with Meirakiophile appearing in the role of the pursuing lover. In light of the lengthy passages lifted directly from Plato, Kallikoite's closing observation that, as far as drinking is concerned, they need nobody else's example, may also be read as a witty reference by Aristaenetus to his use of literary models: "no need for a further quotation from another author" (see Arnott 1982, 316–17).

1. **Kallikoite:** "Beautiful Bedfellow."
2. **Meirakiophile:** "Youth Lover."
3. **Laconian hounds:** Spartan dogs were famed for their speed and keenness in tracking prey. The simile is taken almost verbatim from Plato, *Parm.* 128c.
4. **consolation enough…:** An extended quotation from Plato, *Phaedr.* 240d, which describes the disgust of a boy faced with an elderly lover.
5. **As the old saying…:** Again a direct quotation from Plato's *Phaedrus* (240c).
6. **Say one of the youths…:** The entire passage is taken from Plato, *Rep.* 474d–475a. Aristaenetus has Meirakiophile behave like the lovers of boys, who see something attractive in any youth and find euphemisms for all possible flaws. The parallel between lovers and wine addicts likewise comes from Plato.
7. **look among ourselves:** The link between women and drunkenness is very common in antiquity, especially in comedy.

LETTER 1.19

The speaker of this letter, Euphronion, tells the story of an actress/hetaira, Melissarion, who manages to leave her socially disreputable profession by getting herself pregnant by a wealthy and handsome man. Out of love for the child, he makes her his legitimate wife, and Melissarion marks her change in status not only through a transformed lifestyle but also by changing her name to Pythias. The part of the story prior to when she meets her husband-to-be, at a time when she was at the height of her artistic success and had many paramours, presents her in a situation modeled almost verbatim on an anecdote from Hippocrates, *On the Nature of the Child* (7:490 Littré); for a detailed discussion of Aristaenetus's allusive technique here, see the introduction (pp. xxvii–xxxv). It is interesting to note that Melissarion's career trajectory from actress/hetaira to legitimate wife finds a parallel in the life of Theodora, who would become the bride of the future emperor Justinian, a marriage made possible through Emperor Justin's passing of a law (between 520 and 524) permitting actresses to wed men of any rank provided they give up their profession (see the introduction, pp. xv–xvi).

1. **Euphronion:** "Well Intentioned."
2. **Thelxinoe:** "Enchantress."
3. **By Hera:** As the goddess of marriage, Hera is a fitting deity to be invoked for the following story.
4. **Melissarion:** The name, "Little Bee," suggests a woman flitting from lover to lover.
5. **musician:** The Greek word, μουσουργός, is the same used by Hippocrates in his anecdote about the performer seeking an abortion.
6. **Melissarion socialized with the richest men…:** This entire passage is closely modeled on the account of Hippocrates mentioned above.
7. **I ordered her to do what I knew had to be done:** In Hippocrates's account the pregnant girl aborts the fetus by jumping vigorously up and down while kicking her buttocks with her feet.
8. **Eileithyia:** Goddess of childbirth.
9. **by the two goddesses:** Demeter and her daughter Persephone; this is a typically female oath.
10. **purple cape:** See *Ep.* 1.4 note 4.
11. **by Dione:** Mother of Aphrodite by Zeus, according to Homer, *Il.* 5.

LETTER 1.20

A prison guard writes to a fellow guard, recounting how a young man, incarcerated for adultery, seduced the prison guard's own wife. It is ironic that the narrator cannot resist telling this humorous incident, though it made him a laughing stock, as he himself laments. For the victimized husband as a butt of laughter, one may compare the story of Ares and Aphrodite in Homer, *Od.* 8.266–366, in which the aggrieved spouse, Hephaistos, likewise exposes his own humiliation to the great amusement of the gods.

1. **Phylakides:** "Guard."
2. **Phrourion:** "Custodian."
3 . **Eurybatos:** A proverbial scoundrel. A more detailed account of his particular quality as an escape artist appears in the Suda (ε 3718 Adler).

LETTER 1.21

The letter's narrator describes the frustrating predicament of Architeles, whose beloved Telesippe grants him every liberty with her except intercourse. Ironically, the names of each "lover" include the word for "fulfillment" (τέλος), though the desired end is precisely what is withheld. Architeles is forever stuck in the preliminaries (ἀρχή), as the first part of his name suggests.

1. **Phaleron:** Old harbor of Athens.
2. **For a young man's cravings…:** Quotation from Plato, *Ep.* 7.328B.

LETTER 1.22

This letter tells of a hetaira who wins back the devotion of her lover by feigning interest in another man. The epistle is linked to *Ep.* 1.5 through its identical though reversed correspondents (Alciphron and Lucian), its theme, and its closeness to comedy (see the introduction, pp. xxii–xxv). The names of the protagonists recall characters from Menandrian comedy, and the plot evokes specific elements of the *Perikeiromene*, with jealousy playing a key role in either case (see the introduction, pp. xxiv–xxv).

1. **Glykera:** Glykera, Doris, and Polemon are characters in Menander's *Perikeiromene*.

2. **Charisios:** Charisios is the name of the protagonist in Menander's *Epitrepontes*.

3. **you know what the boy is like:** Recalls a similar expression in *Ep.* 1.5 ("you know what a womanizer the boy is").

4. **For many men disdain what they can readily have:** Evidently a recollection of the sentiment presented in the previous letter, *Ep.* 1.21.

LETTER 1.23

The letter writer, Monochoros, laments his bad luck both in love and in games of chance: he is so distracted by desire that he undermines himself when gambling, while his rivals use the money they win from him to buy precious gifts for his rapacious beloved. The connection between dice play and love is already established in the Archaic Greek poet Anacreon, who features Eros as playing with knucklebones (fr. 398 *PMG*), an image further elaborated by Apollonius of Rhodes at the start of *Argon.* 3. The speaker's name, Monochoros, probably reflects a position in a game where a player has been hemmed in to a single space (χώρα) and hence loses.

1. **Monochoros:** "Checkmate."
2. **Philokybos:** "Dice Lover."

LETTER 1.24

Mousarion reports to her beloved Lysias how she was confronted by a group of suitors, who criticized her for being devoted to a single man (for a reversal of this motif, see *Ep.* 2.13, where a hetaira worries that her lover has left her because she goes with other men). Like the hetaira of *Ep.* 1.18 Mousarion is not interested in financial profit, but where Meirakiophile cares for youthful lovers in general, Mousarion has committed herself to one individual, who—at least according to the other suitors—does not even stand out for his good looks. The motif of a hetaira's devotion to a single lover is here inspired by Lucian, *Dial. Court.* 12 (see notes below and introduction to *Ep.* 1.25).

1. **Mousarion:** The name Mousarion is appropriate for someone who works on stage.
2. **Lysias:** See note 3 below.

3. **you've deafened us…:** This passage is an almost verbatim quotation from Plato's *Lysis* (204c–d), where Hippothales is said to bother his friends with constant praise of the boy Lysis. The name of Mousarion's darling, Lysias, surely is meant to evoke the character from Plato's dialogue. It is, moreover, noteworthy that the man for whose sake Ioessa in Lucian, *Dial. Court.* 12, rejects all other suitors is likewise called Lysias.

4. **And so beautiful…:** There is a gap here of about twenty-six letters in the manuscript.

5. **satyrs:** Hybrid creatures with a horse's tail and grotesque features, who belong to Dionysus's retinue.

LETTER 1.25

In this letter Philainis complains that her sister Thelxinoe has tried to steal away the object of her desire, Pamphilos, during a symposium. As in *Ep.* 1.24, Aristaenetus draws on Lucian, *Dial. Court.* 12, here closely following his model's description of the all-too-obvious flirtation between Lysias and a rival hetaira—especially in the details about the cup and the apple. Indeed, Aristaenetus seems to have split his Lucianic source into two parts, using the beginning of that dialogue as a model for *Ep.* 1.24 and its subsequent portrayal of an amorous symposium as a model for the present letter. His allusive evocation of one text (by the very author who appeared as letter writer in *Ep.* 1.22!) in two juxtaposed epistles may suggest something about Aristaenetus's method of composition, namely that *Ep.* 1.24 and 1.25 were conceived together in response to a reading of the Lucianic dialogue.

1. **Philainis:** This is the name of a fourth-century B.C.E. Samian hetaira who allegedly authored an erotic handbook, fragments of which survive.

2. **Petale:** Petale is likewise a hetaira's name (possibly from πετάννυμι, "to spread wide"), appearing as the title character of a comedy by Pherecrates and also acting as a correspondent in Alciphron (4.8 and 9).

3. **Pamphilos:** "Lover of All," a typical name for lovers in New Comedy.

4. **Thelxinoe:** "Enchantress" (addressee in *Ep.* 1.19).

5. **Tarentine tunic:** Tarentum, a Greek colony in the south of Italy, was famed for its fine fabrics.

LETTER 1.26

The speaker, a public courier named Speusippos, praises Panarete for her stunning beauty and expressive dancing. During the imperial age, pantomime was a popular form of entertainment, in which a dancer, accompanied by music and song, enacted little scenes, often taken from Greek mythology. This letter is unique in containing two references (one to a mime named Karamallos, another to Constantinople) that have been used for determining an approximate date for Aristaenetus (see the introduction, pp. xiii–xiv); a further chronological clue may reside in the profession and name of the letter writer (see note 6 below). It is a nice touch that a courier, whose job it is to deliver messages, must communicate with his beloved by post (is the implication that he is off elsewhere transporting other people's letters?).

1. **Speusippos:** "The Courier Who Hastens on Horseback."
2. **Panarete:** "The One Endowed with Every Talent."
3. **Polymnia:** In the imperial age this muse served as patron goddess of dance and pantomime.
4. **Pharian Proteus:** A sea deity thought to live on the island of Pharos opposite Alexandria. Proteus is endowed with the gift of prophecy but tries to elude those asking for his advice by morphing into various animals and objects (see Menelaus's encounter with Proteus in Homer, *Od.* 4.351–659).
5. **Karamallos:** Various mimes of this name appear in our sources, which makes identification difficult (see the introduction, pp. xiii–xiv).
6. **public courier:** The system of state couriers, established already under Emperor Augustus, was in use until Byzantine times. The service was reformed under Diocletian (284–305) and Constantine I (306–337), being split into two parts, an express and a regular track. The former, known as the *cursus velox*, or ὀξὺς δρόμος, utilized horses and mules as opposed to oxen. As Speusippos's name suggests, he works as a courier on the express track. The fact that the letter reflects Constantine's reforms presents us with an additional *terminus post quem* for Aristaenetus.
7. **new Rome:** That is, Constantinople. The reference to this city gives us a secure *terminus post quem* for the dating of Aristaenetus. Constantinople, previously known as Byzantium, was rebuilt as the new capital of the Roman Empire and consecrated on May 11, 330 c.e., by Constantine I. The name change and the city's characterization as the "new Rome," however, are already attested for 324 c.e.

Letter 1.27

The letter recounts a coy flirtation between a young man and a woman who, while pretending to find her suitor repellent and ostensibly rebuffing his advances, engages him in erotic banter suggesting her interest. The name of the letter's addressee (Amynandros, "He Who Fends Off a Man") may indicate that he has a similar relationship with the speaker.

1. **Klearchos:** "First in Glory."
2. **Amynandros:** "He Who Fends Off a Man."
3. **considering how incredibly smug he is about his beauty:** A verbatim quote of Alcibiades's description of his own self-love in Plato, *Symp.* 217a.
4. **Philon:** From φιλεῖν, "to love." The woman's suggestion that the youth gave himself a speaking name to reflect his self-image as a lover might be read as a metapoetic comment on the way Aristaenetus gives his characters fictitious names.
5. **... trading beauty for beauty—and indeed a lot for a little:** This passage is modeled on Plato, *Symp.* 218e, where Alcibiades describes how he hoped to trade his beauty for Socrates's wisdom.
6. **Libethrians:** Though living in the region of Pieria, the traditional home of the Muses, this people was said to be exceptionally uncultured; the expression "more unmusical than the Libethrians" was proverbial.
7. **by the two goddesses:** See *Ep.* 1.19 note 9.
8. **the wind permits you neither to drop anchor nor to sail:** A phrase from Aeschylus (fr. 250 Radt) that became proverbial.

Letter 1.28

Nikostratos complains to a friend about the fickleness of his beloved Kochlis, whose unpredictable behavior he is unable to comprehend (first she acts as though in love, then she spurns him again). The situation resembles that in *Ep.* 1.17 (see the introduction to that letter), but contrary to the speaker there, who resolves to persevere in his suit, Nikostratos gives up (even though he bears the Greek word for victory in his name), offering free rein to his friend Timokrates to pursue this capricious woman.

1. **Nikostratos:** "Victorious Army."
2. **Timokrates:** "The One Honored for His Might."
3. **measure a white surface with a white tape measure:** A proverb (see

Sophocles, fr. 330 Radt; Plato, *Charm.* 154b) indicating the impossibility of forming a judgment (the στάθμη, or "tape measure," is usually red; see Homer, *Il.* 15.410; *Od.* 21.121).

4. **Kochlis is named for her crookedness:** Nikostratos derives Kochlis's name from the Greek word for a shellfish with a spiral shell (κοχλίς or κόχλος). Once again a character's interpretation of a name may be taken as a metapoetic comment on Aristaenetus's practice (see *Ep.* 1.27 note 4).

5. **changeable as a slipper where one size fits all:** Literally, "more changeable than a cothurnus." The cothurnus was a soft leather boot worn by tragic actors, which equally fit the left and the right foot.

6. **she uses my soul like Penelope her loom:** Penelope promised to choose another husband as soon as the burial shroud for Odysseus's father Laertes was finished. However, by unraveling at night what she had woven during the day, she managed to postpone this moment for a long time (Homer, *Od.* 2.93–109). Note how Aristaenetus plays with this image already in the preceding lines, where Nikostratos claims that Kochlis often "unravels" the hope that she had kindled in him before.

Letter 2.1

The situation of this letter—an intermediary pleads on behalf of his friend with a hetaira who is angry at him for a perceived offense—is reminiscent of Menander's *Perikeiromene* (see *Ep.* 1.22): after Polemon has offended Glykera by cutting off her hair in a fit of jealousy, Pataikos observes that "when a lover is in trouble the only means left to him is persuasion" (497–498) and thereupon tries to reconcile the girl with her lover. As in *Ep.* 1.5, 1.11, and 1.22, the speaker, Aelian, bears the name of an earlier epistolographer. Indeed, the prominence of rural imagery in the second part of the letter may be read as an homage to this author, who composed a collection of twenty *Rustic Letters.* In particular, the striking comparison that the speaker draws between a woman and fruit (ὀπώρα) recalls Aelian's letters 7 and 8, where a hetaira called Opora reflects on the significance of her name and the transience of female beauty. Aristaenetus underlines the importance of such vegetal imagery by naming the addressee Kalyke ("Flower Cup").

1. **Kalyke:** "Flower Cup."

2. **Please, Persuasion, be present ... send:** An almost direct quotation of Menander, *Epitr.* 555–556. While the hetaira Habrotonon in the play asks

Persuasion to aid her speech, Aelian here asks for help in the writing of this letter.

3. **a shadow's shade:** An echo of Pindar, *Pyth.* 8.95, where man is described as "a shadow's dream."

4. **Furies' deadly revels:** The Furies are spirits of vengeance, originally for the spilling of kindred blood, here transposed into the erotic sphere.

5. **Watch out lest, as the proverb says, we snap the string by stretching it too tight:** The proverb is known as early as Herodotus, but the context in which it is used is closely modeled on Lucian, *Dial. Court.* 3.3, where a mother warns her hetaira daughter not to test the patience of a lover.

6. **sheathed in Babylonian gold:** That is, the success of a lover's embassy to a hetaira depends on his coming with money. Babylon was proverbial for its wealth.

LETTER 2.2

Euxitheos declares his boundless love to Pythias, whom he spotted while praying to the gods in a temple. Falling in love at a sanctuary or during a religious festival is a widespread motif in ancient erotic literature (see, for instance, the story of Acontius and Cydippe in *Ep.* 1.10). It might well reflect a real-life phenomenon, as religious events provided one of the few occasions for the encounter of the sexes in a world where women were largely confined to the home.

1. **Euxitheos:** "The One Praying to the Gods."

2. **Pythias:** The name suggests a woman associated with Pythian Apollo at Delphi.

3. **my arms were still outstretched in prayer:** It was a common practice in ancient Greece to pray by holding up one's arms with palms turned toward the sky.

4. **supplicating the gods on my own behalf:** This supplication (ἱκετείαν κατ' ἐμαυτόν) might be read as Aristaenetus's implicit opposition of this letter to the previous one, where the speaker was supplicating a woman on behalf of another man (ἱκετηρίαν ὑπὲρ Χαριδήμου, *Ep.* 2.1).

5. **your slave:** The motif of erotic slavery (*servitium amoris*) is often evoked in ancient literature; in particular it is a characteristic feature of Roman love elegy. Euxitheos's willingness to enslave himself is contrasted with Pythias's characterization as a free woman.

6. **Zeus, transformed:** An allusion to three erotic exploits of Zeus, who slept with Europa in the form of a bull, with Danae in the form of golden rain, and with Leda in the form of a swan.

LETTER 2.3

A newly wed woman here laments the neglect she suffers from her husband Strepsiades, whose sole concern is to practice his oratory. The husband's name clearly recalls that of the hero in Aristophanes's *Clouds*, who goes to study rhetoric with Socrates. Early in that play Strepsiades curses a matchmaker (προμνήστρια, *Clouds* 41) for inducing him to marry his luxury-obsessed wife (*Clouds* 46–55). Aristaenetus cleverly inverts this scene by presenting the female perspective: in this case it is the wife who complains to her matchmaker cousin (προμνήστρια) about the rhetoric-obsessed Strepsiades.

1. **I am grasping a wolf by its ears:** A widespread proverb, known in both Greek and Latin (*auribus teneo lupum*), that Aristaenetus has his speaker explain.

LETTER 2.4

Hermotimos tells a friend of an erotic encounter with his beloved, the serving girl Doris, who managed to sneak out of her master's house at night on the pretext of fetching water.

1. **Doris:** A typical name for a female servant (see *Ep.* 1.22 note 1; see Menander, *Perikeiromene*).
2. **like a bright star rising:** It is a commonplace of erotic literature to compare the beloved with a star or other heavenly body.
3. **Her cheeks reflect ... hard to describe:** These lines are an almost direct quotation from Philostratus. Aristaenetus has transposed the description of the Persian princess Rhodogoune at *Imag.* 2.5.5 to the serving girl Doris.
4. **we did what came next:** The speaker teasingly breaks off his account at the most titillating point, leaving what follows to the reader's imagination; for such erotic aposiopesis, see *Ep.* 1.2 note 2.

LETTER 2.5

A young virgin, inexperienced in love and appropriately named Parthenis, writes to a female friend about how she suffers the pangs of desire for a lyre-playing youth who lives next door. The situation of a girl torn between her love and sense of propriety is modeled especially on Apollonius's depiction of Medea in *Argon.* 3 (see notes 6, 7, and 9), though with no hint of the tragic consequences of betraying one's family and country.

1. **Parthenis:** "Virgin."
2. **Harpedone:** "Yarn" (see note 10 below).
3. **exudes musical understanding and hard-won skill in singing:** These words are inspired by Philostratus's description of the famous mythical flute player Olympus (*Imag.* 1.21.2).
4. **Achilles:** The hero appears as the most handsome Greek who came to Troy in Homer, *Il.* 2.673–674.
5. **Chiron's pupil:** Achilles was educated by the centaur Chiron, among other things in playing the lyre. It is interesting to note that the "Education of Achilles" is the subject of one ecphrasis in Philostratus's *Imagines* (2.2)—when the speaker says that she knows what Achilles looked like from "the pictures [πίνακες] at home," one might be tempted to understand this as a metapoetic reference by Aristaenetus to this Philostratean source.
6. **I clasp my ever-pounding chest…:** Detailed descriptions of love's symptoms are a staple of erotic literature, starting with Sappho (31 Lobel-Page). Here the most thoroughgoing reminiscences are to the portrayal of lovesick Medea in Apollonius, *Argon.* 3.
7. **My thoughts leap … twists and turns:** These lines present a close rewriting of a famous erotic simile in Apollonius, *Argon.* 3.756–760, that compares Medea's pounding heart to the flickering reflection of light from a bucket of water.
8. **torch-bearing god:** Eros, who is often represented holding a torch, which symbolizes the fire of love.
9. **Away with shame; away, good sense…:** This exclamation mimics the one of Medea at Apollonius, *Argon.* 3.785–786 ("away with shame; away with glory").
10. **find some thread, perhaps, or yarn:** This passage may underlie the choice of the addressee's name, as the Greek word ἁρπεδόνη means "cord, yarn."

11. **mysteries:** Cults requiring initiation. Members were prohibited from revealing the secret rites.

LETTER 2.6

The speaker (whose name is not transmitted in the manuscript) sends an indignant letter to his rival Phormion, who gloats about having snatched away his beloved. So as to hide his disappointment, the spurned lover acts as though the girl is a terrible catch. His sarcastic praise of the new couple and wishes for a long life together wittily invert motifs of ancient epithalamia (wedding songs); see notes 2, 3, and 4.

1. **your thoughts are sky-high:** The Greek verb ἀεροβατεῖς (lit., "you walk in the air") is used in Aristophanes's *Clouds* (225, 1503) to characterize Socrates; here, of course, it refers not to a philosopher's lofty thoughts but to the arrogance of the rival in love.
2. **May her face be a match for yours:** In epithalamia it is customary to praise the beauty of bride and groom; here they are imagined as equally ugly.
3. **May you enjoy the fruits of each other's company for a long, long time:** The epithalamic wish for a long and happy life together is turned into a gleeful hope for never-ending misery.
4. **spitting image of its father:** Normally the resemblance of a child to its father (a frequent motif in epithalamia) was taken as a welcome sign of legitimacy; here the speaker's wish is malicious, as he wants the child to be as ugly as its father.
5. **the sword has found the sheath it deserves:** The proverb-like phrase (see English: "there's a nut for every bolt") in all likelihood contains an obscene double entendre.
6. **Cadmeian victory:** A victory that comes at a great loss to the winner. The phrase alludes to the founding of Thebes by Cadmus: following an oracle, the hero had to get water for a sacrifice from a spring guarded by a dragon. He eventually defeated the monster, but all his men were killed during the fight.

LETTER 2.7

The scenario depicted in this letter, with a serving girl seducing her mistress's lover but then being caught by her *in flagrante*, is reminiscent of

ancient mime. This subliterary genre, about which little is known for sure except that it offered popular entertainment in the form of brief sketches, seems frequently to have dealt with the topics of adultery and betrayal. One may, for instance, think of the so-called *Moicheutria* ("Adulteress"), a mime fragment found on papyrus, which shows a married woman trying to force her slave into a sexual relationship though he is in love with someone else. Similarly, in Herondas's *Mimiamb* 5, a woman wants to punish her slave for his infidelity to her. In this letter the topic of sexual rivalry is combined with the motif of erotic preference between young and mature love, which has a long history in ancient literature, going at least as far back as Aristophanes's *Ekklesiazousai* (893–923). Upon discovering that her young slave girl is having sex with her lover, the mistress attempts to persuade him of her superiority as an experienced woman—by leaving the outcome open, the letter, written from one man to another, invites the reader to reflect about his own preferences.

1. **Terpsion:** "Joy."
2. **Polykles:** "Much Renowned."
3. **a Sicilian filching unripe grapes:** An ancient proverb applied to someone who would steal anything, even objects without value. The reference to Empedocles here is an emendation, though a plausible one, since the philosopher could be understood as an archetypal Sicilian.

LETTER 2.8

The letter writer Theokles is married to a girl he loves but is now struggling with his illegitimate passion for her mother. One could take the story as an inversion of the Hippolytus/Phaedra myth, where a stepmother falls in love with her husband's son. Zanetto (in Conca and Zanetto 2005, 375–76) suggests, however, that the epistle might be inspired by Ovid's account of Myrrha's love for her father, who unwittingly ends up sleeping with his own daughter (*Metam.* 10.298–502). Theokles's hesitation to court a woman who calls him son and whom he has often addressed as mother could evoke the (tragically ironic) terms of endearment exchanged between Myrrha and Cinyras: "maybe, using a name appropriate to her age, he called her 'daughter,' and she said 'father' to him, so that the crime would not lack its proper names," *Metam.* 10.467–468). Theokles's plea to the gods to avert such impiety is furthermore paralleled by *Metam.* 10.321–322: "O gods, I invoke you, O piety and sacred laws of the family, prevent this sacrilege and

oppose my crime." This closing prayer is appropriate coming from someone named "Glory of the Gods." Moreover, it is interesting to note that this
letter picks up the motif of young versus mature love, which was central to
the previous text (*Ep.* 2.7).

1. **Theokles:** "Glory of the Gods."
2. **Hypereides:** The name of a famous fourth-century B.C.E. Athenian
orator, most of whose speeches do not survive. He appears as an addressee
also in Alciphron (4.3), where he is praised for his defense of the hetaira
Phryne. By taking him up again here Aristaenetus may suggest that Hypereides was a figure to whom one could turn in erotic crises.
3. **Arignote:** "Well Known."

LETTER 2.9

Forsaken by his beloved, a lover tries to win her back, not by blaming the
girl, but by feigning concern that the gods might punish her for breaking
her oath. In *Ep.* 1.10 Acontius had similarly worried that Cydippe might
suffer by perjuring herself, but while the lover's fear in that instance was
genuine (she has unwittingly sworn to marry him, and he keeps his worry
to himself), here it seems a calculated attempt by Dionysodoros to both
scare the girl and present himself in a good light. It is ironic that erotic
oaths were traditionally said not to be punishable if broken, a commonplace already found in Hesiod's *Catalogue of Women* (124 Merkelbach-
West); see also Plato, *Symp.* 183b ("they say that oaths do not exist in matters of love"), and *Ep.* 2.20. Perhaps the speaker is here counting on the
fact that his beloved is "naïve and youthful" enough to be unaware of that
tradition and hence susceptible to his ruse?

1. **Dionysodoros:** "The Gift of Dionysus."
2. **Ampelis:** "Young Vine."
3. **Dike:** Goddess of justice.

LETTER 2.10

Philopinax is in love with the image of a girl he has painted, which does
not and cannot respond to his touch. His predicament resembles that of
Pygmalion, who was struck with passion for a statue of his own creation
(see Ovid, *Metam.* 10.243–297), though the medium in which Philopinax

works clearly puts him at a further disadvantage: taking a two-dimensional portrait to bed is bound to be even less satisfying than embracing a three-dimensional statue. While the gods reward Pygmalion by making his statue come to life, Philopinax ends his letter with a prayer for a living version of his beloved that evidently remains unfulfilled. Interestingly, he does not want to replace his painted girl with a real one but envisions the two side by side, the juxtaposition itself allowing him to appreciate the living beauty. Ancient authors report various cases of agalmato-/iconophilia (see, e.g., Pseudo-Lucian, *Am.* 15–16, on a youth who had sex with Praxiteles's Knidian Aphrodite), and the topic seems to have been a popular one in rhetorical exercises (Philostratus, *Lives of the Sophists* 2.18, mentions a speech by Onomarchos of Andros delivered in the voice of an image lover, and Severus of Alexandria, *Ethop.* 8 (= Libanius, *Ethop.* 27), composed a character sketch, or *ethopoieia*, on the following topic: "What would a painter who painted a girl and fell in love with her say?"). Like Lais in *Ep.* 1.1, who owes her existence to the author's verbal power, the painted beloved of Philopinax is a product of artistic skill, and the letter can be read as a further reflection on the constructedness of Aristaenetus's epistolary loves (see Höschele 2012, 176–82). An intriguing (in)version of the motif is to be found in Alciphron 4.1, where the model/statue addresses her creator: Phryne invites her lover, the sculptor Praxiteles, to make love to her/her image in a temple precinct (see Rosenmeyer 2000).

1. **Philopinax:** "Image Lover."
2. **Chromation:** "Pigment."
3. **Phaedra, Narcissus, and Pasiphae:** To console himself in his misery, Philopinax evokes three mythical examples of unnatural desire more wretched than his own: Phaedra committed suicide over the unrequited love for her stepson Hippolytus, Narcissus pined away with desire for his own reflection, and Pasiphae copulated with a bull and gave birth to the monstrous Minotaur, half bull and half man.
4. **For the spring bears the image…:** The sentence conflates the beginning and end of an ecphrasis that Philostratus the Elder gives of a painting representing Narcissus: "The spring bears the image of Narcissus, even as the painting represents both the spring and the whole story of Narcissus" (*Imag.* 1.23.1) and "For the youth stands over the youth standing in the water, or rather over the youth who looks at him and seems like someone dying of thirst for his beauty" (*Imag.* 1.23.5). By evoking the two phrases that frame the image in Philostratus, our text wittily suggests that Philopi-

nax "saw" the painting of Narcissus in the art gallery imagined by the *Imagines*, whose speaker poses as an art critic and purports to offer brief discourses on pictures he has encountered in a Neapolitan villa.

5. **a word crouches at their very tip:** The painted girl looks as though she is about to speak. This is a widespread topos in ecphrastic literature; see, for example, Asclepiades (43.3 Gow-Page; *Anth. plan.* 120.3) on Lysippus's Alexander statue: "the bronze resembled one about to speak."

6. **She, however, remains silent...:** In ecphrastic literature the absence of voice is often said to give away the artificiality of a statue or portrait (e.g., Erinna, *Anth. pal.* 6.352.4: "if he had given her voice, she would be entirely Agatharchis"); here Philopinax amusingly associates the silence of the image with the unresponsiveness of a hetaira.

LETTER 2.11

The speaker, who has tried to ban his love for a hetaira by getting married to a respectable woman, finds that he loves both at once and struggles to understand why he cannot keep them both under the same roof. The motif of simultaneous passion for multiple beloveds is widespread in ancient erotic literature; in particular, the letter appears to be closely modeled on Ovid, *Am.* 2.10, which envisions a similar situation and likewise illustrates the effect of a double passion through the image of a ship being tossed this way and that by contrary winds (vv. 9–10). In this light the speaker's opening wish to consult experts in love might be read as a metapoetic reference to earlier authors who depicted this predicament, such as Ovid.

1. **Sosias:** The significance of Apollogenes's name is not evident, but it is worth noting that Sosias is a common name for comic slaves, who are often asked for help in matters of love.

LETTER 2.12

The usual advice given to a man was to choose someone of his own social class as a bride (see, e.g., Callimachus, *Epigr.* 1 Pfeiffer). The speaker of this letter describes his mistake in marrying a woman of lower status, who—contrary to his expectation—has become as insolent and demanding as a spoiled, rich woman. Ultimately he resolves to kick her out.

1. **Euboulides:** "The One of Good Counsel."

2. **Hegesistratos:** "The One Leading an Army."

3. **desire is often born from pity:** See Achilles Tatius 3.14.3: "Pity often procures love."

4. **Deinomache:** "Terrible in Battle."

5. **I show her the threadbare coat…:** Euboulides imitates the gesture of Strepsiades in Aristophanes's *Clouds* and quotes the words that the comic character addresses to his wife ("O woman, you are laying it on too thick," *Clouds* 55); the allusion is explicitly signaled ("as in the comedy").

6. **The bear is in the room…:** An ancient proverb attested already in Bacchylides (fr. 6 Snell-Maehler).

Letter 2.13

Chelidonion, a hetaira, worries that her lover has abandoned her because she has to be with other men to make a living—a problem also presented in Lucian, *Dial. Court.* 12, though from the perspective of the jealous male, and inverted in *Ep.* 1.24, where potential lovers criticize a hetaira for devoting herself to only one man (see introduction and notes to *Ep.* 1.24). Here Chelidonion imagines herself in the role of Ariadne and her lover as Theseus, since he left her while she was asleep. In the myth the hero Theseus fled from Crete together with the princess Ariadne, after she had helped him kill the Minotaur and escape the labyrinth. Yet he abandoned his sleeping companion on the island of Naxos, where the god Dionysus subsequently found the girl and married her. Chelidonion hopes that Philonides will be not only Theseus to her but also Dionysus, though the letter leaves it open whether her wish is fulfilled. It is interesting to note that this epistle is one of the very few that refer in detail to the act of writing (see also *Ep.* 1.24 and 2.5).

1. **Chelidonion:** "Little Swallow."

2. **Philonides:** "Love Child."

3. **Megara:** A city on the coast between Athens and Corinth.

4. **by that quiver of yours:** Chelidonion imagines her beloved as Eros.

Letter 2.14

Melitta writes to her lover Nikochares, filled with joy about their recent reconciliation: an (unspecified) plot against them had led to a quarrel, but their mutual passion withstood the trial. That lovers have to guard them-

selves against the resentment of others is a widespread motif in ancient erotic literature. Thus Catullus, for instance, prompts his beloved to exchange innumerable kisses and mix up their count "lest no malevolent person can be jealous of us when he knows that there are so many kisses" (*Carm.* 5.12–13).

1. **Melitta:** "Bee."
2. **Nikochares:** "The One Rejoicing in Victory."
3. **Melissarion:** Diminutive of Melitta, a common hetaira's name. See also *Ep.* 1.19.
4. **you stretched your finger…:** This seems to have been a salutatory gesture.

LETTER 2.15

Two women scheme to satisfy their respective desire for a man in the other's household (in one case for the husband, in the other for a slave). Once again the situation resembles a scenario such as might have occurred in ancient mime (see the introduction to *Ep.* 2.7).

1. **Chrysis:** "Goldie."
2. **Myrrhine:** "Myrtle." Both names are typical of comedy. The myrtle plant was closely associated with Aphrodite.
3. **Euktetos:** "Well Bought" (a reference to the purchase of the slave), but also "Good to Possess," in a sexual sense.

LETTER 2.16

Myrtale writes to her lover Pamphilos, complaining that he does not care for her anymore but is crazy with desire for another hetaira, who plays hard to get. Blaming her love and easy availability for his loss of interest, she decides to forswear her passion and resist any possible advances from now on (but is her aim merely to spur him on?). It is a common motif that rejection kindles desire (see note 7 below), and emotional attachment to a single lover can prove detrimental to a hetaira's trade (in Lucian, *Dial. Court.* 12, for instance, Ioessa finds herself in a similar situation, as she has eyes for no one but Lysias).

1. **Myrtale:** "Myrtle."

2. **Pamphilos:** "The One Who Loves All."

3. **often you pass … seen it:** A quotation from Alciphron 4.7.1, where Thais (who bears the same name as Myrtale's rival; see note 6 below) complains that Eutychides has stopped showing interest in her after devoting himself to the study of philosophy.

4. **I never shut you out:** That is, Pamphilos never found himself in the situation of an *exclusus amator*; similarly Ioessa to Lysias in Lucian, *Dial. Court.* 12.1 ("Never have I left you at my door, saying, 'There is another man inside'").

5. **then I would have seen … and showing it:** A reversed quotation of two phrases from Lucian, *Dial. Court.* 12.2 ("You, O Ioessa, have ruined him by loving him too much and showing it … you will see him completely inflamed with desire and truly crazy with passion in turn").

6. **Thais:** The name of a famous hetaira linked with both Alexander the Great and his general Ptolemy I Soter.

7. **You pursue her … from afar:** The idea of erotic pursuit already appears in Sappho (1.21 Voigt): "If she flees, she will soon follow you." For the idea that men go after what is hard to get, see Callimachus, *Anth. pal.* 12.102 (1 Gow-Page; 31 Pfeiffer), whose speaker compares his desire to that of a hunter ignoring the easy prey: "Such too is my desire: expert in pursuit of fleeing prey, it flies from what lies right there" (vv. 5–6).

8. **worth four cents:** Literally, four obols, a sum indicating little value.

LETTER 2.17

A lover having been warned off by the girl he desires, because she is already in a relationship, declares that his love will make him persist despite any possible dangers. It is a commonplace of ancient erotic literature that a lover will endure any peril, even death, for the sake of his beloved (see, e.g., Phaedrus's speech in Plato, *Symp.* 179a–b).

1. **Epimenides:** "Son of Persistent."

2. **Arignote:** "Well Known"; see *Ep.* 2.8, where the speaker is married to a girl of this name but longs for her mother.

3. **I already live with someone:** The Greek word σύνοικος ("someone who lives in the same house as another") suggests that the girl is a concubine.

4. **a youth of such qualities is killed:** The threat is a real one, since under Athenian law a man could kill another if he caught him *in flagrante* with a member of his household.

5. **"With it, or on it"**: Spartan mothers are said to have told their sons when they went off to battle that they should return either with their shield or on it (i.e., dead; see Plutarch, *Sayings of Spartans* 241F).

6. **I choose either marriage with delight or death:** The same sentiment is attributed to Acontius in *Ep.* 1.10.

7. **Let the dice's cast come up either all or nothing:** Literally, "let the dice that have been cast now be either three times six or three"; these are the highest (eighteen) and lowest (three) possible scores in dice play.

LETTER 2.18

This letter tells of a hetaira and her pimp, who fool a young man by respectively posing as a modest woman and a magician. Against payment the pimp performs erotic spells destined to kindle the girl's desire, and she plays along with the act—until they have robbed the young lover of all his money. With its tale of deception, magic, a shady woman, and a pimp, the text recalls the characters and situations of mime. Its generic affinity to these popular sketches is underlined by several references to the world of the theater.

1. **Mantitheos:** "Divine Prophet."
2. **Aglaophon:** "Glorious Voice."
3. **Thelxinoe:** The name also appears in *Ep.* 1.19 and 1.25; its derivation from θέλγω ("to beguile") is particularly suggestive in this tale of love and magic.
4. **a wolf ... gentlest:** A quotation from Plato, *Soph.* 231a.
5. **As her beauty ... fire:** A quotation from Plato, *Phaedr.* 251b. That love enters through the eyes is a widespread motif (e.g., Xenophon, *Eph.* 1.3.2; Achilles Tatius 1.9.4; 5.13.4; Paulus Silentiarius, *Anth. pal.* 5.226).
6. **[...]:** The text has a lacuna here, in which the pimp must have been introduced.
7. **like a Cretan...:** A proverb referring to someone who pretends to be ignorant of something that they, in fact, know very well. In antiquity Cretans were known as notorious liars.
8. **magic wheel:** The Greek word (ἴυγξ) refers to a bird, the wryneck, which was bound to a revolving wheel and used in magic incantations. It is famously invoked during the magic rite performed by Simaitha in Theocritus, *Id.* 2, who repeatedly chants: "Iynx, bring my man back to the house."

LETTER 2.19

After hearing a youth sing before her door, a woman questions her servant girl about him and upon learning of his love asks her to invite him back. This is one of the rare instances in which a lover's song before the beloved's door (*paraklausithyron*) actually achieves its aim (for the more typically unsuccessful attempt, see the next letter, *Ep.* 2.20, and *Ep.* 1.11).

1. **Archilochus to Terpander:** The names of two famous early Greek poets, perhaps because in the youth's wooing of his beloved the medium of song plays a crucial role.

2. **youthful revelers … in the dead of night:** These lines refer to the *komos*, the traditional nighttime procession following a drinking party, in which revelers streamed out into the streets, making a general nuisance of themselves and singing songs before the door of their beloveds.

3. **not in a dream but wide awake:** The Greek phrase (οὐκ ὄναρ, ἀλλ' ὕπαρ) goes back to Homer's *Odyssey*, where it refers to Penelope's prophetic dreams (19.547; 20.90). The contrast is also a favored expression of Plato's (e.g., *Phaedr.* 277d; *Rep.* 7.520c).

4. **Sirens:** See *Ep.* 1.1 note 16.

5. **Hippothales … you'd know him at once just by his good looks:** The same is said *by* Hippothales about the beautiful youth Lysis in Plato's dialogue of that name (*Lysis* 204e). In a characteristic and witty reversal of his model, Aristaenetus thus turns Hippothales, who appears as the speaker in Plato, into the one spoken of.

6. **through their kisses weaving their souls together…:** The idea that a kiss allows the lovers' souls to mingle often appears in erotic epigram, starting with an epigram attributed to Plato (*Anth. pal.* 5.78): "When kissing Agathon, I stopped my soul at the edge of my lips—for the bold one came as though wanting to make a crossing."

LETTER 2.20

This letter seems to be inspired by a passage in Plato's *Phaedrus* that famously compares the desire of a lover with a wolf's hunger: "As wolves love sheep, so lovers desire boys" (242d). Transforming the pederastic constellation into a heterosexual one, Aristaenetus shows us a woman who adamantly rejects the advances of a suitor named Lykon (from λύκος, "wolf"), as she doubts the sincerity of his oaths. It is interesting to note

how the letter self-consciously points out the clichéd stereotypes of erotic persuasion employed by the youth, and it is tempting to understand the woman's refusal as a sign that she knows and sees through the standard tropes of this tradition (e.g., "You yourself say that your oaths don't reach the ears of the gods").

1. **Okeaneios:** "Oceanic."
2. **Aristoboulos:** "The Best Counsel." The significance of the names in this context is not evident.
3. **Lykon:** The name emblematizes the lover's predatory nature (for an explicit comparison between Lykon and a wolf, see below).
4. **in the rude manner of a Scythian:** The Scythians, a nomadic people living north of the Black Sea, were often used as an example of uncultivated barbarism.
5. **you camp out ... blanket:** This phrase combines two passages from Plato's *Symposium*, describing the behavior of the lover and Eros respectively (183a: "camping out on door steps"; 203d: "always being on the ground and without a blanket, you sleep ... by the doors").
6. **an oath forever ready on the tip of your tongue:** The expression is similar to one in Lucian, *Dial. Court.* 7.3, about the readiness of young men to swear their love.
7. **For as wolves ... after women:** See the introduction to this letter.
8. **You yourself say ... the gods:** See the introduction to *Ep.* 2.9.
9. **wolf ... gaping mouth:** A proverbial phrase designating a person with vain hopes, mostly attested in comic writers (e.g., Aristophanes, fr. 350 Kassel-Austin; Euboulos, fr. 14.11 Kassel-Austin; Menander, *Aspis* 372–373).

LETTER 2.21

The speaker envisions himself as judging the beauty of his beloved against that of all other women (see *Ep.* 1.12) and finds that she has no equal. He then gives a description of her stunning features (see *Ep.* 1.1) and swears his eternal love to her.

1. **Habrokomes:** The name of the romantic hero in Xenophon of Ephesus; see note 7 below.
2. **judging one against the other:** The motif of a beauty contest ultimately goes back to the Judgment of Paris but is also present in various erotic texts, such as Rufinus, *Anth. pal.* 5.35 and 36, or Alciphron 4.14.

3. **For your charms … as the proverb says:** The proverb as it appears, for instance, in Zenobius (1.36) is "The Graces are nude," meaning that the Charites give their gifts without holding back.

4. **There's no need for you to wear a crown…:** The idea that a woman does not need a crown, because her own beauty (here her hair) is sufficient adornment, might be inspired by erotic epigrams, such as Meleager, *Anth. pal.* 5.143: "The garland on Heliodora's head is withering, but she herself shines forth as the garland's garland."

5. **And just as a rose … women far behind:** Again the image seems to be inspired by an epigram (see Rhianos, *Anth. pal.* 12.58.3–4): "Empedocles is so much more radiant [than the other boys of Troizen], as a lovely rose outshines the other springtime flowers."

6. **take us captive with your eyes…:** The erotic power of the beloved's eyes recalls a motif found in Meleager, *Anth. pal.* 12.101, where Myiscus shoots the speaker with his eyes, a poem adapted by Propertius (see 1.1.1: "Cynthia was the first to capture pitiable me with her eyes").

7. **Let this, therefore, be my one rightful pursuit … to listen to her chatting:** An almost verbatim quotation from Xenophon, *Eph.* 2.4.1, where the same is said of the lover Habrokomes, who bears the same name as the speaker here, and his love toward Anthia.

LETTER 2.22

This letter, the last in the collection, breaks off in the middle, and we do not know whether other texts followed and, if so, how many. Its plot is that of an erotic novella in the style of the so-called *Milesian Tales*, a genre that influenced Apuleius's *Golden Ass*, which in turn inspired stories such as those in Boccaccio's *Decameron*. A woman, who is surprised by her husband while sleeping with another man, cunningly pretends that her lover is a burglar. It is not clear how the text ended, but we may assume that the woman's suggestion to guard the thief overnight gave the adulterous pair the opportunity to continue what had been interrupted by the husband's unexpected return and facilitated the lover's escape. One might compare the "Tale of the Tub" in Apuleius, *Golden Ass* 9.5–7, where an adulterous wife, surprised by the sudden return of her husband, hides her lover in a tub, which she later pretends to have sold to him. While the husband examines the tub's interior for possible defects, the wife has sex with her lover on top of it, even as she directs her husband in his inspection.

1. **Charmides:** The name of a beautiful youth who was Socrates's interlocutor in Plato's dialogue *Charmides*, which deals with the question of *sophrosyne*, or temperance (Aristaenetus alludes to this dialogue in *Ep.* 1.1 [note 8] and 1.3 [note 9]). Could it be that the speaker's name thus ironically contrasts with the following tale of unbridled lust?

2. **Eudemos:** This name possibly evokes the disciple and editor of Aristotle (see the *Eudemian Ethics*). If we are indeed meant to think here of these figures who are normally linked with serious philosophical discourse, it might be a bit of play on the part of Aristaenetus that he allows us to overhear them conversing humorously about adultery.

3. **the Eleven:** A reference to magistrates in classical Athens, who were responsible for prisons.

Bibliography

Anderson, G. 1993. *The Second Sophistic: A Cultural Phenomenon in the Roman Empire*. London: Routledge.

———. 1997. "Alciphron's Miniatures." Pages 2188–206 in part 2, *Principat*, 34.3 of *Aufstieg und Niedergang der römischen Welt: Geschichte und Kultur Roms im Spiegel der neueren Forschung*. Edited by H. Temporini and W. Haase. Berlin: de Gruyter.

Arnott, W. G. 1973. "Imitation, Variation, Exploitation: A Study in Aristaenetus." *Greek, Roman, and Byzantine Studies* 14:197–211.

———. 1974. Review of O. Mazal, *Aristaeneti Epistularum Libri II*. *Gnomon* 46:353–61.

———. 1982. "Pastiche, Pleasantry, Prudish Eroticism: The Letters of 'Aristaenetus.'" *Yale Classical Studies* 27:291–320.

Bast, F. J. 1796. *Specimen editionis novae epistolarum Aristaeneti*. Vienna: Blumauer.

Bianchi, N. 2008. "Appunti sulla tradizione manoscritta e la ricezione di Aristeneto." *Exemplaria Classica* 12:135–43.

Bing, P. 2009. *The Scroll and the Marble: Studies in Reading and Reception in Hellenistic Poetry*. Ann Arbor: University of Michigan Press.

Blume, F. H. 2009. *Annotated Justinian Code*. Edited by T. Kearley. 2nd ed. Online: http://www.uwyo.edu/lawlib/blume-justinian/ajc-edition-2.

Boissonade, J., ed. 1817. *Lucae Holstenii epistolae ad diversos*. Paris: Bibliopolium Graecum-Latinum-Germanicum.

Borg, B., ed. 2004. *Paideia: The World of the Second Sophistic*. Berlin: de Gruyter.

Boswell, J. 1980. *Christianity, Social Tolerance, and Homosexuality: Gay People in Western Europe from the Beginning of the Christian Era to the Fourteenth Century*. Chicago: University of Chicago Press.

Boyer, A. 1701. *Letters of Wit, Politicks and Morality ... also Select Letters of Gallantry out of the Greek of Aristaenetus*. London: J. Hartley.

Brenous, J. 1938. *Aristénète: Lettres d'amour*. Paris: Belles Lettres.

Brown, T. 1707. *The Works of Mr. Thomas Brown in Prose and Verse; Serious, Moral, and Comical.* Vol. 1. London: S. Briscoe.

Bungarten, J. J. 1967. *Menanders und Glykeras Brief bei Alkiphron.* Ph. diss., University of Bonn.

Burri, R. 2004. "Zur Datierung und Identität des Aristainetos." *Museum Helveticum* 61:83–91.

Ceccarelli, P. 2013. *Ancient Greek Letter Writing: A Cultural History (600 BC–150 BC).* Oxford: Oxford University Press.

Conca, F., and G. Zanetto. 2005. *Alcifrone, Filostrato, Aristeneto: Lettere d'amore.* Milan: Rizzoli.

Cribiore, R. 2001. *Gymnastics of the Mind: Greek Education in Hellenistic and Roman Egypt.* Princeton: Princeton University Press.

Drago, A. T. 1997. "Due esempi di intertestualità in Aristeneto." *Lexis* 15:173–87.

———. 2007. *Aristeneto: Lettere d'amore; Introduzione, testo, traduzione e commento.* Lecce: Edizioni Pensa Multimedia.

Floridi, L. 2012. "*De Glaucia inmatura morte praevento:* Riflessioni su Auson. ep. 53 Gr." *Eikasmos* 23:283–300.

Gager, J. G., ed. 1992. *Curse Tablets and Binding Spells from the Ancient World.* Oxford: Oxford University Press.

Gallé Cejudo, R. J. 1999. *Aristéneto: Cartas eróticas; Introducción, traducción y notas.* Madrid: Ediciones clásicas.

Gibson, R., and A. D. Morrison. 2007. "Introduction: What Is a Letter?" Pages 1–16 in Morello and Morrison 2007.

Gleason, M. 1995. *Making Men: Sophists and Self-Presentation in Ancient Rome.* Princeton: Princeton University Press.

Goldhill, S. 2009. "Constructing Identity in Philostratus' Love Letters." Pages 287–305 in *Philostratus.* Edited by E. Bowie and J. Elsner. Cambridge: Cambridge University Press.

Harder, M. A. 1993. "Thanks to Aristaenetus...." Pages 3–13 in *Polyphonia Byzantina: Studies in Honour of Willem J. Aerts.* Edited by H. Hokwerda, E. R. Smits, and M. M. Woesthuis. Groningen: Forsten.

———. 2012. *Callimachus: Aetia.* 2 vols. Oxford: Oxford University Press.

Hercher, R. 1873. *Epistolographi graeci, recensuit, recognovit et adnotatione critica instruxit R. Hercher.* Paris: Firmin Didot.

Hinds, S. 1998. *Allusion and Intertext: Dynamics of Appropriation in Roman Poetry.* Cambridge: Cambridge University Press.

Hodkinson, O. 2007. "Better Than Speech: Some Advantages of the Letter in the Second Sophistic." Pages 283–300 in Morello and Morrison 2007.

———. 2013. "Aelian's Rustic Epistles in the Context of His Corpus: A Reassessment of Aelian's Literary Programme and Qualities." Pages 257–310 in *Lettere, mimesi, retorica: Studi sull'epistolografia letteraria greca di età imperiale e tardo antica.* Edited by O. Vox. Leece: Pensa Multimedia.

Hodkinson, O., P. Rosenmeyer, and E. Bracke, eds. 2013. *Epistolary Narratives in Ancient Greek Literature.* Leiden: Brill.

Holzberg, N., ed. 1994. *Der griechische Briefroman: Gattungstypologie und Textanalyse.* Tübingen: G. Narr.

Höschele, R. 2009. "Catullus' Callimachean *Hair*-itage and The Erotics of Translation." *Rivista di filologia e di istruzione classica* 137:118–52.

———. 2012. "From Hellas with Love: The Aesthetics of Imitation in Aristaenetus's *Epistles*." *Transactions of the American Philological Association* 142:157–86.

———. 2014. "Greek Comedy, the Novel, and Epistolography." Pages 735–52 in *The Oxford Handbook of Ancient Comedy.* Edited by M. Fontaine and A. Scafuro. Oxford: Oxford University Press.

Jacob, A. 1988. "Une épigramme de Palaganus d'Otrante dans l'Aristénète de Vienne et le problème de l'Odyssée de Heidelberg." *Rivista di studi bizantini e neoellenici* 25:185–203.

Jenkins, T. E. 2006. *Intercepted Letters: Epistolarity and Narrative in Greek and Roman Literature.* Plymouth: Lexington.

Johnson, W. J. 2010. *Readers and Reading Culture in the High Roman Empire: A Study of Elite Communities.* Oxford: Oxford University Press.

Jory, E. J. 1996. "The Drama of the Dance: Prolegomena to an Iconography of Imperial Pantomime." Pages 1–28 in *Roman Theater and Society.* Edited by W. J. Slater. Ann Arbor: University of Michigan Press.

Kapparis, K. 2002. *Abortion in the Ancient World.* London: Duckworth.

König, J. 2007. "Alciphron's Epistolarity." Pages 257–82 in Morello and Morrison 2007.

Kuefler, M. 2001. *The Manly Eunuch: Masculinity, Gender Ambiguity, and Christian Ideology in Late Antiquity.* Chicago: University of Chicago Press.

Lesky, A. 1951. *Aristainetos: Erotische Briefe; Eingeleitet, neu übertragen und erläutert.* Zürich: Artemis.

———. 1957. "Zur Überlieferung des Aristainetos." *Wiener Studien* 70:219–31.

Letters of Love and Gallantry: Written in Greek by Aristaenetus. 1716. London: Bernard Lintot.

Licht, H. 1928. *Liebesbriefe des Aristainetos.* Dresden: P. Aretz.

Luchner, K. 2009. "Pseudepigraphie und antike Briefromane." Pages 233–66 in *Pseudepigraphie und Verfasserfiktion in frühchristlichen Briefen.* Edited by J. Frey, J. Herzer, M. Janßen, and C. K. Rothschild. Wissenschaftliche Untersuchungen zum Neuen Testament 246. Tübingen: Mohr Siebeck.

Magrini, P. 1981. "Lessico platonico e motivi comici nelle lettere erotiche di Aristeneto." *Prometheus* 7:146–58.

Maricq, A. 1952. "Notes philologiques." *Byzantion* 22:357–72.

Mazal, O. 1968. "Die Textausgaben der Briefsammlung des Aristainetos." *Gutenberg-Jahrbuch* 43:206–12.

———. 1971. *Aristaeneti Epistularum Libri II.* Stuttgart: Teubner.

———. 1977. "Zur Datierung der Lebenszeit des Epistolographen Aristainetos." *Jahrbuch der Österreichischen Byzantinistik* 26:1–5.

McGill, S. 2010. "Plagiarism or Imitation? The Case of Abronius Silo in Seneca the Elder's *Suasoriae* 2.19-20." *Arethusa* 43:113–31.

Meyer, W. 1905. "Der accentuirte Satzschluss in der griechischen Prosa vom IV. bis zum XVI. Jahrhundert." Pages 202–36 in vol. 2 of *Gesammelte Abhandlungen zur mittellateinischen Rythmik.* Berlin: Weidmann.

Morello, R., and A. D. Morrison, eds. 2007. *Ancient Letters: Classical and Late Antique Epistolography.* Oxford: Oxford University Press.

Müller, K. K. 1884. "Neue Mittheilungen über Janos Laskaris und die Mediceische Bibliothek." *Centralblatt für Bibliothekswesens* 1:333–412.

Nissen, T. 1940. "Zur Rhythmik und Sprache der Aristainetosbriefe." *Byzantinische Zeitschrift* 40:1–14.

Olson, R. S. 2010. *Tragedy, Authority and Trickery: The Poetics of Embedded Letters in Josephus.* Washington, D.C.: Center for Hellenic Studies.

Pagès, J. 2009. *Aristènet: Lletres d'amor; Introducció, text revisat i traducció.* Barcelona: Fundació Bernat Metge.

Rosenmeyer, P. 1994. "The Epistolary Novel." Pages 146–65 in *Greek Fiction: The Greek Novel in Context.* Edited by J. R. Morgan and R. Stoneman. London: Routledge.

———. 1996. "Love Letters in Callimachus, Ovid and Aristaenetus Or the Sad Fate of a Mailorder Bride." *Materiali e discussioni per l'analisi dei testi classici* 36:9–31.

———. 2000. "(In)versions of Pygmalion: The Statue Talks Back." Pages 240–60 in *Making Silence Speak: Women's Voices in Greek Literature and Society.* Edited by A. Lardinois and L. McClure. Princeton: Princeton University Press.

———. 2001. *Ancient Epistolary Fictions: The Letter in Greek Literature.* Cambridge: Cambridge University Press.

Schmitz, T. A. 1997. *Bildung und Macht: Zur sozialen und politischen Funktion der zweiten Sophistik in der griechischen Welt der Kaiserzeit.* Munich: Beck.

———. 2004. "Alciphron's Letters as a Sophistic Text." Pages 87–104 in Borg 2004.

Sheridan, R. B. B., and N. B. Halhed. 1771. *The Love Epistles of Aristaenetus.* London: J. Wilkie.

Slater, N. 2013. "Lucian's Saturnalian Epistolarity." Pages 207–18 in Hodkinson, Rosenmeyer, and Bracke 2013.

Stirewalt, M. L. 1993. *Studies in Ancient Greek Epistolography.* Society of Biblical Literature Resources for Biblical Study 27. Atlanta: Scholars Press.

Stowers, S. K. 1986. *Letter Writing in Greco-Roman Antiquity.* Library of Early Christianity 5. Philadelphia: Westminster.

Swain, S. 1996. *Hellenism and Empire: Language, Classicism, and Power in the Greek World, AD 50–250.* Oxford: Clarendon.

Sykutris, J. 1931. "Epistolographie." Pages 185–220 in Supplementband 5 of *Paulys Realencyclopädie der classischen Altertumswissenschaft.* Edited by G. Wissowa and W. Kroll. Stuttgart: Metzler and Druckenmüller.

Temkin, O., trans. 1956. *Soranus' Gynecology.* Baltimore: Johns Hopkins University Press.

Thraede, K. 1970. *Grundzüge griechisch-römischer Brieftopik.* Munich: Beck.

Trapp, M. 2003. *Greek and Latin Letters: An Anthology with Translation.* Cambridge: Cambridge University Press.

Ureña Bracero, J. 1993. "La carta ficticia griega: Los nombres de personajes y el uso del encabeziamento en Alcifrón, Aristéneto y Teofilacto." *Emerita* 61:267–98.

Vieillefond, J.-R. 1992. *Aristénète: Lettres d'amour; Texte établi et traduit.* Paris: Belles Lettres.

Voiture, M. 1701. *Familiar and Courtly Letters to Persons of Honour and Quality.* 3d ed. London: S. Briscoe.

Whitmarsh, T. 2001. *Greek Literature and the Roman Empire: The Politics of Imitation.* Oxford: Oxford University Press.

Zanetto, G. 1987. "Un epistolografo al lavoro: Le *Lettere* di Aristeneto." *Studi Italiani di Filologia Classica* 5:193–211.

www.ingramcontent.com/pod-product-compliance
Lightning Source LLC
Chambersburg PA
CBHW030549030726
47495CB00004B/1184